BUT NAMES WILL NEVER HURT ME

LINDA Y. ATKINS

For Bill
Linda Atkins
8/20/04

 CHICAGO SPECTRUM PRESS

CHICAGO SPECTRUM PRESS
1-888-BOOKS-80
1-888-266-5780

Printed in the U.S.A.

10 9 8 7 6 5 4 3 2 1

ISBN: 1-58374-101-1

As always–for Tom. How blessed I am!

ACKNOWLEDGMENTS

My love and thanks to my beloved Tom for being so patient in listening to all my ideas, and for reading and re-reading the manuscript so many times, and each time, offering wise advice.

My love and thanks to Jenny who diligently read the manuscript in its infancy, and offered great suggestions along with lots of love and encouragement.

With affection and heartfelt thanks to Melanie McGown for working her magic one more time in creating the perfect cover design.

My thanks to Jerry Hall, homicide detective, Jefferson County Police Department, retired, who patiently answered my questions about police procedure and crime scene investigations.

Thanks to Marley, for being you.

PROLOGUE

John Bradley was dying and he knew there was nothing he could do to change that. The wounds inflicted by his unrelenting attacker were too numerous and too brutal in their intensity not to be fatal. He had underestimated the temperament with which he had been dealing. Now, he would pay for that mistake with his life.

He writhed in pain, twisting and turning to ward off the attack, in spite of instinctively knowing that any defensive effort would be in vain. The blackness which, up until now, he had been able to hold at bay, slowly and completely enveloped him like a heavy, inky mist. Its deadly embrace, at first so repugnant, now felt strangely comforting. In the end, he was not the master of the game, only one of the pawns, used, then cast aside when no move was left to play.

It was over. Forever. Slowly, he allowed himself to stop living.

Tumbling forward, he crashed to the floor.

PART ONE

CHAPTER ONE

"Hilary, help me."

Dead asleep and not at all pleased by the uninvited, as well as unexpected interruption, Hilary Adams was in no hurry to "help." She rolled over in bed. The phone, which she had angrily grabbed after several demanding rings, slipped without resistence from her hand. Still dazed from being awakened so abruptly, she fumbled half-heartedly about before successfully retrieving it. With one eye still stubbornly closed, she squinted at the digital alarm clock on her night stand, trying to focus. Even without her contacts or glasses, she could easily see the oversized iridescent orange numbers shouting back the time. Three-ten a.m.

Trying to shake herself awake, Hilary strained to place the vaguely familiar voice at the other end of the line. But the effort was useless. Her eyelids were too heavy; her mind mush. Burrowing deeper beneath the warm bedcovers, she listlessly propped the receiver against her ear with a pillow and mumbled into the mouthpiece, "Don't you know it's the middle of the night?"

Hearing nothing but silence, Hilary screwed her face into an impatient frown. "Okay, whoever you are, call my office between eight-thirty a.m. and five-thirty p.m." Firmly, and not too nicely she added, "Goodbye."

Hilary Adams was no stranger to desperate calls from desperate clients after hours. But this was ridiculous. "I should have known better than to list my home phone number for the convenience of all the kooks and crazies in the world," she muttered to herself. About to slam the receiver down hard to make her point, she heard a plaintive cry, "Hil, wait. It's Susan."

It took only a split second for the caller's identity to register. Hilary sat bolt upright; her eyes wide-open. Kernels of popcorn which had fallen unchecked from her hand while she watched an old Betty Davis movie earlier that night scattered everywhere like flying white bullets. Furiously rubbing her eyes, Hilary again, inadvertently let the phone drop. After bouncing once, it hit the floor with a thud. "Damn it!"

Leaning over the edge of the mahogany four poster, she tried unsuccessfully to recover it, but it lay just out of reach, stubbornly nestled between the folds of the flowered and ruffled bed skirt. Tugging on the phone's dangling twisted cord, she watched helplessly as it began spinning in tight concentric circles like an out of control plane taking a nosedive. "I'm here, Susan. Hold on," Hilary shouted into the air. "Don't hang up on me. I just need to get hold of this darn phone."

Impatient, she yanked the cord's rubbery coil, this time successfully retrieving the elusive receiver. Hilary placed it once more to her ear, but heard only agonized sobbing. "Susan, what's going on? What's wrong?"

"Susan" was Susan Emmett-Bradley, one of Hilary's closest friends—a friend whom she had first met when both were freshman law students at the University of Louisville. Now, twenty-one years later, Susan was a highly regarded Circuit Court Judge; Hilary, a very successful criminal defense attorney in Louisville, Kentucky.

In a small hoarse whisper, Hilary heard Susan answer, "John's dead . . . murdered, and I—"

At first, unable to grasp what she was hearing, Hilary rocked backwards as if slapped. Her head banged against the fabric tufted headboard, but Hilary didn't feel a thing. "W—wait, John murdered? What hap—"

"Hil, I can't say any more over the phone," interrupted Susan. "The police are here at the house asking me all sorts of things."

Taking a sharp breath inward, Hilary's mind raced. As a lawyer, she had so many questions, but as Susan's friend, she knew instinctively to ask only one. "What can I do?"

"Can you come over?"

"I'm on my way." Peeling back the covers and throwing her legs over the side of the three foot high canopied bed, she added, "Hold it together 'til I get there. And most importantly, *don't* talk to the police without me being present."

Without another word, Hilary replaced the receiver and flipped the switch on the bedside lamp. Her cat, Marley, who had been resting contentedly on top of one of Hilary's old sweatshirts spread out over the bed's down comforter, stretched with catlike disinterest, opened one bronze colored eye, then curled up once more into a contented ball of orange fur. Hilary bounded out of bed, throwing a loving backward glance at her prize Persian. "Gosh, Marley, how can you go back to sleep after that?" Reaching for her well-worn flannel bathrobe at the foot of the bed, she muttered to herself, "I can't believe this." She shook her head in amazement. "This can't be happening. I just saw John a few months ago."

She bent down on one knee, lifted up the dust ruffle, extended her arms as far as they would reach, and successfully grabbed up her pink terrycloth mules from underneath the bed.

Shuffling into the bathroom on rubbery soles squeaking noisily against the dark hardwood floors, Hilary quickly splashed cold water on the mottled freckles which covered her face like a mask of subtle beauty marks, then turned, retraced her steps, walked the length of her bedroom and opened the door to her darkened closet. After absently pulling on the dangling overhead cord, she remembered for the umteenth time, that she hadn't replaced the light bulb which had burned out sometime the week before. Since she rarely got up most days before seven-thirty, the lack of light hadn't proven a critical priority. Before now, that is. Resigned to groping blindly about in the dark, she didn't waste time, in spite of the sensory handicap, in finding her favorite pair of size four "Levis" hanging on a hook right inside the door, and an oversized cable knit sweater which she had meant to take to the cleaners several days ago, but somehow, had never found the time. *There's something to be said for procrastination*, she thought.

Quickly, Hilary grabbed a tortoise-shell barrette which had been carelessly dropped on the dresser the night before, gathered up her long, curly, copper colored hair into a ponytail of sorts, and hurried to unlock the backdoor.

CHAPTER TWO

The adrenaline Hilary always counted on in tough situations was finally kicking into high gear. She could feel it working its magic. The fact that only hours before she had been physically and mentally exhausted after defending a client in a two week murder trial was all but forgotten. Right now, she had to concentrate on only one thing—doing all she could for Susan.

Because of the hour, traffic was minimal. Hilary pressed hard on the accelerator, inching well past the speed limit. *What the heck,* she assured herself, *if I get stopped, I have the best or worst of explanations, depending upon how you look at it.* To Hilary, the risk was worth it, in spite of receiving two speeding tickets within the last six months.

At any other time, the drive to Susan's home, a large Tudor set back from the road and neatly tucked behind a row of bushy evergreens, was a short one. But tonight, to an anxious Hilary, in spite of what her speedometer warned was breakneck speed, the five minute drive down Bardstown Road, a well-traveled two lane thoroughfare voted "the best street in Louisville" with its colorfully eclectic shops and casual laid-back bistros, seemed endless.

Like Hilary, the Judge lived in the Highlands, one of Louisville's oldest and most cherished neighborhoods located close to downtown. Though cosmopolitan and sophisticated, this section of the city, dotted with nineteenth century pastel colored Victorian style homes, with wraparound verandas, brick sidewalks and wrought iron gates, still managed to maintain that comfortable, laid-back Southern charm which Louisvillians are so proud of, and so good at unabashedly showing off.

The temperature was plummeting, but it was the shock of the news just shared by her friend that made Hilary's teeth chatter and her body shiver. Not knowing what to expect, she could sense her muscles tensing. She swallowed hard. Absently rubbing the back of her neck, while keeping the other hand firmly on the steering wheel, she wondered, *If I'm cast in the role of lawyer as well as friend, can Susan stop being a judge and act like a client? More importantly, what can I possibly say right now, tonight, to get her through these first few hours?* Gripping the wheel hard, this time with both hands, Hilary, with characteristic resolve, quietly accepted the obvious. She would have to wait until she got there. Then, she would know what to do. In the meantime, however, Hilary couldn't help thinking back. . . .

Several weeks before, at Susan's urging, Hilary had met Susan for a quick bite to eat at The Jefferson Club, a private, members only restaurant on the twenty-ninth floor of the PNC Building. When Hilary arrived, she was surprised to see Susan already waiting, a glass of chardonnay half empty, in her hand. Because it was in the middle of a workday, and so uncharacteristic of Susan, Hilary had kidded her about "drinking on the job."

"Maybe a little glass of wine will help," had been the terse reply.

Knowing that Susan would explain her rather cryptic comment in good time, and not wanting to appear overly concerned, Hilary raised an eyebrow, but said nothing. And, true to form, after lunch had been ordered, and without much prompting, Susan did finally open up.

Before she began however, Hilary remembered how Susan had nervously looked around the room, in an apparent gesture to assure herself that no one was listening, then suddenly lowering her voice, had haltingly announced, "I guess there's no nice way to ease into this, so just let me get it out, then we'll talk, okay?"

Hilary nodded as Susan took a deep breath, then dropped a bombshell.

"John and I are through!"

"Come on, Susan. What are you saying? You and John—you both seemed so—"

Interrupting, Susan asked, "'So' what? Happy? Not for a long time. I can't take his moods or his temper any longer. Enough's enough."

It was the last thing Hilary had expected to hear that day. She didn't want to argue with Susan, but Susan's intractable position, even for Susan, seemed a bit drastic. After all, she and John had been married for over fifteen years. "Maybe you need to think about this a little more before you take steps you'll regret," Hilary urged.

Again, furtively looking over her shoulder before continuing, Susan tried to smile. "Let me make it a little clearer. Maybe then you'll understand. . . . John and I haven't been intimate for months. Any discussion between us is now limited to the weather and, for convenience only, each other's respective schedules." Taking another nervous sip of wine she proclaimed, while sitting rigidly on the edge of her seat, "This time, there's no going back."

Again, Hilary was at a loss as to how best to respond. Hampering her further was the fact that she hadn't seen John since absently waving to him over a punch bowl and shouting, "Happy Holidays" at a crowded Christmas party—an opportunity hardly sufficient to assess John's current mental state.

But in a vain attempt to calm her, Hilary, who had known John since undergraduate school, pointed out what everyone else had long ago accepted—that John had always been a rather brooding, complex fellow. So, the behavior which Susan had just described probably wasn't anything to worry about. Nothing had changed, other than Susan's and John's lack of personal interaction with each other, which, Hilary gently suggested, could only be remedied by Susan and John patiently confronting whatever it was, together.

Patience however, was not in Susan's vocabulary. She had been adamant that day. According to her, something was wrong with John and she was not going to tolerate his behavior any longer. The only question left in Susan's mind, was how and when to tell John of her decision.

At the time, Hilary dismissed such declarations, which had never been brought up since, as "typical Susan"—always wanting to control, contain, and manage everything and everyone. Now, however, Hilary couldn't help but wonder—did Susan's concerns, expressed so angrily that day at lunch, have anything to do with what had happened that night?

Turning onto the Park Boundary Road, Hilary saw police cars everywhere, either blocking Susan's driveway or parked in a checkerboard pattern across what once had been Susan's beautifully manicured lawn. She could see curious neighbors, some clad only in bathrobes with blankets thrown over their shoulders, huddled together, waiting in the cold drizzle, their umbrellas softly bumping up against each other, as they gossiped among themselves and kept anxious eyes trained on the police coming in and out of Susan's front door.

Nervous, Hilary tried to steady herself—this was no time to feel weak in the knees. Expertly, she weaved in and out amidst the dozens of blue lights flashing in unending rotation, searching frantically for a place to park, finally spotting one just big enough to squeeze into with her black BMW Z4. Not bothering to lock it, even though it was her pride and joy next to Marley, Hilary quickly crossed the street, deftly managing, in spite of her haste, to dodge police cars, an awaiting ambulance, and the coroner's ominous shiny black station wagon parked at the bottom of Susan's gently sloping driveway.

Taking the terraced stone steps two at a time, while hanging onto the gracefully winding black wrought iron railing for balance, Hilary reached the front door, presented her lawyer identification card to the uniformed officer standing just outside, then quickly jabbed her index finger hard against the doorbell, and waited patiently as the chimes rang throughout the house like muted church bells.

Within seconds, the door was slowly, tentatively opened. A face, devoid of color, as well as expression, peered around the door with a vacant stare.

With a sense of shock, Hilary realized it was Susan. The always self-assured Judge was hardly recognizable. Although dressed impeccably in a navy blue double-breasted suit, white silk blouse, and cultured pearls, she looked tired and scared—two adjectives which Hilary never would have used before in describing the Honorable Susan Emmett-Bradley.

Without a word, Hilary gently pushed the door inward and pulled her friend to her.

Burying her face in Hilary's shoulder, Susan cried, "Thank you so much for coming."

Once inside, Hilary gently extricated herself, closed the door behind her, and in a rush of words which tumbled out unchecked, asked, "What happened?"

Susan dabbed at the several tears that defiantly rolled down her checks, streaking what little face makeup remained and smearing shreds of dark clumpy mascara into raccoon-like circles around her pale blue eyes. "That's just it. I—I don't know what happened. When I got home tonight, I found John dead, lying on the floor in the library. There was blood everywhere and—"

Unable to continue, her body convulsing into gut-wrenching sobs, Susan covered her face with her hands. For support, Hilary leaned against the heavy oak door and put her arm around her, while at the same time barely avoiding a near collision with the evidence technician unit from city homicide.

Hilary could tell that the unit had been there for some time. The shear volume of sealed manila envelopes stacked haphazardly in the front hallway on a large faux finished parson's table, revealed that the unit had already collected and catalogued a substantial amount of forensic evidence.

Keeping her arm protectively around Susan, Hilary whispered, "I'm here now. You don't have to handle this alone; I'll help you through it." Looking around, Hilary added, "Right now though, we're obviously very much in the way, so let's get out from underfoot and allow the police to do their job."

Neither waiting for, nor expecting a response, she took Susan firmly by the hand and steered her toward the kitchen and away from the library with its steady hum of activity. As she passed by, Hilary tried to avoid the horror in that room, but found she couldn't help stealing a curious glance in that direction. She caught nothing more than a brief look, blocked in part by the usual gaggle of police personnel, but that brief look was enough to send a shiver down her spine.

Crime scenes, and Hilary had been to many, were often horrifically violent. This one was no exception. The room, cordoned off by bright yellow police tape, was in chaos. Blood splattered papers, shards of glass, and books pulled from massive built-in bookcases, were positioned in helter-skelter fashion, as if carelessly picked up and tossed about in the wake of a devastating tornado. John Bradley's body was in the middle of it all, positioned face upward, encased in a black rubber body bag which had been placed perpendicular to the leather sofa. Fringe, girding a green and russet plaid chenille throw, was still clutched tenuously in his right hand. Like everything else, it would not be disturbed until permission was given by the coroner, and the scene was cleared by the lead detective. In the interim, the area was being meticulously processed to determine how the crime was committed and to find evidence pointing to a particular suspect. She could see evidence techs busy shooting the scene from every angle with still photos and videotape. Another investigator was taking measurements, which Hilary knew would be preserved first in a rough sketch, then developed into a more detailed drawing for future use, if need arose, by police and prosecutors.

The coroner, still in attendance, was bending down on one knee, clearly intent upon his task of securing plastic bags over John Bradley's hands in an attempt to preserve any forensic residue that may have lingered there. If the police were lucky, the killer, in his apparently frenzied struggle with Bradley, may have unwittingly left behind a trail of valuable trace or impression evidence.

With Susan still in tow, Hilary choked back a wave of nausea and continued in the direction of the kitchen located at the rear of the house. Unlike the rest of the grand old mansion, in which the graceful beauty of a bygone era had been carefully preserved, the kitchen was a modern, sterile looking room, bathed in tones of unrelieved black and white.

Hilary and Susan sat down on two of the high white wooden and caned bar chairs which had been positioned by design to face each other across the narrow uncluttered counter top.

With her body sagging like a rag doll unable to sit upright, Susan slumped forward in her chair, and buried her face in her hands. Leaning towards her, Hilary murmured, "Just let go. This has been an awful shock. I'm here to help and listen when you're ready to talk, but take your time; this is just too much to handle all at once."

Hilary reached over and smoothed Susan's hair, cradling her face. "I'm not pushing you to say or explain anything until you are ready. Just remember, I'm here when you need me, and for as long as you need me."

While Susan sat gently crying, Hilary, with caring concern, quietly studied her friend. The two had met at the local Brandeis School of Law when seated next to each other in Contracts. As usual, Hilary had been running late, and as luck would have it, by the time she finally arrived, the only seat available was one next to Susan in the front of the room—the last place Hilary wanted to be; the first and only place Susan would have considered.

Physically, Susan looked now, very much as she had then—tall and fine featured with perfectly coiffed shoulder length champagne blonde hair, an elegantly formed patrician nose, and a Cindy Crawford beauty mark on her cheek. In law school, Susan Emmett, as she was known then, was referred to as the "Ice Queen," a nickname which she had tried for years to shed but without success. Even now, it was indiscreetly used by colleagues on the Bench who envied her winning track record with the Court of Appeals, and snidely bandied about by lawyers who felt threatened by rulings adverse to their clients' interests.

Always her champion, since that very first day in Contracts, Hilary explained away Susan's uncompromising temperament as nothing more than a rigidly fixed value system. Hilary had long ago accepted, that in Susan's straight jacketed world, no allowances could be made. Everything was black or white, right or wrong, empty or full. And during the past several months, in trying to follow that brand of uncompromising philosophy, Hilary watched helplessly as Susan heedlessly created even more difficulties for herself.

The Judge was nearing the end of her first term, and with the primary just around the corner, had already begun a grueling schedule of nonstop campaign appearances at every "weeny" roast and fish fry which extended a greasy invitation. While there, she was expected to beg people not only for their vote, but subtly ask for their money as well. It simply wasn't Susan's style. She hated it and it showed. But it was a necessary evil of political life.

Once again, her opponent was the well-liked and well-connected, Edward Arpel. Seven years before, Arpel had been defeated by only a slight margin. This time around, he told constituents that he intended to claim what should never have been lost in the first place.

In spite of Arpel's bravado however, the polls reported that Susan maintained a consistent lead, albeit slim. But that slim lead could easily vanish like snow in the desert, now that the local Bar Association indicated in its election poll results, made public just three days before, that its membership was no longer solidly behind the incumbent. Susan's support had eroded and abruptly fallen like a rock when Susan recently issued several pretrial compliance orders which, to the very powerful defense bar, limited their ability to have open-ended discovery. Hilary knew that those lawyers would now not hesitate in placing their bets and their money on Susan's very motivated to please, by promising everything to everyone, opponent.

"Is there anything I can get you, or anyone I could call?" Hilary asked.

Gently dabbing at red puffy eyes with a white linen handkerchief, Susan tried to answer in between involuntary spasms that at times, left her gulping for air. "Not really, Hil. I've already contacted my family in Pittsburgh. They'll be in sometime tomorrow. As for friends, you're the only one I want to talk to right now. And you know the media will alert everyone anyway." Pausing briefly she added, "I never thought I would hear myself say this, but for the first time in my life, I'm thankful that John and I had no children."

Trembling, she said, a despondent tone in her voice, "Right now, there's nothing I can do but relive this nightmare, like a videotape stuck on instant replay." She closed her eyes tightly. "Over and over, I watch myself in slow motion, finding John lying on the floor in the library. So bloody. And so . . . dead."

As Susan again gasped for air in between disjointed sentences, Hilary leaned across the counter top and took

Susan's hands in hers. "What time did you come home tonight?"

Susan shook her head slowly. "I don't remember exactly. It was late. Obviously too damned late. You know these campaign schedules. Between making personal appearances and doing my real job, I have no time for anything else." Wringing her hands, she added, "If I had just stayed home tonight, or come home earlier, maybe this would never have happened."

Angrily, Hilary grabbed her arm. "Don't ever say such a dumb thing again. It's a blessing you weren't here. Has it crossed your mind, you could have been killed too?" Seeing the look of fear in Susan's eyes, Hilary lowered her voice, and in a calmer tone asked, "Where were you tonight anyway?"

Susan cast her eyes downward and began twisting the thin gold wedding band wrapped around her long narrow finger. "At the office. Tonight was the only chance I had to catch up on a docket jammed because of last week's judicial conference in Chicago, and this never ending campaign schedule. I'm just so tired of it all."

Abruptly getting up from her chair, Susan demanded, "Why are you even asking me where I was and when I came home? Honestly Hil, you're beginning to treat me like one of those criminals you love to represent. Who cares? Only one thing matters now. Some animal came into my home and murdered John while I wasn't here."

Susan's angry outburst caught Hilary by surprise. "You're right. Force of habit I guess for a criminal defense attorney." Placing her hand over Susan's, she explained, "When you called, I came as your friend. But this friend is also a lawyer." Smiling, she added, "Look at it this way, it's an added bonus—you get two for one."

Susan looked away, then noiselessly walked toward the window, and for several seconds peered out at the predawn darkness. "Hilary, before you got here, all I could think about was, who could have done this? John had no enemies. Certainly no enemies capable of murder. Then I thought maybe, just maybe, the killer was trying to get back at me—some convicted defendant out on bond, or disgruntled plaintiff who lost money and took his rage out on John when he couldn't find me." With her voice rising, Susan screamed, "Don't you understand? All this may be my fault."

"Susan, you're certainly not to blame for this."

"How do you know?" she asked defiantly.

"Because I do, that's all." Trying her best to distract her, Hilary asked, "What have the police told you?"

Susan turned away from the window and once more faced Hilary. "That force of habit you just referred to, doesn't let you stop playing the role for a minute does it?" She folded her arms across her chest. "I've been told almost nothing. What I do know came from your friend, Lieutenant Peter Elliott. But believe me, that little bit of information adds up to what I said before—almost nothing."

Until that moment, Hilary had no idea that Peter was there at the house. Since Susan was the only person who knew just how deeply Hilary and Peter had, at one time, cared for each other, and if the truth be told, probably still did, Hilary appreciated Susan's unerring discretion in referring to Peter as merely a "friend." Trying hard to ignore her rush of emotions, Hilary concentrated on the situation at hand. "So tell me what Peter told you, even though you think it was 'almost nothing.'"

Sighing, Susan answered, "There were no signs of forced entry, and they think the killer attacked John from behind."

"Then they must believe that John knew whoever killed him."

With her voice shaking, Susan answered absently, "I—I guess so. But then you'd know more about that sort of thing than I would. They found no signs of forced entry, so that makes sense."

Abruptly, Susan walked back to her seat and sat down. "Please, do we have to do this now? I can't talk about it anymore. You're asking way too much of me."

Patiently Hilary answered, "I hate to remind you, Susan, but you, of all people should know. You're going to have to answer these questions and more, sooner or later."

CHAPTER THREE

Susan's immediate reaction to Hilary's prediction was to lay her head on the counter top and turn her face toward the wall. In any murder investigation, Hilary knew this to be the proverbial "calm before the storm." The police might now be busy collecting all the physical evidence they could from the crime scene, but it wouldn't be long before they'd begin questioning Susan in earnest, forcing her to recount in detail what she had experienced that night. Now was the most critical time, just after the crime had taken place, when evidence and memories were still fresh. Susan's input would be crucial.

Taking advantage of the temporary lull, Hilary glanced around the kitchen which she could see had already been thoroughly processed by the police. Black, dusty fingerprint residue was everywhere. Noticing for the first time, that the coffee pot's orange indicator light was still on, she got up and walked towards it. Picking up the stainless steel carafe and shaking it, she found that it was full. But only one cup had been placed next to it. If John had been expecting someone that evening, that person obviously hadn't been invited to stay for refreshments.

Looking closely, she found nothing in the kitchen to be out of place, out of order, or out of the ordinary. All Hilary could think of was how exceptionally neat Susan and John were—as if no one actually lived in, or enjoyed, this house. Guiltily, she remembered the dinner dishes piled high in her own sink that evening, placed there with the usual solemn vow to get up a little earlier and clean up the mess. Making a covenant like that with herself always made Hilary feel a little better, even though she knew that in all likelihood, those dishes wouldn't be rinsed or even stacked in the dishwasher until her cupboard was bare and there were no more dishes for her to dirty. *Obviously, Susan and I couldn't be more different.* Hilary's mental comparisons between households was abruptly interrupted however, by a voice she knew well—that of Lieutenant Peter Elliott.

Hilary had known Peter for some time, at first, through cross-examination of him in her representation of criminal clients. They shared a mutual respect for each other's abilities, and over the years, had come to deeply care about each other on a personal level as well. With regret, Hilary had let the opportunity for more than just friendship, pass. For her, it was still too soon after her husband Jack's unexpected death.

"Judge, I hate to intrude, but—"

When he began speaking, Hilary's back had been positioned towards the doorway. Upon hearing his voice, she turned slowly and faced him.

"Hil!"

She took delight in his obvious discomfort.

"I knew the Judge was expecting a friend; I didn't know that friend would be you."

Trying not to appear obvious, Hilary shyly studied Peter in his brown tweed sport coat, "ColeHan" loafers that were always shined to a high gloss, and thought, certainly not for the first time, what a good looking man he was. Six feet tall, medium build, but thin, with sandy colored hair and wire rimmed glasses, he was the epitome of the intellectual gumshoe. Using the vernacular currently in vogue, he was every inch the "sensitive, new wave" kind of guy whom women reading *Cosmopolitan* are told exist, but can never find.

With a perverse sense of pleasure, Hilary saw the hint of a blush begin to spread across his face. It was nice to see she still had that effect on him. Hopefully, she was not having the same visible reaction towards him. It was enough that she felt her toes tingling—at least that condition wasn't visually obvious to others. "Hello, Peter," Hilary managed to say without falling over her words.

Looking suddenly ill-at-ease, Peter answered formally, "Nice to see you, Counselor, though not under these circumstances. But then, it's not nice for anyone, is it?"

For a second his eyes bore into hers. Long enough for her to get the message—he hadn't quite gotten over her, even yet. But that was personal. Very personal. This was business, and she knew he intended to keep it that way. She did too.

"No. It isn't nice for any of us. But I'm glad you're here. It makes this a lot easier somehow."

Her compliment seemed to diffuse the awkwardness of the moment. Peter even managed a smile.

"I appreciate that." Looking sideways at Susan, he added, "Investigations like this are even more difficult when you know the people involved. I hope you understand. I have a job to do."

Hilary decided to answer for both of them. "We understand, Peter."

"Well then, in order to get the job done, I need to ask the Judge some questions about tonight. You're welcome to stay if you wish, Hilary."

"Thanks. I'd like to. I'll try not to get in your way. Promise."

Peter slowly shifted his gaze, and for the first time, rested his full attention on Susan. "Judge, if you feel up to it, we need to talk about some things."

Sitting up straight, still sniffling, though trying to hide it, Susan answered, "Ask me whatever you feel you need to." She pointed to another chair. "And please, do sit down."

Peter nodded his head slightly in her direction but remained standing, as if some degree of formality had to be observed. "Why don't we just start with something simple—like what time you came home tonight?"

Fleetingly, a half-hearted smile played across Susan's face. "You and Hilary think alike. That's one of the first questions she asked." Distractedly, she drummed square tipped fingernails on the smooth granite counter top while glancing at her watch. "I came home around six or six-thirty. John wasn't here yet, so I checked the answering machine to see if he had left a message. He had—something like, 'I'm running late; don't know how much longer I'll be. Go ahead and have dinner without me.'"

Looking up at Peter, Susan explained, "Work had piled up while I was out of the city last week, so I decided to return to the office."

"And what time was that?"

"I don't know exactly. Since I got back downtown around seven-fifteen, I guess I left here around seven or a little thereafter. I went directly to my office and started dictating Opinions and Orders which needed to be entered today."

"Take any breaks?"

"No. I didn't look up until around midnight. When I realized how late it was, I quickly closed up shop and left."

While quietly jotting down notes, Peter asked, "Before you left the house, did you leave a note telling your husband where you were and when you expected to return?"

"Yes. I always leave little 'Post-it Notes' right here on the kitchen counter." Glancing quickly around the kitchen Susan added, "Since it's gone now, I gather he read it when he got home, then disposed of it. Have you seen it?"

"No. But that's probably because the evidence techs have already processed this room. Did your husband call while you were at the office?"

"No. He would know that if I went back to the office, it was for something important. He wouldn't bother me."

Peter's right eyebrow lifted slightly, almost imperceptibly. No one else would have noticed, but Hilary knew him too well. Something about Susan's answer bothered him. And that bothered Hilary.

"Was it ususal for your husband to be late for dinner?"

Before answering, Susan again stole another quick look in Hilary's direction. "Not really. Recently though, he's been a little later than usual." It didn't escape Hilary that Susan's voice had a wistful yet angry twinge to it. As evidenced by his next question, Peter had noticed it too.

"I gather this upset you?"

"What exactly are you asking?" Susan shot back.

Not bothering to look up while flipping over a fresh page in his spiral notebook, Peter explained, "I think I asked if it bothered you."

"Of course it did. But my husband owned a business which demanded a great deal of his time."

"What kind of business was your husband in?"

"He and his partner, Jake Stein, owned a medical supply company."

Looking at her long and hard, Peter suggested, "I gather then, that your husband's absences created some friction between the two of you."

"I didn't like the arrangement, but then, I didn't have much choice," Susan answered hotly.

"Whoa, just a minute here, Peter," interjected Hilary. "I know you need to question Susan, but just where do you think you're going with this? Aren't we getting just a little far afield?"

Appearing not in the least put out, Peter answered evenly, "Maybe we need to get your role in this discussion clarified. Are you here as the Judge's attorney or friend?"

Hilary could feel a slow burn tweak her cheeks. "To set the record straight as to my 'role in this discussion,' I'm Susan's counsel as well as her friend. And as such, I want you to know for that record, which you seem to be so meticulously maintaining, I think your questions stink."

"Earlier, both you and the Judge accepted the obvious—I have a job to do. So, right now, I'm doing what I get paid to do. Believe me, I wouldn't be asking these questions if I didn't absolutely have to."

People and things never change, Hilary thought as she and Peter continued to glare at each other like two tigers fighting over a kill. *He just has to get the last word in.*

"Lieutenant, Hilary's just looking out for my welfare—a thankless task that she's performed, without complaint, for years. I guess at this point though, it's a tough habit to break—like some others she has." Susan turned to Hilary. "I don't need to be protected."

"But—"

"Hilary, please. I may be a little shaky right now, but the Lieutenant's right. Even you warned me—I'm going to have to answer these questions sometime. It might as well be now. And don't look so worried. I'm much better since you've been here with me. I *can* handle this."

Facing Peter head-on she explained, "I'm sure you can understand that what you're asking me is very painful to think about. But I know I have to talk about these things, regardless of how it makes me feel. So, please continue with your questions. I know they're necessary."

CHAPTER FOUR

"Maybe it would be easier on all of us if I asked some background questions first. We could go from there."

Susan nodded her agreement; Hilary wisely decided not to offer any lawyerly resistance.

"Tell me about your husband's business."

Hilary watched as Susan meticulously smoothed out the folds in her skirt and settled back in her chair before answering. "As I've already told you, my husband was in the medical supply business, servicing both hospitals and doctors' offices all over town."

"Any particular reason why your husband was putting in so many long hours?"

"I wouldn't know. John never talked much about the business. I gathered though that he and Jake were having some sort of disagreement."

"Over what?"

"You name it. Problems between John and Jake weren't anything new. They had very different personalities, very different styles. I could never quite understand how they remained business partners for over seventeen years. But something kept them together, no matter how much they disagreed."

"What was your relationship with Jake Stein?"

As if taken by surprise, Susan leaned forward in her chair and fixed a steady gaze on Peter. "I'm having a hard time

figuring out what that has to do with my husband's—"
Gulping, she added, "death."

Peter gave no reply. He stood, waiting, expectant.

I almost forgot how good he is at this passive aggressive style of questioning, Hilary thought. Leaning forward, she counseled, "Answer if you feel up to it, Susan. Peter just wants to get a handle on John's friends and relationships with others. That's all."

With a sigh, Susan replied, "I still don't know what that has to do with me." She put her hands up to her face, momentarily covering her eyes. "Everyone knows I didn't particularly like Jake. He was John's business partner; nothing else. Therefore, John and I together, saw him infrequently, for very short periods of time, and only when necessary."

"When did your husband's partnership with Jake Stein begin?"

"They met in medical school. Not long after, John quit school due to financial difficulties. To put it simply, he was flat broke. Then Jake dropped out too, but not because times were tough. Jake just didn't like working that hard. Besides that, Jake had been offered a job with the state crime lab and decided forensic work was what he really wanted to do, at least for the short haul."

Susan got up and retrieved a glass from the corner cabinet, filled it with water from the sink, took a long slow sip, then continued. "It wasn't too long afterwards, that John and Jake decided to pool what few resources they had and go into business together, selling prosthetic devises and hospital equipment and supplies. Against all odds, they were quite successful." Taking another drink of water she asked, "Who would have thought?"

Sensing that more background information might be useful, and too, that Susan could use a few moments of relief from Peter's questions, Hilary interjected with, "Peter, I'm sure you're going to want to know how Susan and John met, so let me explain, since I guess I was the matchmaker.

"John, Jake, and I all went to undergraduate school together. That's how the three of us first met. Then when I went to law school, I introduced Susan to John. 'And the rest,' as they say, 'is history.'"

As if only half listening, Peter didn't immediately respond. From all outward appearances, he seemed focused only on moving his pen back in forth in determined strokes across the lines of his logbook, an exercise resulting in nothing more than nonsensical doodles and scribbles. Finally, after what Hilary thought to be an interminable period of time, he looked up. "Thanks for the additional info. As ususal, you seem to be one step ahead of me, Counselor."

Turning to Susan he said, "As Hilary explained earlier, in any investigation, we first try to get a handle on the victim—their habits, their routine, their friends, their business associates, things like that. It allows investigators to get a fix on the victim as a person, which in turn, helps lead us to the killer." Peter's jaw flinched but not his gaze. "I'm not asking these questions to harass you. I just need background." He tapped his pen on the note pad. "Can you handle talking about things like that?"

"I thought that's what I was doing," Susan answered.

Nodding absently, Peter said, "I'll try to make this as brief as possible." As if choosing his words carefully, he asked quietly, "In the last several weeks, did you notice anything unusual in your husband's behavior?"

Susan thought for a moment. "Yes. I guess you could call it unusual, even though John always did have a tendency to be moody. Lately though, I'd describe him as more than just moody. In fact, I was so concerned, I even talked to Hilary about it." Rolling the white linen hankie she had been holding into a ball she added, "I guess the best description I could give is, he seemed worried, preoccupied. Something was bothering him, but he didn't want to talk about it."

"Was that unusual?"

Susan took a deep breath as if for added support. She looked downward. "Unfortunately, it was not."

"Did you and Mr. Bradley have children?"

"No. John never wanted them."

"Does Mr. Bradley have any family besides you?"

"He was an only child, very close to his parents. Unfortunately though, they died in a car accident about eighteen months ago. Their deaths were a terrible shock. Truthfully, I'm not sure he ever completely got over it."

"How about friends?"

"With my career, his business, and the campaign, we didn't have much time for entertainment. Any recent socializing was for purposes of political expediency. John was rather reclusive anyway, so if I had to name John's friends, that would be difficult. His world was his business," Susan explained, her voice trailing off.

Distracted by a noise in the hallway, Peter turned and looked behind him. "I can see that the technicians are about ready to clear out, so I need to get going too. But before I do, just a few more questions. Feel up to walking me through what happened when you arrived home tonight?"

"If I have to." Hesitantly, with eyes tightly shut, in a voice barely audible, and with hands gripped tightly to each side of her chair, Susan began describing what she had seen and felt. Hilary and Peter listened without interruption as she began.

"When I got home, I parked the car in the garage, then walked around to the front of the house. As expected, the front door was locked. Once inside, I remember thinking it odd that lights were still on in the library, but figured that John had just forgotten to turn them off."

"Did your husband routinely go to bed at a certain time each night?" asked Peter.

"Yes. John liked to be in bed by ten, so I didn't expect to find him downstairs, if that's what you are asking."

Susan waited for a moment as if expecting Peter to respond. When he didn't, she continued. "I called out, but there was no answer. Dropping my brief case and keys on the drum table in the center of the front hall, I glanced at the mail, then stepped into the library, at first not taking much notice of anything until I walked toward the sofa."

Incredulous, Hilary blurted out, "You didn't notice anything unusual up to that point?"

Silent for several seconds, Susan, with head bent, tried to explain. "You have to understand. I wasn't expecting anything unusual. When I entered the room, the first thing I noticed out of the ordinary was a table lamp lying on the floor. Then I realized blood and papers were everywhere." Looking up at Peter she said, "It was truly as if my mind could only comprehend a little bit of horror at a time.

"It seems unimaginable to me now, that I didn't see John before that point in time, but I didn't. I—I don't know how to explain it other than there was a spilt second of denial that anything was actually wrong. As if my mind couldn't or wouldn't accept what my eyes were actually seeing." Susan stared at each of them. "Does any of this make sense?"

Hilary said nothing. After all it was Peter's Q and A session. She just wanted time to take it all in; she'd sort it out later when she and Susan were alone.

Ignoring Susan's question, Peter asked, "What did you do then?"

"I—I think I just stood there. Staring. Willing John to move or say something. It's odd, but for some reason, I didn't feel any fear; I didn't feel danger, and I don't know why. I felt only a compelling need to move towards John; to touch him.

"I remember reaching for what I think was his left hand. Trying, I guess, to feel for a pulse, even though instinctively, I knew there wasn't much hope John would still be alive."

"Did you move the body?"

Susan shuddered. "'Move the body?' No, of course not," she whispered. "He was lying face down. It's strange, but for some reason I kept thinking that his hair looked too dark, as though it was wet—like he had just stepped out of the shower and hadn't dried off yet."

"I don't follow," said Peter.

"It's hard to describe. His hair was sticking straight up in all different directions, like a clump of 'pigtails.' But as I stooped down next to him, I realized that the 'pigtails' were matted clumps of dried blood. His chest, near his throat had been cut, and I—" At that, Susan began to sob again, her shoulders involuntarily heaving with every word. She tried to speak but couldn't.

Without waiting for another question to be asked, Hilary interrupted. "Peter, I've kept out of this as long as I can. Susan really needs to rest. Can't we continue this?"

Obviously irritated, Peter snapped his note pad shut, then placed it and his pen in the left breast pocket inside his sport coat. "I need to run a few errands and then get downtown anyway." Though still looking at Susan, he directed his comment to Hilary, "I know she's worn out." Reaching out, he placed his hand on Susan's shoulder. "I'm sorry about all this, Judge. Sometime later on today, after you've had a chance to rest, I'll give you a call."

Without further comment, Peter turned and walked toward the hallway, leaving Hilary and Susan alone once more.

Not willing to accept any resistence from Susan, Hilary ordered, "Come on. You've been up almost twenty-four hours straight, and you need your rest. I'll help you upstairs."

"Hilary, I can't rest. Not until we've had a chance to talk. I mean really talk. As my lawyer, and not as my friend. I have to tell you something. Now! It can't wait any longer."

For the second time that night, Hilary felt a shiver go down her spine.

CHAPTER FIVE

While en route downtown that morning, Peter decided to make a detour. He knew from experience, that he had some lag time before he reported back to the city's police chief—two hours at least, since that was how long it would take the evidence techs to finish sorting and logging in all the physical evidence taken from the scene. In any investigation, each item had to be carefully checked for correct labeling and numbering in order to preserve the integrity of the chain of custody—a chain which began at the crime scene, and continued unbroken, even when transporting the items to the state crime lab for analysis, fifty-five miles away.

Peter also knew that at this time of the morning, homicide would be in the middle of a shift change, from night to day squad. Unfortunately, due to the time frame in which the newest murder had occurred, incoming detectives would receive no information other than a "squawk" over the radio—a brief message covering only the basics of the crime—the tentative identification of the victim, the location of the crime, the suspected cause of death, and identification of any known suspects.

Since no other information, other than preliminary reports, would be available yet, activity on the Bradley murder would be minimal until new information was received from the evidence unit as well as the medical examiner's office. In the interim however, police work didn't come to a screeching halt. There were still plenty of loose ends to be tied up and leads chased down before valuable information on other unsolved homicides withered on the rumor vine, or died from lack of attention.

Peter had to accept the inevitable however—the push to find John Bradley's killer would be felt soon enough. A high profile case, as this was sure to be, could easily cannibalize all other cases still open on the books. It was unspoken department policy—all the Bureau's energy and resources would be expended on the case which garnered the most public attention. Bradley's was made to order—a particularly grisly homicide on the "nice" part of town, the victim married to a well-known public figure. The rationale for speed in this investigation was obvious. Efficiency looked good to the press and the public. And that was what mattered most to the top brass.

Detectives who had been at the crime scene, while no longer inside the victim's house, would still be on the clock. In conformance with Peter's standing orders, several would have begun a neighborhood canvass to discover if anyone had seen or heard anything suspicious. And at least one detective would stay with the body as it was transported to the medical examiner's office, to preserve the all important chain of custody.

It didn't matter that these detectives were assigned night shift. In cases like Bradley's, shifts frequently lasted around the clock, at least initially. Preliminary reports were due in the office this morning, and when fully transcribed, would be distributed posthaste to the day shift for follow-up. The process would take several hours to complete. After that, Peter knew all hell would break loose, and the quality of police work, which Peter prized above all else, compromised by the haste in which his superiors would order the case solved.

He knew that now was the perfect time to do some independent investigation on his own, before the crime became the subject of gossip on everyone's lips; before the so-called tips from unidentified do-gooders came in, clogged up the system, and wasted precious minutes of a homicide investigator's time.

The drive downtown also gave him the perfect opportunity to think about the unexpected pleasure he felt at seeing Hilary again. As always, she was as elusive as water through his fingers. It was no secret that he had wanted more from her than just friendship, but she wanted and needed time. Smiling, he thought, *For her, I can be patient. No matter how many centuries she makes me wait.*

He had been acutely aware, while talking with the Judge and Hilary, that one name cropped up again and again. From all accounts, this person knew Bradley well, and most importantly, had seen Bradley sometime within the last twenty-four hours. That kind of recent interaction with the deceased made the person's recollections as priceless as a winning lottery ticket.

Even better, Peter's recent conversation with the victim's widow, indicated that chances were slim that this particular individual would have received a courtesy call advising of the tragedy. Therefore, the person's reaction to the news would be genuine. Breaking the news would be left up to Peter, and that was just what Peter wanted. For some reason, he knew this was going to be interesting.

CHAPTER SIX

Susan continued her protestations, but Hilary remained adamant, even though curiosity was getting the best of her. She knew that Susan needed rest, if only for an hour. Whatever it was Susan wanted to talk about, surely would keep for at least that long.

After settling Susan in, Hilary turned off the light, quietly closed the door to the Bradley's master bedroom, and descended the spiral staircase leading to the first floor. So much had changed, and in such a short period of time. Restless, Hilary didn't know what to do first, or where to go next.

Upon reaching the bottom step, she was surprised and relieved to find that all police and medical personnel had cleared out during the few minutes she had been upstairs. The house seemed so quiet; so normal. For a moment, the calm gave rise to a desperate, illogical belief that perhaps John's murder had never really happened after all.

But Hilary's attempt at self-deception was short-lived. As if to cruelly confirm the brutal reality of the past few hours, she saw that left behind, was a taped outline, memorializing the location where John's body had been found. She put her hand out to steady herself, but in so doing, inadvertently touched a chalky substance which she noticed too late, clung to most of the antique cherry furniture in each of the downstairs rooms. It was a ghostly reminder of where the city's evidence technicians had attempted to lift fingerprints from various surface areas in the house.

"Ugh." Hilary furiously wiped her hands against her jeans, trying to transfer the dusty powder to her clothes. In spite of her efforts however, the gritty substance stubbornly stuck to her fingers like wet paper on smooth glass. For a second, she shut her eyes, sensing nothing but the relentless ticking of the massive grandfather clock in the front hallway.

An overwhelming feeling of depression hit hard. "Don't do this," she warned herself. "Things have to be taken care of." Moving tentatively, she side-stepped the library with its horrific reminders and headed back toward the kitchen where the unemptied coffee pot was still waiting. Since photographs had already been taken, and the area dusted for prints, Hilary decided, with a shrug of her shoulders, to be practical and drink what had already been prepared.

She grabbed a fresh mug from one of the kitchen cabinets. By now, the coffee was jet black in color, syrupy in consistency, and more than strong enough to chase away the dull lethargy that was beginning to overtake her. She knew that this was her body's normal reaction to stress after an emergency. All systems were beginning to shut down. She would have to fight to stay awake, and coffee, in spite of its advanced age, would surely do the trick.

Hilary glanced at her watch for the first time since she had arrived that morning, and noticed with surprise, it was well past eight-thirty. Her secretary, Maria, would be in the office by now. She reached for the wall phone and punched in the seven digit number.

On the second ring, she heard a cheerful, "Good morning. Adams & Adams. May I help you?"

"Hi, Maria. It's me. How's everything going?"

"Can't tell yet. I just got in the door. Where are you anyway?" she demanded. "I thought you'd be here by now."

Haltingly, Hilary explained. "I know this is a lot to throw at you, Maria, but there's no way to sugarcoat it." Taking a deep breath, she said, as gently as she could, "John Bradley was murdered last night. I'm still at Susan's where it happened, and I don't know for sure, how much longer I'll be here. To be safe, don't count on me for at least another hour or—"

"Oh, my word," interrupted Maria. "Who did it?"

"At this point, I don't think the police have a clue."

"How awful for Susan. Is she all right?"

"Not at the moment. But you know Susan. She'll handle it."

"I know she will. It'll just take a lot of time. But then, I don't have to tell you about that, do I?"

Hilary said nothing. It was still too painful to talk about. But Maria was right—Hilary did know all about grief and what Susan was about to face in the days ahead. Four years before, Hilary had unexpectedly lost her husband and law partner, Jack, in a scuba diving accident. The two had been inseparable. Since Jack's death, life had never been the same. Well meaning friends had handed out the usual platitudes—that she'd learn to live without him, life went on, and Hilary's very favorite of all—pain eases with the passage of time. As she had expected, none of these well-worn bromides, so freely given, had worked. There was no miraculous healing. Instead, Hilary only survived, fighting a daily battle to overcome the despair, the what ifs, and the irrepressible longing to be with Jack just one more time. The fact that she was still able to function, gave her hope that one day she could overcome the sadness, and life again could be good. So far however, that hadn't happened. In part, she had to admit, because she wouldn't let it. Peter Elliott was a case in point.

Deliberately changing the subject, Hilary answered, "I'm embarrassed to admit it, but with all that's gone on, I can't remember what's on my calendar for today. Could you take a look? It's in the usual place—the middle drawer of my credenza."

"Sure. Hold on while I get it." Hilary was put on hold, but only for a few seconds. When the phone was picked up again, Maria was panting furiously. "Give me a minute to catch my breath."

"Are you all right?"

"I'm fine. Really. It's just that the news about Susan has really knocked my socks off, that's all."

Hilary could hear the pages of her calendar being flipped back and forth with dogged determination. While waiting, she took the opportunity to reach into her purse in search of a paper and pen. Finding a scrap of paper proved no problem—one was tucked inside her wallet behind her sister's photograph. Finding a useable pen however, was another matter. She spotted two long forgotten "Bics" in a zippered side pocket, but after scribbling furiously on the scrap of paper, she quickly discovered that each was out of ink. Undaunted, Hilary again fished around the bottom of her purse, finally globbing onto an eyebrow pencil with just enough of a stubby brown point to accomplish the task. "Ready when you are, Maria."

"Okay, here we are—February 19th. If I can read your writing, it looks like you have a ten-thirty hearing with Judge Dunn. It's on the Commonwealth's Motion for Sonny Hill's probation to be revoked.

"Then let's see, at eleven-fifteen, you're scheduled to be in federal court on a detention and bond hearing. If you'll remember, the magistrate's clerk called late last Friday and asked if you'd accept an appointment to represent an indigent defendant nabbed along with three others for importing and distributing several kilos of cocaine. Looks like the feds even have some nice photos of the operation while in progress." Chuckling, Maria quipped, "Obviously, this one's going to call for a very creative defense."

"Remember, there're always two sides to everything," Hilary gently chided. "You know that. Besides, the accused may see the error of his ways without too much persuasion and want to enter a plea to the charges."

"Yeah, yeah, sure. You can only hope."

"We'll see. What's next on the agenda?"

"At twelve-thirty, you're locked into being the guest speaker at the monthly meeting of the Women Lawyer's Club. According to the agenda they sent over, between the chicken pot pie and the pie ala mode, you're to lecture on the oh so subtly sexist topic, 'Even a Woman can be a Successful Criminal Defense Attorney.' Damn, I hope you didn't come up with that."

Hilary laughed. "You know better. Does that sound like anything I'd write?"

"No. But then it doesn't sound like anything you'd talk about either."

"Maria, sorry to ask this of you, but—"

"But you want me to call and cancel with the lady lawyers."

"Yeah, and do me another favor—don't let them talk you into an alternate date. I don't want a rain check on this lecture."

Maria chuckled. "I hear ya."

"One more thing, even though I'm almost afraid to ask—what's my afternoon look like?"

"One appointment—with a new client at three-thirty. When I screened the initial call, Mr. Hornecke told me he'd been arrested on a First Degree Sodomy charge involving his five year old son. The arrest was made on a direct indictment returned by the Grand Jury two days ago."

"When is he scheduled for arraignment?"

"Arraignment's set for Monday at nine o'clock in Judge Thaler's court, with bond set at fifty thousand full cash. And before you ask, I already checked. Bond was posted immediately."

"Good. Money must not be a problem then."

"Apparently not. And it gets better. Hornecke asked what your retainer was for a Class A felony. I told him thirty-five thousand up front. 'No problem,' he says. 'I hear she's the best.'. . . I guess that means you're hired, huh?"

Laughing, Hilary replied, "You take such good care of me. What's it look like after my conference with this Mr. Hornecke?"

"You're free and clear."

"Good. In the meantime, this is what we need to do. Go ahead and cancel not only the lady lawyers, but also my ten-thirty appearance on behalf of Sonny Hill. Explain to Judge Dunn's secretary the reason why we have to re-schedule, even though I'm sure the word's already gotten out. Secure another court date for sometime in the next two weeks if the Court and prosecution can accommodate. Then call Sonny. He should be ecstatic since it means a couple more weeks of freedom before he gets jerked back to serve the ten years he has waiting for him on the shelf. Just remind him he better not run. If he does, he'll forfeit his bond of ten grand and me as his lawyer. That should keep him local while we wait for the next court date."

"What about the bond hearing at eleven-fifteen?"

"I'll be there. But warn the clerk I may be a few minutes late. Also, since I haven't talked with our new client yet, I'd like a few minutes with him before we see the Judge. When you call, ask if she could arrange that with the U.S. Marshals who'll be bringing him in from central holding.

"I guess that should cover it, Maria. . . . Oh, wait, except for one thing. When Sam, our intrepid investigator, finally decides to make an appearance at the office today, ask him if he could meet me sometime early evening. He knows Susan and I'm sure he'd like to help any way he can. As usual, thanks Maria. I know you'll keep a lid on it 'til I get there. See you soon."

Hilary carefully replaced the phone and sat down to finish her coffee. In spite of the awful taste, it was keeping her alert and halfway in control. She hadn't quite finished however, before she was startled by her name being called. It was Susan. She wanted to talk.

Trying to smile, Hilary wearily got up from her chair.

CHAPTER SEVEN

After showing his badge to the doorman, and being assured that his arrival would not be announced to the occupant he sought, Peter took the private elevator to the twentieth floor of the high rise structure located just across the parkway which bounded Cherokee Park in the heart of the city's Cherokee Triangle, and knocked on the massive front door of the pricey 1400 Willow condominium unit. Within easy walking distance of bike trails, running tracks, the popular Heine Brothers' Coffee house, and the well-known Bristol Bar & Grille, the condos, for the most part, were occupied by a strangely compatible mixture of well-to-do retirees; busy professionals who didn't want the hassle of household maintenance; and transient, newly divorced yuppies who eschewed making decisions any more life altering other than how best to successfully re-establish a foothold in Louisville's social scene on a Friday night.

At first, hearing nothing, Peter knocked again. Finally, after another interminable amount of time, the door was pulled open with an impatient yank. Peter immediately flashed his badge, but got no verbal response—just a silent waving gesture indicating that Peter was permitted to step inside. Momentarily taken aback by the reception, or more accurately, the lack thereof, Peter hesitated.

"Well, would you like to come in?" the man asked with a touch of irritation in his voice. "I can't imagine what I could do for one of Louisville's finest at eight o'clock in the morning, but I'll do my best."

Quickly, Peter introduced himself. "Mr. Stein, I'll take only a few minutes of your time."

Peter crossed the threshold and looked down the long hallway into the living room area. The room, monochromatic and ultramodern from the furniture, which was all chrome and glass, to the objects d'art which Peter recognized as the expensive stuff he had seen earlier at the trendy Edenside Gallery on Bardstown Road, was corner to corner, utterly tasteless. The carpeting was white; the walls were white; the translucent open weave draperies, twisted in great cascades of shimmering fabric over metallic white drapery rods were white; the sofa, a camelback which hosted four overstuffed cream colored pillows with oversized gold gesso tassels, was white brocade. As a finishing touch, three accent chairs, upholstered in wide shiny ribbons of white and ivory, were set on the periphery of a fringed, Persian area rug, its colors resonating, in uninterrupted monotony, the same muted tones of ivory, white, and beige. The effect on Peter was dizzying, like being caught in a whirling blizzard of blinding, gaudy excess.

After closing the door, Stein turned and strolled into the living room ahead of Peter. Smiling, he said, "You don't need to comment on the decor. Believe me, I had no idea what that idiotic designer was going to do. I guess though, there's nothing I can do about it now, except pay the bill." His gaze fell once again on Peter. "But, then you didn't come here to talk about wallpaper, furniture, and fabrics, so what's this all about?"

Dressed in charcoal gabardine slacks, a black cashmere jacket, foulard tie and five hundred dollar tassel loafers that reminded Peter of sissy ballet slippers, Stein picked up a sleek gold Rolex watch from the bleached wood coffee table and wrapped it around his left wrist. After securing the clasp, Stein urged, "Come on, Lieutenant, we've exchanged pleasantries. Again, what can I do for you?"

Peter hated guys like this—guys that were seemingly a little too perfect, at least in appearance. Stein's brown hair, streaked with blond highlights in just the right places, was immaculately combed; his face was a dark artificial tan; his body muscular and fit like a prize fighter. Obviously Stein had the time and the bucks required for a personal high maintenance regime. Question was, how did he find the time to run a business too? Shrugging, Peter decided there was no need to spoon-feed the bad news to him. Anxious to see Stein's reaction, Peter announced, "John Bradley was murdered sometime last night or early this morning."

Peter watched closely for what he thought would be the inevitable signs of shock and revulsion, some level of emotion indicating that news like this had registered. Instead, Peter witnessed nothing. Stein merely sat down on the white on white sofa and stared into space, saying nothing.

Peter took a seat in the chair closest to the couch. His question, "Are you all right?" was met with more silence. Peter tried again. "I know this news must be a shock."

Without skipping a beat, Stein responded dully, "It is that, Lieutenant."

Peter waited for more of a reaction, but none was forthcoming. He decided to try stoking the fires of a conversation once more. "Sorry to have to ask you this, but when was the last time you saw him?"

Stein screwed up his mouth in disdain as if the memory of that last meeting was unpleasant. "That's easy. I saw him yesterday. At the office. As usual, we didn't have much to say to each other, or at least nothing noteworthy enough to share with the police." He added, "Unless, of course, you're interested in wooden arms and legs, hospital bedpans or rectal thermometers. Because if, for some reason you are, I can get you a really good deal, but it has to be a big volume purchase."

"I'll keep the offer in mind," replied Peter evenly. "But let's get back to Bradley."

"Okay by me." Stein crossed one leg over the other and picked at a piece of lint tucked inside his trouser cuff. "But keep in mind, as indelicate as it may sound, because of what you've just told me, I obviously have a lot to do."

"Well, I certainly wouldn't want to keep you any longer than necessary." Peter opened his coat and sat back in the chair, trying hard to get comfortable. But he could have saved himself the trouble—getting comfortable in this mausoleum was impossible. "Notice anything unusual about your partner yesterday?"

"Nothing out of the ordinary." Stein looked away before continuing. "Since you'll hear this anyway, I might as well go and ahead and say it. John and I may have been partners, but frankly, we didn't really like each other. We were partners because we had to be, not because we wanted to be. But don't take that all too obvious leap of logic that since I didn't like him, I must have murdered him."

Leaning forward, Stein said, "Let me make it simple for you. I didn't murder John Bradley, even though lately, he'd become more of a liability than an asset to the company, and a royal nuisance to me personally."

In nineteen years of law enforcement, Peter thought he had seen everything, but Jake Stein defied all the rules. Most people, undoubtedly out of fear, go out of their way in a murder investigation to make themselves likable, thereby giving the impression they're incapable of committing an act as heinous as murder. But here was Stein, acting like a lightning rod, just begging to be number one on the city's hit parade of possible suspects. Something wasn't adding up.

Curious, Peter asked, "I guess you know then what my next question is going to be, right?"

Cocking his head sideways, Stein replied, "Ah, let me guess. I suppose you're going to ask me where I was during the late night, early morning hours of February 18th and 19th?" He stood up and stretched. "I was right here, safe and sound in my cozy little condo. If necessary, a friend can verify that, since that friend was here too, if you know what I mean."

"Does this 'friend' have a name?"

Stein chuckled. "Most friends have names. But in this case, for the time being, I've given you more than enough information. All you require is reassurance that I wasn't at the Bradley residence at the time of the murder. Now, you've got it. That means I'm not your man."

"Well, it's interesting that you mentioned you weren't at the 'Bradley residence' last night." Peter smiled. "How could you possibly have known that John Bradley was killed at his home? I don't remember sharing that little piece of information with you."

Seemingly unruffled, Stein answered, "Since I saw the deceased as recently as late yesterday afternoon when he was leaving the office, and it's only around 'eight-ish' now, one could conclude that John was most likely killed during the intervening hours at his home. If I were a betting person, which upon occasion I am, I'd place the smart money on that kind of deductive reasoning, wouldn't you? But then, you're the detective, not I. Far be it from me to tell you how to do your job."

"You still haven't answered my question. Who was with you last night and for how long? Sorry, if you think I'm prying, but I need an answer."

Leaning toward Peter, his eyes narrowing, Stein warned, "We need to get something straight. I know that you're just doing your job. And I can assure that I will cooperate in any way that I can, in spite of the fact that there is nothing right now which would compel me to talk with you." Quietly he added, "John was my partner. Regardless of the differences we may have had, he certainly didn't deserve to be murdered.

"So, for now, you'll just have to trust me. I was here at home last night. Someone else was here as well." Stein absently looked down at his splayed fingers, so perfectly manicured. "Whatever else you can say about me, I'm still a gentlemen. And if I don't have to divulge my guest's identity, then believe me, I'm not going to. Any further information on the subject will be given only upon my arrest. And I doubt very much that you're prepared to do that . . . at least not right now."

"Listen Stein, I just need some simple answers. No one is accusing you of murder. But you're right—that could change. Cooperate and we'll get along just fine. Push me around anymore, and you'll see just how nasty I can get. Do we understand each other?"

"Whatever you do, Lieutenant, don't threaten me. Ask the questions you feel you have to, then leave."

Peter knew he was getting nowhere fast. Stein was right. Peter had no authority to force answers to any of his questions. It was time for a different approach. "I'll make this short.

What was going on with your business that necessitated Bradley putting in long hours?"

Stein crinkled his brow. "Honestly, I wouldn't know. If John put in long hours, then he did it without telling me or anyone else at the office."

"I've been told that the two of you weren't getting along and because of that rift, Bradley had to devote more time to the business."

"As I said before, that 'rift' as you call it, is old news which everybody and his brother knows about. It's no secret that John and I didn't agree on a great many things. So what! I have nothing to hide. What's your point?"

"Just this—right now, everyone is a suspect in this murder. And the more you talk, the more I think you may be my best bet."

Stein stood up, towering over Peter. "There's just one problem with that kind of thinking. I didn't do the crime. So why then would I admit to something I didn't do?"

Bending down, he opened a glass cigarette case, placed like a theatrical prop in the middle of the coffee table next to several issues of *Architectural Digest*. Reaching inside, he removed a long thin brown tiparillo, and rolled it gently between his fingers. Placing it next to his nose, Stein inhaled deeply, but never lighted up. Peter figured it a ploy to buy time before answering.

"While Bradley and I were partners on paper, we were otherwise totally independent of each other. There were areas that I took care of. Areas he took care of. Generally speaking, I took care of the sales end of it. John, on the other hand, liked to handle books and keep up with all the latest information regarding any new equipment on the market."

As if out of breath, Stein sat down and shook his head. "Don't ask me how, but it was a system that worked. Maybe because it allowed us to stay out of each other's hair." He turned full face and stared at Peter. "How's that for an explanation?"

Peter decided it was again time to switch gears. "When you saw Bradley at the office, did you notice any signs of depression?"

"Let me explain something," Stein said patiently. "I went to med school for about six months. It didn't take long for me to realize that I didn't want to become a doctor, let alone a doc specializing in mental illness. I just never assimilated those feelings necessary for treating people suffering from emotional problems. Therefore, I certainly don't feel qualified now to make a judgment call as to whether my late partner was down in the dumps in the clinical sense, or just being his usual miserable self."

"Was the business experiencing any financial problems?"

"I believe you heard me say earlier that finance was John's department, not mine. All I know is, I got my take every two weeks and John never so much as breathed a word that we were in any kind of trouble. Our profits were up and our debt ratio down—my own simple kind of accounting system that lets me know all's right with my world. We have a CPA who oversaw John, so perhaps you should check with him if you have any lingering doubts. Frankly, after what you've been telling me, I should contact him myself. Goodness knows, what John had been doing with the books behind my back."

"Have you had occasion to visit the Bradley residence recently?"

"Are you talking in the social or business sense?"

"I don't want to miss anything, so how about both?"

"That's easy. Socially—no. For business reasons—infrequently. The few times I did go, I always felt the need to go around to the back door, as if I were the dog, the delivery boy, or the hired help. Who would want to submit to that kind of treatment very often?"

Pushed for time, Peter began buttoning his coat and got to his feet. "This little discussion has been enlightening to say the least, but fortunately for both of us, it's over. I must caution you, don't plan any trips out of town without first telling me. And at all times, play it smart and make yourself available to my detectives. I have a feeling that you and I are going to get to know each other real well before this is all over with." He handed his business card to Stein. "Any questions before I leave?"

CHAPTER EIGHT

"I'm in here, Susan." Slightly raising her voice she added, "In the kitchen."

Hilary heard Susan's heels hitting against the hardwood floors like the clickety-clack of a metronome set at a fast clip. Even the plush Oriental area rugs did little to muffle the sound. "Didn't you promise me that you'd rest for awhile?"

"Yes," Susan answered irritably as she entered the kitchen. "But I couldn't sleep. Each time I closed my eyes, all I could see was John, lying in all that blood." She shook her head. "I don't think I'll ever sleep again."

"Of course you will, but it's going to take time. Be patient with yourself." Hilary got up and hugged her friend tightly. "I just wish there was something I could say to ease the pain. But all I can do is be here when you need me." Hilary turned and got another mug from the kitchen cabinet. "I'll never forget how you were there when I needed help. Looking back, I don't know what I would have done without you. Now it's my turn to take care of you. So let me do that, okay?"

Susan took the offered cup, poured a cup of coffee for herself, and sat down at the kitchen counter in the same chair she had occupied earlier. She reached over and touched Hilary's arm. "I really do need your help."

"You know I'll do anything you ask." Hilary sat quietly, ready to listen.

Still trembling with what Hilary attributed to the after-effects of shock and exhaustion, Susan managed a small, wan smile. "You may think I'm asking too much of you."

Hilary smiled reassuringly. "We're better friends than that. Whatever it is, you know I'll help."

"I don't think you understand. I need to talk to you like client to lawyer." Unflinching, Susan stared at Hilary. "Are you comfortable with that?"

Susan's question startled her, but Hilary didn't want to show it. She blinked hard as if trying to re-focus, then slid her hand over Susan's in an attempt to reassure her. "Susan, as your friend, you know you can tell me anything. Just keep one thing in mind though—whatever it is that you want to say to me while invoking attorney-client privilege, is something altogether different. I'm no longer your friend. And you are no longer a judge. You have become my client."

"I've got to confide in someone, and preferably that someone is also my lawyer." Susan looked away. "I don't think it's really that serious anyway."

"So then, what's the problem?" Hilary asked, relieved.

"It's not a problem, actually." Susan bit her lower lip. "Although I guess it could be."

Hilary inched forward in her chair. She didn't like the sound of that last remark, but in spite of her concern, managed to light-heartedly say, "This is intriguing. Tell me more."

Swallowing hard, Susan answered, "To be honest, I'm afraid I didn't answer the Lieutenant's questions as fully as I probably should have." She licked dry lips then continued. "I left something out."

Wrinkling her brow, Hilary replied, "Is that all? Well, that can be easily corrected the next time you talk with Peter. No big deal. He'll understand."

"Hil, it's not that simple; it's more complicated than that." Taking a deep breath, Susan explained, "I don't intend to correct it." As she had earlier that morning, Susan abruptly got up from her chair and walked toward the window, turning her back to Hilary. "It's hard to know where to begin. Frankly, it's embarrassing to talk about, but I know I don't have much choice."

Hilary watched as Susan leaned against the counter top for support.

"As I told you before, John's been having problems for quite some time. He never confided in me, so what they were exactly, I couldn't tell you. I just saw the repercussions—behavior that was erratic, in some cases, inappropriate. Even more embarrassing, other people were beginning to notice, so it wasn't reserved only for my benefit. In the beginning, I tried to help, but John wouldn't let me. He shut me out, totally."

"What do you mean by 'inappropriate' behavior?"

"Constantly losing his temper and threatening to sue people with whom he did business."

Hilary said nothing. She had to keep reminding herself that even though Susan was her friend, right now, her friend was speaking as a client. It was time to listen, not talk. Questions could be asked later. Hilary knew only too well, that clients tend to be communicative only initially, when their pain, their trauma is at its greatest. Often, after a client has had time to think the situation through, in a light most favorable to them, the truth is often compromised for the benefit of their lawyer.

With her back still turned toward Hilary, Susan slowly began to talk about what had been bothering her. "Last night when I came home and found John, I did exactly what I told you and Lieutenant Elliott I did. I walked into the library; I went over to John; I felt for a pulse." Pausing, Susan then added, "But I neglected to say that I removed something from John's hand when I tried to feel for a pulse—"

Hilary's eyes opened wide. She couldn't believe what she had just heard. "Why would you do that?"

Susan whirled around. "Don't dare question me that way. I know what I did would raise some eyebrows, but all I took was a crumpled piece of paper—crumpled, but not so much so that I couldn't still read part of it. Luckily, there wasn't much blood on it, which looking back was surprising considering all the blood that seemed to be pooling around him otherwise."

Shocked by what the Judge had admitted, Hilary demanded, "What was so important about that particular piece of paper, that you would risk being charged with tampering with physical evidence?"

With blue eyes turning a cold hard grey, Susan replied, "Calm down. I knew what I was doing. The evidence, if indeed it *is* evidence, was just a letter—addressed to John, sent to John's office address, and signed by a Dr. Parker."

Pacing the length of the kitchen floor, Susan continued. "I don't know what made me notice it, let alone pick it up. But I did. It really wasn't much different from the rest of the papers strewn about, except that it was typed on light blue paper." With her voice fading, Susan explained, "I guess that's what caught my eye, initially at least."

Impatiently, Hilary demanded, "Okay, I'll bite. What did the letter say?"

Susan hesitated.

Impatiently, Hilary asked, "Well, are you going to tell me?"

"I can only paraphrase—"

"Right now, that will do."

Haltingly, Susan recounted what the doctor had written—that John's tests had again been returned with negative results; any further concerns John might have, should be discussed with one of the specialists recommended previously.

When Susan finished, Hilary asked, "Does any of that make sense to you?"

"No."

"Anything else in the letter?"

"That was it. There wasn't even a date on it. What's even more curious, our family doctor, Paul Hanley, has treated John since we were first married. Paul's also a personal friend, so if there had been any kind of problem, I would have expected John to contact Paul."

Susan slumped back down in the chair opposite Hilary and rubbed her forehead. "Bottom line, I have absolutely no idea what John was up to, and frankly, I'm scared to death just thinking about the possibilities."

Trying to assuage her friend's understandable fears, Hilary said, "Well, let's just take it one step at a time. I'm sure John's problem wasn't life threatening to him or to you. If it had been, you would have been notified."

"Then what was wrong with him?" In frustration Susan pounded the table with her fist. "Why couldn't he come to me about this? If ill health was at the root of his erratic behavior, why not talk to me about it?"

"I'm sure he just didn't want to alarm you, that's all. You know how men are." Hilary dug her hands into her jeans pockets and absently rattled the loose change left there after her last trip to the grocery store. "Where is this letter anyway?"

Since Susan had angrily buried her head in her hands, Hilary could barely hear her answer. "Upstairs in my brief case."

Hilary touched Susan's arm, compelling her to lift her head. "Susan, look at me."

Dutifully Susan obeyed. "What?"

"Tell me why you hid the letter. On its face, it seems harmless."

"For privacy reasons." Smoothing her hair back behind her ears, then clasping her hands in her lap, Susan added, "God only knows what the letter means, and here I am in the middle of a campaign. John was acting so strangely, it could have meant anything. And right now, politically, I can't afford surprises." She began stirring her coffee, which by then was stone cold. Without looking up she asked, "How can I find out what was going on with him? Should I call this doctor he was seeing?"

"No," Hilary answered emphatically. She had to think fast. "Let's see—they'll be scheduling the autopsy for sometime today. That should give us a few preliminaries about John's physical condition at time of death." Hilary grabbed the scrap of paper she had used when talking with Maria and began writing. "I'm making a note to ask Peter. He's the lead detective, so he'll have to be in attendance. There's no reason, as your attorney, why he wouldn't tell me if the preliminaries revealed something unusual."

Wearily Susan answered, "Okay. At this point, I can't ask for much more than that. To be honest, I'm not sure I'm anxious to know."

"What's the name of that doc—the one who sent the letter to John?"

"Someone named Franklin W. Parker."

"Written on letterhead with an address?"

"Yes, an office located on the other side of town. Where, I don't exactly know. In fact, I don't think I've ever been to that part of town."

Hilary smiled. That answer was so Susan. "Okay. I'll check it out. I've already talked with Maria about contacting Sam anyway. When I get back to the office, I'll ask him to find out about this Dr. Parker. All you have to do, is sign a release for the records."

Hilary reached over and reassuringly squeezed Susan's hand. "In the meantime, find some comfort in the fact that it's beyond your control. You can do nothing about this now, so let's not fall on swords trying to right what you did in a moment of panic." Hilary bit her tongue to prevent herself from adding, "Unfortunately, it's already a done deal anyway."

Susan started to speak but was interrupted by the telephone. The sound made them both jump. Susan picked up immediately. "Hello?"

Still reeling from what she had heard, Hilary just sat there, unable to do anything but listen to Susan's monosyllabic responses. "Fine. . . . Yes. . . . No."

Curious, Hilary mouthed, "Who is it?"

"Ah, just a moment." Susan cupped the phone with her hand. "Lieutenant Elliott. He's on his way downtown."

"What does he want?"

"He wants me to meet him downtown this afternoon. He'd come to the house, but apparently there's some evidence he wants me to look at in the property room at headquarters."

Susan didn't wait for a comment from Hilary. She again put the phone up to her ear. "Lieutenant, you said one-thirty or five o'clock—are they the only times you have available?"

Hilary waved her arms wildly to gain Susan's attention. "Lieutenant, I'm sorry, could you hold again, please?" With exasperation she asked, "What is it, Hil?"

"I know I'll be tied up until at least four," Hilary whispered. "Tell Peter we'll both be there at five. I don't want you going by yourself." Hilary grabbed the phone from her. "Never mind. I'll tell him myself."

"Hi, Peter. Hilary. I know your request to see Susan isn't a formal one, but I'd like to be with her just the same, strictly as her friend, of course. Five o'clock would be best for me."

"Then five it is," came Peter's reply. "The post mortem is now scheduled for sometime early this afternoon anyway, so five o'clock would probably be better for me too."

"Great. See you then." No matter the circumstances, Hilary had to admit, she was elated at having the opportunity to see Peter again, and so soon.

After firmly hanging up the phone, Hilary turned to Susan and said, "Now, show me that letter."

CHAPTER NINE

Following his disconcerting conversation with Jake Stein, Peter had decided to drive straight downtown. Upon arrival, he carefully maneuvered his unmarked vehicle into the parking garage at headquarters, then entered the second floor squad room where he was surprised to see only four detectives still signed in for the day shift. The rest were already clocked out investigating other cases, or following up on what few leads had trickled in on the Bradley murder.

He found a note taped to his chair advising that the coroner had called. Bradley's autopsy had been rescheduled for ten o'clock that morning. That meant he had little time to scan the preliminary reports already awaiting his review.

Peter's desk top, aside from the prelims, was littered with messages from newspapers and t.v. reporters wanting to know if the police had a suspect yet, and demanding to know when the department would be granting interviews. Without a second thought, he decided the best way to handle an attempted invasion by the media was to toss all the pink telephone slips with their "please call" messages into the wastebasket.

His gut told him the Bradley investigation was going to be complicated. The murder was too clean, and it was evident, even at this stage, that a whole lot of digging would have to be done just to get all the information he needed on the victim. Only when that was complete could he start concentrating on the killer.

Peter looked at his watch and decided he still had time to start his customary "to do" list. *And the first thing I need 'to do' is stop thinking about Hilary.*

Organizing priorities was Peter's trademark—it was how he began every investigation. And if he had his way, this case was going to be no exception to that rule, regardless of any outside pressures he may feel being exerted on his department.

With a quickened step which belied his mounting fatigue, Peter walked from his glassed-in private office to the main squad room. "Listen everybody. There's going to be a meeting this afternoon at four o'clock. If DeAngelo and Rigger call in, tell them about it. For the rest of you, I'm writing it down in big letters on the chalkboard so there won't be any excuses like, 'I didn't know about it.' The meeting's been set for a time when the day shift is just about to get off, and the evening shift is just about to come back on. So everyone should be here—no excuses given; no excuses accepted. The faster we get the grunt work done, the better shape we'll be in when we get the forensics back from the lab."

Peter's attention was caught by the sound of a groan winding its way from the back of the room. "But Boss, my kid's in a basketball playoff this afternoon. His team's got a chance at the 'Sweet Sixteen,' so it's real important that I be there." Banging his hand on his desk, he added, "I knew something like this might happen, so I asked off a long time ago, just in case."

"Sorry, Burjinsky. Tell the kid you'll give him a rain check."

Grabbing his coat, Peter added, "I'd like to stay and listen some more, but I'm out of here. If anything breaks, you know how to get hold of me. I've already put together and posted in my office, the ususal list of things that must be done today, so you all have your assignments. As they say in the movies, 'Round up the ususal suspects.'"

CHAPTER TEN

With blue lights flashing, Peter drove to the medical examiner's office located in the basement of the government center, a four story, modern, characterless building, which housed offices for a variety of county-wide agencies. *Nobody likes to go there, probably not even Dr. Pressano,* he mused. But then, it was the only place he could think of, right now, that could possibly provide some answers.

He entered the chief medical examiner's suite and immediately felt the chill and smelled the smell of death. Shirley, the medical examiner's receptionist was busily typing in information on the computer while eating what looked to be a leftover breakfast burrito from McDonald's. She didn't bother to look up from the monitor. "Hey, Peter. Not to rub your nose in it, but you're late. Doc's been looking for you, so I suggest you get in there pretty pronto."

"Yes, Miss Shirley." Peter mockingly saluted and clicked his heels.

"Don't mess with me, young man," she answered with a laugh. "You know how difficult I could make your life."

Peter helped himself to a pair of medical "greens" from the linen closet and opened the double-wide steel doors which separated the reception area from the examining room. Taking off his sport coat, he donned the short-sleeved top and pulled on the drawstring pants.

"It's about time you got here, Peter my boy," bellowed Dr. Gabriel Pressano, Kentucky's chief medical examiner. "If I could have, I would have started without you. Don't you know the dead wait for no one?"

"Sorry," Peter mumbled. "You know how it is, Doc. Too much to do; too little time."

Pressano chuckled. "I'm just kidding you. I know it's tough to get here on such short notice." Pressano pulled on a pair of surgical gloves, handed a pair to Peter, then covered his silver hair with a surgeon's green paper bonnet. Moving his lumbering six foot seven frame over to the stainless steel draining table, he pulled the suspended microphone which had a foot operated transcription system, close to his mouth.

"Peter, let's see what we've got here."

"Doc, before you get started, I think you should know. The deceased was the husband of Judge Emmett-Bradley."

Pressano closed his eyes and grimaced. "I'm sorry to hear that. She always struck me as one fine woman."

Pressano pulled back the white sheet which had discreetly covered the body and began dictating his findings. "From information received from the Louisville Division of Police, which matches the toe tag on the deceased's left foot, the body before me has been identified as that of John Michael Bradley, a white male, age forty-six. Upon examination, the scalp hair is matted with dried blood. Rigor mortis is well-formed in all muscle groups.

"From information provided by my assistant, the body, upon receipt by this office, was clothed in what appeared to be, in spite of the great quantity of blood found thereon, a button-down, blue oxford cloth, long sleeved shirt; a brown tweed sweater vest, fastened with wooden buttons; tan corduroy trousers; brown and tan argyle socks; and tan 'buck' oxford lace-up shoes. Upon removal of the outer layer of clothing, the deceased was found to be wearing red plaid 'Jockey' brand boxer shorts and a white short-sleeved tee shirt. Upon searching the pockets of all exterior clothing, no items were found. Lieutenant Peter Elliott, who is in attendance, has advised that all valuables were taken from the body and placed in evidence bags by evidence technicians. No other items or materials were found in the pocket areas.

"Now, again looking at the unclothed body before me, it is that of a well-nourished male with an estimated weight of one hundred and eighty two pounds, a measured height of seventy-four inches. Examination of the exterior of the body reveals multiple stab wounds on the victim's chest and back with particular concentration in the fleshy area of the scapula. The right hand and wrist reveal seven linear cuts ranging in length between a quarter, to one and one-half inches. Two are located on the wrist itself, with the remainder on the hand, specifically, two on the anterior portion, and the last three located on the palm, directly below the index finger.

"A five and one-half inch by one and three-quarter inch deep sharp instrument wound is present in the upper chest and shoulder area. Extensive soft tissue hemorrhage is identified. The path of the injury is sixty degrees downward and thirty degrees lateral.

"Also identified is a one-half inch by one-sixteenth of an inch linear laceration, present on the right forearm." Pressano bent down and adjusted the "mike."

"There are—"

"Sorry, Doc. I know your standing rule—don't interrupt during an autopsy, but I gotta ask. Do those small lacerations indicate what I think they do?"

"Yep. The victim, at some point, must have tried to fight off his attacker. All these collateral lacerations were the result." Pressano looked across at Peter over gold rimmed reading glasses. "Now may I continue?"

Peter smiled and nodded. "Sorry. I just needed to be sure."

"Continuing on then, there are two areas of blunt force trauma present within the soft tissues of the right forehead. The first of these is a superficial laceration measuring one-half inch and extending from the medial surface of the right eyebrow, upward, approaching the hairline then veering to the right, terminating at the lateral margin of the right eyebrow. The second area of trauma is similar in appearance and size, located just one-eighth of an inch below the first. Otherwise this area is unremarkable."

Fascinated, in spite of the mounting nausea which left him almost gagging, Peter watched as Pressano made the "Y" incision down the length of the body's torso. Seconds later, the dictation continued. "The lungs appear normally inflated. Total transection of the left brachial artery and vein is present however, within the wound site. Extensive soft hemorrhage in and around the injury. There are aspirated contents of gastric material within the bronchial tree."

"Doc, please, speak English for me."

"It means the stab wounds to the victim were inflicted with a great deal of force, ripping the artery and vein in half. At the time of death, food was still in the victim's stomach and he vomited the contents into his lungs. Not pretty I know, but that's what happened; it helps pinpoint time of death.

"Again, picking up where we left off, there is no hemorrhage within the scalp. The brain is of normal convolutional pattern. Examination of the arteries at the base of the brain reveal them to be of normal distribution and dimension."

"Doc, this is really important. If there was anything mentally wrong with Bradley, would you necessarily see evidence of it in an autopsy?"

"Why do you ask?"

"Because the widow told me the deceased had been exhibiting some rather uncharacteristic behavior lately."

"Peter, to give you an example—with a neurological condition such as premature dementia, I would expect to find some increased neurofibrillary tangles, consistent with that disease. But I don't see anything like that, and quite frankly, I wouldn't have expected to in a person forty-six years of age, although it does happen. Nor do I see any evidence of tumor or cyst in any part of the head. So, physiologically, he looks to have been in fine shape. Now his psychological health is something else again and, as you know, wouldn't show up during a post-mortem."

Pressano moved away from the table and began pulling off his surgical gloves. "Final diagnosis: death attributed to the stab wounds to the chest. No other discernible evidence of disease. Tissue and blood work-ups may show something else, but I doubt it. Time of death, roughly nine-thirty p.m. to two o'clock a.m., give or take." Off the record, he added, "Sorry Peter, but I can't pinpoint the time of death any better than that."

Wearily, Pressano shook his head as he looked at the body in front of him. "What a tragedy. He was young, nice looking. Now he's mutilated and almost unrecognizable. When you see the Judge, tell her how sorry I am."

Pressano accompanied Peter through the double doors, into the reception area and held out his hand. "Okay, Peter, pony up. You owe me a cigar. Where is it?"

Peter reached inside his sport coat which he had thrown over a chair. "Here. As a doctor, you should know how bad these are for you."

Pressano laughed. "We all die of something, sooner or later."

"Before I go, one more thing as you puff away. Anything out of the ordinary about this 'post'?"

"Nope, not that I saw. From the look of the stab wound to the chest, which resulted in total transection of the artery, I can take an educated guess and tell you that the killer was likely right-handed.

"The bumps and cuts on the face and forehead were most probably the result of the deceased falling forward and possibly hitting something. From what you described of the crime scene, I agree with the coroner—at the time of the initial attack, Bradley was probably in a sitting position. Someone no doubt came up from behind and stunned him with the first of several stab wounds to the back which were superficial. Once the deceased was somewhat immobilized, the killer then stabbed him in the chest, most likely in a left to right motion, creating what could best be described as a slicing action. That's probably when Bradley attempted to stand up but instead fell forward. By that time though, he was undoubtedly bleeding profusely and close to death.

"The preliminary results of the microscopic and toxicology examinations will probably be available sometime next week. But I don't expect to find any surprises there either. He looked pretty healthy. No evidence of disease.

"The photographs which I took during the post will be available sometime today. I concentrated on the stab wounds, getting good close-ups of the lacerations. I don't know whether you'll be able to match that wound with any particular knife, but who knows? I gather you didn't find a knife in close proximity to the body—correct?"

"No. But we've collected several from the kitchen area. When we send them to the state police crime lab, maybe we'll get lucky."

"Peter, keep in touch. And thanks as ususal for the cigar. Everyone has a secret vice, don't they?"

"Yeah, you're right about that. I just wish I could figure out what John Michael Bradley's was."

CHAPTER ELEVEN

After carefully studying the letter from Dr. Parker, which Susan had wrested, just hours before, from John's lifeless hand, Hilary was convinced that in order to protect her client, she had no ethical alternative but to remain silent about the letter's existence. According to the rules of evidence, it was the client, not the lawyer, who maintained the privilege not to disclose. The only applicable exception would be if the lawyer's services were sought or obtained for the purpose of enabling the client to commit a crime. Since that was not the case here, Hilary could communicate to no one, the action her client had already taken.

So, feeling confident that she was snugly cloaked in privilege, and knowing that for the time being, nothing else could be done at Susan's, since Susan had stubbornly and inexplicably insisted that she would be going to the office, Hilary said goodbye and walked, as if in a daze, to her car.

The chill in the early morning air felt good on her face even though it numbed her fingers and toes. She had to admit, if forced to be honest, it was a relief to be by herself. Worn out with worry and shock, Hilary had a lot to think about before she started what she knew would be a long and difficult day. The sadness she felt was overwhelming; John's death, still incomprehensible.

Trying hard to keep from crying, Hilary thought how much she had truly liked John, in part, because she knew that he was one of those people you could count on; someone you could trust. She absently slowed her pace. . . . Or was he?

In light of what Susan had told her, Hilary began to wonder about her perceptions of John and Susan as a married couple. Had those perceptions been skewed, albeit subconsciously, because she wanted her friends to be happy, therefore, she convinced herself they were? When she was with them, John had always seemed so devoted to Susan, so committed to their relationship. But if, as Susan claimed, that wasn't true, then what went wrong, and why hadn't she seen it? Sighing, Hilary got in and started the car.

John had always been so quiet, so insular—as if he held secrets no one would understand, or, if known, care about. He never talked about his family or himself. Conversations seemed intentionally geared toward others and what they were doing, not what was going on in John's world. And those few times when John talked about business, the only subject which he seemed comfortable in discussing, he was always quick to apologize for appearing too self-absorbed.

How then, could someone so smart, so handsome, and so well-educated, who owned a successful business as innocuous as selling medical supplies, end up brutally murdered?

Even more nagging, did Susan know more than she was telling her lawyer and best friend? Was the letter from Dr. Parker the only thing Susan had held back, or was that just the very least of it?

Pulling into her driveway, Hilary leaned against the steering wheel, and for the first time since she was awakened by Susan's unexpected phone call, wept.

CHAPTER TWELVE

At the appointed hour, all eight homicide detectives, from both day and night shifts, showed for the first formal briefing on the Bradley case. Pleased, Peter moved quickly to the front of the rectangular shaped squad room. "Okay, everybody, let's get started. We've got a high profile homicide on our hands, and already, the chief has been on my ass asking why we haven't arrested anyone yet. And, as all of you know and understand, when my ass gets chewed, yours closely follows."

Looking around the room, Peter asked, "So, with that said and out of the way, what have we got so far?"

He waited, but no one said a word. "Come on people, let's share the wealth here. Greene, we'll start with you and Shapero. Give me a rundown of what you've been doing since I last saw you."

Greene and Shapero were veteran cops, each with twenty years on the force. Partners for five, they had become so close, the two could now finish each other's sentences. They were alike as two peas in a pod; as different as night and day—Shapero a bachelor, newly divorced for the third time; Greene a family man, married to the same woman for twenty-five years; Shapero, a towering six foot four; Greene, barely five feet six in his specially made elevated shoes; Shapero a brash transplanted New Yorker; Greene, third generation Louisvillian and proud of it. Their "Mutt and Jeff" physical appearance, contrasting temperaments and styles, surprisingly brought out the best in each, perhaps Peter thought, because their relationship was so clearly grounded in mutual respect.

"Well, Boss, like we're supposed to, we've been shakin the trees, checking the victim's whereabouts during the seventy-two hours before he unexpectedly 'bought' it. Hate to admit this, but we haven't come up with shit." Shaking his head, Shapero added, "If the last few days were any indication of what the rest of this poor slob's life had been, the guy was already walking around comatose. He just didn't know it. Everybody we talked to confirmed he didn't do much of anything, or go anywhere. Just your regular kind of guy—you know plain, like mayonnaise. Believe me, he was so straight, my own saintly grandmother would have lost interest."

"Shapero, thanks for the run down on what you think Bradley's quality of life was. That's all very interesting, but I need to know about his habits, his routines; you know, the ususal stuff."

"That's just it. After talking with those who should know, what I just described was 'the usual stuff.' According to them, Bradley never deviated from routine—in the office by nine, and generally remaining there all day except for some outside calls he'd make on clients and wholesalers. At the office, he stayed pretty much to himself, never kibitzing with staff; a real loner. That's what I meant when I used the word, 'boring.'"

"Who did you talk to at Bradley's office?"

"His secretary, Mary Jane, who by the way, looks and acts just like her name. She told us it wasn't anything out of the ordinary for Bradley to close his door and lose himself for a good part of the day, supposedly working on company books and keeping up with the latest in the industry."

"What about lunch appointments, or phone calls he'd receive during the business day?"

Smiling, Greene said, "We asked about all that. Mary Jane told us he rarely went out. Had the same lunch every day—tuna on rye, hold the mayo, washed down with a diet coke. If he did go out, it was to scheduled appointments, which he himself made. Details were never disclosed to his secretary. Most incoming calls were business related. Any personal calls were generally from the wife."

"Wait a minute," interrupted Shapero. "There was one exception to that. Remember? Mary Jane said that a while back, there was some woman who used to call a lot. At first, Bradley's pants were on fire to take the calls. But after a few months, Mary Jane said he acted pissed, as if talking to this lady was something he had to do, not what he wanted to do."

Interested, Peter asked, "Come up with a name, by chance?"

"Hope to. Mary Jane promised to check her phone logs and get back with us. Apparently, even though the mystery woman wouldn't leave her name, she may have, on at least one occasion, left a phone number," offered Greene.

"As you say, let's hope," Peter answered. "Find out anything else while you were there?"

"Tried, but couldn't get much. Talked with office workers, mostly sales people," interjected Shapero. "Looking at my notes here, there were twelve in all—seven guys, five gals. Due to Bradley's death, though, not everyone was there. And those that were, weren't really working, just worrying each other to death about what kind of future they now had with the company."

"Did Jake Stein's name come up?

"Yeah, but only in passing," replied Greene. "But you know, come to think of it, when his name did come up, every last one of them acted like they were afraid to talk about him."

"I got that impression too," agreed Shapero.

"Then that's something you two need to follow through on. By the way, did you run into Stein while you were there?"

"Nah. Stein was a no-show today. But his secretary," Shapero said with a smile, "some dish with double 'D's,' explained that he'd called in saying, 'he'd be there when he got there.' According to her, he had some important outside business to attend to first. I asked her if she knew what that meant, but she just looked at me with jaws going a mile a minute with what smelled and looked like a wad of blueberry bubble gum and said, 'Jake never tells me anything about where he's going, 'cause he says its easier to lie when you don't know the truth.'"

"Get outta here," Peter laughed. "She said that?"

Shapero clasped his hand to his chest. "Honestly, I felt like I was talking to a child, but being the gentlemen that I am, I decided not to take unfair advantage." Shapero looked over his shoulder at the rest of the squad and lowered his voice. "Instead, strictly as follow-up, I made a date, well sort of a date, but not really a date, for lunch tomorrow.

Greene winked, "All business of course, Boss."

Shapero began fidgeting with the key ring attached to his belt loop. "Hey, there's nothing wrong with what I did. I'm just gonna follow through like you told us to. You never know what you can find out in a more informal atmosphere. Trust me, this is gonna be *nothing* but hard work."

"Ah, shut up, Shapero," whined Burjinski, whom Peter knew was still smarting from the rebuke he had gotten earlier. "You always get the good stuff to do in an investigation. Why is that?"

"We all have our talents, some more hidden than others," Peter laughed. "I must say though, even for you, this is a little over the top."

"Ah c'mon, Boss, you know I wouldn't do anything I shouldn't."

"Not yet, you haven't." Peter looked at him sternly. "And it better stay that way."

Peter let that sink in, then turned to Greene. "While Shapero's attention was drawn to chest level, I hope you weren't similarly distracted. What did the other employees have to say?"

"Well," began Greene in his well-known slow southern drawl, "we just asked about Bradley & Stein in the general sense. But, it was the damnedest thing, none of them would say anything about the company—good or bad." Shrugging his shoulders, Greene added, "Considering that we were interviewing them altogether though, which was dumb now that I think about it, their lack of cooperation was none too surprising."

"How many employees were absent today?"

Greene turned to his notes. "Five unaccounted for."

"Generally, how would you collectively describe the employees that were there, since that's how you chose to interview them, which, by the way, isn't how I want them interviewed in the future."

"I know. I know we screwed up, but that's just the way it turned out," Greene answered defensively. "First impression, I'd describe them as a friendly, but pretty competitive group. Seems it was fairly common knowledge that Bradley and Stein remained partners only out of necessity due to mutual business obligations."

"That's pretty consistent with what I heard from the widow and Stein himself," Peter volunteered. "How about any public disagreements, physical altercations between them—anyone see anything like that go on?"

"No one witnessed any words between them, but everyone agreed, they gave each other a pretty wide berth when they were in the office. It helped I guess, that Stein was the rainmaker. In that role, he was expected to be out drumming up business ninety percent of the time. Bradley though, from what we learned today, was supposed to have a more hands on approach with the sales force."

"Who did the hiring and firing?"

"Bradley. He also did the training," replied Shapero. "As we already told you, no one said anything negative, but we, or at least I, got the impression that even though he was more of a presence in the company, Bradley wasn't real approachable." Shapero looked over at Greene. "You agree?"

Greene nodded, then pulled out his notes. "I asked them if they could describe Bradley in ten words or less. They chose less and I wrote the descriptions down—'intense,' 'nice looking,' 'quiet,' and 'neat.' Sounds like a boy scout, don't he?"

Peter ignored this last comment. "What's on the agenda for follow-up, besides Shapero's luncheon plans?"

"We're scheduled to meet tomorrow with each of the employees, individually, fifteen minutes apart."

"Dig deep," grumbled Peter, "especially when interviewing employees who've been reprimanded, or past employees who've been discharged, then dictate your report as quickly as possible. Have it on my desk tomorrow evening."

Peter turned halfway around and focused his attention on the other side of the room. "Bunker and Thompson. What've you found out about evidence gathered at the scene?"

Bunker quickly threw the sports page down on his desk as if it were a snake ready to bite, then leaned forward covering it as best he could with his big beefy elbows. "Evidence techs picked up lots of smudges and five identifiable prints. Two belonged to the deceased and his wife. They have a housekeeper, Mrs. Mencken, who comes in three days a week to cook, do the laundry and clean the house, so most probably one of the remaining unidentified latents belongs to her, so—"

"I don't want to hear the word, 'probably,'" interjected Peter. "Make sure you verify that tomorrow, first thing. Anything else?"

"Yes, Sir." Fidgeting, Bunker continued, his elbows still stretched outward trying hard to conceal the basis for his earlier inattention. Peter could see big ovals of sweat begin forming on each side of Bunker's light blue cotton sport shirt. *Nervous was good*, Peter reminded himself.

"We also collected some papers found on the floor, near the body, as well as on the couch where we think Bradley was sitting when attacked. First impression—they seem to be just a bunch of contracts with various pharmacies, hospitals and nursing homes. We're checking out all the individuals who signed on the dotted line. In all, nine contracts; all signed within the last ninety days."

"I know it's early in the game, but notice anything out of the ordinary about any of them?"

"I haven't had a chance to really study them, but one had a note attached, indicating that Bradley wanted to talk with Stein about canceling, then suing the guy." Bunker momentarily forgot about the sports page he had so diligently tried to conceal, and as Greene had done before him, pulled out his spiral note pad, part of every homicide detective's investigative arsenal. "I jotted the name down here somewhere. Yeah, here it is. Richard Waylander—some high roller affiliated with Our Lady of Lourdes Hospital. We're in the process of setting up an appointment with him, but it has been tough going. Waylander isn't too eager to see us—says he really doesn't know anything about Bradley. Either way, I don't look for much from that interview."

"Regardless, stick with it. What about other evidence taken from the scene and collected during the autopsy?"

This time, Thompson took a turn. "We already transported blood samples collected during the autopsy, as well as the victim's clothing, Bradley's fingernail scrapings, seven kitchen knives, and some other miscellaneous items found at the residence, to the crime lab for comparison analysis."

"Who's doing the examination up there?" asked Peter.

"Wendy's the serologist who accepted the items for chain of custody purposes, so I guess she'll be the lucky one."

"What's the expected turn around time?"

"Things were slow, so she thought she could get to them pretty quickly. As to an exact time, I got the usual song and dance—she'll call when she's got some results."

"What did you ask for on the request form?"

"Hair, blood, and fiber comparisons as to all items submitted, which included the deceased's clothing, a pillow from the sofa which appeared to have blood on it, the lamp and lamp shade which were on the living room floor next to the body, and a piece of rug cut from the area located directly beneath the body."

"Are photos of the scene back yet?"

"Yeah. But they were delivered just before this meeting, so we haven't had a chance to look at them. Included, should be a photo, as well as measurements of a bloody partial shoe print found in the area separating the library from the hallway. Since it didn't match the tread on the suede bucks worn by Bradley, we're hoping it's a decent lead."

"That's the best news I've heard all day," muttered Peter half to himself. "Anything else?"

Bunker volunteered, "We figure the killer must have been wearing gloves due to the lack of prints, other than the five or so found in the library that we already talked about. With the weather the way it is though, I guess it wouldn't have made Bradley uneasy, the fact that his guest kept gloves on."

"Well then," Peter replied, "with what we know so far, I think we can safely assume that the killer was invited inside." Peter moved to the middle of the room so that he could more easily see everyone. "The front, side, and back doors were all locked, and Bradley's key was located in his pants pocket at the time of death. When I asked the Judge about keys to the residence, she told me no one else had one other than she and Mrs. Mencken. And before you get your hopes up, Mrs. Mencken isn't exactly a viable suspect. She's sixty-two, and has been with the Bradleys for years. In fact, she worked previously for the Judge's mother and dad, both of whom now live in a nursing home in Pittsburgh."

Peter stopped and thought for a moment. "Just to make sure though, Bunker, I want you and Thompson grilling her tomorrow. You never know—she could have given the key to someone, or someone may have helped themselves to the key when the lady wasn't looking."

"Will do, Boss."

"Thompson, when the evidence techs processed the body, did they find anything unusual in the victim's clothing?"

"Nothing. Just keys, a money clip, assorted change, and a handkerchief."

"Do we know what doors or locks those keys open?"

"Nope. I figured since you were personally interviewing the Judge, you could ask next time you saw her."

Peter nodded. "Who did the neighborhood canvass?"

"We did," Burjinsky and Moffatt replied in unison.

"Anything worth mentioning?"

"So far, a bunch of nothing," Moffatt explained. "The next door neighbors at 168 Park Boundary Road weren't home last night. We heard from neighbors on the other side, at 164, that the Boysens, who live at 168, are 'wintering in West Palm.' And before you even ask, the neighbors at 164 heard and saw nothing. There's quite a distance between the houses, so no surprises there. From what we could gather, the Bradleys seem to have kept pretty much to themselves; no one knew them all that well."

"Okay. Good start. And just so we have something to show the Chief, get those reports written up and on my desk within the hour."

Peter's gaze fell on two detectives in the corner of the room. "Now, last but certainly not least, DeAngelo and Rigger—what do you two have?"

"Lieutenant," began DeAngelo, while taking up for his partner who was, as usual, engrossed in eating a Reese Peanut Butter Cup, "you told us to tail the Judge, which we did. All day."

"And?"

"You won't believe it but the Judge's been at the Judicial Center from eleven o'clock a.m. on. She's still there, I guess.

And due to keeping an eye on her all day, we didn't do much of anything else. Billy here though," referring to his partner, "talked with some of the court personnel while I stayed outside watching the Judge's office."

Luckily by then, Detective Billy Ray Rigger had swallowed most of his Reese Cup, but what hadn't been eaten was still visible, in the form of tiny dried specks on his clip-on, made in Taiwan, made to look like real silk, tie.

Rigger picked up the narration begun by DeAngelo and explained that he had talked with all four circuit court clerks and secretaries on the seventh floor, including the Judge's own personal staff, but had nothing noteworthy to report. "I asked if anyone had seen the Judge on the night of the murder. None of the secretaries or the clerks I talked to had worked late that night—no trials were going on. And the bailiffs of course, had all left by four-thirty, so they didn't see her either. The guards who were there today at the courthouse checking purses, briefcases and every lowlife that came through the revolving doors, work only day watch, but I got the names of those who work the night shift. There are three of them, and they work every night, Monday through Friday. I made arrangements to talk with them tonight after this briefing's over." Glancing at Peter, Billy Ray said, "I guess that's all I have, Sir," then abruptly sat down, narrowly missing the table leg with his pointy-toed genuine pigskin cowboy boots.

Peter looked around the room one last time before dismissing the squad. "As I said, this is nothing more than a start. There is a lot to do. Follow up until those leads you got today are dried up. Then I want you to follow them up some more. Burjinski and Moffatt, I know you're pulling double duty as backup on all other cases, but when called upon, make yourselves available to assist on this one.

"Before we call it a day, I need to share what I learned this morning at the 'post'—Dr. P puts time of death at between nine-thirty p.m. and two o'clock a.m.– but that's real flexible. The large laceration in the chest area severed an artery and very simply, John Michael Bradley bled to death.

"I'm meeting with the Judge right after this. Before I forget though, I need those photographs that were just developed. Earlier today I asked her to come over to look at the evidence which had been collected, but since Bunker and Thompson are one step ahead of me, and have already transported them, photographs will have to suffice." Turning to Thompson, Peter asked, "Before you took the victim's clothing to the lab, did you photograph each article, and if you did, are those photographs included in that packet you have in front of you?"

"Yes, Sir. Everything was photographed. The lab said each developed without any problem, so we should have a pretty good record of everything connected with this case."

"Good. I guess that's it," Peter said. "Each team—check in with me tomorrow morning. Depending upon what I hear, I'll schedule another briefing to exchange information. Meantime, no one should, for a second, think that a shift lasts only eight hours. During this investigation, shifts go around the clock. For those of you who have to be in court to testify on other matters, ask the prosecutor if you can be on call, so you don't waste time waiting around to testify. Keep up the good work."

With that, Peter gathered up his papers and left the room.

CHAPTER THIRTEEN

Peter looked out from his second floor window which was speckled with a dusting of snow, made grey by the perennial grime that sadly seemed part of every downtown government building. In the waning daylight, he could see Hilary and the Judge trudging down Seventh Street, then trying to cross Jefferson against busy rush hour traffic, their stride hampered by a slippery slush that appeared to be accumulating at an alarming rate of speed.

Hilary, he could see, was wearing that black coat with the faux fur collar that he liked so well. He remembered with painful longing, how her long, red hair, which fell just past her shoulders in gentle waves, always felt so soft, smelled so sweet. Smiling, he watched with fascination as it was now being picked up and tossed about in all directions by the harsh late winter wind blowing in from the Ohio River. Hilary, as ususal however, appeared unconcerned—her step remained deliberate, her expression determined. She was so beautiful. *Hilary, you still take my breath away.* He leaned against the window, his gaze following her every move until she disappeared through the front door of police headquarters.

Three minutes later, the intercom announced that Peter had visitors. He quickly straightened his tie, grabbed his sport coat which he now regretted leaving in a ball on the corner of his desk, and ran a hand roughly through his hair. He then walked through the squad room, empty but for two detectives busy scribbling notes, their necks cocked sideways, their shoulders cradling telephone receivers, to the reception area where Hilary and the Judge stood waiting.

"Thanks for coming," he said, trying a smile. For a moment he allowed himself to wonder if Hilary still shared those old feelings that just minutes before, he had found impossible to ignore. He took a deep breath and decided to direct his attention to the Judge. That was safer. "I apologize for keeping you downtown so late, especially since the weather is turning bad."

"That's all right, Lieutenant," she answered. "I guess it can't be avoided. I was down here anyway, getting things squared away at the office. Since I couldn't bear to stay at the house, it provided my only safe haven."

He couldn't help but notice how pale and utterly exhausted she looked; Hilary, however, appeared her usual self—intent upon getting down to business and, in the process, committed to getting answers. Quickly, Peter escorted both to his private office, closed the door, and pulled up two mismatched wooden chairs, scarred by decades of abuse, each listing dangerously to the side at twenty degree angles, like ships in distress. He noted Hilary immediately positioned herself on the edge of hers and planted both feet firmly on the floor, succeeding nicely in lessening the uncontrollable wobble. Judge Emmett-Bradley however, sat expressionless, appearing totally unaware of her surroundings or the precariousness of the seating arrangements.

"So, what's this all about?" Hilary asked expectantly.

Not immediately answering, Peter moved to the chair behind his desk and slumped down, his chin resting on cupped hands. "There were two reasons why I asked you here tonight—one, so that you could help us, which is the most obvious. And two, in helping us, I'm assured that you remain current with what is going on in the investigation. It's been my experience that often, families feel out of the loop in criminal investigations because they're not kept well-informed. That's not going to happen in this case. You'll be kept advised every step of the way." Peter looked at the Judge, expecting some outward expression of relief at receiving such an assurance; instead, he received a question. One he hadn't expected.

She spoke slowly, thoughtfully. "Not that I minded, since it gave me a sense of security, but why were two detectives stationed outside my home and then outside my office today, watching my every move?"

Surprised, Peter asked, "How did you know they were detectives?"

A hint of a smile formed. "Remember, Lieutenant, I'm a Judge. I'm paid to see a lot of things that other people may not notice." She leaned forward in her chair. "I have to be honest though, they seemed a cut above the ususal courthouse regulars whom I'm so used to seeing on a daily basis. I think that's what tipped me off."

Peter chuckled to himself. "And I thought those two would blend in so easily." Looking downward, not wanting to face her directly, he absently rolled a paper clip back and forth between his thumb and index finger, buying time, trying to get his thoughts together. The silence was awkward, but he knew he had to phrase this just right. Quietly he explained, "Frankly, the detectives assigned to you were there for your protection, because—"

"I don't understand," interrupted the Judge.

"It's simple. Right now, I don't know who killed your husband. It could have been anyone. And your husband may not have been the only target."

Susan shrank back in her chair and bowed her head. He felt badly about the pain that last comment caused, but he had no choice. "Judge, we now believe that your husband knew his killer; however, we can't rule out the possibility that whoever that individual was, may have been after you. That's why I'm taking every precaution. You're going to be watched closely for the next forty-eight hours."

Susan lifted her head and stared at him. "I knew it. I even told Hilary this may be my fault. The killer wanted me, not John."

"Now hold on a minute. We don't know that for sure," Peter answered reassuringly. "We're just taking some precautionary measures." He got up from his desk and walked slowly over to where Susan was sitting and stood in front of her, his arms folded. "I know this question is also going to be painful, but I have to ask."

"Then just ask it," she answered impatiently.

"Have you made arrangements for Mr. Bradley's funeral?"

"Yes. This morning." She clasped her hands together and placed them in her lap. "It's set for ten o'clock, day after tomorrow at Highland Presbyterian Church. Burial at Cave Hill."

Quietly, Peter advised, "Just so you know, at least two of my men will be at the service, as well as at the internment."

"Why?"

"Believe me, there's good reason for this precaution. I don't want to alarm you unnecessarily, but killers often like to attend their victim's funerals. As hard as this is to understand, psychologists think they like having their work affirmed publicly; they enjoy seeing, close-up and firsthand, the pain they've inflicted on the victim's loved ones. On the off chance that your husband's killer will show, we're going to be watching and taking notes. We want to know who's there that shouldn't be."

Peter watched sadly as the Judge's eyes opened wide with horror. She shivered before answering. "Do whatever you have to do, Lieutenant."

Peter turned and picked up a large brown envelope that had been placed in the center of his desk. It hadn't escaped him that Hilary's eyes had been riveted on it throughout the discussion. *Nothing gets by her does it?*

"When we talked earlier, my intent in asking you to come here today, was for you to look at various items collected by the evidence unit. My detectives were way ahead of me though, and have already transported those exhibits to the crime lab. Because of that, I'm going to ask you to examine photographs that were taken of the crime scene and also of Mr. Bradley's clothing worn at the time of his death. Take your time and look at them carefully. Afterwards, I'll ask some questions if you feel up to it. Since they were just delivered, I haven't had time to look at them. I'll do that after you're finished."

Gesturing, Peter directed both women over to a small stainless steel table set in the corner of his office and placed the sealed envelope in front of them. Quietly he left the room and pulled the door shut behind him.

*** *** ***

Hilary and Susan glanced at each other, shrugged their shoulders and sat down side by side.

"Are you ready for this?"

"No," Susan answered angrily. "But like everything else, do I have a choice?"

Carefully opening the ungummed flaps of the string-and-button envelope, Hilary pulled out the contents, but only halfway. On top were fifteen color photographs taken by the medical examiner during the post-mortem. Quickly, before Susan could see them, she separated them out. Susan averted her eyes until all such photos were returned safely inside the envelope. Hilary and Susan then began concentrating on those that remained—photographs which depicted John's clothing, as well as the area wherein he was found. They looked at them for several minutes. Though Susan's fingers trembled, Hilary was surprised to see that her client was able to view them all. She watched Susan studying each photograph, one at a time, saying nothing, then turning all of them, face down, on the table in front of her. After each photograph had been viewed in this fashion, Hilary replaced them, alongside the others in the brown paper envelope.

"Do we need to talk about anything?"

Susan shook her head, then covered her face with her hands. "No."

Again, Hilary couldn't help but think back to that earlier conversation when Susan had confided her decision to no longer tolerate John's behavior. Uncomfortably, Hilary asked herself—was she failing to press for explanations because Susan was a friend? . . . Would she treat any other client with such deference? . . .

With a muffled sigh, Hilary decided that today was not the day to tackle weighty questions. *Maybe tomorrow . . .*

Hilary, with the packet in hand, got up, turned the knob on the door to the outer office, and walked towards the squad room to an awaiting Peter. Out of earshot from Susan, she explained, "Susan looked at all but the autopsy photos. She has nothing to add which she believes would be of value." She looked at Peter for several seconds, but he didn't respond.

"Are you listening to me?"

"I heard what you said, Counselor."

Hilary glared at him. "Can't you understand? It's just too soon for her to be looking at something like this. It's tearing her up to see these photos. For the life of me, I don't know why you want to put her through this."

Patiently, Peter answered, "Hilary, we've had this discussion already. Both you and I know this is the best time, even though it is probably the most painful, for someone to contribute what they know. This is when memories are fresh and powers of recall are at their best. If the Judge can't handle it today, perhaps in the next few days, she could look at them again."

Hilary knew he was right, but still felt she had to verbalize the obvious. She couldn't let Peter's zeal to solve the case compromise her friend's emotional as well as physical health. "Peter, I know she's a material witness, but remember, she's also a widow."

Again, Peter didn't answer. He glanced past Hilary in Susan's direction, then walked back into his office. Hilary followed. Looking directly at Susan he said, "Earlier, we talked a little about problems that you believed your husband was experiencing in the last several months. Have you given any more thought as to what may have been the basis for this concern, and the reason why he was behaving as he did?"

Hilary watched as Susan took a deep breath. She stumbled over her words. "I—I have thought of little else in the last several hours. But I haven't come up with anything new or different." She sat silently for several seconds then added, "Since I felt the need to leave the house and go to my office today, I haven't had a chance to look through John's personal and business papers which are in his desk in the library. They may provide some kind of answer."

Hesitantly, she explained, "On the key ring which your detectives collected from John's pocket, is a small gold key that fits the locks on each drawer in this desk. John always kept them locked; I never invaded his privacy. There was no need before all this happened. If you could retrieve that key, Lieutenant, we could search those drawers together."

"When can we do it?" asked Peter.

"I expect to be home most of tomorrow morning, ironing out any last minute problems which might crop up with the funeral arrangements. If you would like to meet me there, say around nine-thirty, we could do it then."

"How about ten-thirty?"

Susan nodded and sighed. "If that's when you want to do it, that's fine by me."

Peter jotted down the time on his desk calendar. "I'll bring the key ring with me so you can examine it and hopefully identify every key on it. For obvious reasons, the key ring was the one item not taken to the crime lab."

Almost as an afterthought, Hilary believed, Peter turned to her and asked, "Would you also like to be there tomorrow morning?"

"Yes, I would, thank you," she answered cooly. "I intend to stay at Susan's tonight, so we'll both see you tomorrow at ten-thirty."

Retrieving their coats, Peter quietly advised, "In the meantime, Judge, if you think of anything that may be of help, anything at all, let me know." He studied Susan closely, then added, "Most important, think about whether the photographs which you looked at tonight are truly representative of what you saw when you first arrived back at the house early this morning." He smiled. "I'll see you both tomorrow."

Hilary's heart sank. *Did he know?*

CHAPTER FOURTEEN

After the meeting at headquarters, Hilary walked Susan to her car, then returned to the office to check messages and tie-up loose ends left dangling due to her preoccupation with John's murder.

One loose end she could not neatly tie-up however, was the new client being held on charges of cocaine distribution whom she met for the first time that day in federal court. After just two minutes with him, she knew that representation of this angry two-time loser named Enrique Lewis was going to be a nightmare. She was not looking forward to it.

Checking his past criminal records revealed that this wasn't the first time Enrique had seen the inside of a jail cell. Though only twenty-three years of age, he was already a seasoned veteran with two state convictions under his belt, a status which earned him the dubious distinction of being tagged a persistent felony offender in the first degree. But in spite of his revolving door relationship with the criminal justice system, the state invariably gave Lewis a break each time he was prosecuted, by amending the original charges of trafficking, to the lesser charge of possession.

To Enrique Lewis however, who would sooner spit than say thanks, the reduction in charges was no break; it was an entitlement. So with his most recent conviction, he copped an attitude, along with a plea, and ended up serving three out of a five year sentence at Kentucky's maximum security facility, Eddyville. The parole board had decided that for the sake of society, prolonged incarceration was necessary. As a result, Enrique, already homicidally angry, was given a twelve month deferment, twice, in spite of the fact that statutorily, he was eligible for parole after serving only one year.

Since all attorney-client jail conferences are required to be "contact visits," Hilary met with Enrique face to face, in a claustrophobic five by six foot holding cell with only an emergency intercom button for protection. Depending upon how busy the corrections officers were that day, any cry for immediate assistance in opening a locked jail door, could go unanswered for several minutes. For this reason, jail visits always made Hilary uneasy. But something about Enrique made this visit even more uncomfortable. He was hostile and uncooperative, not unlike a lot of clients, but there was something else too, that unnerved Hilary. Even now, she still couldn't put her finger on it. She glanced at the file once more. Nothing. Picking up a pen, she made a note to have Sam accompany her the next time. Sam was insightful. Maybe he could figure it out.

But Enrique's problem wasn't the only factor motivating Hilary's return to the office that evening. She wanted to dictate some notes she had scribbled down in shorthand while interviewing Herman Hornecke, the other new client she had met with today. In Herman's case, she felt confident that a successful defense could be mounted, but it would take months before a trial date was secured. In the interim, the pretrial process would be tedious, expensive, and publicly embarrassing.

Herman Hornecke's case was sad, but unfortunately, in child custody battles, it was fairly unremarkable. During her initial meeting with him, Herman had reluctantly disclosed that he and his estranged wife, Judith, had recently separated.

Living apart however, had not resolved their irreconcilable differences, so Herman had petitioned the court for dissolution, and that's when all hell broke loose.

According to Herman, during their embattled seven year marital union, the parties engaged in a pattern of not so pretty behavior, acted out over and over again—he strayed, then as a catharsis, confessed the details of his sinful behavior. Afterward, Herman would plead for absolution, and suffer the inevitable tongue lashings he knew would follow from a sanctimonious and initially unforgiving Judith. Then, after hours of uninterrupted groveling and humiliation, Judith would open her arms and welcome Herman back like a loving mother with a recalcitrant child.

The honeymoon period wouldn't last long however, before some inexplicable magnetic force would again pull Herman back to his voyeuristic pursuit of finding the best in striptease, lap dancing, and other mindless sexual distractions, thus prompting the mutually destructive tango to start all over again.

Unfortunately, with his last foray into the exotic, Herman convinced himself that he had found true love—a sometime dancer named, Holly. And after a period of soul-searching and enchanted evenings in Holly's third floor walk-up, Herman decided to ask Judith for a divorce. But Judith, who hadn't worked a day since her marriage, had long ago decided that she needed to stay at home with their son. She had grown accustomed to the comfortable lifestyle Herman provided. Divorce was the last thing Judith wanted.

But this time, Herman remained adamant, and in a show of newly found resolve, promptly moved out, and in, with Holly. Weekend visitations with his son were enjoyed without concern, at Holly's apartment, until Judith got wind of the unconventional arrangement. Livid, she asked the court to halt the weekend visits until a home study by social workers could be conducted. Like most romantic triangles, somebody had to get the squeeze—Judith decided early on, she'd be the one applying the pressure.

After meeting with the parties and hearing all the testimony however, the court felt that in the best interests of the child, and without more specific evidence that the child was being harmed, weekend visitation should continue. Unfortunately, the court's good news was short-lived since it wasn't long after that, that Herman was arrested on a district court warrant charging him with first degree sexual abuse and sodomy of his son. The warrant was issued based upon a sworn affidavit being filed by none other than Herman's estranged wife. Finally, she was going to make him pay.

Like most issued on the district court level, the criminal warrant was rather lacking in particulars. But the allegations, regardless of their shortage of detailed information, still met the standard for probable cause. Therefore, when the so-called evidence was presented to a district court judge, who by training and experience, was predisposed to err on the side of caution, the warrant was promptly signed, and then, just as promptly, executed. The result—Herman was arrested, booked and fingerprinted.

Hilary closed Herman's file, tossed it back down on her desk, and sat there wondering how two people who had loved each other enough to marry and have a child, could end up hating each other enough to do this. Sadly, Hilary knew, regardless of the outcome, no one was going to win. Herman's reputation as a well-respected CPA would be irreparably damaged; Judith would become even more bitter and spiteful;

and the little boy would forever be torn between two warring parents who professed to love him.

Not often did Hilary allow herself to dwell on the unhappiness of her own life, but the sadness that had permeated the last twenty-four hours brought back painful memories. Carefully, she picked up a double photograph frame that had been placed on the perimeter of her desk. The photograph on the left was that of Jack, her late husband; the photograph on the right—one that had been taken of them together while on a belated honeymoon to Jamaica. It had been such a glorious vacation—taken on the spur of the moment upon realizing that any chance for taking a vacation in the very near future would be slim once their partnership, Adams & Adams, Attorneys-at-law, was formed.

Jack, who had graduated magna cum laude from law school two years ahead of Hilary, had been an associate, soon to be partner, with the largest law firm in Louisville. But after marrying Hilary, Jack decided to give up his quest for a lucrative partnership with Rosse, Fenner, Fuller and Smith. He wanted instead, to practice law with his wife, and he knew he wouldn't have to do much of a hard sell after a honeymoon in Jamaica.

When they returned after ten days in paradise, Hilary put aside her feelings of apprehension and, satisfied that Jack knew what was best, resigned from the Public Defender's Office and eagerly threw herself into readying their new offices.

To their surprise and delight, the practice had gone well from the start. Each partner had brought an established client base, and each dutifully respected the other's areas of expertise. Jack practiced mostly corporate law and civil litigation; Hilary concentrated in criminal defense. It was a perfect partnership and a perfect life, until almost two years to the day later, when Jack died.

They had decided to take a few days off and travel to Grand Cayman after jointly trying a three week products liability case. Both were exhausted but ecstatic after securing a half million dollar judgement for their client, a third of which was soon to be theirs. It was the first real vacation since they had opened Adams & Adams, and they desperately needed the break.

Grand Cayman was chosen since neither Hilary nor Jack had ever been there, and the brochures, which they poured over night after night, promised an island which would provide everything each of them looked for in a great getaway vacation.

Several years before, Hilary had tried scuba diving but while going through the certification process, had experienced a panic attack in forty feet of water. After that, she could never again bring herself to put on a wetsuit and goggles. So while Jack pursued his passion for scuba diving at Grand Cayman, Hilary waited on the beach, getting a great tan, in spite of slathering on layers of sun screen, drank pina coladas, and read trashy romance novels, an indulgence she would never have engaged in anywhere else.

On the last day there, Hilary agreed to wait on the beach while Jack went in for one final dive. The weather was perfect and the dive promised to be exciting—the exploration of a shipwreck off the eastern coast. It was an opportunity Jack did not want to pass up.

An experienced diver, Jack knew the importance of the buddy system, but for some reason, on that day, he became separated from his diving partners in waters laden with jagged coral.

After the body was recovered, officials on the island speculated that Jack must have thought he could swim though the tight aperture between the rocky formations which protectively surrounded the wreck. But in his haste to explore, Jack got stuck, and in a desperate attempt to dislodge himself, punctured the hose to his regulator and drowned.

That was four years ago and still, Hilary longed to feel the never forgotten embrace of the smiling blond staring at her from the gold picture frame she held in her hands.

Jack was the reason why she had never allowed herself to commit to Peter. When she and Peter became close, Jack was still too much a part of her life; she couldn't and wouldn't let go. The thought of sharing a future with someone else was tantamount to being adulterous. Even if that someone else was as special as Peter Elliott.

She looked lovingly at the photographs she had picked up, then with a sigh, set them down and turned off the lights. Enough pity. She had a lot to do before she got to Susan's tonight. First, she had to return home, pack some clothes and most importantly, rescue Marley. Thankfully, Susan shared Hilary's love of cats, especially Marley, so Marley was in for a rare treat—being an overnight guest at Susan's. She could hear his contented purr already.

CHAPTER FIFTEEN

At eight-thirty, Hilary rang Susan's doorbell with a suitcase in one hand and a disgruntled Marley, imprisoned in his cat carrier, in the other. While she waited, she couldn't help but think about the irony of it all. Less than twenty-four hours ago, she had stood on this same doorstep and rung this same doorbell. . . .

In vain, Hilary had tried throughout the day, to convince Susan to come and stay with her, at least until after the funeral. But Susan stubbornly refused, adamantly arguing that she needed to face the situation head-on. And in Susan's mind, that meant "staying put."

Since Hilary agreed with Peter that until the identity of the killer was known, there was a small chance that Susan might still be in danger, Hilary believed she had no choice—she and Marley had to move in with Susan, at least for the night. *There was safety in numbers,* she thought, *and most convincing, Marley was a killer cat.*

***   ***   ***

"I've started dinner, Hil, but it isn't much, believe me. Just a lot of odds and ends left by friends and neighbors that—"

"Don't be silly," interrupted Hilary. "You know me. I eat everything. Right Marley?"

Hearing his name, Marley looked over at Hilary, uttered a half-formed meow and settled himself where it was warm—right in front of the fireplace in the living room.

Hilary noticed that for the first time since John's death, Susan looked somewhat rested. Dressed casually in slacks and a pink cashmere turtle neck sweater, she seemed softer, but yet fully in command of her devastating circumstances, and her heretofore vacillating emotions.

"Dinner is going to take a while, so how about a drink in the meantime?"

"Sure. What have you got?"

Poking around a wet bar neatly tucked inside a converted antique chifforobe, Susan, replied, "From the looks of things, anything you want."

"Well then, I'll be picky and have a beer. Light if you please."

After getting Hilary's beer, and a glass of red wine for herself, Susan plopped down on the couch, and curled up into a ball, pulling her legs up under her. "You don't mind if we sit in the living room, do you?"

Hilary, in the midst of a gulp of frothy beer, shook her head. The unanticipated jarring motion sent foam up her nose. "Sorry," Hilary exclaimed as she scrambled for a napkin.

But Susan didn't seem to notice. Looking around the room as if checking to see if everything was in its proper place, Susan said, "I usually relax in the library but I can't muster the courage to go in there tonight, even though everything has been cleaned, and the rug removed." She bowed her head, "I'm not sure I'll ever be able to go in there again."

Looking over her shoulder, Hilary could see that the library, located further down the front hallway, was dark and closed off by elegantly shuttered french doors. She touched Susan's hand which lay lifeless beside her. "As I said, let's take one step at a time, okay? You don't even need to think about going in there tonight, tomorrow, or the next day. What you do need to do right now, is relax."

Susan, who had been staring straight ahead as if in a daze, confided in a whisper, "I'm also not sure if I can ever again relax or stop worrying. I keep thinking about what Lieutenant Elliott said when we left his office today." Turning to face Hilary, nervously rubbing her hands together, she exclaimed, "I think he knows what I did—that I removed something from the scene of the crime."

Hilary shared her uneasiness about Peter's comment made earlier that day, but warned herself that it was best to hide any display of concern to Susan. "Don't borrow trouble. He doesn't know anything of the sort," Hilary replied in a tone of voice that she hoped projected optimism, not just wishful thinking. "Besides, even if he did, what's he going to do about it?"

"But maybe—"

"No buts, no maybes. He'd just be guessing. And anyway, this isn't the right time to discuss it with him."

Taking another sip of beer, Hilary suggested, "Let's just concentrate on other things."

"I'd like to," Susan answered wistfully, "but it's not all that easy."

After sitting quietly for a few moments, listening to Marley purr and the fire crackle, Hilary put down her beer on the coffee table and tapped Susan's arm, coaxing Susan to face her. "Before I forget, I wanted to fill you in on my meeting with Sam this afternoon. We had a chance to talk just before you and I went over to police headquarters. First thing tomorrow morning, he's going to pay a visit to Dr. Franklin Parker. Since John's deceased, we'll argue there no longer exists any doctor-patient privilege, and that Parker has to cooperate."

Susan ran her finger around the rim of her wine glass, but said nothing. She didn't appear to be listening.

"Who knows? Parker may have nothing of importance to tell us. If that's the case, we may never have to divulge anything to Peter. In the meantime, let's just wait until we hear back from Sam."

Again, Susan remained silent, so Hilary continued, but this time carefully changed the subject. "Before we have dinner, why don't you tell me a little more about those locked drawers in John's desk. Have you ever seen what's in there?"

Susan shook her head slowly. "Not really. I've been in the library when John had the drawers open, but I never looked over his shoulder to see what they contained. Since all our personal papers are in the bank's lock box, I just assumed that any papers under lock and key in his desk were connected to the business. That made it none of my concern; or so I thought at the time." Susan turned and looked directly at Hilary, her eyes bright but impenetrable. "Why did you ask if I had seen inside those drawers?"

"Only because we know one thing for certain—something was going on with John; bothering him to such a degree, his behavior was affected. If he wrote anything down about it, it's probably going to be in those drawers. Think about it—no one would lock drawers in their own home if they didn't have something to hide, would they?" Without further comment, Hilary felt it best just to let that last comment sink in. Idly watching the embers flickering against the fire screen, she asked, "Anything else go on today?"

"Nothing really. Lots of phone calls, including people from John's office."

Leaning back, Hilary asked, "I hate being nosey, but do you have any idea how much John's interest in the company is worth?"

Susan closed her eyes and rubbed the back of her neck. "It sounds stupid, I know, but I have no idea. You know how John was. Everything was a secret, especially about his business dealings."

"Didn't that bother you?"

"On some level, I guess, but I've always had money from a trust, set up by my grandparents, to fall back on. The annual distribution and accrued interest is placed in a segregated account, in my name only." Dismissively she added, "Like 'Topsy' it just grows on its own. In fact, I never look at the statements of account. John was the named trustee, so he always handled any investments we made with the principal."

"Where are those records?"

"I suppose they could be in any number of different places." Looking hard at Hilary she asked, "First you ask questions about contents of locked drawers, then questions about trusts and finances—where are you going with this?"

"Oh, nowhere really," Hilary said offhandedly, though her mind was racing with all sorts of possibilities. "You know I'm just a criminal practitioner, which means I know nothing about trusts or estate planning." Laughing, she added, "So, with that in mind, I think I'll just keep my big mouth shut. That way, my staggering ignorance doesn't show."

"I think you intentionally sell yourself short in order to throw people off track. I want you to know, you're not fooling me," Susan said with a wink. Placing her wine glass next to Hilary's beer, she asked, "Not to change the subject, but do you think that I need detectives assigned to me for forty-eight hours?"

Hilary tried to shrug off Susan's concern. "I don't want you worrying about the slim, and I mean very slim, possibility that you're the killer's real target. Call it a gut feeling, but I don't think the killer was after you. I think whoever killed John meant to kill only John. Now the question is, who wanted John dead?"

To herself, Hilary added, *And when we find that out, I think we'll also find the answer to another question, equally as interesting—why?*

CHAPTER SIXTEEN

"Everyone, listen please."

His captive audience stared back, saying nothing.

"I know. I know you're upset. John's death is a blow to us all, both personally as well as professionally. But unfortunately, Bradley & Stein is a business, and you are employees hired to work at this business. Because of that, we need to keep our minds on our work, at least for a couple of hours today. Tie up all loose ends, then go home. Since the funeral is tomorrow morning, I will see you all here sometime tomorrow afternoon. If you need to talk with me, I'll be in the office and available all day today."

Hearing a muffled sniffle, he added, "I know this is rough, but we will all get through it, if we work together. I'm here if you need me."

As he strode from the lobby and into his navy, mauve and turquoise office, Jake turned to his secretary and demanded, "Get me some coffee with the usual."

The "usual" Vivian knew meant coffee with a drop of cream, a pinch of sugar, and a sliced bagel with a dollop of strawberry jam squished between each half.

When she returned with breakfast in hand, Jake was busily throwing papers around in a hundred different directions, not caring that in his haste, some were being shredded like a tax evader trying to hide a paper trail from the IRS.

"Jake, tell me what you're looking for, and I'll help you find it; that is if I can in this mess you've made," she said as she set the tray down on his desk.

Not for a second halting his flurry of activity, Jake answered, "Vivian, believe me when I tell you that I wish you could, but let's face it, filing just isn't what you do best." He sat back on his haunches and threw the pages he was holding up in the air. He stared at her. "But if you really want to help, I'm looking for that damn partnership agreement I drew up with John. All I know is, it was in this mess somewhere." Standing up and dusting off his trousers, Jake said, "Hell, I can't waste any more time on this. Get the company lawyer on the phone. I want five minutes with him after I've read a copy of that agreement that you're going to tell him he needs to fax over. And that faxed copy better say what I hope it's going to say, because I sure paid him enough to word the agreement just the way I wanted."

Skittering around him like a frightened mouse, Vivian answered, "Yeah. Okay. Sure, Jake." Quietly, she turned and opened the door to the outer office. "I'll get him on the line."

Jake watched with silent approval as she exited. He hadn't missed the new outfit Vivian was unabashedly showing off that day—a baby blue angora sweater set with matching stirrup pants that stretched as far as they could without snapping from the pressure, while meandering down endlessly long legs, finally to be tucked under tiny little feet teetering on gold flecked spiked heels. *What a woman*. He hired her because she looked, well, like women should look. Nice and feminine, with nothing left to the imagination. He smiled. Paying her rent, spotting her for a new Mustang convertible and paying for a wardrobe that Dolly Parton would die for was worth every penny. When it came down to the important things in a secretary, it didn't matter that Vivian couldn't file, couldn't type, and couldn't find the "on" button to the computer even with the assistance of a red arrow pointing directly at it. Vivian had other skills. Most importantly, she knew when to keep quiet and how to keep a secret.

Jake sat down hard in his button and tucked leather swivel chair and looked out the window at the grey cheerless sky. *Just when murder has finally provided me with the perfect way out of this partnership and the perfect entree into another. Thank God, with my nemesis about to be placed six feet under, I won't have to listen to anyone ever again before I make decisions. That is if Drummond did what he was supposed to do.*

Jake's daydreaming was interrupted by Vivian opening the door to inform him that the fax had come in, and that Nick Drummond, Esquire would be only too happy to make himself available for consultation.

"Good. Bring it in."

Vivian did as she was directed, then with eyes fluttering coyly, and in a little girl voice which was music to his ears, asked, "Ah, could I maybe have a little longer lunch break today?" She picked nervously at last week's french manicure. "I have an appointment, and it's real, real important that I keep it." She walked towards him and bent forward over Jake's desk; her voluptuous breasts clearly visible as they threatened to spill out over her black lacy "Wonderbra."

Jake found himself no longer looking at her face, listening to her mindless chatter, or thinking about partnership agreements. Nervously he answered, "Right, whatever makes you happy." With great effort, he pulled his eyes away from her. "But before you leave, did anything go on in the office yesterday that I should know about?"

Puckering her lips into a sassy pout, Vivian looked at him teasingly. "Well I guess you could say something went on but—"

Irritated at being so shamelessly toyed with, he demanded, "C'mon, c'mon, out with it. We have a lot to do today."

"Why can't I ever finish a sentence without you shouting at me?" Vivian blubbered.

Jake could see the tears start to well up in her eyes. She really knew how to make him feel badly. "Okay, okay. Sorry. Quit that and tell me what happened."

Vivian hesitated. "I was waiting for just the right time." She fiddled nervously with the top button on her sweater.

"Are you going to tell me?"

"Jake, hold on." She sat down, slowly crossed her legs and bit her lip sullenly.

"All right, you've made your point," he admitted, his eyes narrowing in anticipation of the worst.

With her forefinger, she traced the outline of her collagen enhanced lips while trying to explain. "The police were here and they're coming back around ten this morning. They said they want to re-interview everybody. But this time, they're going to talk with each of us, one at a time."

"Oh that's great."

"Now, don't be mad and get your undies in a bundle. They didn't mean to leave you out. They asked where you were yesterday. I told them you were really busy and had left word you weren't to be disturbed—that you were deep into shock and in a state of full-blown mourning." Looking up at him she cocked her head sideways. "I did good, didn't I?"

"Sure. You did just great, Vivian." To himself he thought, *With that kind of help, I could be looking at life without parole.* "Now, what else did the police stick their nose into?"

"Nothing really. It's hard for me to remember—that was so long ago. Let me think."

Jake watched as her eyes drifted to the ceiling and her index finger moved from her mouth to the corner of his desk where she began tapping it lightly, irritatingly. Blinking hard as if that would jar her memory, she said, "I think they wanted to know a couple of things really. Like they wanted to know all about John, and if anything unusual had happened in the last few days." She hesitated, "Oh, and I almost forget. They asked about you too."

"They asked about me?" Leaning forward in his chair, Jake asked, "Well, tell me, what did they want to know?"

He could see that she was nervously picking at her nails again. A bad sign.

"Oh, Jake, you won't get mad, will you?"

"Do I ever get mad? C'mon, just tell me," he encouraged in low tones.

Again, batting her baby blues she answered, "Nobody said nothing. Nothing at all. They just said that you were really, really nice."

Jake smiled, then burst out laughing. "That's the biggest crock of you know what that I've ever heard."

Vivian bowed her head, absently twisting a lock of curly blonde hair.

"Didn't anybody say anything bad about me? I'm disappointed; or maybe I should be worried."

"To be honest, they'd be afraid to say anything bad. But I'm sure," she added, "even if given the chance, they wouldn't want to."

"Cut it out, Viv." Jake took out a cigarette and lit it. He inhaled deeply.

"I thought you quit."

Ignoring her, Jake asked, "What else did they want to know?"

"Nothing."

"Okay, we'll leave it at that, for now." He leaned back in his chair. "Besides the police making an impromptu visit, what else went on here yesterday?"

"It was so weird. Everybody just walked around in kind of a fog, saying they couldn't believe John was dead—that he'd been murdered. I can't either." Softly, she added, "He was such a nice man."

"I know you liked him, but we need to move on."

Standing up he ordered, "Find out what everybody says to the police during their interviews today. And don't give me that dumb blonde routine either. I know you can find out all that crap without any trouble. I also need to know what the police are looking for, so find that out too."

"Well, the police did say that they'd have a search warrant when they came back."

"And when did you think you were going to give me the low down on that?"

"I just did!" Defensively, she got up and inched towards the door. "I don't know why you're always on me. You know I'd do anything for you."

"Yeah, I know." He smiled, pulled out his wallet and handed her a crisp one hundred dollar bill. "Knock yourself out."

Grabbing it, she said playfully, "If you want me to get the 'poop' on what everybody's saying to the police, then I guess I better skedaddle. Here's the fax you wanted from the lawyer. I'll leave it on the couch. Right here."

"And one more thing," he said, lowering his voice. "Don't ever, and I mean ever, talk to anybody about our little secret. That remains between the two of us. Got that?"

Vivian nodded her head. "Promise."

"Just remember who pays you." He watched to see if his message had sunk in, then turned on his heel. "Close the door behind you on your way out." Mumbling to himself, he said, "Whoever heard of the word, 'skedaddle?'"

CHAPTER SEVENTEEN

Ten minutes later, having dialed the number himself, Jake was on the phone with the bespeckled, always very nervous Nick Drummond. He began the conversation without salutation. "What did you think you were doing when you drew up this so-called partnership agreement you just faxed over? I paid you to protect me, not screw me."

"Wait a minute," answered Drummond. "You can't talk to me like that."

"To be honest, Nick, when I read this, I began wondering how in the world John and I ever hired you as our corporate lawyer."

Jake could hear Drummond breathing heavily over the phone. He hoped he was hyperventilating. "Oh, now I remember. You were cheap. That's why we hired you. Guess we got what we paid for."

Angrily Jake hit the phone's speaker button, then stood up and began pacing. "Let me tell you something, Drummond. This time you screwed up big time by not putting a buy-sell clause in this partnership agreement. And because of your screw up, I'm screwed up." Bending down, placing his mouth within half an inch of the speaker box, Jake shouted, "Right now there's only one thing that keeps me going, and that's knowing I'm not alone in this. You're in it with me, all the way. I hope you've paid your malpractice premiums, because when I'm done taking you to the cleaners, you'll wish you'd never aspired to do anything but bagging groceries at the local market." Slamming his hand down on the desk he added, "I'll take everything you have, and everything you ever hoped to get. Kiss it goodbye, Drummond, because it's all going to be mine."

"Wait a minute. I can explain."

"Do it fast then."

"When the contract was originally drawn up, you and Bradley were close friends. Based on that, you opted to omit a buy-sell clause in the contract. Therefore, it was agreed that when one of you predeceased the other, the company would cease to exist, and the partnership would dissolve as a matter of law. That's why the contract was drawn up the way it was—it was your decision."

Jake sat back down in his chair and tried to think. "Well isn't that a convenient excuse." His hand was sweaty as he angrily reached down and gripped the receiver. This is the last thing he had expected. "Listen, I don't remember it happening that way. And I don't remember it happening that way for a very good reason—it never did. As our lawyer, you never once advised that it would be in each of our best interests to have a provision in the agreement that allowed the surviving partner to purchase the interest of a deceased partner."

"Let's get something straight," Drummond answered defiantly, though his quivering voice belied his bluster. "I can't be expected to read a crystal ball. You were apprised at the time, of all the possible ramifications if that provision wasn't part of the deal. You both were savvy businessmen—you especially. Fortunately, I made notes contemporaneous with the contract being drawn up. And those notes confirm that you were told what would happen if you didn't include a buy-sell clause and one of you died—the company would automatically dissolve as a matter of law."

Not wanting to listen to Drummond's self-serving recollections any longer, Jake cut him off. "How the hell am I supposed to know if those notes were made at the time we entered into the partnership? For all I know, you could be fast and furiously writing them out this minute, 'contemporaneous' with this conversation."

"That's just it. You really don't know for sure. But that's how I'm going to remember it. And if push comes to shove, that's how I'm going to testify about it." Chuckling, Drummond added, "I know you're upset because you're caught between that old rock and a hard place. But if you wish, I'll be glad to assist you in your contract negotiations with Bradley's widow. That's the very least I can do. Of course my fee nowadays is three hundred and fifty dollars per. Take it or leave it."

"You'll be hearing from me," warned Jake, as he slammed down the receiver. He sat back, thinking for several minutes and letting his anger settle. Then slowly, he leaned forward and picked up the phone once more, dialing a number he knew by heart.

"Hi," he whispered, a smile spreading across his face. When he heard her voice, he was a different person. All of a sudden, nothing was as bad as it seemed. "I know I shouldn't have called, but I'm missing you, as usual."

He could hear her laugh.

"Me too, you. But I can't talk."

"That's all right. I knew you'd probably be busy. All I wanted was to hear your voice, and know you were all right." He put his feet up on the desk and sat back in the chair. "Have I told you lately how very much I adore you? . . ."

CHAPTER EIGHTEEN

Peter showed up promptly at ten-twenty-five with an added bonus—a bag full of goodies from Louisville's most popular bagel shop—Dooley's. "I never come empty-handed, especially this early in the morning."

Susan took the offered bag and peeked inside. "They look wonderful, Lieutenant. Thank you. Obviously, as a good hostess, I can't say 'no' to this."

"Morning, Peter," Hilary chimed in as she hurried down the stairs while fastening the last pearl button on her silk blouse. "Glad to see you brought some real food. Susan's into this health kick thing—fresh squeezed orange juice, wheat germ, and yogurt with granola. Believe me, it tastes as awful as it sounds."

"I was hoping I could win you over with a bag full of dough," he said with a grin.

Hilary looked at him sideways, surprised, but strangely pleased by the comment. For now however, she decided to ignore it. Maybe later she'd try and figure out its significance, if any.

*** *** ***

After setting out the half dozen bagels and cream cheese on a Waterford cut glass plate, along with a carafe of freshly brewed coffee, Peter, Susan and Hilary sat down in the formal dining room at a twelve foot long Queen Anne table with its graceful outwardly curving claws, and stared at each other across a centerpiece that looked like a three dimensional reproduction of an eighteenth century still life. For thirty minutes they each forced themselves to engage in inane conversational banter about anything and everything, excluding of course, the real reason Peter was there that morning.

But when the bag quickly emptied, and polite chitchat abruptly stopped after "safe" topics of conversation were throughly exhausted, Hilary found she could no longer put off the inevitable. Looking over at Peter she asked, "So what have you found out?"

Before answering, Peter swallowed his last bite of bagel, then chased it with a gulp of black coffee. "Unfortunately, there's not much to tell. I haven't had a chance to talk with the detectives on the night shift yet, but I will once they're back from nine o'clock court. All five were subpoenaed for hearings this morning. I expect them back around eleven."

Leaning forward, he wiped his mouth with a three by five napkin emblazoned with Dooley's well known logo. "So far, I can tell you that the neighbors heard and saw nothing that night." Absently, he picked at bagel crumbs and a glob of blueberry cream cheese left on his plate. "Just in case though, we left our cards, asking them to think about it. We'll follow up just in case, but I think, for all practical purposes, that's going to prove a dead end."

"Well, that's not surprising," sighed Susan. "Given the distance between our homes, and the fact that it was dark outside when John was attacked, I guess I shouldn't have expected anyone in the neighborhood to have witnessed anything unusual that night."

Peter nodded. "We knew going in, that if that line of inquiry paid off, it would be one hell of a long shot. You'd be surprised though, how often people call the police about a tidbit of information they had forgotten about. So don't give up. We haven't."

Trying hard to squelch her disappointment, Hilary asked, "So what else are you doing?" She knew that as time wore on, leads would dwindle, memories would fade, and the chances of finding the murderer would diminish in equal measure.

With a tinge of irritation in his voice, Peter answered, "I know how frustrating this waiting is, but it's still very early in the investigation."

It didn't escape Hilary that Peter immediately turned his full attention to Susan—*obviously a softer touch*, she thought.

"I think what's going to be most informative Judge, is what Detectives Shapero and Greene find out from your husband's employees. Generally speaking, the people with whom you spend eight waking hours a day, five days a week, seem to know a whole lot more about you than even your family. In some cases, more than you want them to know."

Susan made no comment, nor showed any reaction other than an almost imperceptible shrug. Surprised and disappointed by her indifference, Hilary remembered how, when Jack died, she had pestered island officials until they gave her all the details of their investigation. This wasn't like Susan to be so passive. Looking hard at her friend, Hilary wondered, not for the first time, whether the letter from Dr. Parker, which Susan had yanked from John's hand on the night of the murder, was the only piece of information Susan had chosen to ignore and failed to disclose. In spite of her misgivings however, she forced herself to concentrate on the conversation. After all, Susan was a client, and Hilary knew, clients didn't always tell the whole story. She shouldn't expect more from this client just because Susan was a friend.

"Remember too, we've got some good physical evidence as well—a partial footprint, fibers scraped from underneath Mr. Bradley's fingernails, and blood splatters that will be compared with his blood standard to determine DNA. If all the DNA doesn't match up, it's a good possibility, the killer unknowingly left something behind during the struggle." Turning to Hilary he added, "It may not sound like much, but it should give us a starting point at least."

"Seems like we should have been well past the 'starting point' by now," Hilary argued.

"If I could spin the clock ahead to get answers, I would. But unless you find the murderer bending over the body, investigations like this take time. And I don't need to tell either of you, investigations have to be done right, or the resulting prosecutions won't hold up."

"I know; we both know you're right. It's just so hard—"

"So why don't we get off dead center then by starting with this key ring," Peter suggested. From inside a brown five by seven mailing envelope, which he had earlier placed on the counter top, Peter pulled out a key ring which, according to the evidence report and the notation on the front of the envelope, had been found in John Bradley's right trouser pocket. "Recognize it?"

Susan read the note on the envelope, then taking the key ring in her hand, cautiously turned it over, her eyes closed. Holding it tight for a few seconds, she answered, "The key ring is definitely John's." Opening her eyes, she held it out in the palm of her hand so that Peter and Hilary could examine it. "See? It still has the six keys on it that he always carried with him."

Susan then began separating the keys one at a time, explaining with each, what it locked and unlocked. "This first one opens all four doors to the house—one key fits all. This next one opens the front door to John's office; the smaller key next to it unlocks John's private office at the company."

Holding up the next one, which was smaller and more ornate, Susan explained that it opened the locks to both John's credenza and desk located in the library. "This other key opens our joint safe deposit box. And this last key, the sixth key, was John's key to the Audi still parked in the garage."

Once again holding the keys tightly in her hand, Susan seemed to hesitate. "One thing puzzles me though." She smiled and shook her head. "It's such a small detail, I'm not sure I should even mention it, but the note on this envelope describing the location where these keys were found, bothers me."

Gently, Susan placed the key ring on the counter. "I guess you'd have to understand how meticulous John was about his keys, his handkerchief, his money clip, and assorted change that were always in his trouser pockets."

"I'm not following," Peter answered with a quizzical look on his face.

"John always carried his handkerchief and keys in his left front trouser pocket. His money clip and loose change were then carried inside his right front trouser pocket." Laughingly she explained, "John always said that he felt perfectly balanced that way. I used to kid him about it, but it didn't matter. He never deviated from the routine."

She looked down and picked up the set of keys again, carefully separating each as if peeling an onion. "John was so compulsive in fact, that he would begin each day with the same exact amount of change in his pocket—two quarters, three dimes, four nickels and three pennies. That's why I just thought it odd that the evidence technicians retrieved John's keys from his right front pocket when they should have been in his left front pocket." She looked at Peter and shook her head. "I told you it was silly; I don't know why I even brought it up."

Peter held up his hand. "Don't say that. Habits are very important because deviations from a set behavior pattern rarely occur. It's almost as if the person believes that repeated behavior is necessary for continued good luck or well-being. And because these habits are generally known only to the victim, his family or close friends, idiosyncrasies like this can prove to be of real value in an investigation."

"I don't see the importance."

"Let me explain then. Not knowing your husband's personal habits, I wouldn't have thought twice about where his keys were found. But with what you're telling me now, we may have some insight as to what happened just before the murder, as well as the killer's behavior just after the murder."

"I still don't understand where you're going with this," Susan answered irritably.

Interjecting, Hilary suggested, "Why don't you let me explain it to Susan?"

Peter shrugged.

Interpreting that gesture as permission, Hilary said, "John's assailant may have felt that his tracks were sufficiently covered when he replaced the keys in John's pockets after John had been killed. He never thought about which pocket to stuff them back into. Since the keys may already have served the purpose in retrieving something that the killer wanted, most probably from the desk drawers in the library, that's all that may have mattered."

With a look of horror, Susan cried, "But my fingerprints are on these keys now."

Gently, Peter explained. "We've already checked and found nothing—just some smudges. No identifiable prints."

Susan began crying softly. "You'll never find who did this."

"We didn't expect to find fingerprints on the key chain. More than likely, the killer wore gloves while inside your home, so recovery of fingerprints would be next to impossible. Right now, we believe that this was a planned murder, so the killer took all the necessary precautions, thereby leaving behind few clues."

Between sobs, Susan said, "I'm not trying to be defeatist about this, but it just seems as though we're continually running into brick walls or down blind alleys."

"That's why we need your help. And unlocking the desk drawers in your library is a start."

Suddenly sitting up straight, wiping tears away with the back of her hand, Susan announced in a small but commanding voice, "I guess there's no point in putting this off any longer." She pushed her chair back and stood up. "Let's move to the library and unlock John's desk drawers." Looking hard at Hilary and Peter she added, "I don't know which feeling is the strongest—the hope that we'll find something of real value, or the fear that we'll find something I really didn't want or need to know about."

CHAPTER NINETEEN

They walked tentatively towards the library. For each of them, it was a room crowded with gruesome reminders of never ending unanswered questions. Though thoroughly cleaned and sanitized, the haunting scent of death and the unnatural stillness created when a life ends so violently, was still cloyingly pervasive. Following several steps behind, Peter saw Hilary put a comforting arm around Susan's stooped and trembling shoulders, guiding her carefully but firmly, to the last place Peter knew Susan wanted to be.

Even in the light of day he noticed how oppressively gloomy the room appeared, in part due to the hardwood floors, the built-in floor to ceiling bookcases, and the red oak shutters adjusted purposely he imagined, to obscure what little sunlight peeked through the cloudy February sky.

Standing in the middle of the room, taking a moment to carefully look around and get his bearings, Peter decided it was more than just the physical aspects of the room that seemed so disquieting—it was the irrepressible air of melancholy which seemed to permeate throughout the whole house, no matter what hour of the day.

Silently, Susan and Hilary stood around the massive inlaid mahogany partner's desk like true believers waiting for a sign, as Peter carefully inserted the old-fashioned iron key into the center drawer lock and turned it once to the right. The center drawer, along with the two oversized drawers located on either side, immediately sprung open with a violent lurch, as if bursting at the seams to be released.

Peter slowly pulled the middle drawer towards him along its metal tray, then stood there staring. He had to admit, he wasn't surprised. Susan and Hilary however, each let out a gasp.

What must have been a very neat filing system at one time, was now in total disarray. Papers were bent and crinkled like accordians, shoved haphazardly one on top of the other, some torn almost in half, the pieces now only tenuously connected.

"I can't believe this," cried Susan. "It's a mess." She reached past Peter, trying to grab at the drawer's contents, but Peter caught and held her wrist firmly.

"Don't!"

Susan shrank back. "Sorry," she murmured. "I should know better. It's just that this is such a shock." She put her hand up to her face and mindlessly rubbed slender fingers across her forehead. "While I may not have known exactly what John had in these drawers, I know the contents were never arranged like this." She turned her head away. "John couldn't stand any kind of mess. He had an orderly mind and an equally orderly system for doing things. He would be so upset."

Soundlessly, Peter pulled a pair of white plastic gloves from inside his coat pocket and put them on, mindful of the chance, though minimal, that a viable print may have been carelessly left behind. Bending over, he tugged gently at the several pieces of paper, trying hard to juxtapose them after cautiously smoothing out wrinkles, unfolding creases, and carefully flattening out all the shredded, tattered corners. By the time Peter finished his task, he had created two stacks of papers, each scrap clinging precariously on top of the other; each pile measuring half an inch in thickness.

Having accomplished this, Peter looked back at the drawer. With the clutter of papers cleared away, he found what appeared to be some of Bradley's personal items hidden beneath—a pipe which appeared well worn; a photograph of a much younger Susan in a miniature frame, the glass cracked halfway down the middle; a four by six inch box chock full of fishing lures; and a St. Christopher's medal dangling from a tarnished silver chain, its clasp bent and broken. With his fingers barely grasping each, Peter held the items out for Susan to see. "Do you recognize these?"

"Other than the pipe, I didn't even know John kept things like this. He just wasn't what you would call sentimental." She sat down hard in the brown tweed wing chair that had been placed catty-cornered to the desk. Hilary continued to stand, saying nothing. After a few uncomfortable moments of silence, wherein Susan tried desperately to choke back tears, she said with a catch in her voice, "Lately, John had changed so much, we simply lost touch with one another. And now that he's dead, it's too late to do anything about it." She tugged at the beige afghan which had been draped over the arm of the chair, pulled it downward, and buried her face in it.

"Judge, I know you're dealing with a lot right now, but you can't beat yourself up over what could have been." With care, Peter returned Bradley's personal items back to the drawer, then sat down in the high back leather executive chair positioned directly behind the desk. As patiently as he could, he explained, "What we need to do right now is concentrate on the matter at hand—collecting these papers and determining if there's anything else in this desk which appears out of the ordinary."

Susan sat in silence, apparently unable to cope with what Peter was asking of her. He looked to Hilary for help. Without a word being spoken between them, Hilary appeared to understand his dilemma. She walked over, bent down in front of Susan and from the tenor of her voice, muttered something soothing. *Whatever it was*, Peter thought, *it's quieting the Judge down, which is what I need.*

Turning away from them, he focused his attention on the two side drawers which had also sprung open when Peter inserted the key in the center lock. Pulling both out towards him at the same time, Peter saw that each contained several legal size manila folders suspended in dark green hanging files fastened at the top with coated metallic tips—an arrangement which allowed Peter to glide the folders along the horizontal rod with just a touch of his fingers. At first glance, he could see that each was divided by clear vinyl tabs with lettered inserts, arranged in alphabetical order, beginning with the left-hand drawer and ending midway into the right. He quickly thumbed through the folders, not looking for anything in particular, just satisfying his detective's curiosity.

He noticed that several folders, located in the front of the drawer and measuring about five inches in thickness, were collectively inventoried, "Audit," subdivided into "Internal" and "External," and neatly labeled with dates reflecting the three preceding years.

The next file, equally as voluminous, was found under the label, "Bank Records." Peter pulled it out along with the several audit files and laid them all on top of the desk. Each one would have to be catalogued, then carefully gone over later at headquarters when he could take the time to more thoroughly review them.

In skimming through the remaining hanging file folders, Peter saw that they contained nothing more than canceled invoices relating to household maintenance—past electric bills, water bills, phone bills, and what appeared to be a comparison study of cost increases within the last five years. In all, Peter counted nine manila file folders, each identical to the other, each containing papers neatly mounted on both sides, secured with prong paper fasteners, reference tabs for easy access, and numbers that corresponded with the inventory sheet neatly typed and placed on top. Some clearly pertained only to household accounts, conveniently identifying the company or vendor by name. Others were labeled with names of specific individuals, some of whom Susan recognized, some of whom, even after trying hard to jog her memory, she did not.

Picking up the files one by one, Peter began placing them in a large evidence pouch. "This should be pretty easy to follow up on since all the invoices have an identifiable account number."

Looking down one last time at the drawers before closing them, he paused before securing the tape on the evidence bag. "Hold on. . . . I didn't see these folders hidden behind the hanging files." Stooping down, he reached in and grabbed them with one hand, pulled them out, then spread them open on the desktop. All were empty. "These other files . . ." Peter's voice trailed off as he thumbed through them, "'Waylander, Richard;' 'Parker, Dr. Franklin W.;' 'Leprakalb, Liam;' 'Partner;' and 'Trust Account I,' have been stripped clean." He looked closer. "Only one file labeled, 'Trust Account II' seems to have remained intact."

Susan made no comment; neither did Hilary. But so engrossed was he with this latest find, Peter barely noticed. "From the looks of the double holes punched on both sides of these five manila folders, I guess we can assume that at one time, these files held papers too." He picked up the trust account file and ran his fingers down the two inch expandable spine. It was well-worn. But for some reason, whether closed out, taken elsewhere, or destroyed, all five files were now empty. He looked up and asked, "Know anything about these empty files, Judge?"

Susan shook her head. "Nothing but the obvious. The file labeled, 'Trust Account' must refer to my trust set up long ago by my grandparents."

In giving this explanation, Peter couldn't help but notice how Susan's hands fidgeted—her fingers nervously poking holes in and out of the afghan's almond colored yarn as if playing a game of hide-and-seek. *What was going on here?* He couldn't pin it down. The uneasiness he felt before, inexplicably returned. He stared at Susan hoping to get some sort of read, but conveniently, she cast her eyes downward.

"Who oversaw this trust account—you or your husband?"

Susan took her time in lifting her head and facing him once more. "I hate to admit this, being a lawyer and a judge, but I've never had any reason in the last several years to keep tabs on that account. Since John handled all our finances, including bank accounts and the stocks and bonds portfolio, we thought it best that he oversee my trust as well. He loved to take care of the bills, balance the check books, and monitor investments. They were jobs I didn't relish, so I was only too glad to hand them over."

"Do you know whether your husband kept your personal financial papers at the house or at the office?"

"Both places," Susan answered simply.

"Anywhere else?"

Thinking for a moment, she added, "I think he may also have kept some at the bank. You see, he preferred to do most of the paperwork at the office downtown, but sometimes he worked on bank statements here in the library. Whether he did it here or at the office depended a lot on who was working at the office, and how much time he thought he might have there without interruption. Likewise, his decision to work at the house depended on my schedule—whether I would be home or not."

"Why was that important?"

"John didn't like any kind of distraction when he did the books. The work was tedious, and he said it was too easy to make a mistake if he didn't concentrate."

"So, what you're telling me, is that the contents of the trust account file, since they're not here, could be at his office downtown, or at the bank, right?"

"Yes," she answered quietly. "Either is possible."

"What about these other files that are empty? Know anything about them?"

Susan gave the files only a cursory glance. "No, nothing."

Peter studied her closely, but Susan didn't appear to notice. "Well, why don't we go over them one by one, just to make sure."

"If you insist."

"What about 'Richard Waylander?'" Scratching his head, Peter added, "This is the second time I've run across that name in the past thirty-six hours. From that, I guess it's safe to assume he's had some significant involvement with your husband."

"Could be, but personally, I know nothing about him."

"Okay, then let's try another. What about 'Liam Leprakalb?' Does that name ring a bell?"

Shaking her head, Susan answered, "No. I can't recall ever hearing that name mentioned. But we've recently had a lot of construction done to this old house, and I guess its possible that Mr. Leprakalb was a contractor or subcontractor. Let's put it this way," she added, cocking her head sideways, "that's my best guess."

"Sounds reasonable. What about the file labeled, 'Partner?'"

"I assume it had something to do with Jake Stein."

Knowing that he was running out of time before he needed to be back at headquarters, Peter hastily picked up the next folder. "Last but not least, how about 'Dr. Franklin W. Parker?'"

Even though his head was bent down, out of the corner of his eye, Peter noticed Susan glance quickly in Hilary's direction before answering.

"I believe he's a medical doctor. That's all I know and I'm not even sure about that. Paul Hanley has always been our personal physician, so if John saw someone else, I wasn't aware of it."

"Have you seen any correspondence, statements, or anything of that nature from this Dr. Parker?"

"I could have, but I wouldn't have paid much attention."

Raising his eyebrows, Peter asked, "Wouldn't statements from a medical doctor be rather important to you?"

"Receiving something in the mail with a doctor's return address wouldn't necessarily mean John was his patient. Since John was in the medical supply business, it wouldn't be unusual for him to receive correspondence from physicians at his residence as well as at his office."

Peter thought for a minute, then suggested, "I guess that's a possibility, but don't you find it strange that Dr. Parker was the only doctor identified in these files? Not even your long time personal physician, Dr. Hanley, had a file in these drawers." He looked at her quizzically. "Why do you think that is?"

Susan stood up and angrily threw down the afghan, then slowly walked over to where Hilary was standing next to the window. She played with the shutter, moving the wooden rod up and down before answering. The repetitious movement bothered Peter. He wondered why she was stalling.

"There could be several explanations. First, I probably haven't seen Paul for any kind of medical problem in over two years. Second, I have no idea how often John purged old bills." She turned around, folded her arms and stared back at him, her jaw set. "So logically speaking, if I didn't receive a bill from Paul Hanley for at least two years, there wouldn't be much use in maintaining a file on a nonexistent account, would there? Only the audit files cover a period of three years." Gesturing toward the files spread out on the desk, she added, "And we don't exactly know the time span on these others, do we?"

"Judge—"

Holding up her hand—a sign that she was not to be interrupted, Susan continued. "Of course there could be a another explanation as well. Most of the time, Paul never charged us for office visits. John was always giving him samples of this, that, and the other, so I gather the two of them construed the arrangement as a trade-off." She paused for a moment, then angrily asked, "Does that answer your question?"

Peter smiled. "I've hit a nerve, haven't I, Your Honor."

Quickly interjecting, Hilary pronounced, "I think that's enough for today, don't you, Lieutenant?"

CHAPTER TWENTY

Two hours later, Peter was still fuming over his most recent encounter with the Judge and Hilary Adams. Without much doubt, he knew the Judge was hiding something, or to give her the benefit of his doubts, she was afraid of something. And Hilary, he reasoned, was doing her utmost to protect her—like always.

Since the squad room would be relatively quiet except for the rat-a-tat-tat of the secretary's computer keyboard, Peter decided that this would be the best time to more carefully examine the files he had just retrieved from the Bradley residence. But before he went back to his office, he made an impromptu visit to the evidence unit on the lower level. He had a hunch, which he hoped would pan out, that prints might be lifted from some of the items he had just brought in. Luckily a tech was available and took the offered items for immediate analysis. Peter paced back and forth in the reception area, but after twenty-five minutes of waiting, was told the results were not what he had hoped. The lab found only one latent—belonging to the victim. The remainder were nothing more than smudges. Discouraged, Peter picked up the files and trudged upstairs to homicide.

With his arms full, he slammed the office door shut with a kick, then plopped his heavy load on the desk top. After throwing his coat over the nearest chair, he opened the evidence pouch and spilled its contents onto his desk. Taking one file at a time, he leafed through each, quickly realizing nothing much made sense except for the obvious—the IRS had been unusually interested in inspecting and verifying the Bradley & Stein partnership returns.

From what he could tell, for the last three years, the agency had conducted a thorough inspection of Bradley's accounting records, including analyses, as well as confirmation of alleged business transactions. At the end of the third examination however, the auditors found nothing substantive, even though the first two examinations had listed exceptions which in turn, prompted the agency to search and re-search twice.

After placing the audit file back down on his desk, Peter next turned to the equally expansive file entitled, "Trust Account II." Again, it was evident that Bradley had been quite thorough in his documentation. *Almost too thorough,* Peter thought to himself as he reached over, grabbed the phone and deftly dialed a number he knew by heart.

"Commonwealth Attorney's Office. How may I direct your call?" asked the receptionist. After identifying himself, Peter was immediately put through to the person requested—Senior Deputy, Larry Benovitz.

Detective and prosecutor had known each other for years, both professionally, and personally, often meeting after work at BW3s for a beer to discuss pending cases and the latest women in their lives. Benovitz was well liked and respected throughout the legal community; by some, even feared. He was hardworking, honest, and most unusual for a prosecutor, accessible not only to the police and crime victims, but to courtroom opponents as well. His no bullshit attitude was why Peter liked him and often sought out his advice, even though Larry's personal appearance belied his boundless abilities. Prompting the most negative comments was Larry's side-swept thinning hairdo, parted just above his right ear in a failed attempt to hide an ever increasing circular bald spot located directly on top. His clothes, outdated twenty years before he even bought them, made him look like an unmade bed; his socks never matched either his suit or each other; and his ties, wide as a baby's bib, were always inappropriately adorned with Disney cartoon characters, even when arguing the most serious of cases before the highest appellate court in the Commonwealth. Regardless of his appearance though, Larry won by persuasion, because Larry Benovitz was a lawyer who possessed that rarest of all combinations—clarity of reason and an innate ability to artfully get his point across.

"Hey, Peter. Haven't seen you for a while. What's up?"

"I've got a favor to ask."

"Name it."

"How about a fast study on the subject of trusts?"

Benovitz chuckled. "It's not everyday I get a request like this, but right up front, I've gotta warn you, I haven't thought about trusts since law school, and for a damn good reason. I deserved a 'D' in the course, but by some miracle or mistake, I made a 'C.' Now, knowing that much, do you still want advice on trusts?"

"You're all I've got, which has to be better than nothing, right?"

"Not much, believe me. But I've warned you." In a clipped voice, Benovitz added, "Hate to cut this short, but I needed to be in Judge Morrison's court five minutes ago, so exactly what's the legal issue here?"

Knowing that the social chitchat was over and it was down to serious business, Peter struggled to pull the bulky folders open with the one hand that he had free. Finally succeeding, Peter answered, "Wish I knew enough to tell you. All I have here is one of two file folders, three inches thick, labeled,

'Trust II,' which may or may not have relevance to the Bradley murder case. Everything else we've looked at so far has come up a big fat goose egg, so we're quickly running out of options. All we know for sure is, the deceased was compulsive about financial records, keeping most of them under lock and key in his desk at the residence, where, I might add, he was killed."

Quickly flipping through the file as best he could, Peter continued to provide Benovitz with a thumbnail sketch of what he thought they were dealing with. "From what I read here, the Judge has something called an 'expressly executed trust.' She's the 'designated beneficiary.' The deceased was the named 'trustee,' and the Judge's grandparents, the 'grantors.' I've also got a copy of the terms created by the old guy's will, but they make no sense to me whatsoever, so— "

"Wait. Before you go on, you've told me everything but what's most important. How much money are we talking about—nickels, dimes, dollars, what?"

"Dollars—a little more that two million of them."

"Whew! I had no idea the Judge was so well-off. I guess she comes by her hoity-toityness naturally then."

"I didn't realize you disliked her."

"Let's just leave it at this—the lady sometimes has an attitude."

Peter could hear Larry take a deep breath before continuing.

"Maybe I shouldn't mince words here. I'll make it short—as I said, I'm in a hurry. When I was a first year law student, Susan Emmett was a senior. Back then, she was bearable, but demonstrated a potential to be insufferable. She was smart though. I'll hand her that. And all the professors kissed her probably very lovely ass when she was editor in chief of law review, but I always thought she was nothing more than an intellectual snob with an insatiable ego. Just the right combination for a judge, don't you think?"

"Well, I— "

"Not to interrupt, but the one thing I never understood, was how she and Hilary Adams remained such good friends. I know you and Hil had a thing going at one time, so I won't get into it, other than to say that with her, you get what you see. She's bright, honest and up front, but those aren't qualities I'd ascribe to Susan, except for the intelligence part of course. There's no question—the Judge is a fine legal scholar, but as I said, on a personal level, something's just not right."

"I appreciate your comments. As I said, I don't know the Judge personally, only professionally. And in that context, I've always thought that she was fairly reasonable. But anything I can learn about her other than what I've seen in the courtroom, is helpful to say the least."

Peter put down his notes and picked up the file again. "Getting back to this trust business—how about setting up a time whereby you and I could take a look at it?"

"Okay, but give me a second to look at what I've got going on today."

Peter could hear Larry tapping out selections on his electronic calendar.

"Looks pretty tight. Four-thirty might work though," he said slowly. "Tell you what, if that's convenient, I'll go ahead and draw up a subpoena duces tecum for all of Bradley's bank records, to include the trust account. If I can find a gopher to go over and pick up the records this afternoon, I'll have them ready when we meet at four-thirty. How's that?"

"Great," Peter answered enthusiastically. "That'll make my life a whole hell of a lot easier. See you then. And thanks."

CHAPTER TWENTY-ONE

No sooner had Peter hung up the phone, but Shapero and Greene, whom he had seen lounging outside his door, trooped in with ear-to-ear grins on their faces. He was hopeful their expressions meant good news. No doubt about it, they were very competent investigators, especially Shapero. That is until Shapero got served with divorce papers six months ago, and went into an immediate tail spin. Lately though, he appeared to be towing the line. *It was a good thing,* Peter thought, *because Shapero was fast running out of chances, no matter how good he was in the field.*

"What's up?" they asked, almost in unison.

"Well, why don't you tell me," Peter urged. "And whatever it is, it better be something good because so far, it's been a really lousy day."

"Well then, your day is finally looking up," answered Greene, beaming. "Today, we spent a very rewarding several hours at Bradley & Stein getting the skinny on Bradley. From what we've heard so far, he may have had a little 'honey' on the side."

"Hear this rumor from a reliable source?"

"Remember the day after the murder, when Bradley's secretary told us about a woman, who up until a few months ago, was regularly calling her boss?"

"Yeah. So?"

"Well, Mary Jane remembered this broad calling in a panic one day, saying she had to reach Bradley immediately.

Unfortunately for her, Bradley was out-of-pocket for the day and no one knew when he'd be back. So Mary Jane invited her to leave a number where she could be reached on the off chance Bradley called in for messages. I guess whatever had gotten the woman bent out of shape was important, because the lady agreed to do just that." Greene stopped his monologue just long enough to catch his breath, then continued.

"Mary Jane, compulsive neurotic that she is, told us the first day we talked with her, that she may have kept the phone number and that she'd look for it the first chance she got. We asked her about it again today. And we got lucky. Turns out, she did keep it. We dialed the number and guess who answered?" For effect, Greene waited several seconds, saying nothing.

Irritated, Peter snapped, "I haven't got all day. Who the hell was it?"

"None other than attorney Caroline Witten."

Peter, who had been leaning back on the rear legs of his chair, came crashing forward with a loud thump. "Is this secretary sure that the woman who'd been calling Bradley was the same woman who left the phone number?"

"Absolutely." Loosening his tie, Greene sat down on the edge of Peter's desk. "You gotta understand, Lieutenant. Mary Jane had a humdinger of a case on Bradley. Believe me, she made it her business to know everything she could about Bradley, including who called him. What really pisses me off is, she could have told us that first day who the lady caller was. You know damn well she called that number herself that day, just to keep tabs on lover boy."

"You're probably right," Peter agreed. "Any indication that there was anything actually going on between this secretary and Bradley?"

"Nah. Not a chance. This office romance thing was as one-sided as an argument with yourself. From what we could tell, Bradley didn't even acknowledge her existence, except when he needed something."

"Well," Peter said, "I guess there's only one thing to do. I'll have to get to the bottom of this by making an appointment with the very attractive Caroline Witten." Peter closed the trust files and stood up. "And just so no one thinks I keep all the glory jobs for myself—like interviewing Ms. Witten, I also have the unpleasant task of following up with Jake Stein today. In anticipation of that, I don't think I'll eat lunch."

"I hear he can be a real S.O.B.," offered Shapero, who, during the entirety of the conversation, had been bent on busily picking at his shirt sleeve—trying to dislodge what looked to be a piece of dried ravioli which had landed there, Peter guessed, sometime during lunch. Peter watched in amazement as Shapero reached over and dipped his fingers into Peter's drinking glass, then applied the water droplet to his sleeve.

"Do you have to do that?" Peter asked.

"Sorry. Forgot there for a second it wasn't my water."

"Obviously." Shaking his head, Peter asked, "Before you two write up your final investigative reports, what about the rest of the employees you interviewed—turn up anything at all?"

"Not really. We got pretty much the same kind of comments we got the first time around. We did find out though, that Bradley would be absent, without explanation, for hours at a time. He had a car phone and a beeper, but rarely answered the phone or responded to the beeper, either one. So most of the time, nobody knew where he was which apparently irritated Stein no end."

"Did you two think to retrieve phone logs?"

"Yes, Sir," piped up Shapero. "We got copies of Bradley's phone logs, so we can trace all calls he made from the office during the last six months. But there's a bunch of them, so it's going to take a while."

"You've gotta understand," whined Shapero, "Mary Jane was constantly looking over our shoulder like a nosey mother-in-law. But in spite of her, we did have a chance to look through some papers stacked on top of Bradley's desk and credenza. Most of them though, with few exceptions, were duplicates of what we'd seen in Stein's office."

"A search warrant will get us a much better look," Peter suggested.

"And we're in the process of getting it."

"What about your lunch with Vivian? How'd that go?"

Shapero rolled his eyes. "Well, all I can say is, I should get time and a half for what I have to do for this department. And by the way, I'm turning in an expense voucher for this lunch. I took her to Vincenzo's, and of course, she ordered the most expensive items on the menu, complete with a split bottle of asti spumonte. The total came to sixty-four dollars and six cents, including tip. I put it on my credit card and surprisingly, even with my overdue balance, they took the charge. But I know I can't afford to make the minimum monthly payment now. So to make a long story short, when can I expect to get reimbursed?" asked Shapero, out of breath.

Peter chuckled. "You never give up, do you? I'll see to it right away. But you better have gotten some worthwhile information while you were busy wining and dining this so-called witness for two hours."

"No question," Shapero answered a little too anxiously. "The lunch was worth it. From what she said, Bradley's not the only one involved in disappearing acts. Stein is too, but I couldn't get anything more out of her than that. Whatever he's been doing, or wherever he's been going, she knows what it is, but she's not saying." Shapero stood and straightened his tie. "But just wait until I work some more Shapero magic, then I'll get some answers." He kicked the ravioli crumb, which had finally fallen from his sleeve, under Peter's desk. "Anyway, I'll try and follow through with her."

"What does that mean?" Peter asked.

Shapero smiled. "Don't worry. There won't be any more expense vouchers submitted. Promise."

Peter just looked at him. What could he say? Shapero wouldn't listen anyway.

Greene got up to leave. Obviously, he too had heard enough. Shapero though, never one to take a hint, held back. "One more thing—when she told me where she lived, I ran the address through county property and found out it's owned by some outfit called, 'Jakorp' which it doesn't take a genius to realize means Jake Stein. Hell, the guy isn't even clever."

"I think I've talked with Jake Stein long enough to know he's far from stupid," Peter argued. "He knows all the ins and outs of anything he wants to know about."

"Not to switch subjects," Greene interrupted, "but while Shapero was doing his thing, whatever that thing is, I talked to Billy Ray over at the courthouse. He wanted a message passed on to you. All the guards who were on duty the night Bradley was killed have been contacted and their statements taken. Only one remembers a woman leaving the courthouse around midnight, give or take a few. He said it must have been the Judge because she took the elevator to the underground garage where all the judges park. And only the judges have keys to that particular elevator."

"Is there a point to this?"

"I looked up the 911 call report. It was clocked in at one-fifty-six a.m. According to the Judge, she placed that call just after she discovered the body. Considering it only takes twenty minutes, tops, to drive from the courthouse to Park Boundary Road, there's a lot of time unaccounted for."

Sighing, Peter answered, "Thanks for breaking the numbers down for me." Tired, he rubbed his eyes. "I guess that means I need to talk with the Judge again. But maybe it's just this simple, unlike everything else in this case so far—maybe she made a stop at an all-night grocery store on her way home."

"I guess that's a possibility, but if that's her excuse, she had enough time to shop for a month's worth."

Ignoring that last remark, Peter grabbed his note pad. "While you're both here, I need to bring you up to speed on what Thompson and Bunker have been up to. First off, one of the prints lifted by the evidence unit belongs, no surprise here, to the Bradley's housekeeper, Mrs. Mencken.

"Also Bunker and Thompson have already begun talking with some of the folks listed on the contracts and other papers found near the body. Richard Waylander wanted to cancel one of those contracts with Bradley, so he especially, can't be crossed off the list. Even better, Waylander also had a loud argument with Bradley just last week, during which time he threatened to kill Bradley."

Looking down at his notes, Peter said, "Bunker and Thompson are splitting the remaining names on that list and should be finished by the end of this week. In the meantime, continue what you're doing and I'll see you tomorrow, same time, same place. Now get going."

CHAPTER TWENTY-TWO

Before attending John Bradley's funeral, Hilary scheduled a brief meeting at her office located on the top floor of the Kentucky Home Life Building with private investigator, Sam Monroe. Since his "suite" as Sam called his two room bare bones office was right next door, it was convenient to meet at Adams & Adams, even though the hour was a little too early for both.

Old friends, Hilary and Sam shared a unique relationship. They had met eighteen years before as adversaries when Hilary was a fledgling criminal defense attorney, and Sam an FBI agent assigned to represent the government on Hilary's first federal case. That was just before Sam retired and set up his own P.I. firm. Now, at the age of sixty-three, Sam's's once conservative appearance, consisting of pin striped suits, spit shined shoes and crew cut hair, had given way to a graying ponytail, khaki "Dockers," comfortable "Timberland" boots and wool cardigan sweaters. His eyes, bright and shiny, were periwinkle blue, Hilary's favorite color. His face, full of lines and creases from too much time in the sun, earned while engaging in his one undiluted passion—fishing, was kind and thoughtful.

Kindred spirits, they appreciated each other's abilities, enjoyed each other's company, and respected the other's opinions even though at times, those opinions could not have been more diverse.

Sam kept a full schedule performing surveillance work for several other attorneys, but Hilary's cases always took precedence. As a result, Sam was part of the package when Hilary was hired by a client accused of criminal activity. Not only did the client retain her services, they paid for Sam's as well. If they didn't, or wouldn't, Hilary refused representation.

Having arrived early, and not yet quite awake, Hilary stifled a yawn then propped her feet up on her desk and waited until she heard the familiar sound of Sam slamming his office door and shuffling into her reception area with the usual, "Hello, hello" greeting.

"In here, Sam."

He poked his head in, entered, and rubbed his hands together, a sign that Sam was ready to get going.

"Care for coffee?"

Sam hesitated. "Before I answer that, did you or Maria make it?"

"Very funny," Hilary laughed. "You're in luck. Maria made the coffee. Satisfied?"

Sam looked over at Hilary and smiled, his wire rimmed reading glasses resting precariously on the tip of his nose. "Well, in that case, I would love some."

"You know you drink too much of that stuff, don't you?"

Hilary slouched down comfortably in her chair. "So what did you find out about this Dr. Franklin Parker?"

"Anxious, aren't you?"

Hilary smiled knowingly. It was going to be one of those days.

"Just give me a second to get situated so I can at least grab my notes, okay?" Sam set his mug down, and pulled up a chair close to where Hilary was now sitting at her desk. He settled his reading glasses firmly on the bridge of his nose, pulled out what looked to be an almost new, barely used reporter's spiral note pad from his back pocket, and flipped it over to the first page.

"Well, let's see here . . ."

Quickly, Sam recounted that Dr. Franklin Parker was a thirty-nine year old medical doctor who had graduated nine years before, squarely in the middle of his class, from UK med school. His specialty was infectious diseases, but took about anything that dragged itself through the door. His office, which Sam had visited yesterday, was described as far from plush—nothing more that a walk-in clinic frequented mostly by welfare recipients or junkies looking for a quick methadone fix. The six chairs which encircled the small waiting room were, from what he could see, used at the visitor's own risk. Two of them were lopsided, a third, unuseable due to a missing seat cushion. The cracked and stained linoleum floor littered with paper and cigarette butts was so old, it was devoid of all color.

"When I got there, I explained to the frazzled receptionist, who could barely speak English, that I didn't have an appointment, but that I was a private eye investigating the death of one of their patients—John Bradley. And what do you know? Even with an office full of waiting patients, who all looked like they were three degrees from hell, I was immediately ushered in to see the Doc." Sam stood and put his mug on top of the french-style bombe' chest, then pulled out his well-worn wormwood barrel pipe. Hilary knew he wouldn't light it up; his habit was to merely hold it. Somehow, it helped Sam marshal his thoughts. It was a habit she was used to.

"Let me tell you, Hil, waiting in that reception room, even for a few minutes, was worse than any stint in Viet Nam. When his nurse came and got me, I bolted towards Parker's office, which, though small and pretty sparse, was at least clean, with furniture that 'worked.'"

"Had Parker heard about Bradley's murder?"

Sam nodded. "Said he thought about calling the police, but for whatever reason, never followed through. From that, I think it's safe to assume that the police don't yet know of Parker's potential value. That will obviously change though once they get around to investigating that empty file labeled, 'Dr. Parker.'"

"Any problems getting Parker to talk?"

"Surprisingly no—he was anxious to 'spill the beans.'"

"So, tell me."

Chuckling, Sam said,. "Hold on. I'm getting to that." He flipped over another page of his note pad. "According to the Doc, Bradley first came to see him about a year ago, complaining about some non-specific discomfort in the groin-genital area. Parker did a visual, but saw nothing, and more particularly, no telltale evidence of sexually transmitted disease.

"Coming up empty, I gather Parker decided to take a more detailed medical history and learned that Bradley had been experiencing, along with generalized discomfort in the groin area, some pain upon urination. When the Doc asked him how long this had been going on, Bradley told him about a month, but admitted he was afraid to go to his family physician. Too embarrassing."

"So what did Dr. Parker think was wrong with him?"

"At first, a mild urinary infection, sporadic in nature, but warranting the obligatory specimen in a jar. The results though surprised him—no bacteria of any real significance. But just to make sure, Parker took a penile and scrotal tissue swab along with blood tests to definitively rule out any sexually transmitted disease that wasn't readily apparent. Those tests too though, came back negative once the incubation period expired."

"That should have made John happy."

"You would think so, but Parker told me that when he next saw him, instead of being relieved, John argued that something must have been overlooked and demanded more tests be run."

Hilary stood up and impatiently pushed a strand of hair out of her face. She already had the beginnings of a migraine. "This makes absolutely no sense, Sam. Are you sure Parker was talking about *our* John Bradley and not someone else with the same name?"

"No question. The patient was *our* John Bradley." Sam walked cross the room and refilled his cup. "Sit down. There's more.

"Apparently, it didn't take long before Parker felt he was fast running out of options, so he decided to use the direct approach. He asked Bradley if he'd had recent sexual relations with someone other than his wife. Appearing offended, Bradley vehemently denied having strayed, so Parker recommended that he consult a urologist. Bradley however, refused. Parker next asked if Bradley's wife had been experiencing any similar problems. Bradley told him he didn't know. Then, without another word or explanation, Bradley abruptly walked out of the office. The Doc was no stunned, he never sent him a bill."

"And that was the last he ever saw of him?"

"Not quite. Three months later, without a scheduled appointment, Bradley showed up again, demanding that Parker see him right away. Frustrated, Parker's nurse invited him to make an appointment like everyone else. No surprise, Bradley didn't take her up on the invitation; not right away that is. He waited another month."

"Same problem?"

"Nope. This time, John added a new twist. He presented with a red, mottled rash over his trunk, forearms and upper thighs. Parker was told that the rash came and went, but that no one else with whom Bradley had daily contact was experiencing anything like this, including his wife."

Sam took a gulp of coffee, then continued. "Parker, who seems to be a pretty good old doc, repeated every test known to modern science, including a PSA. But once more, came up empty. Since all the tests proved there was nothing physically wrong, Parker came to the one inescapable conclusion that even I would have jumped to, but months before—that it was all in Bradley's head. But just to make certain, he decided to try one more thing. He asked Bradley to submit to a screening for HIV—a test Bradley had previously refused to undergo. This time though, he agreed. But those results too, were negative."

"Whew. I'm relieved for Susan's sake. So, what was left?"

Sam smiled. "To Parker's way of thinking, nothing. So he told Bradley to seek a second opinion. Again, Bradley wouldn't budge. Finally, in a last ditch effort to help this guy who was making himself and everybody else miserable, Parker suggested hospitalization to observe him in a more controlled environment. But true to form, Bradley panicked and bolted; this time though, for only two weeks. Then, like clockwork, he was right back at Parker's office with no explanation for his behavior.

"Once more Parker questioned him about whether he had enjoyed any new sexual partners lately. This time, Bradley refused to answer.

"Needless to say, Parker had had it. He gave John three names—all of whom were psychiatrists. And to save his own ass, Parker even went so far as to put this in a letter sent to Bradley's house. According to Parker's records, it was mailed about six weeks ago."

Sam paused and looked directly at Hilary. "That letter, and the one Susan got out of John's hand the night he was murdered, were probably one in the same."

Hilary looked down and fiddled with the button on her jacket. She knew, without being told, how Sam felt about Susan withholding evidence. "Did he ever see John again?"

"No. Nor did he hear from him. And before you ask, none of the doctors Parker recommended sent him a follow-up consult." Hastily, Sam added, "I don't think that's too unusual though for psychiatrists not to communicate with the originating doctor, especially if the patient wants it that way."

Sam flipped the steno pad over and returned it to his back pocket. "And that is all I have. If it helps I don't know how." He turned and looked at Hilary, his eyes piercing. "What's your gut feeling? You saw a lot more of John than I ever did."

Hilary slid further back in her chair, and swivelled halfway around to where she could see the courthouse from her office window. "I honestly don't know. What you've just told me blows my mind."

Neither said anything for several minutes. Hilary continued to look outside her window while Sam merely looked into space.

Finally, Sam broke the silence. "If you ask me, John Bradley was smarter and better looking than most. Unfortunately though, he could never use his God-given talents because he just didn't like anybody, excepting Susan of course," he mused.

Hilary again twisted around in her chair, stopping to face Sam head-on. "He was just a no nonsense kind of guy who didn't suffer fools easily. And if he thought you were wasting his time, he'd tell you, and often, not too nicely." She chuckled to herself. "Looking back, I realize that any recent interaction I had with John, was incidental to my friendship with Susan. Which leads me to ask, was it my fault or his, that the friendship, which he and I began in college, dissolved?"

"I think you know my answer to that one."

"Oh, Sam, you just say that because you've been infatuated with Susan since you first met her, and you hated the fact she was married to John."

"I'm not going to say she's not an interesting woman." With a wink he added, "But you know, better than anyone else on this planet, where my heart belongs. To you."

Hilary smiled. She did know that, but she didn't return his love, not in the same way. Uncomfortable, Hilary decided it was time to change the subject. Plowing through a stack of papers on her desk, she rescued one located on the bottom and handed it to Sam. It was the letter which Susan had given her only hours after John had been found murdered. The flecks and streaks of blood, fresh then, now looked like nothing more than dirty brown smudges.

"At least we know from this letter when Parker finally washed his hands of John. That should be helpful." Hilary tapped a pen against the ink blotter on her desk. "Just thinking out loud though, even if Parker didn't hear from any of the specialists he recommended, that doesn't mean John didn't contact any of them under an assumed name, does it?"

Grinning Sam answered, "I'm one step ahead of you. I contacted all three whom Parker identified. If they were hesitant to talk, I made it easy by producing the form signed by

Susan requesting that all of her husband's medical information be released. If John Bradley contacted them, they have no record of it. Just to make sure though, I showed them the most recent photograph I have of John, thinking that maybe he used an alias as you suggested. But none of them could ID the photograph either."

Hilary stretched. "Are you telling me that we are at a dead end already?"

"Not yet. Instinct tells me John wasn't the type to blindly follow anyone's directive, including a doctor's. But at some point, when things were really going haywire, he must have realized some type of intervention was necessary. Remember, he reached out to Parker."

"Hate to remind of you of the obvious, but there are lots of doctors out there," Hilary replied wearily.

With a hint of irritation in his voice, Sam replied, "Obviously, John's not going to leave an easy trail to follow—he was too private for that." Sighing, he added, "We're just going to have to contact every psychiatrist and psychologist in town to see if Bradley got the help he needed."

"Ugh," Hilary muttered as she lowered her head on the desk. "I'm glad that's going to be your job and not mine."

"Well, you could help." Sam waited until Hilary looked up before continuing.

"Oh no. I'm not going to play amateur sleuth. Investigation is your deal." She threw her hands up in the air. "I'm too busy for that. Forget it."

"No one is asking you to change professions, little Miss Prim and Proper. But while you're at Susan's, take a moment to snoop through the medicine cabinets and find out if any prescriptions were filled in John's name. It'll take seconds. And who knows? It could be that easy."

Smiling, Hilary answered, "Speaking of being one step ahead, I already thought of that, but found nothing. And not only did I look in the medicine cabinets, I checked his brief case and the glove box of his car. If he had any, he stashed them somewhere else." She got up, crossed the room, and stood next to Sam. "There is one other possibility though. . . . His office downtown. I can take a good look when Peter Elliott and I go down there after the funeral today. But if that proves to be a blind alley, too, then I haven't a clue where he hid them, presuming of course, they were ever prescribed by this still, as yet, unknown doctor."

"What about the toxicology screen? Is it back from the M.E.?"

"Not that I know of."

Hilary grabbed her coat and picked up her purse. "We gotta go, or we'll be late for the funeral." Over her shoulder, as she and Sam walked out, she added, "Check out as many docs as you can in the next few days. From what you found out, I agree—John couldn't have held the lid on much longer. He was smarter than most; pragmatic if nothing else. He'd want an answer. My guess is, John found it."

Hilary turned off the light and closed the door.

CHAPTER TWENTY-THREE

On the day of the funeral, the chapel at Highland Presbyterian Church was filled to capacity with people as well as flowers. The closed mahogany casket containing John Bradley's body had been placed, with a funeral director's sense of the dramatic, directly beneath a beam of sunlight filtering through one of the stained glass windows, and in between two plain wooden crosses, as if to reflect a comforting symmetry between life and death.

Dutifully, Susan had arrived an hour ahead of time to make sure everything was in order and to receive mourners who began showing up as early as forty-five minutes before the ceremony was scheduled to begin.

When Hilary and Sam met at the church, they were each immediately ushered to the front of the sanctuary where Susan and her parents were still greeting guests while patiently waiting to take their seats. Hilary soundlessly embraced Susan, who was dressed entirely in black, gently squeezed Susan's mother's hand and sat down on one of the hard wooden pews, each grouped, one behind the other, in a collection of semi-circles on either side of two carpeted aisles.

Upon his arrival, Jake Stein, who was ushered to the pew directly behind Susan, bent over and whispered something in Susan's ear before taking his assigned seat. Hilary watched in amazement, as Susan graciously, in spite of how she felt towards Jake, looked up and managed a pleasant, though wan, smile.

Knowing that she had only a few minutes, Hilary pulled her attention away from Susan, and curiosity getting the better of her, tried unobtrusively, to look around one last time. Peter's admonition that perhaps the killer would attend, had piqued her interest—she couldn't resist the impulse to see who was there, and more importantly, who wasn't. As expected, most attendees were judges, lawyers, and courthouse personnel. Surely, she convinced herself, the killer wasn't someone in the profession. That was unthinkable!

Out of the corner of her eye, although unable to immediately connect names with faces, Hilary recognized two men, seated to the rear of the chapel and busily taking notes, as homicide detectives. She also noticed the appropriately dour looking funeral director, as he cast a scathing look in Peter's direction, when Peter, looking tense, arrived just as the door to the church was closing, when only standing room was still available. Their eyes met, but only for a second before Peter nodded, then turned away from Hilary to scan the crowd. In that instant, Hilary longed to reach out to him. Chastising herself, she thought, *Put it into perspective, girl, it's just the emotion of the day*.

To counteract a sudden but overwhelming sense of loss, Hilary absently pulled out a hymnal from the shelf attached to the back of the pew in front of her, and turned to page one thirty-five—*The Old Rugged Cross,* which, according to the printed program handed out upon arrival, was the first hymn to be sung. *God, I hope I can get through this*, she thought to herself. Uninvited, her thoughts were flooded with memories of Jack, but Hilary had already steeled herself to expect that reaction. It was always that way when she attended funerals. And this funeral, more than any other, excepting Jack's, was even more difficult, if not impossible, to understand. Silently,

Hilary read the hymn's verses over to herself, hoping to find some comfort in their meaning.

Her spiritual reflections were interrupted however, when the steady hum of whispered comments and the soothing music from the string quartet suddenly stopped. Looking up, Hilary immediately understood. Out from the side door emerged the church's interim minister, Ernest Crabbe, a wizened little old man, with white hair, stooped back, and a look of what must be, as indicated by the set lines and wrinkles which marked his face, permanent consternation.

In spite of his obvious advanced age, however, he moved, as if on wheels, in the direction of the pulpit, his black robes flying behind him, and with a continued expression of dissatisfaction, dramatically raised both hands, signaling immediate silence.

Unfortunately, however, for all his commanding presence, it became quickly apparent, from the content of his sermon, that the Reverend had known John Bradley only slightly. Highland's beloved minister of fifteen years had left the previous summer, so the Reverend Crabbe was only temporary, and it showed. His delivery was halting, as if searching but unable to find the right phrase; his words of sympathy seemed impersonal, offered as if by rote, and at times, insensitive, given the circumstances of John's death.

Seemingly unaware of how hurtful his well-intentioned comments were however, Crabbe droned on in a tone of undisguised righteousness about missed opportunities, the ravages of unanticipated loss, and the tenuousness of life in general. He then concluded his remarks by explaining how these observations related specifically to the deceased whom he remembered as having much to offer, but who was, blessedly, now wrapped in the peace and calm found only on the other side of death. "There," he intoned, "God answers all questions, both legal and spiritual." Upon hearing this, Hilary and Sam couldn't help but squirm in their seats. Luckily though, Hilary saw that Susan seemed not to be listening, as if far away and deep in thought about something else entirely.

There was, at Susan's request, no eulogy. As she had explained earlier to Hilary, Jake would have been the most obvious choice, but when asked, had declined. To herself, Hilary thought Jake's decision not to speak in honor of his deceased partner, was just one more sad commentary on what she had now come to believe was John Bradley's very pitiful existence.

Thankfully, the service lasted only thirty minutes. Afterwards, the mourners filed out row by row, one by one, to awaiting cars for the short trip to the cemetery. Upon emerging from the church after exchanging sad greetings with fellow mourners, Hilary and Sam solemnly stepped into the limousine parked directly behind the hearse, and sat down on either side of Susan.

"I know you've heard this question all morning long from everyone, but is there anything I can do?"

Susan smiled and gripped Hilary's hand. "No. I just need you and Sam nearby. My parents couldn't take anymore. They left to go back home as soon as the church service was over, so they won't be at the cemetery. Believe me, just the fact that both of you are here makes this day almost bearable."

Pulling out a handkerchief from her purse, Susan, in a hushed voice said, "I'm so tired of smiling and saying, 'Thank you for your kind sympathy,' to people I haven't seen or talked to for years. Even my illustrious opponent, Edward Arpel, made an appearance, offering up all those very socially correct, but very pat phrases found in commercial condolence cards." Looking out the window and absently waving as mourners passed by, she added, "I guess I should have been touched that he made an appearance, but I wasn't." Angrily she added, "That man has never uttered a sincere word in his life. And to think I have to continue the campaign after— "

Interrupting, Hilary urged, "Let's not think about that right now. Thinking about things like that will do nothing but upset you more."

Comfortingly, Sam reached over, covered Susan's hand and held it firmly in his. Nodding in his direction, Susan said, "Maybe it's best if we just don't talk."

If the memorial service at the church was short, Hilary was pleasantly surprised when the internment at Cave Hill Cemetery, located just a half mile from the church, lasted a mere ten minutes. After everyone arrived in the somber processional which consisted of over fifty vehicles, each displaying the telltale white flag signaling a funeral procession, Reverend Crabbe offered some additional banal comments as well as a short, but obligatory prayer.

At the conclusion of the service, crying softly, Susan knelt and laid one white, long-stemmed rose on the casket. She then stood and walked unsteadily, her arm intertwined with Sam's, toward the limousine. Hilary followed a step behind.

As agreed, only Sam was to accompany Susan back to the house. Since Hilary's secretary, Maria, had remained there for security reasons during the funeral service, Hilary felt sure, that between the two of them, Susan was in very capable hands.

After saying a tearful goodbye, and promising to call Susan the next day, Hilary gently, but firmly closed the door to the limousine, then walked slowly toward the edge of the cemetery, watching and nodding as the last of friends and acquaintances filed out, somber and tight-lipped. The wind was picking up. It was spitting rain, just enough, Hilary thought miserably, to curl her hair into even tighter ringlets. *What a picture I must be,* Hilary thought. With her hands in her pockets, and the collar of her coat pulled up around her neck in an attempt to stay warm, Hilary patiently stood and waited.

She and Peter had prearranged to meet after the service, so that they could go together to John's office. She wasn't looking forward to rummaging once more through John's personal effects, but Susan had asked her to be there as her representative. Since the search presented unexpected time alone with Peter, Susan didn't have to do much in the way of persuasion.

Looking over her shoulder, Hilary spotted Peter, as he turned in her direction. She waved and he walked towards her. "Are you ready?"

"Ready when you are," he answered with a grimace.

CHAPTER TWENTY-FOUR

Bradley & Stein's parking lot was all but empty. Most employees had taken the day off to attend the funeral, so Hilary and Peter were spared any curious glances as Peter pulled in and parked the department's unmarked navy blue Crown Victoria.

The firm's offices were located in historic Old Louisville, an area revered for its massive and majestic four story brick mansions built at the turn of the century by Louisville's elite. With the growth of suburbia in the nineteen fifties however, the once magnificent residences had been abandoned, sacrificed to encroaching urban blight. But in recent years, after decades of neglect, the area had enjoyed a resurgence of popularity. Overnight, real estate prices soared as the new yuppie generation discovered the value of the past, and rehabbing became the fashionable alternative to subdivision living. Single dwellings, condos and even offices began springing up on every block from prestigious St. James Court eastward to Main Street, following the meandering course of the rough and tumble Ohio River.

Outside and inside the refurbished offices of Bradley & Stein, it was immediately apparent that the owners had taken great pains to strike just the right balance between the elegance of yesterday and the vitality of the present. Entering through the heavy walnut and beveled glass doors, Hilary couldn't help but twirl around in circles in an attempt to take in all of its breath-taking grandeur. Peter, on the other hand, appeared oblivious to its beauty. Without comment, he approached the reception desk in an area which must have been an imposing but sheltered vestibule in days gone by.

"Hi. Peter Elliott, City Homicide." He held out his badge, then snapped it back into its protective well-worn leather case. "This is Hilary Adams, attorney for Judge Emmett-Bradley. I've got a search warrant to inspect John Bradley's offices."

With eyes open wide, the receptionist with lime green hair, similarly colored eye shadow, and, if Hilary could count correctly, nine ear piercings, jumped to attention. "Vivian told me you might be here today. I'm Shelly. Mr. Stein asked me to buzz him when you arrived. Please, have a seat." She sat down and turned her attention towards the phone, then abruptly stopped; her hand held motionless in the air. "Are you really a homicide detective—like on 'Law and Order?'"

Peter laughed. "Yeah. Exactly like that."

Hilary muttered under her breath, but loud enough for him to hear, "You wish."

"Wow," Shelly exclaimed while staring at both of them.

Not knowing what next to say, Hilary and Peter decided to just sit down, taking the two chairs closest to the receptionist's desk. That way, both figured they couldn't help but overhear at least one side of the conversation exchanged between Stein and Shelly when she announced their arrival.

"Mr. Stein, Lieutenant Peter Elliott, and attorney Hilary Adams are here to see you," Shelly explained in a singsongy voice while rolling her eyes.

Pressing the phone's release button after the conversation had apparently ended, she explained, "Mr. Stein wanted me to tell you he's in conference, and therefore unavailable at the moment." Standing up, she added, "So until he can join you, he asked that I show you to Mr. Bradley's office. Unfortunately,

Mary Jane, Mr. Bradley's secretary, took the day off due to the funeral, so I'm not sure if I can adequately answer all the questions you might have. Sorry. As I said, Mr. Stein will be along as soon as possible."

Pointing in the direction of the marbled hallway, Shelley asked them to follow her. At the very end of the hallway, after passing several empty offices and cubicles, Shelly suddenly stopped. "Here we are. This is Mr. Bradley's office." She showed them in, then turned to leave. "I have to go back to the front desk, but if you need anything, just dial 'zero.'"

As soon as Shelley was out of earshot, Peter said, "Boy, she's a welcome breath of fresh air, in spite of the martian look."

"I'll say. She might be someone we need to follow up on."

"'*We* need to follow up on?' Wait a minute here," Peter laughed. "You're up to your old tricks again, aren't you?"

"Sorry," Hilary answered mockingly. "I seem to have gotten carried away with all this cloak-and-dagger stuff. Promise, it won't happen again."

Unconvinced, Peter answered, "I've heard that before."

Trying her best to ignore him, Hilary dropped her purse on the nearest chair and looked around. "This office is unbelievable. It's spectacular. No wonder he liked to spend lots of time here." She looked in the direction of his desk. "Guess though, we should get started snooping around. We certainly want to avoid the watchful eye of Jake Stein."

Just as they were about to take their overcoats off, Shelly knocked and entered carrying a tray with soft drinks, cheese and crackers. "Thought you might need a little bit of a pick-me-up. I know the funeral service took it all out of me, so I can imagine how wrenching it must have been for you, Ms. Adams.

Anyway, please help yourselves, and if there's anything else I can do, just let me know."

"Thanks. You've been very helpful."

When Shelley had quietly closed the door, Hilary unabashedly reached for a handful of crackers. "She's right. I'm starved, so let's dig in."

While Hilary contentedly munched away, she watched as Peter turned towards the desk and gently pulled out the middle drawer. Unlike the desk in the library at his home, the contents of this middle desk drawer were still neatly arranged. Nothing appeared out of place. "Post-it Notes" were assembled by color, ranging from soft pastels on one side, to the more garish "Day-Glow" colors on the right. Paper clips were laid, one on top of the other in rows, each the same length. Pens were organized also by color, each with the company's logo facing upward. Placed next to the pens were a stapler and transparent tape dispenser, each perfectly aligned like soldiers at attention.

Hilary got up and peered over Peter's shoulder. "Wow. What a difference between this desk drawer and the one in the library at his home!" She bent down and looked closer. "How could anyone do any real work with drawers this neatly arranged?" Absently she reached down and picked up a paper clip. "Neatness like this would be a full-time job. I'd be afraid to sneeze in here."

Peter sat down hard in Bradley's executive chair. "This guy was something else." He leaned back and touched the soft leather. "Considering the kind of job my cleaning lady does every week, I'd have paid him just about anything to whip my house into the same shape this drawer is in." He looked up at Hilary. "Was Bradley ever in the Army?"

Hilary thought for a second. "Not that I know of. Why? Are you telling me this is what the Army does to you?" She laughed. "Where do I sign up?"

Still in the process of carefully examining the drawer's contents, Peter answered thoughtfully, "I just don't have any other explanation for this compulsive neatness. It goes beyond normal. The only time I ever saw anything close to this was when my drill sergeant was looking over my shoulder, flipping quarters on my army cot to see how high they'd bounce."

He leaned forward. "Let's look through the rest of these drawers though. My detectives took a look around his desk and credenza area yesterday, but their search wasn't very extensive."

Being satisfied that nothing of value was to be found in the desk's center drawer, Peter and Hilary turned their attention to the two drawers on either side. Both were shallow, measuring only about four inches in depth. When Peter pulled out the left side drawer, they found several writing pads, all neatly aligned according to length and width, with the smaller being on top. Peter removed the tablets, one at a time. They numbered eight in all. Flipping carefully through each, he found nothing—no notes, not even scribbles. When all eight tablets were removed, the drawer was totally empty; not even a smidgeon of dust remained.

Peter pulled the drawer out the full length of its track, then removed it altogether. Again, nothing. He turned his attention to the right-hand drawer, pulling it out as far as it would extend. It too appeared to contain nothing. "That's odd. I would have expected each drawer to be chock full of things—odds and ends, papers, whatever. Anything to show that someone actually worked here." He bent down, his eyes level with the drawer. "Just to make sure, I'm going to pull this drawer out all the way. So, stand clear, Hil."

Hilary watched as Peter tugged at the drawer, but it was positioned in such a way, that in order to pull it out the entire length of the drawer tray, Bradley's personal computer, keyboard, and monitor would have to be moved back several inches.

"Why in the world would Bradley park a PC right in front of his right-hand desk drawer so that it blocks access?"

"Well, maybe that's the reason why it's empty," reasoned Hilary.

Peter glared. "And me being the detective—why didn't I think of that?" He stepped aside. "Stop with the wisecracks and hold the monitor while I try to roll this computer table away from the desk."

Hilary wiggled in beside him, and together they moved the table. Curious, Peter pulled the drawer out all the way, then stuck his head inside. "Something's catching on this drawer. It's not coming out like it should."

Unable to see because Peter was blocking her view, Hilary suggested, "Maybe the wood's swollen."

"Just hold the monitor," he answered irritably. Finally, with a lot of tugging, Peter dislodged the drawer. It was totally empty. He sat down on his haunches and turned the drawer over, but found nothing except a tiny piece of wadded up masking tape. Clearly disappointed, he peeled it off, then stooped down to again look inside the drawer bed itself.

"Wait a minute. Something's stuck in here."

Peter reached in and two seconds later withdrew his hand which now contained a small key covered with masking tape. Ripping off the sticky adhesive as best he could, Peter turned the key over in his hand, carefully examining it. "Looks like another safe deposit box key to me."

Hilary could see the key gleaming in his hand. "That's exactly what it is. May I see it?"

"Sure. Take it."

Turning it over Hilary suggested, "Let's compare it to the one Susan said belonged to their joint safe deposit box."

Peter again picked up Bradley's key ring which he had earlier laid on the desk top, and carefully separated from the rest, the key which Susan had identified as the one belonging to their safe deposit box. He handed it to Hilary.

"They're not the same," Hilary answered, disappointed. "It must belong to another bank."

"That shouldn't be too difficult to track down. I'll just ask the deputy D.A. to issue another subpoena for all banks within a fifty mile radius and go from there."

But no sooner had Peter replaced the key in the evidence envelope, resealed it and marked it with his initials, than the door flew open and there stood Jake Stein, and not with a smile on his face.

"Lieutenant, we meet again and so soon." Turning his attention to Hilary, he added, "And Hilary, how are you? Nice to see you again." Winking, he added, "Even though I can't say the same for the company you keep."

"Hi, Jake." She held out her hand. "Your offices are beautiful. I'm impressed."

"Thanks. Remind me to give you the grand tour of the place later, but only if you're alone."

Peter stepped around from the back of the desk, and moved towards the door. "Mr. Stein, that reminds me. You and I need to set up a time when we can talk again."

"What exactly is it you want?" Jake asked with irritation. "I've already told you everything I know, and some things I didn't think I knew."

Peter smiled. "I'm afraid I have to be the one making the judgment call on that. So while I'm here, why don't we just set up a mutually convenient time to meet?"

"Where are you planning on throwing this party?" Stein asked, a sneer on his face.

"Downtown, at headquarters. Tomorrow, ten o'clock."

Smirking, Jake Stein replied, "I'll be there. But I'm warning you, I'm not staying long, so don't break out the champagne."

CHAPTER TWENTY-FIVE

As agreed, Jake showed up, ten o'clock sharp, at city homicide. Unfortunately, not everyone was as punctual. Peter had an unexpected court appearance that morning which took longer than expected. So, Stein was forced to sit in the squad room cooling his heels and registering his displeasure to anyone who would listen. When Peter finally arrived, forty-five minutes late, Stein was seething.

"I try not to inconvenience people; I expect the same in return."

"Sorry. Couldn't be helped," Peter answered dismissively. "Why don't we go back to my office?"

Glaring, Stein replied, "Before we do that, is a lousy cup of coffee too much to ask for?"

Peter smiled. "At the very least, I think we can provide you with better than a 'lousy cup of coffee.'"

"Your hospitality is charming. Nice to know city government doesn't waste time or money on unnecessary amenities."

When they got back to Peter's office and the door was closed, Peter decided to try and appeal to Stein's fundamental, but so far, well hidden sense of decency. "Let me begin by being candid. No clear suspect has emerged, so we have to focus more on the victim—his habits, his problems, his associations. And to do that, we need your help."

Scowling, Stein replied, "We've been down this road before. John and I weren't buddies, and we—"

"Hate to interrupt you, but you're missing the point. You and Bradley were business partners. As such, you saw him every day of the week; knew whom he associated with, and why. I need to know more about that general work routine, and you're the only person who can walk me though it."

Stein closed his eyes and shook his head. "Not to be difficult, but honestly, Bradley and I rarely communicated, and then only when it was absolutely necessary. Believe me, if we could have faxed each other instead of meeting face-to-face, we would have."

Trying to be patient, Peter answered, "I understand all that, but Bradley made someone else angry enough to kill him. I need to know whether that someone was business related. Hopefully you can shed some light on it for me."

Stein threw his hands up in the air in a gesture of resignation. "I'll tell you what I can, but I'm warning you, this is a huge waste of time—for both of us."

"Let me worry about that." Peter sat down behind his desk and indicated, by pointing to an empty chair, that Stein was to sit as well. "Know of any run-ins he may have had lately, specifically with a customer or supplier?"

"Sure," Stein retorted. "He had lots of them. But just off the top of my head, none of them were that bent out of shape that they'd resort to murder. Being short three bed pans or getting a prosthetic device that was a hundredth of an inch out of whack, just didn't piss people off that much."

"What about Richard Waylander?"

Without hesitation, Stein answered, "That son of a bitch was a royal pain in the ass. Since he became the head of purchasing for Our Lady of Lourdes Hospital, it's been one screw up after another. For years we'd had a contract with them, supplying all their prosthetic devices, from breast prosthetics to lifelike artificial limbs. And although we weren't their major supplier, we also had other limited purchase contracts with them, renewable on a thirty day basis."

"So what went wrong with the Waylander account?"

Stein sat back in his chair and sipped his coffee. "Waylander's purchase orders were always sent in late, so we'd have to dance double fast to get them filled by the drop dead date. And then the bastard would intentionally hold our checks for ninety days, minimum, even though they'd been cut on time by the hospital corporation."

"How did you handle that?"

"When it all started, I told John that if we kowtowed in the beginning and continued these herculean efforts to fill late orders, we could kiss it if we wanted to go back on him later for breach of contract."

"Did Bradley listen?"

"Hell no. As usual, John knew it all, disagreed with me, ate shit, and got us into a real financial bind with our own suppliers. Then when it got really bad, John got hot and was after Waylander twenty-four seven. By then though, it didn't matter."

"So, how did it all shake out?"

"I finally had to take over the account in order to salvage what little I could. John and I were to meet and discuss it, but he got himself killed. How's that for irony?" Stein put the empty cup down on the floor beside his chair and folded his arms.

"Were problematic accounts like Waylander's, the only items on the agenda for that meeting between you and Bradley?"

"No," Stein answered slowly, appearing to choose his words carefully. "We both wanted to continue some earlier discussions we'd had about the partnership's long-term goals. Frankly, John was acting so strange lately, I knew B & S couldn't last much longer."

"Why?"

"Maybe I can explain it better if I give you an example of his behavior." Stein reached over and pulled a cigarette case towards him that he had earlier laid on Peter's desk. He didn't bother to ask permission before lighting up. "One day the guy was reasonable and you could halfway deal with him, but then the next day, he was nothing more than a condescending know-it-all. No one could get near him. And before you ask, no, there was no work-related reason for his behavior—none that I could see anyway."

"How did the employees react to this?"

"I have a hard and fast rule, and everyone who works for me knows it. No employee rats on management; that's just how it is. So if they have the nerve to complain about John's behavior, they didn't get a sympathetic ear from me. John was my partner; they, on the other hand, were nothing but my employees."

Jake stood up, stretched, then sat down again. "As you might guess, after awhile, they didn't bother to say much of anything about John, at least to me they didn't."

"Tell me," Peter asked, "how did Bradley's behavior change in the last several months?"

"Oh, c'mon. That kind of question could take months to answer." He looked at his watch. "I have appointments which I need to get to. How much longer is this going to take?"

Peter decided not to answer. He felt as though he was finally getting somewhere with Stein, even though it was like pulling teeth without an anesthetic. He couldn't afford to lose the momentum by getting sidetracked.

Stein banged his hand on the corner of Peter's desk. "I asked a question."

"I know. I thought the answer was obvious—it's going to take as long as necessary."

Stein attempted to stare him down for several seconds, then shook his head and turned away. "Okay. Let's just get this over with. To answer your last question, John's always been a little moody, a loner, but, I admit, never to the extent he was during the last several months. The changes were subtle, but they were there."

"So I've heard. I need specifics."

"I'm trying, but that's tough to do. You get used to working around problems. And that's where I was with John. I worked around him by limiting my exposure to him. It's not as though I had a lot of choices. He was totally irrational, toxic. But if I was pushed to pinpoint a time when it all really began to go to hell, I'd say it was about six months ago."

"Anything in particular trigger it?"

"Yeah, looking back, I guess there was. One day John just appeared at my office door, demanding that we immediately rearrange business priorities and reassign individual partnership responsibilities. Long story short, John had read some guru's harebrained best seller on innovative management techniques. According to John, if the principles were implemented as recommended by this million dollar huckster, B & S could expect a miraculous increase in its profit margin. Frankly, I thought he was nuts, but said, what the hell."

"Did the changes make a difference?"

"No. And I think on some level John realized that. But he still kept the books and fooled around doing other things that apparently kept him happily occupied. I oversaw all the marketing and handled most of the clients. That way, only a few of our accounts were personally overseen by John. I thought that would cure the problem." Stein smiled ruefully. "But it didn't—I still got phone call after phone call from each of those few clients saying that John hadn't delivered on the contracts. All I know is, in the last couple of weeks, I'd had it and John knew it. As far as I was concerned, the only thing left to talk about was the division of accounts and employees."

"What about other assets?"

"I think John would have been fair. We had to go our separate ways. He knew that."

"Any possibility that you could have resolved your problems and still kept the partnership?"

"No. Our whole corporate philosophy had changed. John wanted to narrow the focus in order to concentrate only on the development of prosthetic devices for atrophied or severed limbs. For me, that wasn't enough of a client base. I'm strictly sales and marketing. To make money, I need volume."

Peter didn't look at Stein when he asked his next question. Instead, he busied himself by drawing squiggles with a felt tip pen all over the edges of the desk top calendar. He hoped he looked nonchalant; he sure didn't feel it. "Was Bradley so much of a problem that it would have been easier for you if he were dead?"

Stein snorted. "Boy, if nothing else, you're direct. Sorry to disappoint you, but no. He was much more valuable to me alive."

"How so?"

"A couple of days ago, I found out there was no buy-sell clause in the original partnership contract."

Peter raised his eyebrows. "Meaning?"

"Meaning there's now no fixed value for John's interest in the partnership. When he died the partnership ceased to exist. If there had been a buy-sell arrangement, I, as the sole surviving owner, would then purchase John's interest, because Susan, as his heir, would be legally obligated to sell John's interest to me at a fixed price."

"So what difference does that make? What would a 'buy-sell' clause have done?"

"Allowed for an orderly distribution of John's business interest since the valuation of the partnership would have been at a set price. To make it simple, I'd be in a much better position if John were still alive and kicking. That way, we could have amicably dissolved our professional association and split the bounty. Right now, I'm looking at losing everything I've spent a lot of years building."

"When did you first learn there may be a problem with the buy-sell term not being in the contract?"

"Twenty-four hours after he had the nerve to come up murdered."

Peter leaned back in the chair and folded his hands, his fingers interlocking. "So, if I'm following you, I guess we can assume that it wasn't until *after* Bradley's murder that you found yourself in a financial pickle. But by then it was too late—right?"

Stein blinked hard, then took a breath as if the wind had been knocked out of him. With a sly smile he countered, "I'm smarter than that. There're much better ways of dissolving a partnership other than physically eliminating one of the parties."

"Maybe. . . ."

Peter reached into the police file and pulled out some notes. "Why would Bradley retain a file folder in his desk at home labeled, 'Partner?'"

Stein stared at him. "I wouldn't know."

"Could Bradley have approached someone else for the purpose of forming a new partnership once yours dissolved?"

"Anything's possible."

"I understand your former partner was frequently absent and didn't respond either to beeper calls or cell phone messages."

"Is there a question in there?"

"Yeah," Peter answered with irritation. "What do you know about that?"

"I know his disappearing acts really hacked me off. For a split second I thought maybe a woman was involved, but that wasn't likely considering his personality."

"Know an attorney by the name of Caroline Witten?"

"Know her? No, but I know who she is—she's the legal commentator on channel four. So what?" Abruptly sitting forward in his chair, Stein pronounced, "Don't tell me John was involved with somebody like that." He shook his head, smiling. "No, that's not possible—he could never handle someone like that."

Peter decided to let Stein's last observation pass without comment. "Ever see Bradley with another woman?"

"Not unless you count Hilary Adams who's cute, but just a little too wholesome for my tastes." Stubbing the cigarette out in his empty styrofoam coffee cup, Stein got up, walked across the floor, and threw it in the trash. "Lieutenant, I've told you everything I know. So again, how much longer?"

"Just a couple more questions." Peter put the felt tip pen down and looked directly at Stein. "Were you at the Bradley residence the night of the murder?"

Stein's eyes narrowed to mere slits. "Did someone see me there?"

"Just answer the question."

"Why in God's name would I go there? Haven't you been listening? It was enough seeing him at the office."

"Don't answer my questions with a question of your own. That isn't how this works. So, one more time—were you there that night?"

Stein stooped down and picked up his overcoat from the back of the chair. He turned, his lip curling. "I'm going to answer you with an invitation. Ask my lawyer. I've cooperated with you as much as I'm going to." Stein yanked the door open. "For the last time, I didn't kill the son of a bitch."

CHAPTER TWENTY-SIX

Peter knew he had to come up with some answers soon. The Bradley case was more complicated than most, but that excuse didn't cut it with the front office. They were quick to remind him that results were what counted—he had seventy-two hours to come up with some.

With his detectives still chasing down leads and hopefully developing new ones, Peter tried once more to huddle with the deputy D.A. Unforeseen scheduling conflicts had forced cancellation of the previously planned meeting, but this time, from the tone of his voice, Peter could tell that Benovitz was ready, even anxious to meet with him. Something had piqued the prosecutor's interest. Peter intended to take advantage of it.

They decided to meet at the Judicial Center, an ultramodern structure, built within the last five years, but already showing signs of abuse by members of the disenfranchised public who weren't happy about being summoned for a day in court. For Peter and Larry Benovitz, it was a centrally located, as well as convenient, place to meet.

"Peter, we've now got all the Emmett-Bradley trust account statements for the last three years." With a smile of satisfaction, Benovitz added, "To put it mildly, even given my limited knowledge, I can tell you a whole lot of something's been going on. Seems as though Bradley's been liquidating a lot of the trust's principal, as well as diminishing the very extensive investment portfolio successfully built-up over the years. As best I can tell, the liquidation process began about nine months ago. It's been fairly steady ever since."

"Was this liquidation legitimate?"

"Absolutely. Bradley was the named trustee of the account. So no questions were asked, only eyebrows raised."

"How'd you find all this out?"

"By looking at the books and talking with the president and general counsel of the bank, Spencer Winslow. The guy doesn't know a damn thing about the practice of law, or even about banking regulations, but he's made ass-kissing a whole new art form, so he'll forever maintain job security with the CEO.

"Lucky for us, he was only too happy to talk about the Emmett-Bradley accounts, probably because it gave him something to fill in the hours. He knew Bradley pretty well; didn't like him much, but I'm beginning to think that reaction was universal.

"Anyway, a few months ago, when Spence was thumbing through the bank's intra-office transaction forms, he noticed that rather large amounts were being withdrawn from the Bradley trust account. These withdrawals were so substantial that even the CEO noticed and asked Spence to keep an eye on it.

"Being the good soldier Spence can be for the obscene amount of money he brings home, Spence casually mentioned to Bradley the next time he saw him, that he noticed a slew of banking transactions, mostly withdrawals, from the trust account. It was a nice way of asking, 'How come you're taking your money from our bank?'"

"This may sound stupid, but since Bradley was the named trustee, what business was it of the bank's?"

"Technically, it was none of the bank's business. But because the money in the Emmett-Bradley account was to say the least, fairly substantial, the bank wanted to protect its bottom line, especially when FDIC examiners were due to make a visit. Bankers are naturally a bit touchy about these things since they have to be in compliance with federal regulations.

"From what I could gather, Bradley told Spence to mind his own damn business or he'd withdraw all the money, not just the trust account monies. That shut Spence up, fast."

"Uncover anything else considered noteworthy?"

"The principal was substantial—in the neighborhood of two and a half mill. Right now though, it's not that flush due to Bradley's systematic depletion."

"What about the possibility that Bradley re-deposited these monies in another account?"

Benovitz scratched his head. "Too simple. He didn't do that. The only other types of accounts at North Star were the Bradleys' joint checking account and a saving's account, same set-up for each. Bank statements show that the savings account had a daily balance of roughly thirty-eight thousand. In the checking account, there was an average daily balance of about twelve."

Benovitz stopped to take a breath, then continued. "Maybe I'm just a poor working slob, living paycheck to paycheck, but I think a twelve thousand dollar cash balance is a lot to have liquid in an account that doesn't pay daily interest. But what do I know, right?"

"Seems like an awful lot of money to me too. If Bradley was as smart and cautious as everybody said he was, this just doesn't square. But then, he was making frequent cash withdrawals. So he may have needed the liquidity."

"Did the Judge have an account in her own name?"

"No. Neither did the deceased, at least not at North Star."

"Great. I guess this means I'll need a search warrant to open up their safe deposit box. Or, I guess I could have the Judge come down and open it up." Hesitating, he added, "My gut tells me that wouldn't be too smart though."

Benovitz nodded. "Not to change the subject, but exactly who are your suspects in this investigation?"

"Too early to say. I can't point the finger at anybody in particular, nor can I eliminate anyone either. So, right now, that's means everybody's a suspect."

"Any news from the crime lab?"

Peter laughed. "Great minds think alike. Just a few hours ago I called the serologist. To add to my problems, she's not done yet, and doesn't expect to be until tomorrow, around four. Hopefully, we'll get a break there."

"Anything promising?"

"I hope. Someone left a man's bloody shoe print near the body."

"That kind of evidence sounds almost too good to be true."

"At first blush maybe, but we could be starting with a flawed premise—that the person who killed Bradley was dumb enough to leave a footprint behind. Frankly, that would make little sense. The killer was too meticulous. So I doubt the shoe print belongs to the killer."

"You don't think a *woman* would be capable of committing a crime like this, do you?"

Peter shrugged his shoulders. "Why not?"

"Because from all I've read, murderers of the female persuasion, don't like knives—something about not wanting to be that close to their intended victims, and generally, not having the requisite strength to carry it out successfully."

"That's true, but this case is different. We think Bradley was sitting with his back to the murderer. If the knife was sharp enough, the killer could have been male or female. The killer needed only average upper body strength."

"So what are you saying?"

"That I can't rule out the killer being female. Therefore, everybody's still a viable suspect, including the Honorable Susan Emmett-Bradley."

Benovitz stared at him in disbelief. "You're kidding! It would never have occurred to me that she could be considered a suspect."

"Why should she be treated any differently from any other whose spouse has been murdered? Generally, they're the first persons we investigate. Are you telling me that because she's a judge, she couldn't commit murder?"

"Maybe that's exactly what I'm telling you, but not for the reasons you think. For one thing, she wouldn't want to be around all that messy blood. And for another, I couldn't picture the Judge whipping herself into that kind of rage."

"Well, as we both know, stranger things have happened. But the investigation's still too new to be turning the screws on anyone just yet. And don't jump the gun thinking she's the killer—we're just not leaving her off the list."

"You know I saw the Judge on the Bench today which surprised me. Somehow, I didn't expect her to be back on the job quite this soon. So much for mourning I guess."

Shrugging his shoulders Peter said, "Maybe the Judge deals with grief by burying herself in work. Some people may even find that brand of stoicism admirable—something like the Kennedys not shedding a tear in public after J.F.K.'s assassination."

"I guess you're right. I admit to having a built-in bias against her. And as a professional who may be dealing directly with her in the future, I don't need to be making any judgment calls." Sheepishly, Benovitz added, "That means forget what I said before."

Peter smiled and patted him on the back. "No big deal. Want to go along with me when I deliver the warrant?"

"Nope. Think I'll pass. But if you want, I'll be glad to help you draft it. We don't want something as simple as that coming back to haunt us."

"I'll take you up on your offer. Which judge would you recommend for the task of signing the warrant?"

"Hamblin definitely. He's quick but thorough, and rarely wrong when evaluating the sufficiency of a warrant. He'll also be sure to give it a bit more scrutiny just because its Judge Emmett-Bradley who's involved. They're friends, but not so close that friendship would influence him one way or the other."

Closing the folder which held the Bradley trust account statements, Benovitz asked, "Anything else I can do for you?"

"Not right at the moment. I'll have the warrant dropped off a little later this morning."

"Sounds good. Keep me posted."

CHAPTER TWENTY-SEVEN

Hilary always had an unerring sixth sense as to when a client was "liked" by the police. And even though Peter had never said so, in so many words, Hilary's mystical intuition barometer, indicating that Susan was a prime suspect in the murder of her husband, was pointing off the scale. No question. Susan was on the short list, if for no other reason, than there was no one else at whom that old proverbial finger of guilt could be pointed. Unless of course, the police were considering Jake Stein. . . .

Hilary had to admit, if she were to stand in Peter's place, she would probably be leaning in the direction of the widowed spouse also, since that was inevitably the first conclusion jumped to by results driven law enforcement. Mostly, she convinced herself, because those conclusions were so easy, as well as so obvious.

After her staff and Sam had left for the day, Hilary closed and locked the office door behind them, kicked off her shoes and quietly padded down the hallway into her law library, carrying a legal pad and popping open a can of "Pepsi" she had grabbed along the way. Pulling up a wine colored barrel chair on wheels, she made herself comfortable at the massive conference table. Again, her feminine intuition told her it wasn't premature to plan some sort of defense strategy for Susan.

Hilary reached for a ballpoint pen, which someone had thoughtfully left behind on the credenza, then pulled the legal pad towards her and wrote one word—Suspects. Several seconds went by. Frowning, Hilary scribbled down only two names which she placed in two separate columns—Susan and Jake.

"Okay, there has to be someone else," she muttered to herself. But after getting up and pacing for several minutes, Hilary grudgingly resumed her seat. Shaking her head, she realized that with what she knew at the moment, she could come up with no other identifiable suspects that "looked good" for John Bradley's murder other than Susan and Jake. And right now, Susan looked a whole lot better than Jake.

With some sense of satisfaction, however, Hilary put in parentheses the words, Employee, Business Associate, and Subcontractors used at Residence. "Well, at least there are some other vague possibles, even if those vague possibles don't as yet, have names," she reassured herself.

Setting pen to paper once more, she wrote the word, Motive. Under Susan's name she listed, Number One—Embarrassment due to spouse's inappropriate behavior. Hilary giggled in spite of herself. "Surely, that's not enough of a motive to kill a loved one, is it?"

Number Two—Greed. Crossing that out as soon as she wrote it, Hilary reasoned that Susan had enough money all on her own, so that couldn't possibly be the inspiration for John's murder.

Number Three—Revenge. In spite of Dr. Parker's letter, the meaning of which she could speculate all day, Hilary knew of nothing definitively indicating that John had done something so egregious that Susan would be furious enough to kill him, rather than just do the obvious, like divorcing him.

Number Four—Infidelity. Again, Hilary laughed. "I don't think so. That wouldn't be the John Bradley I knew. And anyway, that motive goes to revenge, and I've already decided that's *not* a motive."

Number Five—Infidelity of Widow. Hilary thought for a moment. *Turn about's fair play, I guess, but the same gut feelings apply. Susan, just doesn't seem the type, and anyway, as her best friend, I know she would have told me. So that's a dead end too.*

"There's only one more thing to worry about—Opportunity. And unfortunately, Susan had it in spades!"

Hilary sat back in her chair, and stared at the ceiling, thinking. *Opportunity though, just isn't enough. And too, the police and prosecution aren't required to prove motive. . . . So why then do I still have this nagging feeling that Susan's vulnerable?* Try as she might, Hilary couldn't shake the premonition that Susan was in trouble.

Putting her concerns aside, which Hilary decided, if logic applied, were baseless, she decided to analyze Jake Stein's potential. Motive. Well, let's see . . ."

Repeating what she had done before, when analyzing Susan, Hilary wrote down the options with regard to Jake. Number One—Greed. "Makes sense, since John's death means that Jake is the only surviving partner. But unless there's a buy-sell clause in place, the business, as a matter of law, would dissolve. So what would Jake have to gain, and what does that have to do with motive generally?" After thinking about this for awhile, Hilary carefully wrote in the margin—Need more information.

Number Two—Cover-up. *Had Jake done something to irreparably harm the business and John found out about it?* Again, Hilary wrote a note in the margin of the page—Need more information from Susan and the company's accountant.

"Okay, let's look at the category, Opportunity. No question. Jake had it. That's good because Jake's opportunity will deflect blame from Susan." Smiling, Hilary reasoned, *And that means there's another person besides Susan whom the police and jury could consider as an identifiable suspect.*

Hilary knew, worst case scenario, that if Susan was charged with John's murder, her trial strategy would have to include a plausible showing that other viable suspects besides Susan existed. With that kind of strong inferential evidence, it wouldn't be difficult to establish reasonable doubt—thus meriting an acquittal for Susan.

Flipping the page over, Hilary decided to write down, in stream of consciousness fashion, what was bothering her about the murder—those persistent questions that just didn't go away because either Hilary had not enough information, or the information she had, didn't make sense.

"Maybe writing all of this all down will clarify some things." She began her "worry paragraph" as she called it with, Number One—Susan's defensive posture when questioned about where she had been the night of the murder; Number Two—Susan, a Judge, obstructing justice by secreting the letter from Dr. Parker; Number Three—the anger Susan displayed at The Jefferson Club just two weeks before the murder; Number Four—Susan's need to return to the office so quickly after John's death; and Number Five—Susan's apparent lack of fear upon arrival at the house and finding John's body.

When finished, Hilary put her pen down and again leaned back in the chair. It was just so frustrating. The more she struggled to put pieces of the puzzle together, the more she realized nothing fit. Nothing made sense. Her exercise on paper made it clear—the most important pieces to this elusive puzzle were missing.

Discouraged with finding no answers, Hilary muttered, "Another day." Gathering up her belongings, she turned off the light and went home.

CHAPTER TWENTY-EIGHT

Peter decided to take Shapero with him when he conducted the search at North Star. Arriving a little before three o'clock, they immediately took the elevator located at the rear of the underground parking garage to the bank's security offices on the seventh floor.

After introductions, Peter sat down in a cramped office just off the lobby and explained to chief of security, Stan Geroski, that he was there to examine the safe deposit box currently held by John Bradley and Susan Emmett-Bradley.

Sitting directly across from the burly bank officer at a modular desk littered with papers, a sprinkling of paper clips and old fashioned walkie-talkies, Peter asked, "Would you look over the warrant, and if there are no concerns, make the safe deposit box available to us?"

Without saying a word, Geroski leaned across the desk, heedlessly scattering papers in all directions, and with the biggest and hairiest right hand Peter had ever seen, indelicately picked up the search warrant and began reading it silently, then looking confused, began reading it out loud. Peter and Shapero looked at each other, then at their watches. It was going to be tight. The bank closed in an hour and a half.

When Geroski finished reading the original of the three page search warrant and the affidavit in support of it, he reassembled the pages, then returned them in a bundle to Peter. "Looks all right to me, Lieutenant, but then I'm no lawyer. If ya don't mind though, I'd like to make a second copy of it for in-house counsel, and keep the copy you already gave me for our files here in Security. Have any problems with that?"

"Of course not."

Abruptly, Geroski pulled back, scraping the bottom of his chair against the tile floor and stood, grimacing as his pot belly rubbed against the edge of his desk. "Good. If you'll take the elevator to your left and press the 'LL' button, it should take you to where you want to go. The person you need to see down there is Sherry. Explain who you are, why you're here, and that you're waiting for me. I'll see you in five or less."

When Geroski arrived on the lower level of the bank, he identified the safe deposit box as number 437088. Using an internal control code, he and Sherry turned the vault's oversized wheel and opened the huge silver cylinder which marked the entrance. Geroski then motioned for Peter and Shapero to accompany him inside.

"Here we are, Gentlemen." Geroski stopped in front of Number 437088. "Just to make sure that we've produced the right one though, please review the number on the signature cards which reflect the names, John Michael Bradley and Susan Emmett-Bradley, then compare that number with the one assigned to the front of this steel casing."

Peter looked closely. "I have, and they are identical."

"Good. I'll insert the bank's key, then you insert the key you brought with you."

Cautiously, he slipped the key into the lock and turned it. Peter did the same. The lock immediately yielded. Geroski then laid the box down in the center of a long rectangular table and turned to leave.

Anxious to see the contents in private, Peter said, "Thanks for all your help. We'll let you know when we're done."

Geroski nodded, closing the door behind him.

Slowly, Peter peeled back the long narrow steel lid to expose what lay within. "My God, look at that," exclaimed Shapero. "There must be tens of thousands of dollars in this box. What in the hell was this guy into anyway?"

"Cash obviously," answered Peter quietly. "Now I guess we know where at least some of the money went when Bradley dipped into the Judge's trust account."

Peter lifted out several layers of one hundred dollar bills and looked at the mound of cash still left underneath. "This is a lot of money, but I know it can't begin to account for all that Bradley took from the Judge." He sat down looking glum. "What's more, I can't even be sure that this money was withdrawn from the trust account."

Peter took out the note pad and a pocket calculator he had thought to bring along at the last minute. "We'll have to check the bank's visitor log to determine when and how often Bradley opened this box. We can then check the dates against the withdrawals on monthly statements. Luckily, since the search warrant covers all information pertaining to the box, we're legally authorized to get that information today." He added, "Geroski seems to be an okay guy to deal with, so it shouldn't be too much of a pain in the ass."

"Well then, while you're counting all this, why don't I just mosey on over to Sherry's desk and ask to see the log."

"Good idea. Seeing how much money's here, I don't know how long it'll take to count it. From the looks of it though, I'd say it's going to take a while, so don't hurry."

*** *** ***

Fifty-five minutes later, on their way back to the underground parking garage, Shapero asked, "I didn't want to say anything while we were inside, but how much money was in there?"

"I'm probably not accurate to the dollar, but it was close to half a million."

The detective let out a long slow whistle. "I've never in my whole life seen that much money in one place. What was it like counting it?"

Peter laughed. "To be honest, at first it was fun, but then I reminded myself it wasn't mine." Peter unlocked the car and he and Shapero got in. "What'd you find out about the frequency of Bradley's visits to the vault area?"

"Without fail, he came every two weeks; stayed about ten minutes, said nothing, then left with a black attache case in hand."

Pulling the seat belt tight Shapero asked, "So what do you make of all this?"

"I think Bradley was in some deep shit, trying to tunnel his way out using the Judge's trust funds. But why, what for, and for how long, I couldn't tell you."

Looking dejected Shapero mused, "To be honest, I'm not sure we're any further along than we were before. I can't get a handle on anything. What do you think?"

Peter gripped the steering wheel hard. Frustrated, he answered, "I think I need to get a handle on this fast before it gets any more complicated than it already is."

CHAPTER TWENTY-NINE

Back at headquarters, Peter immediately placed a call to Judge Emmett-Bradley's chambers. When it was picked up on the third ring he asked, "May I speak to the Judge please? Tell her it's Peter Elliott."

"One moment, Sir," came the clipped reply. "I'll see if she's off the Bench."

Within two minutes, Susan came to the phone. "Has there been a new development?" she asked anxiously.

Peter swallowed hard. One of the toughest things he had to do as a cop was tell a victim's loved one to be patient and not give up. Investigations took time. Human nature being as it is however, everyone expected answers yesterday. And no one wanted that more than Peter. Unfortunately though, in this case, that didn't appear very likely.

With caution he answered, "I'm not certain I'd characterize this as a 'new development.' Let's just say that there are some things that you and I need to talk over."

He waited for a response but heard only soft breathing. "Are you still there?"

"Can these 'things' as you call them, be discussed by phone?"

"They could, but it would be preferable to meet in person. Since it's past quitting time, how about right now?"

"Right now?" Susan asked, an unmistakable note of concern in her voice.

"Yes, if that's possible."

"Well, I have some rulings that need signing, but after that, I'm free except Hilary was to meet me at my office in fifteen minutes. And at this late hour I can't possibly get hold of her. So—"

"I have no problem with Hilary being present. After all, she's your legal counsel."

"Do I need legal counsel?"

"That's up to you. You might feel more comfortable if your lawyer was with you."

Seconds passed.

"I see. . . . I guess. We'll be at your offices within the hour."

Without another word, the Judge abruptly hung up, leaving Peter holding the receiver pressed up against his ear, echoing a dead connection.

"Strange woman, Judge Emmett-Bradley," Peter said without much expression to Shapero who had been casually sifting through investigative reports generated by detectives on the day shift.

Shapero appeared to ignore the remark. Dropping the reports on Peter's desk he offered, "I think the Judge is holding back and we need to confront her. Remember what Greene said—that the 911 call didn't come in until close to two? If she left the courthouse sometime just after midnight, what was she doing until almost two a.m.?"

Uninvited, the detective sat down in the nearest chair and clasped his hands behind his head as he looked up at the ceiling. "The way I see it, we have two possibilities here—one, she was at the house cleaning something up, or cleaning herself up; or two, she stopped somewhere along the way, not to buy groceries, but to meet someone who had just 'offed' hubby."

Only half listening, Peter continued his search through the latest investigative reports that Shapero had reshuffled out of order, then left in an uneven pile in the center of his desk. "Is the report back from the crime lab?"

"Yep. But it's only preliminary. See, here it is." Guiltily, Shapero looked over at Peter. "Sorry, I put that pile of papers over it."

With the reports clasped in his hand, Shapero quickly scanned the two page, single spaced memo. "Going down the list, Exhibit One, which was the blood sample taken from the deceased, shows Bradley had an ABO blood grouping of O positive. Wouldn't you know, the most universal blood type known."

"Anything else?"

Reading the report out loud, Shapero answered, "Says here, 'Of the materials and exhibits submitted, which included the victim's clothing, the bloody shoe print after it was photographed, and particles scraped from the floor as well as the carpet sample cut from the rug where Bradley was lying, each show an ABO blood grouping of O positive. Too soon for more definitive DNA results. The pillow collected from the sofa where it's believed Bradley was sitting at the time of the attack, shows minute traces of human blood, too limited in quantity for further analysis."

Shapero put the report down and looked at Peter expectantly. "I guess it's possible Bradley scratched his assailant enough to make him bleed a little, but apparently not enough to let us know even what blood grouping he is. Then again, all those specks of blood on the pillow could belong to Bradley."

Peter threw a pencil across the room, aiming for inside of the trash can, but missed, hitting only the can itself with a loud 'ping.' "So, making a long story short, it's a wash."

Shapero picked up the report again and continued to read the lab's findings out loud. "The scrapings from Bradley's fingernails showed no blood and no tissue."

Shapero sat forward in his chair. "There are a couple of things that're interesting though."

"Well, since you have the report, why don't you tell me what they are," demanded Peter.

"There were two navy blue fibers taken from underneath the victim's left thumbnail. As to the bloody shoe print, the lab says it's a man's dress type, size 10 C, with smooth soles and a new set of heels. The lab estimates that the shoe's owner weighs in at about a hundred and seventy-five."

Absently taking notes, Peter remarked, "At least we know that a male, though still unidentified, who weighed one hundred and seventy-five, and wore a size 10 C dress shoe was at the Bradley residence at or about the time Bradley was murdered. That's a certainty. Other than that, we don't know anything."

With a startled look on his face, Shapero asked, "Are you saying you don't think that the person who left the bloody shoe print was the killer?"

Peter took off his glasses and looked at him. "How many times have you seen a killer leave behind a bloody shoe print, like a calling card?" Laughing Peter added, "If it were that simple, we'd just buy a game of '*Clue*' and I could tell the Chief that it was Colonel Mustard in the library wearing a size 10 C shoe, who wielded the knife, with Mrs. Peacock ready to assist. No, my gut feeling is that there were two people there that night before the police were called, perhaps not including the Judge herself. And that complicates matters considerably."

"I don't know how you figure, but you're the boss." Trying to stifle a yawn, Shapero asked, "Where do we go from here?"

"First of all, we're going to follow through with what we found out this afternoon and check out every bank within fifty miles. Because of that key found taped to the underside of his office desk drawer, we know Bradley must have had a second safe deposit box somewhere, other than at North Star. It follows that he'd have some kind of an account at that bank too. But if we find that he hasn't been depositing the missing money in another bank account, then he's been paying out a lotta cash to someone for something." Peter smiled. "And generally speaking, people don't do that unless they have something to hide."

Quickly jotting some notes to himself, Peter continued. "We know a lot more than we did twenty-four hours ago. First, my gut tells me that Bradley and his wife were having marital problems. I don't know the specifics yet, but something tells me that will probably factor into the murder equation somewhere. We also know that Bradley was having, shall we say, constant communications with Caroline Witten. Admittedly, she does a lot of divorce work, so let's assume since the Bradleys were having marital problems, that's why he was talking with her. And last, but not least, we know from the crime lab, that someone, wearing a navy blue wool suit, was in very close contact with the body. That same someone could also be the killer, but somehow, I doubt it."

Scratching his day old whiskers, Shapero, looking somewhat confused, answered, "Your instincts are generally right on the money, so I won't argue."

Peter closed the files. "Not to change the subject, but I haven't heard any comment or received any investigative report about your meeting with Ms. Vivian."

Looking past Peter, Shapero answered simply, "Went real well."

"I hope that means she gave you some valuable information."

"Well, she told me that Stein's away from the office a lot on personal business. Business that nobody knows about but her, and that nobody would believe anyway, even if they were told about it."

"So what the hell does that mean?"

"Apparently, Stein's seeing someone, but whoever that someone is, it's a big secret." Smoothing his hair back, Shapero added, "I turned on the old Shapero charm, but I still couldn't worm it out of her. Said Stein would be furious if she ever talked about his 'secret.'"

"That tells me absolutely jack shit nothing."

Shapero blinked several times before sputtering, "Now hold on, not all's lost. I can talk to her again later in the week, when I'm off duty. That way, I'm not wasting department time, if that's what you think I've been doing."

"Good," Peter answered curtly. "And let me tell you something right up front. This is going to be the very last time you see Stein's secretary until this investigation is over with, unless you come up with some genuine investigative avenue to pursue with her, and that especially means no more fancy meals. Have you got that straight?"

Shapero started to say something, but apparently thinking better of it, turned and walked out the door, quietly closing it behind him.

CHAPTER THIRTY

Edward Arpel was restless and irritable. The campaign was proving to be much more difficult than originally anticipated. The time involved and effort spent were taking an unhealthy toll on his practice as well as his personal life. He wasn't himself.

Suddenly, Arpel got up from behind his desk, reached for a phone strategically located for his clients' convenience on the oval conference table, and angrily punched the intercom button. "When it's convenient Martha, would you step into my office?"

"Should I bring anything with me, Sir?" she asked in her best Minnie Mouse voice.

"No, just yourself," Arpel answered impatiently. "We need to talk about something, that's all. It's nothing important, so don't wear that worried look on your face. It always starts tongues wagging in this place. And God knows, I don't need the aggravation."

In anticipation of her arrival, Arpel sat down once more, but not behind the massive mahogany desk inherited from his grandfather who was one of the founding members of Arpel's law firm. Instead, he carefully chose one of the paired wing chairs placed next to the plush velvet drapes framing palladium windows in his corner suite of offices located in the pricey Citizens Plaza. He needed a moment to collect his thoughts.

At fifty-six, Edward Arpel was still an attractive, some would even say, handsome man. His wavy blonde hair was clipped and cut with calculated regularity, but always appeared slightly windblown, as if no concentrated effort was taken to maintain it. Only Arpel's wife, Muriel, knew that he rose thirty minutes early every morning in order to have the time necessary to make it appear casual, but always stylish. His charcoal grey pin stripe suit was elegant in cut and style and hugged his size forty-two regular frame with the precision that only an eight hundred dollar custom-made suit could effect.

He pulled nervously at the fourteen carat gold scales of justice cufflinks, trying to marshal his thoughts. An almost inaudible knock at his door startled him. He recognized the timid tap as one belonging to his fiercely loyal secretary. "Come in, Martha."

Martha Briscoe was slight in stature. She wore no makeup; her hair crimped and meticulously styled every day, lay flat against her head like a helmet; her suits, always stark black, were each cut just above her ankles, relieved only by a hint of white lace at the neck and cuffs.

Like a scared rabbit, she took her ususal "at attention" position directly in front of the man who had been her boss for thirty-one years, ever since Arpel had been welcomed into the firm—as his grandfather's legacy. It was no secret that Arpel couldn't get along without her. And fortunately for Martha, Arpel openly accepted the cloyingly codependent relationship as a necessary fact of life, and key to his professional survival.

"Martha, sit down. Let's talk." Watching her move uncomfortably around the room, Arpel barked, "Don't take the chair over in the corner; sit down across from me where I can see you."

Looking flustered, Martha answered, "Why, thank you, Mr. Arpel. Thank you very much. But before I sit down, may I get you anything?"

Arpel shook his head. *She never changes.* "Martha, don't you remember? You already asked me that, and I already told you, 'no.' I'm fine; I need nothing. I just thought that perhaps you and I could sit down for a few minutes and have a little chat. We're always so busy with business matters, that I rarely get the chance to just sit and talk with you."

Since Martha didn't immediately respond, other than to stare transfixed, like a deer caught in headlights, Arpel continued unchallenged. "You know what I've always said. Next to Muriel, you're the most important woman in my life." He leaned forward, hoping the gesture would emphasize that point. "Why, just this morning, I was sitting here thinking I didn't tell you often enough, just how much you mean to me. Everyone knows that without you, I wouldn't be half this successful." He could see he was making her blush. It was just so easy.

"Oh, Mr. Arpel," Martha gushed. "You've always been so good to me."

He smiled knowingly. "That's because you've always been there for me—no matter what."

"Of course I've been there for you. That's my job." Looking anxious, Martha cocked her head to one side and asked, "Is there something wrong—is Mrs. Arpel feeling worse? Is there a problem with one of the boys?"

"Oh no, no. They're all fine. At least Mrs. Arpel isn't any worse. And the boys—well you know children, they'll bleed you dry financially," he said chuckling. "But I guess I deserve that since I've spoiled them so much."

"I believe wives and children are made to be spoiled, and yours adore you so. And not just because of the way you spoil them either," Martha said soothingly. "They truly love you."

"You've always understood, haven't you? They're the reason, really the only reason, I work this hard. If it weren't for them, I wouldn't care to continue this never ending rat race. I guess that's why I want that judgeship."

"I know how stressful this practice is for you. And now with the campaign as well, it's just too much." She looked at him hard. "Is there anything wrong?"

Arpel folded his hands in his lap. He wanted to say this just right. Choosing his words carefully, he answered, "I'm not sure I'd call it wrong. Perhaps a better word would be, bothersome." He glanced downward, but out of the corner of his eye he was still able to watch her. She had that quizzical look on her face again. He decided he better get to the point before her imagination got the best of her. "I'm referring to that call we got yesterday from the police, asking if they could schedule an appointment to discuss the Bradley murder. Why would they think I could offer some kind of assistance? After all, I barely knew the man. And it's all I need having questions like that asked at this point in the campaign."

Without waiting for an reply, Arpel asked, his voice soft and sweet, as if sheathed in honey, "Why don't you tell me exactly what they said when they called yesterday."

Looking thoughtful, summoning all her powers of concentration, Martha recounted her previous conversation with the police in painful, extraneous detail. It was all that Arpel could do, to keep from squirming in his seat.

"I remember that when I took the call, the detective merely introduced himself and asked to talk with you, indicating he'd be here tomorrow around ten to gather what he called, 'routine information.' I don't recall anything other than that. The conversation was brief, since you had two clients waiting, and I was busy trying to make them comfortable until you arrived back from court. So, I intentionally didn't talk very long." Pensively, Martha tapped her pen gently against the arm of the chair. "But I got the distinct impression that the gentlemen on the other end of the line, who identified himself as a Detective DeAngelo, didn't want to prolong the conversation either."

"Did you ask him what he was looking for, or more specifically, what he hoped to get from me?"

"No," Martha answered quietly. "I didn't think it was my place to ask questions like that, Sir. Did I do something wrong?"

"No, of course not. It's just that I was hoping to have some clue as to why they thought it necessary to contact me. After all, I've had nothing to do with the Judge or her husband, excepting those few times I've run into them during the campaign. And even then, I make a conscious effort to steer clear of the Judge when I can. There's just something about that woman that makes me uneasy."

"I know. Mrs. Arpel told me she feels that way too—that the Judge always seemed so unreachable."

"Well, she and Muriel are light years apart, that's for sure. I'm a very lucky man to be married to a woman like Muriel, and I know it."

Still trying to engage her in conversation, Arpel added, "I didn't mean to keep you. I just thought I might be able to glean a little bit more information about what to expect. As they say, forewarned is forearmed."

Arpel paused, his eyes narrowed. "By the way, do you recall what my schedule was around the time Bradley was killed? I certainly don't want to inadvertently mis-speak when I talk with the police. I know how important it is to be precise."

"Don't you remember how busy you were, Sir—trying to get that downtown hotel sold for Mr. Bacharach? The deal had to be closed quickly to avoid another tax levy imposed on his payroll. We had gotten down to the wire that day. You left around seven-thirty that evening, saying that you had scheduled a late meeting with the client—something about a last minute problem cropping up. I guess it had to do with the list of fixtures Bacharach had provided for the purchaser. The bank thought there was more inventory than what was originally disclosed, so you were going over to the hotel that night to 'set Bacharach straight.'"

Arpel's eyes lit up; he smiled and relaxed his stiff shoulders. "Yes, now I remember. Thanks for refreshing my memory. Since I left before you did, I don't even know what time you got out of here that night."

"It didn't really matter, but I think it was about eight-thirty. All the documents had to be pulled and copied that night since the closing was scheduled for the following morning at nine."

Disregarding Martha's show of overzealous commitment, Arpel stifled a nervous laugh. "I don't know why I'm so worried about trying to reconstruct what I was doing that night. It's not as though the police suspect me, right?"

"Oh, my goodness, of course not. What would lead you to think that even for a minute? A man of your stature . . . " Her voice trailed off and she blushed again. "I think they're just checking everything and everyone out."

"Whoa, I was just kidding about being a suspect." Arpel smiled. "This whole thing is so tawdry. It has us all unnerved. And in saying what I'm about to, I risk sounding as though I'm nothing more than an insensitive oaf, but Bradley's murder could really swing the vote in his wife's favor. I don't want or need people feeling sorry for her, thinking she must keep her seat in order to put food on the table. Little do they know she has a pile of money—enough to buy and sell all of us without blinking an eye."

Crinkling her brow, Martha asked, "How did you learn that?"

Hesitating, and for a fleeting moment, looking as if caught with his hand in the cookie jar, Arpel replied congenially, "Oh, that's pretty common knowledge. Unlike the rest of us, I hear she doesn't even need to work."

"Well, that sounds lovely. But I for one, am proud to work, and I dearly love working for you. It's been a career I wouldn't give up for the world."

Slowly inching off her chair while trying unobtrusively to glance at her watch, Martha advised, "I hate to remind you, but if there's nothing else, you must get ready for that five-thirty deposition. If you leave now, you'll have just enough time to make it. I have your briefcase packed and ready to go." With her hand on the doorknob, Martha turned and asked, "Since this deposition is set so late, and afterwards, you'll be so tired, why don't I just call and cancel tomorrow's appointment with Detective DeAngelo? I'm sure we can reschedule."

"No, don't bother. We just need to put this behind us and get on with the campaign."

Arpel rose from his chair, patted Martha on the shoulder as she left his office, then quietly closed the door.

CHAPTER THIRTY-ONE

"Here we are again, Lieutenant," she said with a exasperated sigh as she swept through his office door with Hilary following close behind. "Seems like deja vu."

Immediately seeing what kind of mood the Judge was in, Peter selectively edited out the superfluous, and hastily recapped what had recently been uncovered in the investigation. But instead of having the desired effect of deflecting her rage, his narration only seemed to fan the flames.

Pointing her finger, Susan scolded, "You told me in the very beginning that John probably knew his killer. If that were the case, why then haven't you been able to discover who the murderer is by now? This can't be that tough."

Folding his arms across his chest, Peter tried to be patient as he quietly reiterated his initial conclusions. "There's no doubt in my mind that your husband knew his killer. But your husband and his relationships with others was complicated; nothing about him was simple. And when I tell you what we discovered about his recent banking transactions, I think you'll begin to understand why this investigation has become more complex than originally anticipated.'"

Susan looked at him curiously. "What are you talking about?"

Peter took a deep breath before continuing. This was going to hurt, but it had to be done. "Our investigation has found that your trust account, maintained at North Star, was systematically depleted by a fairly substantial amount. What started out as a trust totaling in the neighborhood of a little over two million dollars has been reduced to about half that."

Peter watched as Susan's hand flew to her mouth as she inadvertently let out a gasp. "Oh my God. That's not possible."

Quickly, Hilary grabbed a chair for Susan, then helped her into it. "That's not possible," she repeated. "John would never have done something like that without discussing it first. There has to be some mistake."

Softly Peter answered, "I'm afraid there's no mistake, Judge. Up until nine months ago, your husband was making rather conservative investments with the quarterly interest and leaving the remaining principal to accumulate. Then all of a sudden, he began liquidating."

Susan buried her head in her hands, refusing eye contact with Peter.

Peter hesitated, but only momentarily. He knew he had to go on, no matter how painful this revelation seemed to be for the Judge. Her shock appeared genuine. *There goes motive.* He glanced at Hilary who silently nodded her understanding.

"When was the last time you discussed the trust account with your husband?"

Susan sat up, rigid, trying desperately to stifle her sobs. "I don't know. I felt perfectly secure with John handling our investments, so I never thought it necessary to talk about it. I trusted him to do the right thing for both of us." Looking stricken she conceded, "He was authorized by the trust's own terms to do whatever he felt necessary, but regardless, from what you've just told me, he violated my confidence in him. I—I just can't believe he could have done this to me."

"Do you have any idea what your husband could have been doing with all that money?"

"None whatsoever," came the quick reply. "John was cautious, almost stingy about money. What you're describing is completely out of character." She stared suspiciously at Peter. "Do *you* know what he was doing with the money?"

"Not yet, but hopefully, soon. Just so you know, I also checked your safe deposit box at North Star, incident to a search warrant being executed."

With eyes widening, Susan demanded, "Why would you do that without advising me? Who signed the search warrant?"

"Answering your questions one at a time, I did it because I believed it contained evidence relevant to this investigation. And Judge Hamblin signed it."

Peter didn't want to get sidetracked with incidentals, so he quickly pressed on, not allowing the Judge a comeback. "When was the last time you looked inside that safe deposit box?"

Susan thought for a moment. "I guess I haven't really looked at it since John and I put documents pertaining to the investment portfolio and our wills in it. Why?"

"Before I answer that, did your husband ever tell you not to go to the safe deposit box for any reason, or refuse to give you a key?"

As if affronted by such a question, Susan answered, "No, of course not. But it never really came up for discussion." Susan turned to stare at him and swallowed hard before asking, "Why? What did you find when you opened the safe deposit box?"

"The documents you just mentioned, along with about a half a million dollars in cold cash."

"Good God!" Slumping low in her chair she asked, "Have you tried to follow some sort of paper trail to see whether withdrawals from the trust account matched the dates John opened the safe deposit box?"

"We should receive the log entries by nine o'clock tomorrow. When we get that information, we'll try and compare them to withdrawals made from the trust account as well as your checking account."

Susan shook her head in disbelief. "I don't know what to say. I thought the bank might freeze my accounts, but I never believed, even for a second, there would be any irregularities in getting John's Will through probate. Obviously now, that's not going to be the case."

Peter walked towards the Judge's chair and stood in front of her. "I know you're still reacting to the news I just gave you, but there's something else we learned—something from the crime lab that you and I need to discuss."

Frowning, Susan asked, "Did I misunderstand? I thought you told me you didn't find out much of anything from forensics except very preliminary information."

"And it may prove to be nothing. But affixed to the underside of your husband's left thumbnail, were two fibers. We know that they were navy as far as dye color, and we know that the fiber was worsted wool." Peter looked at her hard. "I think we can assume from this information that someone who was wearing navy worsted wool more than just touched John Bradley's wrist or hand on the night he was murdered."

Slowly, Peter stood up and turned away from the Judge, hoping that a less confrontational posture would be more beneficial in getting a true emotional reaction. "When I arrived at your home that night, I remember you were wearing a navy wool suit—"

"Come on, Peter," Hilary interjected. "Probably a lot of people, police included, were wearing clothes with navy worsted wool fibers that night, so where do you think you're going with this?"

Peter turned around again and smiled at Susan, while answering Hilary's question. "That's absolutely true, but before we go to the trouble of trying to eliminate those other individuals, would you object if we obtained a fiber sample from your navy blue suit?"

"Susan already explained that she touched John to see if he had a pulse," Hilary argued.

"I remember," Peter said evenly. "But in merely checking someone's pulse, you wouldn't expect to find fibers *underneath* the victim's nail."

"So? Even if we were to produce that suit for comparison sampling to the two fibers in question, the results still wouldn't prove anything conclusively."

"Nice try, Hil. But as I explained, it raises some questions, and in order for me to be satisfied, they'll have to be answered by the Judge—your client."

Susan had sat silently during this exchange between Hilary and Peter, turning her head slightly from side to side, watching and listening. But with Peter's final pronouncement that she would be expected to provide an explanation, Susan resignedly answered, "All right. I'll furnish the suit tomorrow morning, or this evening if you'd like to follow me home." Returning his stare, she added, "On second thought, maybe your retrieval of it tonight would be best, since I don't want any questions raised about my complete and full cooperation with the city police department."

"That's fine. I'll just follow you and Hilary to your home tonight."

"If that's what you want," Susan answered coldly. "I must warn you though, the suit was thrown in with the rest of the laundry and is now a mass of wrinkles."

"I don't think the crime lab will mind. As you and I both know, they've seen worse."

CHAPTER THIRTY-TWO

With an introduction so often used, that it now required no thought, he began with, "Ms. Witten, this is Lieutenant Peter Elliott, city homicide. I'm phoning you in reference to the John Bradley murder."

Not surprisingly, he didn't wait long for a response.

"Lieutenant, I think you've been misinformed. I don't deny knowing John Bradley, but it's been a while since I've actually seen him. I'd like to help, but—"

Not to be put off, Peter quickly interjected, "I understand how you feel, but our investigation has uncovered that you spoke frequently with Mr. Bradley. At one time, as often as three or four times a week. That regularity of contact leads me to believe we need to talk."

"Unfortunately, I can't stop you from asking questions, but frankly, I'm under no obligation to answer you. I don't know how you got this information, but your casual use of it over the phone seems a bit reckless. If you want to pursue it, set up an appointment. I don't discuss matters like this over the phone. I know you by reputation, even though I don't do a lot of criminal practice. My only involvement in that end of the business is doing t.v. commentary on criminal cases which titillate the more sensation seeking viewers. Otherwise, I steer clear of them."

"I understand, Ms. Witten, however I need to ask—"

Interrupting, she said, "You're not going to give me a break from this constant barrage of questions, are you?"

"Nope."

"Well then, rather than harassing me by phone, let's just schedule a mutually convenient time to meet."

"Sorry, I didn't know a phone call constituted harassment. But how about noon today?"

"Fine," she said with a sigh of resignation. "Here, twelve noon."

Peter smiled and carefully replaced the phone. *This should be interesting. I've watched and listened to her legal commentary on the local news for a lot of years, but I've never had the pleasure of actually meeting her. As Jake Stein said—she must be some kind of woman.*

CHAPTER THIRTY-THREE

"Sorry to bust in on you like this, Mr. Arpel, but we can't leave anything to chance. I hope you understand. Since you're running against the widow in the next election, we have to interview everyone whose name happens to crop up during a murder investigation."

Patronizingly Arpel answered, "I understand, Detective DeAngelo. I must admit however, I'm somewhat puzzled as to why anyone believes I could be of assistance." Bracing for the onslaught, Arpel nonchalantly adjusted his tie and buttoned his suit coat. "Since I barely knew the deceased, and the widow and I aren't exactly friends, I really don't know what I could offer that would require spending valuable investigative time with me. I'm sure you can understand—the last thing I want or need is my opponent's husband getting murdered." Smiling graciously, and with a wave of his hand he added, "But of course, I'm at your disposal. Please, do sit down."

Looking uncomfortable, the detective did as he was directed while politely explaining once more that it was not his intent to take up too much of Arpel's time. The interview was nothing more than routine.

With care, Arpel folded his hands in his lap, his long fingers interlocking, like pieces of a jigsaw puzzle. "As I said, whatever I can offer, I'm here at your service."

"Great. I wish everyone was as cooperative," answered DeAngelo amicably. "Ah, to begin, I just need to get a little background. . . . Sorry to trouble you, but could you tell me when, and under what circumstances, you first met the deceased?"

"That's kind of a tall order, Detective." Arpel sat motionless for several seconds, saying nothing. The question seemed simple, but still, he needed time to gather his thoughts. The questions had to be answered in just the right tone, with just the right words. After all, he had a campaign to consider. Turning to face DeAngelo directly, he replied evenly, "If I recall, I met Bradley about eight years ago at the Bar Association's annual banquet." Visibly puffing out his chest, Arpel explained, "I was president that year. Susan was testing the waters so to speak in her run for the Bench. She was making all the rounds of the social circuit, trying to garner early support—seeing what heavy hitters she could count on during her campaign. I was thinking of running too, but at that time, had not yet announced my candidacy.

"I remember her husband was standing somewhat off by himself that night. As a courtesy, I went over and introduced myself." Laughing Arpel explained, "Those dinners can be insufferable and it's easy to tire of talking only to legal types. Since I'd gotten to that point already that evening, I walked away from the crowd at the bar and began talking to Bradley who, I was surprised, proved to be a breath of fresh air."

Leaning back in his chair, DeAngelo answered, "I realize Sir, it was a while ago, but can you remember what that conversation was about?"

"Well, let's see . . ." Arpel knew he had to appear neutral. The phrase, "Never speak ill of the dead," ran through his mind like a mantra. "I remember Bradley as intelligent and articulate, but noticeably uncomfortable. He admitted he was there only because his wife had asked him to be; told me he hated any get-together where the attire was what he called, 'forced formal.' I remember being amused. We then went on to talk about his business, which again, if I recall correctly, had something to do with hospitals or hospital equipment. I thought his profession was an interesting one and asked him for his business card, thinking that his expertise might come in handy one day in litigating personal injury cases. Altogether, I guess we talked for about five minutes, certainly not longer than that. We were interrupted by Susan who asked him to accompany her to the dining table."

Arpel looked cooly in DeAngelo's direction, trying to gauge his audience's reaction. There was none. He wondered if DeAngelo was even listening.

"Did you see or speak to him again?"

"Not really. Except, of course, at the usual campaign rallies that candidates and their spouses have to attend."

"How well do you know the Judge?"

"Not very," Arpel answered, hoping not to appear evasive even though his head was bowed and answers like, "Not really" and "Not very" seemed, at best, vague. "I had a couple of cases against her when she was a practicing attorney, so we knew each other, but only in the adversarial sense." He looked up at DeAngelo but could tell that his attempt at humor was lost on the boorish public servant. He continued, laughing inwardly at his own play on words. "Since she became a judge, I've never had the opportunity to be in her courtroom; therefore, I see her rarely—only at campaign events."

Crossing his legs carefully while keeping a steady bead on DeAngelo, Arpel further explained, "I guess you can discern from this that we're not exactly friends or enemies. Our relationship is strictly professional and because of that, I can't say I know her well."

DeAngelo nodded. "I take it then that you've never been to the Judge's home for some sort of social occasion?"

"Not that I can specifically recall."

"Are you saying then that it's possible that you've been there?"

"No," Arpel said with a tinge of impatience. *Why is this guy hanging onto this like a bulldog with a bone? I've answered his question once already.* He glanced at his watch, trying to quickly assess how much time he had before he must leave for a scheduled mediation. "Sorry, I didn't mean to sound annoyed. It's just that I have an appointment elsewhere in just a few minutes." Looking directly at the detective he explained, "To answer your question, I'm just saying that I don't recall for certain. Accuracy, certainty—that's what you want, isn't it?"

"I'm sorry; I'm not trying to split hairs, but I thought you said you never saw the Judge socially."

"I can see you're good," Arpel answered cloyingly. He thought those words would soothe the detective. And from the look on DeAngelo's face, he was right. The guy was putty. "Let me clarify. As a Judge, Susan is expected to entertain, at various times, officers of the Bar. She's also expected to be involved in various civic endeavors in which the Bar is a participant. As a past and present officer of the Bar Association, I may have had occasion to meet with the Judge, along with others, on matters of mutual interest. And it's possible that those meetings may have taken place at her home. I certainly didn't go there as a social guest. All my dealings with the Judge and her late husband have been strictly the result of professional commitments—nothing more, nothing less."

"Then you wouldn't know if the late John Bradley had any enemies?"

He tried a smile with his answer. "Sorry, I can't help you there."

Awkwardly, DeAngelo gathered up his trench coat and stood. "I guess ah that's all I had to ask you." Shaking Arpel's hand he added, "I certainly appreciate a man of your stature taking the time to see me."

"That's all right, my boy," Arpel answered as he patted the detective on the back. "Always delighted to help when and if I can. Such a tragedy. . . . Something you just don't want to get involved with."

DeAngelo paused. "I don't know why I'm even bringing this up, but you handled a case for my grandmother. She didn't have a whole lot. She was injured when an elevator fell. My family never forgot you."

"Really? Well, it's always nice to hear about former clients. What was your grandmother's name?"

"Rose Pellegrini."

"Oh yes, I do remember her, but that must have been years ago." If nothing else, it sounded good, even though if he tried, he couldn't have distinguished Rose Pellegrini from "Adam's cat."

"It was," DeAngelo agreed. "But as I said, my family never forgot you and what you did for my grandmother."

"You flatter me." Moving towards the door, he invited, "I hope that you'll call on me anytime, although as I told you when we started this conversation, I don't know what, if anything, I have to offer you that may be of value."

"Well, we sure do appreciate you giving us your time anyway. I know how really busy you are. But Sir, before I go, just in case, I'd like to reserve the opportunity to see you again if that proves necessary—but I'm almost sure it won't."

Arpel held out his hand. "It's been a pleasure."

Nervously, DeAngelo handed him his card and answered without looking up, "Thank you. The pleasure's been mine."

Arpel watched as the Detective passed through the double glass doors marking the entrance to Shaughnessy, Marks & Arpel, then move towards the bank of elevators waiting to carry him down to street level.

With a smile, Arpel returned to business.

CHAPTER THIRTY-FOUR

"Come in, Lieutenant."

With that very terse greeting, delivered without a trace of a smile, Peter was ushered into a small but comfortable conference room. Like her t.v. persona, Caroline Witten, in the flesh, was a breathtakingly beautiful woman. Dressed casually in a tailored, light blue pants suit, she was close to six feet tall, and brown eyed, with short, chestnut colored hair that shimmered with blonde highlights. Peter couldn't help but follow her every move, watching in appreciation, the cat-like grace with which she carried herself.

"Let's not waste time with this. I'm not in the mood." Her dark eyes were riveted on his. "What is it you need to know?"

Peter threw his coat over a chair and asked, "May I at least have a seat?"

Caroline Witten nodded, but barely.

"Getting to the point, Counselor, I need to know the nature of your relationship with Bradley."

Not blinking an eye, she answered, "Direct. Honest. No bullshit. I like that." She pulled a chair out from under the rectangular conference table for herself, lighthly slid into it, then clasped her hands together as if in prayer. "I loathe playing games, so I'll save you the trouble of punctuating our conversation with probing, but probably irrelevant questions. Instead, I'll give you the abridged, but what I believe, comprehensive version of the truth." Sighing, she added, "Honestly, it'll be a relief to get this off my chest."

Peter noted that her voice sounded troubled. "Please," he encouraged, "tell me."

She leaned across the table in Peter's direction, her flared collar open just enough for Peter to catch a glimpse of generous breasts. It was obvious she was teasing him. At the moment however, he didn't mind.

"Listen carefully. I'm only going to tell this once."

Peter nodded his agreement.

"John originally came to see me for professional services. I guess you, as well as anyone else, can put two and two together and come up with the rest. I'm primarily a divorce lawyer—John came to me about a divorce. But don't jump to conclusions. John didn't come *seeking* a divorce, but to find a way to save himself from *being* divorced. It seems John had a thing about being abandoned, or at least that's what he said, though in not so many words."

She stopped and looked away, not too subtly biting her lip. "During our first conference, John described himself as depressed about his current marital situation with the Judge. But still, he wanted to remain in what he readily acknowledged was a harmful union. The reason was simple—he idolized her. So much so in fact, that even though life with her was nothing short of abysmal, to him, the alternative wasn't even worth considering." Shaking her head, she added, "He truly was one of the most wretchedly miserable clients I think I've ever had. He was so bad, I felt shaky about representing him without the involvement of a therapist.

"But when I broached the subject, he was livid. His state of mind was so unstable though, I felt I had no choice but to continue prodding him. As kindly as I could, I explained that my job was to take care of his legal needs. For his own sake, I didn't want or need to be burdened with emotional challenges fracturing my concentration. Since my professional reputation was at stake, I refused to let that happen—at first that is," she explained wistfully.

"As I said, initially my intentions were above reproach—representing my client's interests to the best of my abilities, especially in this case, where, if a petition for dissolution were filed, the chances that he may be taken financial advantage of by a spouse, who was a judge, were pretty great." Shrugging her shoulders, she added, "I knew also how challenging it would be." She smiled suddenly. "In case you haven't already guessed, I like challenges."

With a quick gesture, barely noticeable, she tucked her hair behind her ears, then once more placed her hands contritely on the table. Closing her eyes, she half muttered to herself, "I just need to say this and get it over with. So, here goes." She took a deep breath. Haltingly, in a small voice, barely above a whisper, she disclosed, "John and I became lovers."

Peter should have known immediately when she advised that she wanted to get something off her chest, that the two had enjoyed more than just a professional relationship, but for some reason, the obvious just didn't compute. Peter's shock was hard to hide.

Looking at his face, Caroline smiled, and with a look of almost fierce defiance spat out, "He was a different sort of man—not obvious in showing his interest like most men."

Feeling uncomfortable for a reason Peter couldn't understand, he looked away from her penetrating stare. After all, he assured himself, he wasn't "most men."

Without skipping a beat, Caroline Witten continued—this time, her voice stronger, more in control. "John would toy with a woman by look or gesture, but he always seemed mysteriously out of reach. And not because he was married to Susan either. You knew instinctively he didn't belong to her or anyone else—John belonged only to himself, and he let you know it.

"He was an endless enigma—introspective, self-contained, but yet, always engaging in frantic efforts to avoid being abandoned by anyone, unless of course, he was the one doing the abandoning." She looked directly at Peter. "As I said, I like challenges, so John became irresistible."

Apparently uneasy with Peter's continued silence, she asked solicitously, "No questions? Have I totally embarrassed you?" She gave him a playful smile.

"Not at all," he answered as he struggled to clear his throat. "I was just caught up in what you were saying. Sometimes, it's best not to comment or interrupt, especially when the subject matter is obviously very sensitive."

Caroline Witten closed her eyes and leaned back in her chair. "Thanks for trying to make it easier, but nothing can. Believe me, I've never before, or since, gotten involved with a client. Professionally, it breaks a canon of ethics that we lawyers swear never to violate. But, as they say, the temptation was great and the flesh weak. I couldn't resist. John became an addiction. So much so, I hate to admit, that I felt better only when I was with him, or knew I soon would be."

She uttered a long, sad sigh and sat up. "In the beginning, John felt the same about me. Unfortunately though, that infatuation didn't last long. After the thrill of it wore off, he seemed to withdraw. He became obsessed with secrecy, and I became obsessed with him. Looking back with some newly acquired objectivity, it was a very sick, very twisted tango."

"How long did the affair last?" Peter asked quietly.

She looked startled by the question. Wrinkling her brow she answered, "I can't really tell you that because the relationship kept changing."

"I don't follow."

"I'm sure you don't," she replied knowingly. She threw her head back. "Hell, this is so damned embarrassing." She laughed that nervous soft laugh again, that to Peter's ears, sounded like a contented purr.

"The first few months were glorious. But then, John changed the rules. He demanded that every meeting be planned down to the very last detail; every telephone conversation be limited to a business-like two minutes. And when we did meet, I was to wear no perfume, no scented hair spray. His reason? So that our clandestine rendevous wouldn't be detected by what he described as Susan's almost bloodhound sense of smell. He said she would never forgive him."

"Anything else change?" Peter asked.

"Yes. John did. He became moody, strange. I confronted him about it, but he acted as if I was the one who was behaving oddly."

Hearing this, Peter couldn't help but think back to one of his first conversations with the Judge when she too had described similar experiences with Bradley. "Can you pinpoint when this change began?"

She put her hand up to her forehead and rubbed it, her beautifully lacquered nails making slight indentations in flawlessly unwrinkled skin. "I guess I could give you a ball park if I looked at my calendar. But it wasn't as if it happened overnight you know. It happened gradually, but once it started, it got worse quickly.

"John began avoiding me. I would wait days for a return phone call. One time, in desperation, I finally threw caution to the wind and told his secretary that it was urgent that he call this number. I guess that's how you finally traced me, isn't it?"

Peter said nothing, but Caroline Witten didn't seem to notice.

"The tattletale had to be John's secretary. Sweet little Mary Jane who was madly in love with John herself and possessive to the point of embarrassment. John told me once that she made his skin crawl—he hated her; but at the same time felt he couldn't get rid of her. According to him, she may have known too much. And believe me, if she did, she wouldn't have been too subtle about using it to her advantage. Frankly, she should be one of the top five suspects on your list."

"Thanks for the tip. I'll take it into consideration. But right now, we need to talk about you. So why don't you go on with your story?"

With a sense of bewilderment, Peter listened as the provocative, hauntingly beautiful Caroline Witten, the epitome of sophistication and charm, related in painful detail, how John Bradley's initial affection turned to nothing more than abuse.

"When we first met for 'afternoons of delight,' we'd go to very swank hotels and waste away hours as if no one else existed. John spent money like it was nothing, buying me anything I wanted."

So, that's where the trust money went, John thought. *Maybe things are beginning to add up afer all.*

She got up from the table and poured a glass of water from a silver pitcher which had been set out on an ornate cherry serving board. "Don't get me wrong. I have a lot of money, so money generally doesn't impress me, but the amount that John parted with, did. I remember he always paid in cash, regardless of the size of the purchase. Needless to say, the wad he carried was quite impressive.

"But the extravagant treatment didn't last long. Within no time, he was taking me to seedy hotels where the check-in and check-out times were by the minute, not by the day. I guess I don't need to get any more specific, other than to say it was awful; he hurt me, but I still wouldn't let go."

Grimacing she added, "Even for me, a fairly liberated woman, John's sexual appetite had become kinky to say the least. He also became fascinated with porno flicks—you know, the really nabby ones in which the faces are never shown, and all the guys wear black socks—like the old Harry Reams flicks where dialogue and plot line are written by perennially pre-pubescent men. That's what he craved. He wanted to humiliate me; get back at me for complicating his life and further jeopardizing his marriage. As I said, he was an enigma. He was exhilarated by risk, but terrified of the possible consequences."

She shivered and took a long slow sip of water. "Finally, when I wouldn't let go of him voluntarily, John just plain dumped me. My work and my health suffered until I finally came to the realization that I had no choice. It took a long time, but gradually I healed, but not on my own. I did it with the help of someone else."

Peter couldn't help but notice how Caroline Witten glowed when she disclosed this.

"That's how I finally freed myself—enough at least to be able to talk about it."

Without further comment, she stood, picked up Peter's overcoat, and handed it to him. "And that, Lieutenant, is all I can and want to tell you. I hope it helps. As I said, I owe John, and perhaps myself, that much."

After hearing that painful monologue, Peter couldn't help but admire her. Instinct told him this was a woman who told the truth no matter what the cost to herself. She obviously wanted no pity. She knew and accepted that the hell she had just described, was of her own doing. But was it?

The only thing nagging him was the identity of the person who had replaced John Bradley in Caroline Witten's affections. But Peter knew he couldn't ask. The information served no investigative purpose. Still though, for some inexplicable reason, that missing piece of information bothered him.

CHAPTER THIRTY-FIVE

Peter stood just to the right of the lectern waiting patiently for the commotion in the squad room to calm down. The noise level was typical for that time of day when shifts changed from a.m. to p.m. A mixture of sounds—detectives making last minute phone calls, clipped conversations between investigators going off duty and those coming on as replacements, phones ringing nonstop, and raucous laughter—all filled the room. Hurriedly checking his watch, Peter took a minute to scan the crowd and count the number of detectives present. Nine. *That's a pretty good turnout, considering.* . . . He wanted no wasted time and no duplicative efforts, so having a meeting like this on a daily basis was a necessity, even if his detectives didn't share his enthusiasm for communal dialogue.

"First off, while waiting for everyone to trickle in, let's go over the crime lab's most recent report regarding knives collected from the drawer in the Bradley kitchen. The results indicate that one of the knives, the one with the twelve inch serrated blade, was found to contain traces of human blood. Not surprisingly, efforts had been made to wipe the blade clean, but unfortunately for the killer, traces of human blood remained, caught under the wooden portion of the handle. DNA says that the blood is a match with Bradley's."

Peter turned his attention to the pile of reports he had placed earlier on the lectern, and pulled out a letter size brown folder, its flap unsealed but securely fastened with a clasp and eyelet. With ease, Peter bent the two pronged clasp together, released the flap and removed seventeen, eight by ten glossy color photographs taken by the medical examiner. He passed them out one by one. "As you can see, these show the deceased's wounds—both front and back. Based on the wound's appearance, Doc Pressano concluded at the time of autopsy, that the wounds were made with a serrated blade. From what the crime lab came back with today, he was right.

"While these photos are being passed, please listen to what is being discussed—everything in this case, no matter how small, may prove important. As I said in the beginning, to prevent duplication, we need to be aware of what others are doing, or have done.

"Now, based on this crime lab report, I think we can safely assume a couple of things. The first is fairly obvious—the killer didn't go to the residence armed with a deadly weapon. Therefore, the killing may not have been premeditated as originally thought.

"Secondly, and this is pretty obvious as well—the killer had to have entered the kitchen at least once that night. Knives were kept in one drawer only—the one underneath the counter top where the coffee pot was located. If you recall, the evidence techs reported that the coffee pot was full. From that, we can assume that the deceased brewed a fresh pot sometime that evening. And, since the pot was full when the body was found, no one had the time, or the opportunity to drink it.

"Taking that a step further, we can figure that one of two things happened—either the killer accompanied Bradley to the kitchen when Bradley began brewing the coffee and retrieved the knife at that time; or the killer returned to the kitchen alone, sometime thereafter."

Slowly, Peter moved toward the center of the room in an attempt to get their full attention. "If we follow that latter scenario to its logical conclusion, upon returning to the kitchen, the killer took full advantage of the opportunity, and at that time, palmed the murder weapon."

Turning around in a semicircle, he looked closely at each of his detectives. "But those are just my initial thoughts—let me throw it open for discussion. What do all of you think?"

Bunker was the first to respond. Without hesitation, he stood, and with a pen held high in the air, like a conductor with a baton, proceeded to punctuate his remarks with great swooping motions to emphasize each point. "I agree with most of what you said, but I think it's a given that the killer was in the kitchen *more* than just one time that night."

"Why so certain?" Peter asked.

"Easy. If Bradley was in the kitchen when the killer took the knife, chances are Bradley would have seen him. That knife's too big to hide, and the kitchen's too open. My guess is the first time the killer was in the kitchen, for whatever reason, Bradley opened that drawer and the killer saw the knife. Opportunity later presented itself, and the killer took it when he was in the kitchen by himself."

As if on a roll and enjoying the attention, Bunker expanded on his working hypothesis—"Maybe Bradley used the utensil drawer to get some kind of measuring spoon for the coffee. The killer saw the knives, but didn't act on it because murder wasn't on the front burner yet. If it had been, he would have stabbed Bradley right then and there, while still in the kitchen. Right?"

Peter saw heads bobbing up and down in agreement. Quietly, he answered the question. "You're on the right track. Something happened in the library which set the killer off—could have been something Bradley said, or something the killer saw. Who knows? And don't forget what Pressano said—the killer most likely stabbed Bradley while Bradley's back was turned. Bradley wasn't expecting it, and the killer counted on that. The killer wouldn't have wanted to take a chance on stabbing Bradley in the kitchen—it would have been too chancy. Bradley was a big guy."

Hearing mumbling and grunting among the ranks, Peter waited until he saw that he again had everyone's attention. "I've noticed that Bunker here, continually used the pronoun, 'he' when referring to the killer. Don't for a minute assume this killer's a man. Keep in mind, it would be relatively easy, even for a woman of average height and build, to stab a man to death when the attack comes unexpectedly from behind. It doesn't take a great deal of upper body strength for that. So, I repeat, don't assume the killer's a man.

"Now, while you're still chewing on that—DeAngelo, I want you to begin a twenty-four hour surveillance of Caroline Witten. Find out who she sees, when, where, and for how long. Give the surveillance two days, then get back with me. I don't know why, but I have a sneaking suspicion that if she's seeing someone on the sly, that someone will soon be told about a little talk she and I had this afternoon. Let's see what happens, if anything."

Turning once again to the mound of papers spread out on the lectern, Peter added, "Before we end this, there's one more report from the crime lab that's worth mentioning. I sent a supplemental request asking them to expedite a comparison of the fibers found in the Judge's navy suit with fibers found underneath Bradley's fingernails. And we have a match!

"I'm going over to the Judge's tonight to have another talk with her about how fibers could have embedded themselves in the blood found underneath her dead husband's fingernails. That transfer wouldn't have happened if the Judge had only, as she put it, 'barely touched his wrist while feeling for a pulse.'"

Changing the subject, Peter turned his attention to Rigger, who, as ususal, was busy eating. "Billy Ray, after you finish stuffing your face, I want you to chase down some information I have about Jake Stein. You can team up with Shapero who's real familiar with Stein's secretary, Vivian. The groundwork, so to speak, has already been laid."

No sooner had Peter said that, than he was greeted with a roar of laughter. Holding his hands up, Peter cautioned, "Okay, okay, settle down. We all know what Shapero does best.

"Greene, since your partner will be busy with Billy Ray, I want you following through in getting those phone logs from Bradley's mobile phone. We need to know who Bradley talked to in the last several weeks. I have no doubt that those are going to prove critical, so get them quickly."

Grinning, Greene answered, "Already served the subpoena. The records have been promised for sometime late today."

"Great. Bunker, Thompson, what's the deal with the Waylander interview?"

"Ah, he's coming in for questioning tomorrow, here at the station," responded Thompson who had thus far been one of the few who had not spoken about his involvement in the investigation. "I would have to say, Waylander's a little bit pissed."

"Well that's just a little bit too bad. Use it to our advantage. I want a full report as soon as that interview is over with. In fact, I may drop in for part of it myself. That is if I'm finished with all those subpoenas being sent to every financial institution in the city and surrounding counties. It's critical that we find what that key, found hidden in Bradley's office downtown, opens. Waylander's still a prime suspect, so make him feel some heat."

Peter began picking up his reports, trying without success to shuffle them back into some type of order. Discouraged, he stopped his efforts and looked out over the room. "By the way, before I forget, which one of you is doing the investigation on this guy, Liam Leprakalb? If each of you has been reading the daily investigative reports, as you're supposed to, you'd know the name popped up on one of the empty file folders found in Bradley's desk at home. He's probably just a transient laborer, but check him out anyway. I turned the name over a couple of days ago to the general assignment box for someone to pick up and run with. So who picked it up, but didn't run?"

Looking around one final time, Peter saw only blank stares and shaking heads. "Okay, nobody has even picked it up yet, so it must still be there. Great! Somebody, and I don't care who, take care of it. The Judge suspects that this Leprakalb character was an independent contractor used by her husband to so some remodeling on the residence in recent months. Let's nail it down.

"If there's nothing else, get outta here. We have murders to solve."

CHAPTER THIRTY-SIX

"Hilary, I know Susan's your best friend, but as her lawyer, you need to point out the obvious–like the importance of telling the truth, the whole truth. You know—that same oath she administers everyday to everyone who's been accused of something. Remind her of the risks involved when a client fails to tell the police everything they know."

Hilary said nothing as she leaned against the wall of Susan's front hallway. Aggravated by her silence, Peter reached out and gripped her arm. "Listen to me and stop fooling around. Your friend is holding back, and unfortunately for both of you, now I know it!"

Angrily, Hilary replied, "Don't talk to me like that again. I know you mean well, but you're in no position to tell me how to run my life, either professionally or personally." Pulling hard on the lone thread securing the bottom button of the cardigan sweater which she had pulled tightly around her, Hilary demanded, "Why don't you just spit out what it is you think you know, that you feel I knew before you knew, and believe you should have been told before this?"

Unable to stifle a giggle, Hilary asked, "Did that make any sense at all?"

Peter couldn't help but laugh too. It hadn't escaped him that when he was around her, Hilary seemed to have that effect on him. She made awkward situations bearable. And he also had to admit, because of the way she made him feel, he looked forward to seeing her, regardless of their differences.

"Obviously," he answered, a joking tone in his voice, "we've been spending way too much time with each other, since what you just said, did make sense to me." He touched her elbow. "But before we go back to what we were talking about before—information which I think the good Judge has been withholding, perhaps you should ask her to join us. That way, we'll save a lot of time." He smiled. "If, during that discussion, you believe I'm inquiring into areas in which I have no right, then you'll have the perfect opportunity to tell me to get some extra constitutional protection in the form of an arrest warrant."

Looking stricken, Hilary answered, "Come on. Are you trying to tell me in some twisted police tough guy lingo that Susan's a suspect?" She gave him a playful smile. "Seriously, you couldn't, even for a minute, believe that. You must be desperate."

"You don't get it, do you? I'm far from desperate." Without asking if he may, Peter walked into Susan's living room, and sat down. Hilary followed him but remained standing.

"As I said, your client and best friend, is hiding something. And I intend to find out just what that something is."

"Fine," Hilary said in a huff. "I'll ask Susan to come downstairs. I can only assume from your less than courteous behavior tonight that this has something to do with the navy suit she was wearing the night John was murdered."

Without waiting for a response, she turned and walked back towards the hallway, then stopped. "Next time, call before you just drop by. It's the courteous thing to do."

*** *** ***

"Hello, Peter."

He turned around to see the Judge standing at the door with Hilary who was half a step behind her. "I hope you don't mind if I call you, 'Peter,'" she said nervously. "And turnabout is fair play—please call me, 'Susan.' We've spent so much time together lately, that the name, 'Lieutenant Elliott,' seems a bit formal. Don't you agree?"

Peter looked closely at her. The words sounded inviting, but the eyes staring back at him lacked any semblance of warmth. "You may refer to me by whatever name you feel most comfortable," he said. "But if you don't mind, I'd prefer to call you, 'Judge.'"

Nervously, she touched her hair and smoothed the collar to her white silk blouse. "That's fine. I guess then I should continue to address you as, 'Lieutenant.'" With her voice shaking, she asked, "What is it you want?"

Guessing that she wasn't used to not getting her way, Peter decided to get to the point, quickly. "I'm here to discuss the results of the comparison studies done on the fibers in your navy suit with those mixed with the blood found under the deceased's finger nails."

Imperiously, Susan demanded, "Don't refer to my husband as 'the deceased.' He was a human being, not just a corpse with blood and fiber under his nails." Wearily, she dropped into a chair directly opposite the one occupied by Peter. She looked up at Hilary and waved her hand toward the couch to her right. "Please, Hilary, sit down."

Hilary did as she was told, then wasted no time in asking, "So what were the results, Peter?"

"The fibers are a match."

"So what? Susan already told you she held John's wrist to feel for a pulse."

Peter looked in Hilary's direction, but then quickly turned to Susan since he didn't want to miss her reaction to what he was about to say.

"Holding your husband's wrist to determine whether there was still a pulse probably would not cause fibers from your suit to transfer to the blood under his nails." He waited a moment, then continued. "The only explanation is, there must have been more contact than what you initially described."

Susan didn't immediately answer. Instead, she got up and walked towards the window and pulled the draperies back. Quietly, as if choosing her words carefully, she turned to both Hilary and Peter and confided, "I'm really very tired of all this. You want the truth? Okay, you'll get it. I'm not up to fighting this anymore."

Appearing flustered by the disclosure, Hilary began giving explanations for her client's choice of words. Only half listening, Peter allowed her to talk all she wanted. It didn't really matter—he wasn't about to buy any of it. But that didn't seem to stop Hilary from trying.

"She's been under too much stress since this unrelenting nightmare began, Peter. She can't hold up much longer. It's just too soon to be questioning her like this."

Before Peter could answer, Susan erupted. "Quit it, Hilary. Stop making those damned excuses for me." Then, in a quieter, gentler tone, she added, "You're such a good person—good lawyer, good friend." With tears streaming down her face she asked, "How can I begin to tell you all that I need to, so that you'll understand? I can't hide behind you anymore. And you can no longer protect me." She bowed her head. "I'm not the person you think I am."

Silently, Peter watched and listened, waiting for the right opportunity to participate in the conversation. But it was obvious, Hilary and the Judge had forgotten he was even there. He knew instinctively, that this was going to be an important turning point in the investigation. Judge Susan Emmett-Bradley's seemingly impenetrable exterior was slowly disintegrating. It was the break he had been waiting for.

Straining for just the right words and the right intonation in his voice, he asked, "What really happened after you left the Judicial Center on the night of your husband's death?"

Looking squarely into Peter's eyes, which were now riveted on her, Susan cooly answered, "I don't have anything to say that's any different from what I told you before. I never lied to you. I just didn't tell you everything." Her mouth curved upwards. "Being selective wasn't too difficult actually. You just never asked the right questions."

"Wait a minute, Susan," Hilary interjected. "We need to talk about this before continuing. You—"

"It's no use. I'm too tired to repeat this twice. I have nothing to confide only to my lawyer, and I have nothing to hide from the police. It's out of my hands."

With a look of frustration Hilary answered, "Fine. Continue, then."

"As I told you before, on the night of John's death, I came home about six or six-thirty, ate, then went directly back to the office. To be candid, it would be accurate to say I rushed out of the house. I wanted to avoid John.

"I had flown back from a judicial conference the night before John was killed—a day earlier than expected. I wasn't feeling well. In fact, I was feeling so wretched, I didn't even take the time to call John and tell him about my decision to come home early. I just hopped an earlier flight and caught a cab back to the house. My unexpected change in plans seemed to upset him."

Breaking the tension, if only temporarily, Susan said, "I hope you don't mind if I smoke. I'd given up the habit, but since all this happened, I've gone back to it with a vengeance." She opened a cigarette box found on the mantel, reached in, and with shaking fingers, grabbed a long slender cigarette. After lighting it and taking one slow draw, she continued.

"The next day, after the chilly reception I had received the night before, I talked with John briefly—just long enough to tell him I'd be home for dinner, and after that, would be going directly back to the office, where I remained until sometime a little after midnight."

"Then why did it take you so long to call 911?" Peter asked. "And before you answer that, let me advise you, your call was logged in over an hour and a half later. Since it takes only about twenty minutes to drive from downtown to your home, what was the hold up?"

At this, Susan became noticeably uncomfortable. From experience, Peter assumed she was trying to quickly assess just how much more she'd have to explain in order to satisfy him. Then, as if innately realizing Peter knew just what she was thinking, Susan appeared to make up her mind.

"I guess it's obvious, isn't it? There are only two possible explanations. I either stopped off somewhere, or I immediately came home, and somewhere between twelve-thirty and two o'clock killed my husband. Are we on the same track?"

Peter smiled. "So much so, I think you're a mind reader. So I'll ask you again. Where were you?"

Haughtily, Susan replied, "What happens if I refuse to tell you? Are you prepared to take me downtown?"

Hilary started to speak, but Peter interrupted by holding up his hand. "It's your call." Shrugging his shoulders, he added, "It makes no difference to me. We can do it the easy way, or the hard way." For Hilary's sake, he suggested, "In making up your mind, perhaps you should first take a few minutes to discuss it with your lawyer. It's ladies' choice."

Not skipping a beat, Susan answered evenly, "Thanks for the opportunity to talk with Hilary, but I've already made my decision. Finding out everything is just a matter of time anyway. At this point, I figure I have nothing to lose." Lowering her voice she added, "Maybe telling everything will give me back my piece of mind.

"So, here's the whole story, Lieutenant." Glaring at him, her voice cold and impersonal, she explained, "As I told you before, when I arrived home that night, or early morning, to be exact, and walked into the house, John was already dead. I really didn't notice the body right away. I still don't know why; I just didn't. And no, I can't explain why I wasn't panic-stricken when I did find him, but I wasn't."

Speaking slowly, as if straining to remember, Susan explained, "What I do remember was revulsion and something else—" She stared into space, her jaw clenched. "Relief!"

"Susan, please," Hilary cried.

"Hilary, let me say this. I need to."

Susan turned and faced Peter again. "I remember thinking that the decision was now out of my hands. He was dead. To make sure though, I did touch John's wrist to feel for a pulse—that part was also true. But I did something more."

She stopped. Peter waited while she distractedly drummed her fingers on the mantel.

"Are you going to continue?" he finally asked after several seconds of uncomfortable silence.

"I took something out of his hand," she answered. "It was a letter from a doctor whose name I didn't recognize. It was the same doctor whose name was on one of the those file folders which we found at the house—a doctor named, Franklin W. Parker."

Peter turned to Hilary and asked curtly, "Did you know about this?"

Before Hilary could form a reply, Susan answered for her. "She didn't know until later, long after I had already been questioned. And when I did tell her about it, I swore her to secrecy. She's my lawyer so don't blame her for the non-disclosure. It's my fault."

Hilary nodded, then offered, "I know what you're thinking, Peter. But when I discovered what had happened, it was already a done deal, and there was nothing that could be undone about it, so get over it."

"Don't be flip with me in your interpretation of what's right and wrong. This is serious. Your client obstructed justice, pure and simple. And don't try and sanitize it to protect her either. It's not going to work. Don't forget, she's a judge for Christ's sake!"

"All right," Hilary answered between clenched teeth. "But there's no harm done. In fact, Sam Monroe, my P.I., has already done some of the legwork for you. But don't thank me or anything."

"And don't expect me to either," Peter answered coldly. "You did nothing but compound a wrong."

Putting her hands on her hips, Hilary replied, "Before you get so high and mighty, aren't you forgetting one little point of law that's critical here? It's called attorney-client privilege. I know all you police officers hate to hear this, but ethically, I'm only obligated to involve the police when I believe my client is willfully suppressing or destroying evidence being actively sought in an investigation. If the rules were otherwise, you'd be able to lock up just about everyone you question. Face it.

It's human nature—no one ever tells everything, especially to the cops. And in this case, you didn't know the so-called evidence even existed."

In spite of his attraction to her, Peter was livid. No matter how cutely she tossed her curly red hair around when she was mad, or stomped her tiny foot when trying to make a point, he wasn't buying it this time. "Save it for the jury. Maybe you can find some poor schmuck who's taken in enough to ignore the obvious. Otherwise, I think the evidence, though admittedly circumstantial, may be sufficient to put your client in prison for a good long while."

He gazed at the Judge and for the first time, saw fear rather than defiance in her eyes.

With eyes narrowing, she said, "I think that's enough, Lieutenant. We know you could tie up my career, as well as my life, in a maze of legal maneuverings for months, and in so doing, irreparably damage my reputation. I don't need that, so I'll do as you ask. Just let me finish my story, then you can decide what you need to do."

Peter nodded agreement, and Susan began once more.

"As I said, I didn't arrive back at the house until very late. I stopped off to see someone and remained at that location for, I'd say, at least half an hour, maybe longer. And before you even try—don't ask. I'll never willingly disclose this person's identity."

Perplexed, Peter asked, "Don't you realize that keeping information like that a secret is a luxury you don't have? Sometime, whether it's now or in the future, you'll have to identify this person you're trying so hard to protect."

Susan appeared well past the point of even trying to hide the mental anguish that ultimatum unleashed. In a small but defiant voice she answered, "I won't tell you. And that's final.

I can tell you though, this person had nothing to do with John's death."

"I don't care what your opinion is about this person's involvement. Your attitude leaves me with no other alternative but to take you downtown. Unless of course, you stop these delaying tactics and start cooperating."

Suddenly, without warning, Susan turned, her face white as a sheet. She stumbled, seemed to suddenly loose her balance, and with knees buckling, slumped to the floor, her head hitting the hardwood. Peter and Hilary rushed forward only to find Susan out cold, with a laceration to the back of her scalp. Already, they could see blood spilling around her head like a bright red halo.

"Oh, my God," cried Hilary. "We've got to call an ambulance and get her to a hospital. She's bleeding to death!"

"Calm down. The fastest way to get her there is to take her in my squad car. I'll radio Suburban that we're on our way. In the meantime, while you gather lots of blankets to cover her, I'll wrap my jacket around the wound."

Peter started to take off his jacket. He could see Hilary wasn't moving. "Don't just stand there," he barked. "Do as I said and hurry."

While Hilary scurried around the second floor, opening and slamming shut what must have been every closet door she could find in search of warm blankets, Peter tied the arms of his herringbone tweed jacket around Susan's head, holding it in place while praying that in his single-minded quest to capture the killer, he hadn't created another, perhaps innocent casualty.

Galloping down the stairway, two steps at a time, Hilary shouted, "Here are two blankets; help me wrap them around her to keep her warm."

Surrounded in a tight cocoon of bed covers, Susan stirred and opened her eyes. Slowly, as if drugged she whispered, "My head. I remember hitting it somehow after feeling as if I was about to pass out."

"Don't say anything," Hilary urged. "You lost some blood when you fell, but it's just a little cut in the back of your head. It's nothing to worry about. Just to be on the safe side though, Peter and I are driving you to the hospital. You must stay calm. Are you in pain?"

"No," Susan answered almost in a whisper. Trying to raise her head, she looked over her shoulder. "Look at all this blood. I look like I've been in a car accident." She looked up anxiously. "You two aren't telling me the truth, are you?"

As quickly as he could, Peter explained, "Head wounds, no matter how small, can be very bloody. But you're awake and alert and that's all that matters." Stroking her hair he whispered gently, "Now, I'm going to pick you up and carry you to the car while you hold onto Hilary's hand."

Somewhat quieted, but still softly crying, Susan allowed him to pick her up and carry her to the back seat of the car. Out of the rear view mirror, Peter could see her clinging tightly to Hilary's hand. He was worried about the Judge suffering a concussion, so he issued a stern directive. "It's important that you keep talking to Hilary. Please fight falling asleep. Okay?"

Barely moving, Susan answered, "But I'm so tired. All I want to do is sleep. Please, just let me sleep while we're in the car. I promise I'll talk when we get to the hospital."

"No. You have to stay awake until we get there. Hilary talk to her; ask questions; make her count backwards, anything to keep her alert. If she has a concussion, it's important to keep her conscious."

Quickly, Hilary took control of the situation as Peter backed out of the long driveway with the car's blue lights flashing and siren screaming. "Susan, listen to me. You know I can be a real pain in the rear, so cooperate. It's only a few minutes longer until we get to the hospital. Once there, you can do whatever you want. In the meantime though, you must do as Peter said, so start talking. To make it easy, I'll ask questions that you can answer without a whole lot of effort. So, with that in mind, let's start with you telling me what's on your docket for tomorrow."

Again looking in the rear view mirror, Peter could see how unresponsive Susan was, not only verbally, but physically. She lay listlessly across Hilary's lap, a blank stare on her face. The bleeding had subsided somewhat, but even from the front seat, he could see that her face looked ashen.

"What's wrong with me? I can't remember. I can't remember anything that I have on the docket tomorrow. What's wrong with me?"

"Nothing's wrong," Hilary answered. "Not a thing. I don't have a cut on my head to use as an excuse, and I can't remember what's on my calendar for tomorrow. But you need to stay awake even though you don't want to, so let's try and figure your schedule out. Since it's a criminal docket week, you must have some criminal cases scheduled, right?"

Groggily, Susan answered, "Yes. I remember I have a trial starting tomorrow at nine o'clock. I think it's a theft case but I can't seem to remember." Looking terrified, Susan cried, "I just can't remember."

Hearing the rising panic in voice, Peter interrupted and in a soothing tone said, "Don't worry so much. You're fine. Just the trauma of being knocked out for a few seconds can shake you up for a bit. Believe me, you're going to be all right. Do you understand?"

Neither woman answered in words. The only visible response Peter could see was Susan gripping Hilary's hand even more tightly.

With tires screeching, Peter pulled up to the emergency entrance. Orderlies and nurses appeared out of nowhere and quickly wheeled Susan inside the hospital.

After preliminary information about how Susan had sustained the injury was given to the dour looking clerk at the admissions desk, Hilary and Peter were quickly ushered to a crowded waiting room, with the promise that they would be told about Susan's condition when information became available and hospital personnel could take the time to deliver it. Not before.

PART TWO

CHAPTER THIRTY-SEVEN

While awaiting news, they huddled side by side in sling-back vinyl chairs, each chair connected to the other like conjoined twins. Hilary nervously wrung her hands; Peter hung his head and stared at the floor.

"Hil, she's not going to die. She's going to be fine." As if trying to convince himself, he argued, "It's only a bump on the head which has probably caused a slight concussion. Let's not get carried away until we know the full extent of the injury, okay?"

Hilary looked at him, hard. It sounded good. And she wanted to believe it, but wanting something didn't always make it so. "Okay, okay," she answered listlessly. "I'm just no good in emergencies. They scare me too much." She was shaking all over, with teeth chattering so loudly that another waiting room visitor looked at her with concern.

"How about a cup of hot chocolate?" Peter asked as he stood up and stretched. "There's a machine right over there." Smiling, he added, "And while I'm doing that, try not to shake yourself to pieces. I'll be right back." Bending down, he gently caressed her cheek which, as if by magic, made Hilary's face tingle all over.

Minutes later, Peter filled her outstretched hands with a steaming cup of the promised hot chocolate. She felt better as soon as she drank it.

"Oh, that does taste good. Thanks." Taking a few sips more, Hilary asked, "How long do you think it'll be before we hear something?"

He put his hand on hers and kept it there. "It shouldn't be too much longer. I promise."

They sat there in companionable silence, sipping their drinks, and waiting. Whether warmed by the hot chocolate, Peter's soothing words, or a combination of both, Hilary found she could fight her mounting fatigue no longer. As if it was the most natural thing to do, she comfortably leaned her head on Peter's shoulder and soon fell sound asleep, until abruptly awakened by a loud gravely voice.

"Are you two here with Judge Emmett-Bradley?"

Hilary immediately opened her eyes and sat up straight. For several seconds, she had trouble realizing just where she was. Then it dawned on her. The hospital. Susan. Looking up, she realized that the voice she had just heard, must belong to the person standing right in front of her—a nurse who could only be described as unnervingly formidable. Taking quick stock, Hilary estimated she was about five feet ten, and two hundred pounds of pure muscle. She reminded Hilary of a sumo wrestler, fully clothed.

"Yes, we are," Hilary and Peter answered in anxious unison.

Now instantly awake, Hilary rubbed her eyes and sat up. "How's she doing?"

"She's doing just fine and so is that little baby of hers."

Hilary glanced over at Peter who looked as puzzled as she. The nurse however, didn't seem to notice.

"The Judge's injury involved a small laceration requiring only a few stitches to close. We'll go ahead and admit her just as a precaution, but most likely, she'll be released sometime this afternoon."

Hilary and Peter continued to sit there dumbstruck. The words weren't registering. Susan was fine, but what was this about Susan's 'little baby' doing fine?

Hilary recovered first, quickly assuring the nurse that she would certainly stay with Susan as long as necessary. "You said the baby was fine, too. Are you certain of that?"

"Yes," the nurse answered slowly, her eyebrows knitting together in a "v" just above a red bulbous nose. "Everything seems to be a-okay. But as the doctor recommended, she needs to see her obstetrician as soon as possible—tomorrow would be best. But right now, there's a strong fetal heartbeat and nothing to worry about. Still smiling, the nurse turned to leave, then, as if an afterthought asked, "You did know about the baby, didn't you?"

Still shaken, but realizing she had no choice if she was to save the nurse any unnecessary embarrassment, Hilary replied, "Of course we did. We're thrilled about it."

Peter nodded in silent agreement, a forced smile on his face.

"Oh, I'm so glad. It's always such happy news to tell family and friends that the little one is all right." With that, the nurse turned and walked away, the heavy rubber soles of her white orthopedic shoes, squeaking noisily against the newly polished linoleum.

Staring after her, Hilary murmured, "I guess I'm going to be a godmother. . . ."

CHAPTER THIRTY-EIGHT

Detectives Bunker and Thompson weren't pleased with their assignment—there was nothing glamorous about interviewing Richard Waylander, head of purchasing for Our Lady of Lourdes Hospital, but the two veteran detectives had no one to complain to except each other. Today's directive to do the interview and do it promptly, hadn't come only from the Lieutenant. It also came from the top brass at the front office. So personal feelings as to what they thought they should be doing, didn't begin to enter into it. They knew to do exactly as they were told.

All of the homicide detectives, not just Bunker and Thompson, had begun to feel the heat from department superiors, as well as the press. Like so many other high profile cases which aren't immediately solved, questions as to why nothing seemed to be happening became an instant hot topic for local television commentators and radio talk show hosts. Unquestionably, department superiors were always sensitive to complaints from constituents. And with their years of experience, the top brass knew the inevitable result—subtle but immediate reprisals from the Mayor. So the blame was shifted, and quite naturally thrown, at the rank and file. The old adage, "shit rolls downhill" was heard often around headquarters. And, as luck would have it, that day, it rolled straight downhill onto Detectives Bunker and Thompson.

But they weren't the only targets. The remaining detectives in the unit hadn't exactly escaped the pressure either. On a fairly regular basis, tempers flared and patience took a hike in direct proportion to too much stress, too little sleep, and too much frustration associated with shifts that lasted so long, detectives met themselves coming and going.

The Bradley case was particularly galling because they knew the murderer wasn't a stranger to the victim. Therefore, because it wasn't a random killing, which could arguably lack any connective motive, the list of possible suspects was unusually short. So, even the police began asking themselves, why couldn't they narrow that short list even more and make an arrest?

Both Bunker and Thompson, hoping against hope to make that arrest, in spite of their misgivings about Waylander's involvement in the crime, zealously prepared for the suspect's visit by talking with employees at the hospital, as well as employees of Bradley & Stein. Each person contacted, confirmed what Bunker and Thompson had learned from other sources—there was no love lost between Bradley and Waylander. According to all accounts, even from the beginning, it had been a bitter dog fight with no sign of letting up until conveniently, Bradley got murdered.

Peter and his squad had openly questioned whether business problems like the rather pedestrian ones described as existing between Waylander and Bradley could conceivably escalate into cold-blooded murder. The evidence supporting such a theory was thin—"overkill" in every sense of the word. But, on the other hand, it wasn't hard for police to convince themselves that their contrived interest in this suspect might be justified, given that threats had been exchanged between the two. After all, there were no other "possibles" aside from Jake Stein and the Judge. And time was fast running out.

*** *** ***

"Mr. Waylander," explained Bunker in a tone well-practiced to be perceived as soothing and non-threatening, "we've asked you to come down to headquarters today so that you could tell us a little bit more about your business relationship with the deceased."

Waylander, who had been fifteen minutes late, for no good reason, was sweating the proverbial bullets. A fussy little man with kinky curly black hair, and sporting feminine looking pince-nez eyeglasses which hung over his chest like a tourist with binoculars, Waylander was dressed in a three piece suit, a shirt cuffed with monogrammed links, and a very expensive silk necktie, perfectly knotted at the base of a prominent Adam's apple. Gesturing with veined hands, unadorned but for a small silver wedding band, he implored, "I'm trying to cooperate, Detective, but I'm beginning to think I'm the only person you're questioning like this. I don't know why I have to keep answering the same questions over and over again. For the hundredth time, I hardly knew John Bradley, and what I did know about him, I admit, I didn't much like."

From information the detectives had gathered, it was common knowledge, at least at the hospital, that Waylander had balked at paying the freight in accordance with the terms recently demanded by Bradley. Because of that, the arrearage had, at one time, become rather hefty, hefty enough that Waylander used it as leverage in his dealings with Bradley when discussing new business that may be up for grabs. Since Bradley wanted the business, Waylander massaged Bradley's greed to his own advantage, even though in the usual scheme of things, it should have been the other way around.

Leaning forward, only inches from Waylander's increasingly florid face, Thompson answered, "Why don't you just begin by telling us about the first time you met Bradley?"

Looking frustrated, Waylander busied himself by diligently but unsuccessfully dabbing a bleached linen handkerchief at the beads of sweat collecting on his face. "Just how long is this whole thing going to take?" he whined. "I need to be back at the office sometime today, you know."

"Yeah, we understand you're a busy man, but bear with us, okay?" replied Bunker.

"If you're expecting me to remember the first, as well as each and every time I met with Bradley," Waylander hissed, "then you're asking the impossible. And no, I'm not trying to be difficult. Maybe, when I explain, you'll understand.

"I'm in charge of purchasing for Our Lady of Lourdes. On a daily basis, I see dozens of suppliers and vendors just like Bradley. After a while, they all look the same; they all act the same; they all talk the same. And if I decide not to renew a contract with one, there are hundreds of them standing in line to take that former vendor's place, at a new, even more cutthroat price."

"How long have you been at Lourdes?"

"Since last spring."

Bunker took out a toothpick from behind his ear and, seemingly unembarrassed, began leisurely digging around his left incisor. The lull in the conversation that this activity caused bothered everyone but Bunker. Finally satisfied that he had gotten to the root of his dental problem, Bunker threw the used cleaning tool in the trash can and asked, "When hired, were you told to keep the same vendors, or were you given sort of a free rein to do whatever you felt was best?"

"I was hired for several reasons, one of which was to evaluate our current vendors and by doing that, cleaning up the billing system. I had ninety days to conduct a due diligence and then give a full report to the hospital's chief financial officer."

"You'll have to forgive me," Bunker said in his most down home accent, "but I'm not very familiar with this corporate stuff, so if my partner, Detective Thompson, or I, ask a question that you think is way off base, just tell us, okay?"

Waylander laughed. "It isn't all that complicated, really. It's just the old axiom of supply and demand at work."

"Did you furnish this 'full report' to the chief financial officer as you were hired to do?"

Barely stifling a grin, Waylander smugly replied, "Absolutely."

"And what did that report say?"

"That certain favored vendors, Bradley included, were gouging the hospital with listing prices that were way out of line in the industry. The old guy I replaced, retired after being in the position for forty-five years. A lot had changed since then. My predecessor wasn't even college educated and had no degree in business—just on the job experience. And while that may have been fine and dandy forty-five years ago, it doesn't 'cut the mustard' today," sniffed Waylander. "It's no longer a simple good old boy network. Now, competitive pricing is the name of the game."

Looking more relaxed and obviously relishing the opportunity to lecture on a subject near and dear to his heart, Waylander continued. "When I produced my report, they then gave me authority to set up a whole new protocol for purchasing, a task which took me another thirty days to get on line. When that was done, I notified all current vendors of the change in policy and offered to sit down and talk with each of them, individually, about what the hospital corporation now expected. I also informed them that their contracts would not be automatically renewed. Instead, each vendor would be invited to make a new bid. That bid would then be reviewed by the chief financial officer, together with my recommendation. Based upon those two factors, a final decision would be made as to whether the bid was accepted and a contract offered."

Waylander paused and looked expectantly at the detectives. "Does that explain everything?"

Ignoring the question, Bunker asked, "So, what was the reaction to this new policy among the vendors?"

"Oh, there was some grousing, but not to me personally. They knew there would be no dialogue about this." With a smile of satisfaction, Waylander explained, "They had to play by my rules now."

"How did Bradley take it?"

Waylander's eyes narrowed, his dry lips curling in an attitude. "He complained, loud and long. Mostly loud. It got so bad in fact, that the week before he was killed, I had to literally throw him out of my office."

"Why?"

"Since my first day on the job, Bradley and I had a running argument over his listing prices for supplies and equipment. Bradley's demands for payment and his ability to deliver were so out of sync, that negotiating terms with him became impossible."

"You're losing me," Bunker said as he scratched his head.

Impatiently, Waylander explained, "Bradley worked on a simple premise. If he didn't get his way, he threw a temper tantrum. His behavior was initially greeted as somewhat of an embarrassment to anyone who had the misfortune of witnessing it. But then his nasty disposition soon got to be so bad that I, as well as others, became convinced that embarrassment was the least of it. I finally had to tell Bradley that our business relationship was terminated."

"How'd he react?"

"Well, he began screaming that he hadn't been paid for the last ninety days and he wasn't going to 'call it a day' until he got his money. I explained to him early on, when I took over the job at Lourdes, that accounting was in the process of reviewing all financials for the last six months. With services, products and equipment that had already either been performed or delivered, Lourdes would attempt to pay in the usual fashion—on a thirty to sixty day pay. If there was a foreseeable delay, the vendor would be timely notified.

"Bradley, like the others, had been advised of any potential delays regarding his account. But those contracts which we called ongoing, or open-ended, were an altogether different story. With them, the vendors knew there would be an interruption in the payment cycle while the hospital determined what its long range budget was going to be."

Waylander again stopped, asking this time for a glass of water. While Thompson was retrieving a pitcher so that Waylander could have all he needed, Bunker decided to press on. The interview was going overtime and as the minutes passed, he was even less convinced than before, that Waylander could be considered a prime suspect. In Bunker's mind, he was nothing more than an impotent little piss ant. If anything, he was surprised Bradley hadn't murdered Waylander in an act of justifiable homicide.

"So, exactly how would this have impacted Bradley's pocketbook?"

"His service contracts were the ones I scrutinized the most, because his prices were the highest. I knew pretty well what the market would bear and Bradley wasn't even within waving distance of the norm. In other words, he was a crook."

"How 'bout making it simple for me."

Waylander's smile was mocking. "Bradley had gotten away with that kind of highway robbery before I got there, but no more. Bradley knew he was losing the account and he could no longer line his pockets with that kind of profit margin. I told Bradley he was a thief. It was obvious—if he wasn't skimming off the top by showing me fraudulent invoices from his suppliers, his markup was unconscionable. Needless to say, Bradley didn't like my brand of honesty. That's what prompted the little altercation between us that I had mentioned earlier."

"So what happened?"

"Just some shouting, scuffling," Waylander answered, his head bowed. "After it was all over, and he had been escorted out, I placed a phone call to his partner. Unfortunately, Stein was out of the office at the time, but he returned my call that afternoon."

Flipping a page in his notebook, Bunker asked, "When Stein returned your call, did you explain the situation to him?"

"I tried." Pulling down his shirt cuff to showcase his cuff links, Waylander added, "In Stein's defense, he seemed to listen to what I had to say. I got the impression this wasn't anything new.

"Anyway, after I went through my litany of complaints, Stein asked me about past invoices that hadn't been paid. I told him all payments were current. The only outstanding invoices were those pertaining to items which had been ordered, but hadn't been received. Until they were, the check wasn't in the mail and wouldn't be, for at least thirty to sixty days after actual delivery. I told Stein that Bradley knew this was the deal."

"Anything else discussed between you and Stein that day?"

"Nothing other than Stein perfunctorily apologizing, saying that he would take care of it and asking if Lourdes might reconsider the decision if he promised to personally serve as the account rep. I told him we could discuss it, but only if Bradley was 'out of the picture.' Stein told me he'd make sure that happened."

Leaning forward in his chair, with a sly, "Cheshire cat" smile on his face, Waylander suggested, "Maybe murder was what Stein had in mind when he told me he'd make sure Bradley was 'out of the picture'—ever think of that?"

That same thought had crossed Bunker's mind also, but he wasn't going to give this little puke the satisfaction of knowing that his suspicions were shared. "Did you ever see or speak to Bradley again after you had him escorted from your office?"

"No, but he did make a phone call to the CEO about me," Waylander explained disdainfully. "Because of that, I got an intra-office memo directing me to attend a meeting that had been set up for the following week between the three of us." Smiling, Waylander added, "But, since somebody murdered him, he was a no show."

Bunker stared at him until Waylander's grin vanished and he turned away uncomfortably. "Sir, was this behavior of Bradley's pretty constant, or was this something you saw only recently?"

Waylander appeared to think a moment before answering. "Bradley was always a loose cannon, and with just the right combination of circumstances, he was capable of going off. He was an angry guy who tried to control everything and everyone. At first, he came across as charming and anxious to please, but it was just a ploy to get what he wanted. And when it became apparent I wasn't going to play his game, he turned ugly, threatening to go over my head and complain to the Board if necessary. I couldn't have that."

Closing his tablet and mindlessly thumping his pen on it, Bunker asked quietly, "Is that why you threatened to kill him?"

Waylander abruptly got up. "This is the end of the line, Gentlemen." Grabbing his overcoat he added, "Except for one final comment—the guy was scum."

CHAPTER THIRTY-NINE

Instead of interrupting the Waylander interview, which, according to his watch, must have been well under way, Peter decided to spend some quiet time sifting though papers found tucked away in a lock box at a bank across town. After several days of searching, he had all but given up on his hunch that Bradley had a second stash of papers, money or valuables at another bank. But this morning, Peter got lucky. At the very last bank for which a subpoena had been issued, he found it—a veritable gold mine, documenting events and places in which Bradley had some involvement during the last few months of his life.

After carefully placing the contents of the lock box in a sealed evidence bag, Peter returned to the office to sort it all out. Once there, he immediately broke the seal, then turned the envelope upside down, allowing the papers to fall unchecked, until they collectively covered the top of his desk like a patchwork quilt.

Trying to put them into some semblance of order, Peter scrutinized, then carefully inventoried each on a lined yellow legal pad. After several minutes spent cataloging one item at a time, he was just about finished with his task, when he heard a half knock, followed by his office door suddenly swinging open. Looking up, he saw Bunker and Thompson beaming like two schoolboys ready to burst with a "show and tell" story. "I guess you didn't notice my door was closed."

"Sorry," answered Thompson, "but we just finished with Waylander and thought you might want to know what we found out."

Taking his glasses off and rubbing tired eyes Peter answered, "I would. Sorry I didn't make it back in time to be there. I got sidetracked as usual. How did it go?"

With hands burrowed deep in his pockets, absently jingling spare change, Thompson answered for both. "Real well for Waylander."

"What does that mean?"

"It means that I don't think he murdered Bradley. Granted, he was less than cooperative, but I think he's just scared like everybody else in this mess of a murder."

Peter glanced over at Bunker who was vigorously nodding his agreement. "Find out anything that *was* worth pursuing?" Peter asked, too tired to hide his disappointment.

"As a matter of fact, yeah." As if taking Peter's question as an open invitation to make himself comfortable, Bunker casually slid into one of the two chairs facing Peter's desk and slouched down, his bulky frame expanding sideways like a squished rubber ball until it reached the outer edges of the seat. "Let me tell you—if I was Jake Stein, and half of what Waylander said was true, I'd have been as pissed as hell with Bradley."

"Pissed off enough to kill him?" Peter asked. Suddenly what the two detectives were saying had his undivided attention. He laid his pen and inventory list down and listened.

"It looks that way to us," answered Thompson. "Let's put it this way, I've got plenty to put in my investigative report." Laughing he added, "That should keep the guys upstairs happy. If they want a name, I think we've got it."

"Anything to get them off my back," Peter grumbled as he got up from his chair and turned to walk out the door, intending to grab some coffee from the secretary in the outer office. He was only too delighted to hear that Stein may be his man. Maybe they were finally about to crack this.

"Wait. There's something else I wanted to tell you," Bunker offered as he began twisting around in his chair trying to get up. "Just to make sure we weren't zeroing in on the wrong person, Thompson and I also hunted down those persons whose names were on other contracts found scattered at the scene. There's nothing there. Every one of them gave pretty much the same story—each had recently terminated their business relationship with Bradley due to Bradley's bizarre behavior. And true to form, just like what he did with Waylander, Bradley threatened to sue all of them for breach. Their reaction was pretty universal—they invited him to go piss up a rope."

Finally successful in his repeated attempts to separate his generous behind from the chair, Bunker added, "We thought that maybe Bradley went ahead anyway and hired a lawyer to make good on his threats, so, just to make sure, we checked—no suits had been filed at the time of death."

Stepping away from the open door to his office, Peter walked back to his desk and sat down. The coffee would have to wait. "While you two are here, it's probably a good time to talk about what I found out today. I finally found the other safe deposit box. The results were well worth the effort."

As Peter began talking, he noticed Detectives Thompson and Bunker were quietly joined by Detectives Greene, Shapero, Burjinsky and DeAngelo. His office was now almost full.

"Inside the bank box were literally hundreds of hotel and motel receipts, each signed in what appears to be Bradley's handwriting. Only thing different was the name—instead of Bradley, each was in the name of what looks like, if I can read it right, R. O'Neill. Unfortunately, the signatures, especially the last name, are scribbled, barely legible. Obviously, Bradley wanted it that way—he paid for everything in cash."

Greeted with looks of bewilderment, Peter suggested, "Let's talk this out. Common sense tells us he didn't go to these places alone. And, chances are slim his wife was the type. So, the guy had to have a girlfriend. And from the dates on the receipts, these activities went well beyond the time he broke up with Caroline Witten. Which means there was someone else."

Scratching his head, Shapero was the first to respond. "I don't get it."

Peter picked up his yellow legal pad. "Listen while I read from this list. Aside from hotel receipts, there were receipts for all sorts of weird shit like arcade games, girlie shows, blue movies, and massage parlors—behavior which ties in perfectly with what Caroline Witten described. And the dates on the receipts were fairly new—within the last several months.

"And, for what it's worth, mixed in with all those receipts, were several corporate documents indicating Bradley was in the process of starting up a new company—something called, 'Body Parts.'" Seeing that Shapero was about to open his mouth, Peter added, "And don't ask. I don't know at this point whether that info figures in or not."

Peter threw the legal pad back on the desk. "Right now, that's all I've got. Not to switch gears, but more came in today from the M.E." He leaned down, opened the lower drawer to his credenza and pulled out a one page, single-spaced report.

"The drug screen showed positive. Bradley had been taking some kind of barbiturate, which means someone had to prescribe it. And since neither Dr. Parker nor Bradley's personal physician prescribed any type of barbiturate, that means one of you will be assigned to check out all the pharmacies close to Bradley's home and office, to determine the name of the doc who did." Looking around the room, he asked, "So who's gonna do that?"

"Barbiturates? There's no way we're going to find out who prescribed a barbiturate," whined Burjinski. "We could chase that rabbit all the damn day, especially if the guy was into using phony IDs."

"We run with what we have," Peter answered sternly. "To make it more interesting, the drug screen also indicated that Bradley had ingested alcohol that evening. It wasn't much, but the combination of booze and barbiturates could explain why the killer was able to do such damage. Also lends more credence to the theory that a woman could be capable of committing this murder."

Looking around the room, Peter asked, "Before we go any further, what's going on with those cell phone logs? Have we got a trace yet?"

"*I* did the trace," answered Billy Ray Rigger as he sauntered through the door. "Sorry, I'm late," he mumbled as he walked towards the center of the room. "I know you gave that assignment to Shapero, but he got caught up with a witness, so I picked up for him." All eyes turned to Shapero who remained silent.

Shuffling in next to Burjinski, the heels to his boots making a scraping noise against the linoleum, Billy Ray shrugged his shoulders, setting the fringe on his rawhide cowboy jacket in a frenzied swinging motion. "None of what I found makes any sense though.

"Some of the calls, Bradley made to his office. Each lasted less than a minute. Other calls were traced either to his residence or to clients—pharmacies, hospitals and two rehab centers. Again, like his calls to the office, they were short."

Referring to notes, which Peter could see Billy Ray had scribbled on an assortment of wrinkled scraps of papers, each depicting a prominent logo of a bucking bronco, Billy Ray explained, "And then there were the other calls—to be exact, there were one hundred and thirty-three calls in all, to four different women. Two of the women work as exotic dancers. The other two are penny ante hustlers on Main and Twenty-eighth Streets, with arrest warrants dating back to 1995 when each was a juvenile. Since then, nothing's changed much. The hookers on Main still have the same pimp and they still get tossed pretty regularly by Vice. Coincidentally though, they both have the same lawyer—Caroline Witten. And a quick check of the arrest records shows Ms. Witten never fails in getting them sprung within five minutes of their prints being inked."

Peter noticed how quiet the room had gotten. Information like this never failed to pique prurient interest. Where it was leading though, Peter didn't have a clue. He motioned for Billy Ray to continue.

"When I interviewed the two exotic dancers, known as Lula and Dawn, they first off told me they didn't know anything about a John Bradley. But when I showed them his picture they changed their minds. Both recognized him as, 'Rick'—a 'john' interested in being part of 'three in a clutch.'"

"Whoa, what a guy!" shouted Burjinsky.

Amid cackles of laughter and snide comments about Lula and Dawn, Peter again interrupted Rigger's remarks by asking about the two hustlers on Main.

"I could only find one of them. But they room together. And the one I talked with—Sheila, seems to know all about Brandi, so I figured it was as if I was talking to both of them. They also work as 'love partners' for various clients. And yep, both of them have worked over John Bradley whom they also knew as, 'Rick.' Like the other two, they never heard the name, Bradley, and could only identify him from his photo. According to Sheila, he was a guy who was strictly into kinky stuff—lots of 'S & M.'"

With each detective straining to hear, Rigger droned on with the lurid details. Peter decided to let him roll with it, resisting the impulse to ask questions.

"According to these ladies, Bradley, or 'Rick,' had a routine that was never broken. Like clockwork, after each 'S & M' encounter, he would break down and, as they described it, bawl like a baby and apologize for doing dirty things to them. Then he'd promise never to do anything like that again.

"Fortunately or unfortunately, depending on your viewpoint, Bradley though, wasn't a man of his word. Within a week he would be back, begging for more, and willing to pay whatever price the ladies wanted, which got to be more and more exorbitant.

"After the 'love lessons' were over and done with in what even the ladies called, 'sleaze joints,' Bradley, unlike most johns, insisted on leaving the room first, always wearing a heavy starched white shirt, silk tie, expensive suit, and carrying a black attache case. Another rule—no one but Bradley touched the attache case."

Interrupting, Peter said, "When Shapero and I went to First Star, the lady told Shapero that Bradley always carried a black attache case when entering and leaving the bank vault. It has to be the same one."

Writing a note to himself, Peter urged Rigger to continue.

"According to all of 'em, these sexual encounters had been going on for about six months and occurred often enough for Bradley to have become a 'regular.'"

Stuffing his already crumpled notes into the front pocket of his hip-hugger jeans, Rigger added, "Oh, and before I forget, as I said before, the pay was good, so the ladies didn't mind doing anything they were asked to do."

"Man, who would have thought Bradley would have had the balls to be involved in something like that?" mused DeAngelo. "Shit, Bradley must have found his own little brand of heaven right here on earth. And who would have thought it, married to that tight-assed Judge?"

"Enough," interrupted Peter sharply. "Anyone would think from listening to all this that we'd never seen or heard of this before. Let's not forget—Bradley was like a lot of other dead guys we've investigated whose private peccadillos become unfortunate public embarrassments for the family left behind. And remember too, this particular victim was married to a well-respected Judge who still works and lives in the public eye. So no more snide comments about her anatomy or anything else, until we know exactly where this is taking us." Looking directly at DeAngelo he asked, "Have I made myself clear?

"And let's follow up on this 'Rick O'Neill' alias. We're making progress. I can feel it."

CHAPTER FORTY

After Peter said a hurried goodbye and left the hospital, Hilary's thoughts were crowded with self recriminations. As Susan's best friend, she should have known, or she should have guessed, that Susan was pregnant, even if Susan hadn't confided in her. Thinking back, the signs were all there—Susan's disposition had changed as had her appearance. Even before the murder, Susan complained of chronic exhaustion, but Hilary had unthinkingly chalked up Susan's irritability and lack of energy as nothing more than stress associated with the start of the campaign.

Now, sitting alone in the hospital waiting room, Hilary's thoughts turned to one thing—who was the father of Susan's baby?

Startled when the E.R. doors were suddenly flung open, Hilary turned just in time to watch as orderlies transferred a sleeping Susan to the obstetrical floor for further observation. Worn out by the interminable waiting and numbed by the latest revelation, Hilary listlessly picked up her coat and prepared to follow Susan to her designated room. The same E.R. nurse who had brought them the shocking news the night before, told Hilary that there was now little chance that Susan would spontaneously miscarry—her condition was stable.

With Susan safely on her way upstairs, Hilary pulled out her cell phone, hastily grabbed the night before, and checked in with her office. She then took the elevator to the third floor where she stopped at the nurses' station to inquire whether it would be possible to see Susan, now that Susan had been admitted. The nurse on duty told her that she was welcome to go on in—the last time she had checked, the patient was awaiting her doctor ordered breakfast.

As directed, Hilary followed the oversized black arrows, painted on brightly colored walls, to the east wing. With each step, all she could think of was how best to face Susan with what she now knew. Outside room three twenty-four, which the nurse had identified as Susan's, Hilary took a long deep breath and pushed hard on the heavy wooden hospital door.

Three twenty-four was a private room, painted in shades of neutral beige with equally colorless draperies, drawn tightly shut, successfully concealing the room's only window. Overall, the effect was what Hilary had expected—institutional and dreary. Taking only a moment to get acclimated to the low lighting, she tiptoed inside, and avoiding Susan's gaze, went directly to the window where she gently pulled back the draperies, allowing the early morning light to filter into the room.

"There, that's better," she said quietly as if talking to herself.

After a long, uncomfortable silence, Susan asked, "You know, don't you?"

Without turning, Hilary answered, "If you're talking about the pregnancy, yes. I know." She couldn't bear to look at Susan. It was too painful. Susan hadn't trusted her.

Having no other place in the tiny room to go, Hilary moved slowly from the window to Susan's side and tentatively placed her hand on Susan's.

"We were so worried when you fainted last night." In a feeble attempt to lighten the moment, Hilary added, "I'm glad it's nothing more than being a little bit pregnant."

Susan closed her eyes, then turned away from her.

"Please don't shut me out again," Hilary implored. "I know you're worried about the baby, but I just spoke to the E.R. nurse who said everything is going to be just fine. In fact, you'll probably be going home sometime this afternoon. Keeping you here for awhile was just a precaution—nothing more than that."

With her eyes still closed, Susan murmured, "What would I ever do without you?"

Hilary laughed. "In all honesty, I don't know."

Feeling some innate need to put physical distance between them before continuing, Hilary turned and cautiously moved a few feet away from the bed. She didn't want to look at Susan when she said what was on her mind.

"I know this probably isn't the best time or place, but I'm going to say it anyway." Hilary lowered her voice. "I wish you had trusted me with your secret. You know I would have helped you, but you never gave me the chance. You have no idea how worried I've been about you."

"I *do* know how worried you've been—you're always taking care of me." Susan sighed. "It's never been the other way around, has it? Even when Jack died, I should have been comforting you, but you were the one comforting me because you didn't want anyone feeling badly, or worse yet, feeling sorry for you. This time though, I'm going to try being the strong one in order to keep this baby happy and healthy."

Looking down at Susan who appeared so vulnerable in her hospital issued gown, Hilary said, "I know you will. And I'll be here to help you and the baby any way I can."

Trying hard to hide the anguish she felt, Hilary moved even closer toward the window. "It just really bothers me that you didn't tell me. Try as I may, I can't get past that."

Grabbing at the sheets and pulling them up to her chin, Susan answered, "I don't expect you to understand. I'm not sure I would if I were in your place." With her jaw set, she added, "Obviously, there's someone else involved and I need to protect him."

Struggling to sit up in bed, Susan pleaded, "No one would believe that I had nothing to do with John's murder, if my involvement with this person became known." With her face contorted in anger, Susan asked, "Did you forget that I'm running for re-election? How could I explain it? Not only am I an adulteress, I'm pregnant with another man's child. Don't you see? I had to have time to sort it all out. Why can't you just understand that and let it drop?"

Taken aback, Hilary didn't know what to say. Was Susan angry at being caught, embarrassed by an unexpected pregnancy, or was there something more? Just when she believed that nothing or no one in the world could again shake the foundation of her being, Hilary found herself unable to understand the words and actions of her own best friend.

Seemingly unaware of her discomfort, Susan went on. "You see only the good in people, even in people like those wretched killers and child molesters you so matter-of-factly defend. Your perspective on life is that everyone has *some* basic goodness. That's what makes you the kind of advocate that you are. I'm the opposite, and so is just about everyone else in the world. We see people and things as they really are."

Devastated, Hilary slowly murmured, "I thought I knew you. You're my best friend . . . a judge . . . " Seeing that Susan had again turned her head away, Hilary said, "Look at me. Please. You're making me feel as though I never really knew you."

For several seconds, Susan shut her eyes tightly. "I'm sorry you feel that way, but right now, I can't do anything about it. There are things in everyone's life that are just too personal, too private, even to discuss with your best friend. Can't you understand?"

Trying again to explain herself, Hilary replied, "Of course I can understand and accept that. But let me remind you—your acknowledgment to me that you and John hadn't been sleeping together for some time was neither too personal nor too private to disclose. How could the situation in which you find yourself now, be much different?"

"That's unfair of you," Susan shot back angrily. "Believe me, I wish I had never confided in you. I shouldn't have. It didn't do either of us any good. It made you uncomfortable, and me, miserable. I don't need to talk about my failures which, according to John, apparently even extended to the bedroom."

"That's ridiculous. Stop it. You're anything but a failure." Wrinkling her forehead and leaning her head to one side, Hilary said, "I hope to hell you're not telling me that you had an affair with another man just because John made you feel inadequate in the bedroom." Walking towards the bed, she asked, "That isn't what happened, is it?"

With an impatient sigh, Susan answered, "It's all so complex. Who knows who did what to whom first. For a long time, I think I knew John was probably having affairs. I also had a sixth sense, being married to him for as long as I was, that those affairs weren't what the average person would call normal."

"What are you talking about?"

Before answering, Susan listlessly ran her fingers through her hair, its long length falling well past her shoulders. Her voice was cold. "Let's just say I had the misfortune of seeing rather explicit evidence of it when John stupidly left something in one of his coat pockets—photographs, which, by anyone's standards, were sexually graphic to say the least."

Angrily, Susan put one long slender finger up to her mouth and bit down hard. Hilary heard the nail snap; Susan however, appeared oblivious. "It was almost a year and a half ago. I was cleaning out John's pockets so that I could gather up his clothing to be delivered to the dry cleaners. I'll never forget it. There were six pictures—all of the same woman, just different poses."

Susan stopped and reached for a tissue that was on the nightstand. With her hand visibly shaking, she continued. "After seeing those photographs, I thought I was in a position to confront him and finally learn the truth. But I couldn't have been more wrong."

Realizing how upset Susan was becoming, Hilary warned, "Maybe we shouldn't talk about this. You need to be resting and—"

"No," Susan interjected. "You wanted to know the truth. Well here it is." In an apparent effort to calm down, Susan lay back before continuing.

"Right after I found the photos, I called John at the office. He came to the phone immediately, but I was so upset, I could barely talk. I remember just blurting out, "You need to come home right away. We have to talk.

"He kept asking what was wrong, arguing that if it were a true emergency, it needed to be dealt with immediately over the phone."

All of a sudden, Susan let out a laugh, but not one of amusement. "Little did I realize that the reason John wanted to know the nature of the emergency was not due to any concern for my health and safety," she said mockingly. "No, of course not. Instead, he wanted the opportunity to quickly prepare his defense before facing me in person. With John knowing the nature of the emergency beforehand, the drive home would provide the necessary time in which to concoct some lame excuse.

"Stupidly, I fell for it and told him what I had found. I asked for an explanation. His response? When I calmed down, he would reward me by coming home. Then we would discuss whatever it was, quietly and rationally like adults.

"Not surprisingly, it took longer than thirty minutes for John to get home. By the time he arrived though, no surprise, he had the perfect explanation for his delay—traffic was bad, so he had thoughtfully stopped to get us a nice little bottle of chardonnay.

"The first thing that struck me was how very calm and thoroughly detached he seemed. When we talked, he handled me as if I was some hysterical housewife who had stupidly misinterpreted something totally innocent.

"After he poured the wine, he had the audacity to ask, 'Now, isn't this better?'" She smiled. "Honestly, looking back, it was like being at a 'Mad Hatter' party where everyone thinks of themselves as being perfectly sane, when in reality, they're perfectly mad.

"I remember thinking that his words that day were carefully chosen for effect—like a well-rehearsed closing argument. He was playing a part; a part that he had down so pat, he must have created it a long time before, just in case."

"What does that mean?"

"It means he was very comfortable with a lie. That's the only way I can explain it. Anyway, he began his explanation by saying that I had jumped to conclusions—that the whole thing was absurdly innocent. Really, Hil, if it hadn't been so sad, it would almost be funny." Susan laughed derisively. "He wanted me to believe that these photographs belonged to someone named, 'Rick.' According to John, it seems this person had inadvertently left the photos in a medical supply catalogue which had been dropped off at John's office. Upon finding them, John explained that he had intended to return them, but had gotten busy, and promptly forgot about them. And before you ask, no, I don't know, nor have I ever met, anyone named, Rick."

Susan closed her eyes. "If you could have seen the expression on his face. He truly believed that he was putting one over on me. What a pompous ass he was, strutting around the room, always with that silly smirk on his face. His tone so contemptuous, so reprimanding. At that moment, I absolutely hated him."

Susan lifted her head and leaning on one elbow, reached for a glass of ice chips which had been placed beside her bed. Swallowing several, she again lay back before continuing.

"So engrossed in his self-serving explanations, John never noticed that I said nothing. His explanations were preposterous, but yet, John made me feel as though I should apologize to him. When his diatribe was concluded, I did ask for a few more details, but that request just made him snicker more. His response? I must not have been listening. He was not going to explain further.

"Finally, I understood. His intent was to make me believe that somehow I was sick for thinking, even for a moment, that finding a cache of explicit photographs, which depicted a naked woman posing in pornographic positions, was nothing to be upset about—it was as normal as carrying around a Sears credit card."

Crying softly, Susan explained, "To survive, I made a promise to myself that I would remain with John for only one reason—to get through the next election. Other than that, he would never again invade any part of my life. I truly believe that John was crazy, dangerous and capable of anything. The photos were absolute proof—John was devoid of inhibition; risk exhilarated him. The only thing I had left was my career, and come hell or high water, John was not going to stand in the way of furthering it."

"So how did that work?" Hilary asked quietly.

"After that, it became an unspoken rule—John did as he wanted and I did the same. When it was necessary for John to enter my world, he would do so only by invitation. That's why people believed him to be so shy and retiring during the campaign.

"The contract worked well until I fell in love with someone else. But thankfully, by then, John was so wrapped up in his fantasy world, he never noticed. For him, the real and the unreal had fused together reflecting a distorted caricature of life. In his world, I no longer existed; I no longer appealed to him. Believe me though, by that time, I no longer cared either."

Exhausted, Susan turned her head and again, pulled the covers tightly around her as if in a soft cocoon.

Hilary was in a tailspin. How could Susan not realize the import of what she had just said? John had scorned her; she was pregnant with another man's baby; and according to what Peter had discovered, John had liquidated her financial holdings and most probably wasted her inheritance on other women, or worse. Susan's motive to kill couldn't get much better.

"That's all I'm going to say right now. Surely, even for you, that's enough."

Trying to ignore her friend's sarcasm, Hilary countered, "Not quite. Aren't you forgetting something?"

Looking puzzled, Susan shrugged her shoulders.

"Aren't you going to tell me who the father is?"

"No. At least not yet. I've called him. He's on his way here. Because of that, I'm going to ask you for one more favor—privacy. He's worried sick about the baby and me." Susan reached out and touched Hilary's arm. "I hope you understand. We need a few minutes alone."

"Of course," Hilary answered simply. Glancing at her watch, she added, "Since it's after nine o'clock, I'm late for court anyway." Gathering up her coat and purse, Hilary said over her shoulder, "Call me when they release you and I'll pick you up."

Pulling the heavy door towards her, Hilary again came face to face with the unexpected—Jake Stein with a handful of sweetheart roses.

CHAPTER FORTY-ONE

Hilary was so taken aback, she was unable to speak. She wasn't alone however—no one else seemed eager to hold forth either. So several long, very awkward moments passed without comment by anyone. Hilary instinctively retreated to the nearest corner of the room, wishing for all the world that she was anywhere but where she was.

Feeling more secure in this comparatively safe harbor, she watched in astonishment as Jake approached her, and unabashedly plucked a single sweetheart rose from the bouquet cascading from his arms. Then, extending his hand, he offered the tiny fragile blossom to Hilary. As if on autopilot, she reached up and accepted it, recoiling as their fingers accidentally touched.

"Well, Hilary, I seem to see you everywhere."

Hilary strained to lift her eyes from the ridiculously extravagant bouquet, bound tightly by a rainbow of colored ribbons. Swallowing hard and looking in Susan's direction, she asked, "Is—is Jake your baby's father?"

Susan and Jake looked at each other and nodded.

Hilary blinked hard; her stomach churned. She turned to stare at Jake. Their eyes met, but Jake didn't flinch.

"I'm sorry," Hilary stammered. "I just can't believe this. I—I thought you two hated each other—that you only tolerated one another because of John."

Shaking her head in disbelief she repeated, "I'm sorry. I just, well I just can't take all this in at once."

Stein seemed to understand her obvious discomfort. Gently, he replied, "I'm sorry. This is an awful lot to throw at you."

Nervously fingering the button on her coat, Hilary answered, "I have to admit, I thought I'd experienced it all, but seeing you here, with a handful of flowers, like a schoolboy on his first date, I couldn't have been more wrong. I guess I've just known you too long. This doesn't seem like the Jake I knew."

Hilary glanced over at Susan and with sadness in her voice said, "But then, this isn't the Susan I knew either."

Ignoring her comment, Jake took three giant strides toward Susan, threw down his floral offering on the nearest chair and gathered her into his arms.

"Darling, I've been so worried about you."

"I'm fine and the baby is too. It was just a scare. Nothing more."

"Well, from now on in, you're going to relax and let me take care of you." Not bothering to turn around and look at her, Jake asked, "Don't you agree, Hilary?"

Hilary's silence however, went unnoticed as did her exit.

***   ***   ***

On her way to the office, though wanting desperately to give in to shock and disappointment, Hilary allowed herself to think about what she had just witnessed, but only within the context of its impact on the murder investigation. As a criminal defense lawyer, she knew that as soon as their sexual relationship became public, both Susan and Jake would shoot like rockets to the top of the known suspects list. Separately or together, the two had the perfect motive to kill John Bradley.

Because of that, Susan could no longer be portrayed as the grieving widow. And Jake could no longer claim the role of long-suffering business partner.

Trying to wind her way in and out of the morning's rush hour traffic without mishap, Hilary made a well-practiced reach for her car phone, and, while keeping a steady bead on the road, quickly punched in the numbers to her office. "Maria, I need to talk with Sam. Has he been around yet today?"

"You're in luck. He was just here, wanting to know where you were. Said something about finally finding the 'shrink.' Hope that makes sense to you, because it sure doesn't to me."

"It makes perfect sense. If he's still there and handy, put him on. If he's gone back to his office, get him. It's urgent."

Hilary waited nervously for Sam to pick up. Finally, after she had half convinced herself that Maria had accidentally disconnected her, a familiar voice asked, "Hey, Beautiful. What's up?"

Like a pricked balloon, Hilary exploded with an accounting of what had happened at the hospital the night before, as well as that morning. Sam said nothing—a silence for which Hilary was grateful. The last thing she needed was Sam telling her, 'Told you so.'

"I hope you have some good news, Sam. Whatever it is though, break it to me gently. I can't stand many more surprises today."

"No *good* news. Just *great* news. Tracked down the psychiatrist yesterday— Dr. Michael Moss Dulensky, III. Told me he'd been treating the patient in question for about a month. I can only assume that since this doctor lives and practices forty miles away in Bardstown, our client must have felt pretty safe in small town USA. He even used his real name."

"So what did this Dr. Dulensky have to say?"

"Actually he divulged more about his former patient than I actually wanted to hear. Believe me when I say there's a lot to tell. But, since you're on the mobile, we better limit this conversation."

"You're right. I just needed to vent. I'm only five minutes anyway, so I'll talk with you as soon as—"

"Wait. One more thing before we hang up. When this doc pulled the patient's records, he found that he'd retained a file folder which apparently the patient had provided during the first visit. That file folder contained medical information from Dr. Parker.

"When he showed me this, I remembered you telling me about an empty file folder labeled, 'Dr. Parker' found in the deceased's office at the house. I guess that explains why the file's contents were missing. They weren't stolen by the killer; they'd already been given to Dulensky."

"Well, that answers at least one question." Over the static of her car phone Hilary advised, "I'm just pulling into the parking garage now, so I'll be in your office in two minutes. See you then."

Rather than waiting in line for the building's notoriously crowded and slow elevators, Hilary took the back steps. Bedraggled and looking as if she had just completed a 10 K run and come in dead last, Hilary walked into Sam's's office unannounced, trying desperately to catch her breath. Without comment she slumped into the nearest chair, but only after ridding it of a bundle of yellowed and dog-eared papers which she stacked haphazardly against the wall.

The office which Sam had leased in the Kentucky Home Life Building for the last fifteen years, hadn't been refurbished, updated, or some would say, decently cleaned, during the entirety of his tenancy. The wall to wall carpeting was pea soup green in a swirling marbled design, popular in the seventies, as was the assortment of harvest gold kitchen appliances found in his kitchenette. The desk, the only furniture of value, was a "find" Sam had stumbled on years before. A honey maple partner's table, placed dead center in the fourteen by sixteen room, it was cozily cluttered with a collage of collectibles—papers, pens, and a big red bubble gum machine, the latter always well-stocked with deluxe sized sour balls in an assortment of citrus flavors. It was Sam's's only indulgence since he stopped drinking and smoking five years before.

Upon seeing Hilary, he immediately picked up the cup of coffee he had waiting on his desk. "Drink this. You need it; then we'll talk."

Grateful, feeling that she might actually live, Hilary answered, "You know Sam, you'd make one hell of a husband someday."

"I've been telling you that for years," he answered, "but you never take me up on my offer."

Hilary laughed, in spite of herself. "Believe me, you'd be very sorry if I did."

Pulling up another chair which he planted right in front of her, Sam began his narrative. "According to Dulensky, Bradley was one very sick fella." Cocking his head sideways, Sam asked, "Didn't we hear almost the exact same description from Parker?"

Hilary managed a wan smile.

"Anyway, after talking with Bradley during several therapy sessions, Dulensky, like Parker, recommended hospitalization, but Bradley, no surprise to anyone, refused. Dulensky figured since John wasn't suicidal and didn't present any danger to others, he wouldn't push it, even though the words, 'mental inquest warrant' were mentioned as an option if John didn't cooperate."

Sam turned in his chair, burrowed through the sheaf of papers lying scattered around the perimeter of his desk, and triumphantly pulled out the fourth edition of the *Diagnostic and Statistical Manual of Mental Disorders, Text Revision,* a guide for professionals, generally referred to as simply, the *DSM-IV*. "I'll try and relate this to you in understandable terms, but I can't promise it'll translate all that well the first time around. I took notes as the Doc talked, but I'll need this *Manual* to fill in the blanks." He scratched his head. "It made perfect sense when Dulensky was talking, but now, I don't know. . . ." Grinning he said, "I'll give it my best shot though."

"Okay, I'm listening," Hilary answered encouragingly. She could barely contain her excitement. Something told her that for the first time, they may be onto something, or at least going in the right direction.

"Dulensky diagnosed John as suffering from something called, 'Borderline Personality Disorder,' a specific type of 'Personality Disorder' which can manifest itself in a whole host of nasty ways.

"According to the *DSM-IV*, and I'm not taking these symptoms in any particular order, the person may demonstrate a 'pattern of unstable and intense interpersonal relationships' which can fluctuate between 'extremes of idealization and devaluation;' impulsiveness that may have the potential for being self-destructive in areas such as spending and sex; and 'marked reactivity of mood,' such as 'irritability or anxiety.' The person 'may display extreme sarcasm, enduring bitterness, or verbal outbursts,' and may 'make frantic efforts to avoid real or imagined abandonment.' This 'perception of impending separation or rejection . . . can lead to profound changes in self image, affect . . . and behavior. . . . There may be sudden changes in opinions and plans about career, sexual identity...'and even the type of people you want to hang with."

Hilary began to interject, but Sam whispered, "Wait, there's more.

"Prompting this grab bag of bizarre behavior can be, 'physical and sexual abuse, neglect, hostile conflict, and early parental loss or separation. . . . ' As indicated by the *DSM-IV*, those events are found to be 'more common in the childhood histories' of those suffering from this disorder."

"So, what does all this mean? If a person has it, is the condition curable?"

"Hold on. I'm not finished."

Hilary listened quietly to all the technical terms referred to in notes taken by Sam during his conversation with Dulensky, and his verbatim references to the "*Bible*" of mental disorders– the *DSM-IV*. Her initial feeling of euphoria was quickly giving way to a sudden feeling of disquiet. She felt an overpowering need to stand up and walk around. Sometimes, it was easier to think on her feet, and this was definitely one of those times.

Remaining in his chair, Sam looked up. She could feel his eyes following her as she walked from one end of the room to the other, the click of her heels barely muted by the worn, almost threadbare carpeting.

"I repeat, that's not quite all there is, you know. Don't you want to hear it all?"

Hilary hesitated, then slowly nodded.

"Since Dulensky only saw Bradley a couple of times, and Bradley's recollections of his childhood during those bare your soul sessions were intentionally sketchy at best, Dulensky was apparently considering several differential diagnoses as well, such as, 'Histrionic Personality Disorder,' which, from what I can tell, has somewhat similar characteristic features.

"Let me preface this next pronouncement by verbalizing the obvious– I'm not an expert. But to me, this disorder seems to fit our boy John to a tee." Stopping a moment to take a breath, Sam walked to where Hilary was standing and said, "But then, I'll let you be the judge."

"Okay, you've still got my attention."

"Persons who suffer from this condition, 'may crave novelty, stimulation, and excitement and have a tendency to become bored with their usual routine. These individuals are often intolerant of, or frustrated by, situations that involve delayed gratification, and their actions are often directed at obtaining immediate satisfaction. Although they often initiate a job or action with great enthusiasm, their interest may lag quickly. Longer-term relationships may be neglected to make way for the excitement of new relationships.'

"When the Doc referred to this section in the *DSM-IV*, he indicated that persons suffering from this disorder 'may seek to control their partner through emotional manipulation or seductiveness on one level . . . a marked dependency on them at another level.'"

"From what you've just read to me, and from what I heard from Susan today, it sounds as though John was the poster boy for either of these disorders, or maybe both, if that's possible." Still unable to accept the obvious, Hilary queried, "But so what? Some of what you've told me could describe just about every client whom you and I have ever represented."

"Yeah, well, the Doc was awfully persuasive. Most interesting, Dulensky was also concerned with the physical symptoms that Bradley talked about, and indicated that there can be another, co-existing complication too—something called a 'Somatization Disorder,' where the patient will complain of multiple physical illnesses–in John's case, the preoccupation with physical complaints associated with sexually transmitted diseases. For John, the fascination proved to be a vicious circle. The fear of contracting such a disease was overwhelming to him, but at the same time, that same fear fed a constant need to take sexual risks."

Sam droned on, describing symptoms and characteristics which Hilary guiltily admitted to herself, had been displayed in small or large measure, throughout her long friendship with John. Listening to the multi-dimensional clinical profiles, Hilary couldn't help but became immersed in emotion, not the least of which was a sense of sadness. There was not much doubt now, that not only did John Bradley die an anguished, horrible death, the life which preceded it was no more than a hellishly roller coaster existence, fueled by nothing more than wretched excess. Could she have helped him? Or had she chosen to ignore the danger signs since addressing them head-on would have been too uncomfortable for everyone? Hilary plopped herself back down in the chair which she had occupied before, and covered her eyes.

Immediately, Sam bent down and knelt in front of her. Taking her hands in his, he said, "Hilary Adams, I know you. You're blaming yourself, aren't you?" He grabbed her gently by the shoulders. "Listen to me. What you learned within the last twenty-four hours was a shock, but there're worse things in this world. So what if Susan's pregnant and doesn't seem to be too upset about it? So what if Jake Stein's the likely or unlikely father, depending on how you look at it? You can do nothing to change them, or the situation they find themselves in.

"And if your concern is for John Bradley. Save it! No one but a professional could have helped him." Stroking her hair he added, "And I'm not even sure a professional could have changed someone so hellbent on self-destruction."

Hilary put her coffee cup down on the floor and leaned back in her chair. "You're right, as usual. It's just going to take a while to accept all this. And too, I have to come to grips with the Susan whom I saw and talked to today. After all, she's still my client."

She looked down at her hands which held three paper clips connected together like paper dolls. "I'm afraid I didn't tell you all that Susan and I talked about at the hospital this morning. She confided some things that I don't wish to repeat, unless of course, it becomes absolutely necessary. Suffice it to say that what you just described about a Borderline Personality's symptoms, and other associated disorders, is right on the money with what she told me."

"So what are you going to do?" Sam asked with concern in his voice. "And Hil, I'm talking about not only John's mental problems, but the information about Susan's pregnancy and who the baby's father is?"

Hilary shook her head. "Right now, I don't know what I'm going to do with it. Who says I have to do anything? Bottom line is, I have a client to protect."

She again got up, this time stretching. "I guess what it comes down to, is whether Peter Elliott asks the right questions. You and I both know there's a fine line between hindering prosecution and doing all you can to make sure a client doesn't get indicted for murder. I don't intend to make it easy for the police to arrest the wrong person."

"Do you really believe the police would be looking at the wrong person if they announced that Susan was now a suspect?"

"How can you say such a thing?"

"Isn't it obvious?" In a softer tone he added, "The legal decisions are always made by you. I do only the investigative work. And you know I like it that way since I don't worry about anyone but you."

"Then don't worry. I'm not making any decisions right now." She smiled. "At least don't worry until after I meet Peter for lunch. In the meantime, I have an appointment with a man who has all sorts of problems with a soon to be ex-wife. She's managed to convince a grand jury that he's guilty of child abuse because he moved in a with a 'professional' woman who's trying to go straight. I'll soon need your help on that case, too. I'll know a little better where we stand after my meeting with him this morning.

"If you're going to be around today, I'll keep you posted about what happened during lunch with Peter." Sighing Hilary added, "Right now though, all I'm worried about is whether Peter's buying. On top of everything else, I haven't had a chance to get to the bank."

CHAPTER FORTY-TWO

After meeting with his detectives, Peter grabbed a much needed cup of coffee, sat down once more at his desk, and took a moment to reflect back on events which had played out late last night and early this morning. Intentionally, he had refrained from mentioning anything about it to his men. Perhaps out of a sense of respect, or perhaps a twinge of conscience, he decided to keep silent—at least for now. Peter had to admit though, if only to himself, that the Judge's collapse had terrified him. One minute she was fine; the next, she was out cold, looking ghostly white and barely breathing. What made it worse, after everything had calmed down, Hilary blamed him for causing the collapse.

Now, several hours later, Peter still had difficulty shaking the guilt, as he again fleetingly relived the chaotic scene as they arrived at the hospital, and later when he and Hilary received the shocking news of Judge Emmett-Bradley's pregnancy. The obvious question—who had fathered the Judge's baby was, right now, unanswerable. Was it John Bradley or someone else? If Peter were to believe the Judge's very candid description of the less than loving relationship she had shared with her late husband, there was a strong possibility that the father of that unborn baby was not John Bradley.

Even more thought provoking for purposes of the investigation, was whether the person whom the Judge had stopped to see, but refused to identify on the night her husband was murdered, was the father.

Loveless marriages Peter could understand; affairs Peter could understand. But what really galled him was the grieving widow role the Judge played with such convincing sincerity, effectively deceiving everyone, including it seemed, her best friend, Hilary.

Now he had to decide whether the Judge had been lying to everyone from the beginning about just some things, or lying from the beginning about most things. Unfortunately, the Judge's delicate condition had put a whole new spin on the investigation. At first blush, it now appeared she may have had one of the oldest motives in the book to kill her husband. She was married, but pregnant, perhaps by another man. So how, Peter asked, would a woman like Susan Emmett-Bradley, used to authority and control, contend with an unexpected development like this? Was she capable of murdering a husband who had become nothing more than a nuisance and an embarrassing inconvenience? And if she was, could he prove it?

CHAPTER FORTY-THREE

Hilary was lucky. She never found it hard to switch gears from one client to another. And that morning, she put that unique ability to the test when she welcomed Herman Hornecke and his wistful looking girlfriend, Holly, to her office.

As they took their seats, she immediately saw that the big hunk of masculine bravado she had met for the first time, only two weeks before, no longer existed. Herman Hornecke now looked beaten. Holly however, looked exactly the same—hair dyed and lacquered with a sticky goo, most noticeably saturating two perfectly twisted spit curls extending the length of her jaw; and though only eleven o'clock in the morning, so gaudily dressed, that the former call girl's former career choice was embarrassingly obvious.

"Good morning. Please make yourselves comfortable," Hilary invited. "May I get you some coffee before we begin?"

"No. No thanks," replied Herman. "I'm really coffeed out."

Hilary turned to Holly. "How about you? Would you like some coffee or another kind of refreshment?"

"No, ah, I don't think so." She looked shyly over at Herman. "Herman said I shouldn't ask for nothing today—that I should just keep quiet. But thank you anyway, Ms. Adams."

Satisfied that the necessary amenities had been observed, Hilary put on her reading glasses and reached behind to grab Herman Hornecke's file. But in pulling the voluminous file, crammed full of police and doctor's reports, off the credenza, Hilary knocked several of her framed photographs to the floor. Holly, in an attempt to be useful, immediately reached over to pick them up while Hilary struggled to balance the contents of the cumbersome file before all the documents tumbled out.

When Herman realized what was happening, he reached over to help, but by then, Holly had successfully retrieved all the fallen photographs. None appeared broken. So Holly began handing them back to Hilary one at a time, after dusting off each with the hem of her short skirt. Just about to hand the last photograph back to Hilary, Holly suddenly stopped and looked at it more closely. "I know this man," Holly exclaimed. "I can't believe it."

Hilary turned to see which one of the framed photographs was still cradled in Holly's hand. There was such a collection of them that Hilary couldn't immediately recall which one she had still not replaced on her credenza. When Holly returned it, Hilary saw that it was a photograph of Susan and John taken the year before, at one of the local state Bar functions. In it, Susan looked unhappy; John looked disinterested.

"That's Rick," volunteered Holly. "He looks just about the same as I remembered him, even though I haven't seen him for a while."

As if realizing what she had said, and that perhaps she shouldn't have said it, Holly quickly shrank back in her chair, casting her eyes downward. "I'm so sorry," she said in a whisper. "I just never dreamed I'd see a picture of someone I knew in an office like this. I mean, I would never have thought, Ms. Adams, that you and I would know the same people." In her excitement, Holly started to bite through the layer of lilac colored lip gloss glistening on her lower lip. "Excuse me. I'm—I'm sorry. I shouldn't have said nothing."

Herman looked over at her and touched her hand. "Holly, Honey, we have a lot to talk about today and you know, time is money. So why don't we just get on with this, okay?"

"Sure, sure, Hermie. I didn't mean to interrupt. I promise, I won't do it again."

Hilary gazed at the photograph, not wanting to ask, but knowing she had to. "It's all right, Holly. This man was my best friend's husband. Tragically, he was murdered. They still haven't caught his killer."

Holly didn't say a word.

Looking only at her, Hilary implored, "It's important that I ask you this." She stared into Holly's vacuous hazel eyes—liquid reflections of a brain that seemed to have shut down or turned off. "You said that you knew this man as, 'Rick.' Was that a nickname you called him, or was that the actual name he gave you?"

In awaiting her reply, Hilary couldn't help but remember Susan's reference to a Rick, who had, according to John, accidently given him some photographs depicting a woman in provocative poses. *Was there a connection? This couldn't be merely coincidence. There has to be some correlation; I just know it.*

Turning her attention once more on Holly, Hilary noticed that, if possible, Holly looked even more uncomfortable than she had before.

"I don't like talking about this," she explained in a quiet voice, "especially in front of Hermie. It was a life I don't have no more. It's embarrassing and I don't want to remember it. So please don't make me tell you about it, okay? Please? I just shouldn't have said nothing. I always open my mouth when I shouldn't."

Hilary leaned across the desk and said to the teary eyed Holly, "I have to know how you knew this man. If it's too uncomfortable for you to talk about in front of Herman, I'm sure Herman wouldn't mind stepping outside while you and I talk by ourselves. Would that make it easier for you?"

Herman looked at Holly. "I know all about your past. If you want me to stay, I will. But if you don't, I won't be offended. You just tell me what is easiest for you."

"Oh, Hermie, I don't want to talk about this. I can't. I just can't. Please, please don't make me." She then began sobbing and rocking back and forth in her chair like a child trying desperately to comfort herself.

Herman got up and put his arms around her. "Holly, if you know something that would help find this man's killer, you need to tell Ms. Adams. If you don't tell her, you may end up having to tell the police, whether you want to or not." Softly he added, "You know, better than anyone, how much I hate the police right now, but each of us has an obligation to help if we can. Ms. Adams thinks you can help, so I'll step outside while you talk with her. If you need me, you know I'll be right outside this door."

Reluctantly, Holly nodded her agreement. Herman bent down and kissed her on the forehead, then quietly walked to the door, opened it, and closed it behind him.

Hilary handed Holly a tissue. After a long, protracted blow, Holly haltingly began to tell what she knew about a man known as, Rick.

With her eyes barely meeting Hilary's, Holly looked pained and confused. "I don't know how to start, except to say he was weird, really weird. I'm sorry to say that because I know he was your friend, but there just isn't any other way to explain it."

"Why don't we begin then with you telling me just how you first met him," Hilary softly suggested.

"I heard he got my name from a couple of other girls who were in the same kind of business I was in. Believe me, if I can ever return the favor, I will. I found out later, they couldn't handle him, so they passed him off on me without telling me anything about what he liked. And for sure, what he liked, not many people would do, including me."

Looking away from Hilary as if embarrassed, she explained, "I know a person like you don't know much about what I used to do, but there are lots of different, well you know, ah specialties. I was known as pretty straight. One thing I don't do is anything with a female partner, so right away this Rick character and I weren't a good match. And those girls knew it when they sent him to me. But when he found out I wouldn't do anything other than a one on one, he took out a pair of handcuffs and told me if I wouldn't do a 'girl guy girl,' he'd 'settle for metal.'"

Listening to this, Hilary could hardly accept that the John Bradley she knew and some stranger named, Rick, may be one in the same man, but Sam's's narrative about the various personality disorders kept nagging at her. She shuddered as Holly continued.

"I don't do 'S & M' either, so at that point, he got really, really mad and asked me real ugly-like, just what I would do. I explained that for a certain price I'd have sex with him, even 'round the world sex with him. Or, if he didn't want to get involved as an active partner, then he could just watch while I did whatever way he wanted me to pose in, with whatever part of my body he wanted showing."

Agitatedly pulling at her hair, Holly turned away from Hilary and looked at the floor. "I hate talking like this." Saying nothing more for a moment, Holly gulped hard then continued, her voice troubled. "None of what I suggested interested him though, so he just up and left. He never so much as even took off his suit and tie.

"I remember too, he had a brief case with him that he never let go of. I remember it 'cause I thought at first, he had some really weird kinky stuff in there, or maybe even a gun."

Wringing her hands, Holly said, as if to explain, "He was just what I'd call a weirdo john. Someone I'd just as soon forget about. And I did, until I saw that picture in your office."

Once more facing Hilary, Holly frowned as if remembering something unpleasant. "I guess you can tell from what I told you so far, I wasn't very good at this kind of stuff anyway. And then, when someone like Rick wanted my services, it made it almost impossible for me to do anything at all." Crying softly she said, "I guess I'm a zero in the sex business too—just like everything else." Lifting up her sleeve to wipe a dripping nose, Holly sobbed, "I don't even know why Hermie loves me because he sure isn't getting any bargain."

At that, Holly burst into tears, so loudly, that 'Hermie' blasted through the office door, grabbed and cradled her in his great big bear arms. Talking quietly, he assured Holly that she wouldn't have to say anything more.

"There, there, Baby. It's all over with." Looking at Hilary, he said, "I think it's better that we meet at another time, Ms. Adams. I need to take Holly home and make sure she's all right. On the way out, I'll make another appointment with your secretary for some time later on in the week. Since the pretrial is three weeks away, we have plenty of time, don't you think?

Not waiting for a reply, Herman Hornecke walked the still sobbing Holly to the reception area, stopping only seconds to obtain a new appointment date.

Hilary closed her inner office door and tried to patiently wait for time to pass before she again saw Peter.

CHAPTER FORTY-FOUR

When Hilary left the office to file a pleading at the clerk's office, and meet Peter at the corner bistro, she saw that the rain, which had poured down in buckets that morning, had now turned to sleet, its crystallized pellets now stinging like miniature ice chips as they stabbed painfully at her face and hands. Quickly, she pushed the release button on her umbrella, expecting it to burst open, protecting her. But nothing happened. She tried again. It didn't budge.

With hands shaking from the freezing rain, Hilary examined the umbrella more closely. The problem was obvious. The stitching which had, at one time, held in place two of the umbrella's metal spokes, was pulled out. Left behind was a telltale signature—teeth marks belonging to Marley. Now, without the necessary support the stitching had previously provided, the metal spokes drooped like daggers. Not immediately giving up, Hilary stubbornly tried once more to open the chute, but the umbrella immediately convulsed inward from the weight of the sleet. She was out of luck. "If I didn't love that darn cat so much, I'd put him up for adoption," she swore under her breath.

With her shoes making a squishing noise with each step she took, and her hair curling into tight wet ringlets suggestive of a bad perm, Hilary walked down the flight of stone steps to the Down to Lunch Cafe. Luckily, Peter had already managed to get a corner table and, knowing Hilary's likes and dislikes, had ordered for both. When he saw her, he waved and stood to help her remove her sopping wet raincoat.

"What a day." Seeing Peter staring, she said, "Don't look at me that way. I know I look like hell. Let me assure you, I didn't start out this way. But my cat ate my umbrella, which I had to stash in the nearest trash bin, and then this rain . . . Oh, never mind." Shaking the water from her coat she moaned, "Obviously, it's a long story and already, a long, loser day!"

Peter laughed. "I was staring at you because you're the only woman I know who looks great, even with wet hair."

Grimacing, Hilary answered, "Thanks, what a compliment. If you like this, it's obvious things can only get better between us. . . . Like they once were," she added, blushing.

"That's my hope," whispered Peter as he turned to pick up their order.

After they had eaten, while conversing in comfortable small talk, they lingered a few minutes longer. But their initial lighthearted discussion, abruptly turned to business, and Hilary again found herself on the receiving end of more information about John Bradley's private life. When Peter had finished bringing her up to date, Hilary said, "I'm not surprised. John's phone logs confirm what I learned quite by accident today, from a client's girlfriend."

Hilary then proceeded to reciprocate Peter's informational generosity with some of her own by describing her dialogue with Holly, and providing a synopsis of the report received from Sam. She was careful however, not to tell all—just enough to lead Peter into believing that she was being cooperative. Personal feelings aside, she still had a client who may need protection, and swapping a little for what she hoped was a lot, may be her only option at the moment.

After taking in her news without interruption, Peter's eyes darkened; his jaw clenched. Angrily, he shot back, "You could have told me about this missing doctor earlier and saved the department a whole lot of time and trouble. Remember when we had a similar discussion earlier about Dr. Parker's letter?" Grabbing her hand he asked, "Why is it that you always insist on playing the role of amateur detective? As I said, it would have been helpful, not to mention timesaving, if we had known before now, about Dulensky. Damn it, I've been chasing my tail trying to figure out where that Parker file went to. Now, the only file, the contents of which continue to remain unaccounted for, is the one pertaining to the elusive, Liam Leprakalb."

Feeling the sting of his rebuke, but not wanting to show it, Hilary took a last gulp of coffee, then pushed her chair back in anticipation of leaving. "Let me remind you, I really just learned about most of this, and besides, I'm under no obligation to tell you anything." As she wrapped her scarf around her neck, she noticed out of the corner of her eye that Peter wasn't moving.

"Slow down, Hil. There's something else I need to tell you."

Hilary didn't need a second invitation. He had her full attention.

"Did you know that Bradley was having an affair with Caroline Witten?"

Hilary closed her eyes and shook her head. She had known Caroline for years. Women lawyers were a tightly knit group in Louisville, mainly because they felt they had to be—in spite of gender equity being a recognized objective, the practice of law in the South was still very much a gentlemen's club. Women lawyers were tolerated, and by some, only barely. In all her contacts with Caroline, Hilary had found her smart, gracious and politically savvy. So hearing this was more than just disillusioning. "It's too much, Peter. Please, tell me it's just in the rumor stage."

"Sorry. Caroline Witten admitted it. And Bradley was the one who called it off, not she."

"How long ago?" asked Hilary.

"Six months. Why? Know something else you're not telling me?"

"Don't push your luck." Hilary answered with impatience. "It's just that what you've told me about John seems to match a pattern of behavior demonstrated by persons suffering from those personality disorders that Dulensky told Sam about. The person becomes bored and is therefore in constant need of something new and exciting to see and do. In John's case, once Caroline Witten was conquered, it was over. She just didn't know it. John then got involved with other people and things that were not only exciting and new, but offered a hint of danger as well."

"You think you have it all figured out, don't you? This isn't a made for t.v. movie, you know, Counselor." Shaking his head, Peter asked, "Did your operative ever think to ask if Bradley had been prescribed medication for his problems?"

"What do you think? Of course he did. And according to Dulensky, John was given samples of a mild sedative after complaining of difficulty sleeping—too many horrible dreams." With a look of consternation, Hilary said, "Why are you asking me this?" Then thinking for a minute, she said, "Oh, I see, you got the toxicology screen back from the lab. So, what did it say?"

"Smart, aren't you? At the time of death, Bradley did have some type of barbiturate in his system. Enough to indicate that he took it sometime just before death—a finding which leads me to believe that the killer, even though known to Bradley, wasn't expected that evening."

"Then why in the world would John have brewed fresh coffee?"

"I figure he must have made it much earlier. Remember, Susan told us he was expecting someone that evening. But for some reason, neither John nor his guest got around to drinking the coffee." Looking past Hilary, as if talking to himself, Peter added, "Makes perfect sense when you think about it. I've felt all along that more than one person was there that evening—the killer and someone else. And through the process of elimination, the name Jake Stein, immediately springs to mind as one of those two individuals."

Taking a deep breath, Hilary decided that it was best not to comment in light of what she had witnessed at the hospital that morning. Apparently however, her silence set off alarms.

"Anything you feel like sharing?" Peter asked with a disarming smile. He watched her intently.

Damn, he thinks he knows me so well. "Nothing I feel compelled to share right now," she said while lightly patting his hand. "As Susan's attorney, I can't divulge information that falls within the purview of attorney-client privilege. I can tell you though, that I have no independent knowledge as to whether Jake Stein was, or was not, at the Bradley residence the night of the murder."

"I thought your client was the Judge. What's she got to do with Stein, aside from thinking she might be morally obligated to divide the assets and debts of the business with him?"

Looking up at him, as innocently as she could, Hilary inquired, "What makes you ask?"

"Oh, I don't know. Something just doesn't feel right, that's all." He smiled. "Is John Bradley the father of Susan's baby?"

Hilary returned his stare. She had to protect Susan at all costs. With a calmness she didn't feel she answered, "A baby born to a lawfully married couple is presumed to be fathered by the husband."

"Don't preach the law to me, Hil." Peter lowered his voice. "I know that you know who the father is—John Bradley or not. And I also know that you know your client has also become a prime suspect in her husband's murder." Straightening his shoulders, Peter sat back in his chair. "Bottom line, I need to see your client again. And you'll want to be present when I do."

Hilary took another nervous nibble from the last remaining french fry lying in a glob of cold grease on the paper plate in front of her. "Okay, okay, I'll talk to her and get back with you."

"This isn't an open-ended deal time-wise," Peter answered evenly. "I want to talk with her tomorrow. By then she should be feeling better. And that gives you plenty of time to prepare her for what she may have ahead of her."

Peter pushed his chair back and stood. "You'll be hearing from me. Promise."

Hilary smiled gratefully as Peter reached for the check. She didn't offer to pay half.

CHAPTER FORTY-FIVE

Peter gave Hilary until the end of the day to call him about setting up a time to talk with the Judge. But when five o'clock rolled around and still no phone call, Peter decided he had no choice—he would have to make the first move. As he dialed the number, Peter couldn't help but admit, if only to himself, that there was another reason he needed to talk to Hilary Adams. It presented another opportunity to hear her voice.

***   ***   ***

Susan wasn't at all pleased with the news that once again, she was expected to make herself available for questioning. At first, she resisted, explaining that the doctor had warned her about overdoing it. And being interrogated by police, Susan argued, certainly fell into the category of "overdoing it."

Hilary assured her that Peter's intent was not to interrogate, but admitted, given the circumstances, tough questions would be asked. After all, it was Susan's husband who had been murdered, Susan who had found the body, and Susan who had left the telltale navy blue threads under her dead husband's fingernails. Therefore, from a strictly investigative standpoint, at the very least, Susan was a very material witness.

Instinctively, Hilary knew that Susan's best interests would only be served if her client openly admitted her relationship with Jake Stein. To Hilary's way of thinking, only complete disclosure could forestall a legal nightmare. So, in order to have the time to convince Susan of this, Hilary made arrangements to meet with her thirty minutes before Peter was scheduled to arrive at Susan's home.

*** *** ***

"Susan, look at me. Please! As your lawyer and your friend, I'm here for only one purpose— to help you, but I can't do that without your cooperation. At least pretend to listen to the advice I give you. I know you're a Judge, but you are incapable of looking at this situation dispassionately. This case is all about you! And right now, you have no more rights or privileges than any other scared, helpless, unprotected person caught up in a messy murder investigation. You are totally and utterly vulnerable. Remember that, and listen to me."

Met with continued silence, Hilary went on, trying to appear unfazed by Susan's lack of rejoinder. "Frankly, I see no way out other than telling Peter everything, including the name of your baby's father. You and Jake have no choice. Stop protecting him. Jake's a big boy and perfectly capable of taking care of himself. And frankly, since we're being brutally candid here, he shouldn't be taking care of only himself. He should be taking care of you and this baby of his."

To Hilary's dismay, Susan remained silent.

"Can you at least tell me how long this relationship with Jake has been going on?"

"Why does it matter?" asked Susan. "Let's just say it's been long enough for me to realize that I love him, and that I would do anything for him, to include having his baby."

So intent was Hilary in her attempts to talk to Susan, that she failed to see Jake Stein enter the library. Hidden at first by shadows cast by the doorway, she became aware of his presence only when his loud voice filled the room, in direct competition with hers.

"Bravo, Counselor." Clapping his hands together, he added, "I certainly appreciate your loyalty to Susan, and your ardent support of the truth at all costs. You've even convinced me that the truth must be told."

Sighing, Hilary said, "Great. You're just what I don't need right now. So if you wouldn't mind, Susan and I were having a very private conversation." Meeting his piercing gaze head-on, she said evenly, "That means butt out."

Jake chuckled. "Contrary to your present opinion of me, I can only argue that I'm really a pretty decent sort of fellow, once you get to know me. And I can also assure you that I intend to take care of Susan and the baby. Right now, they represent my only interests."

"Hate to disappoint you, but right now, I don't care about your interests, whatever you say they are." Walking past Susan who remained seated on the leather couch, her face disgustingly aglow at the sight of Jake, Hilary asked, "Why are you here anyway?"

"Why do you think?" Jake asked with a hint of impatience in his voice. "Right after Susan talked with you, she called and told me that Lieutenant Elliott was coming over to question her. And if you think that I'm going to let Susan go through this one more time without being here with her, think again."

Hilary turned to Susan, but Susan's only response was to immediately bow her head and say nothing. *So it was true.*

Fortunately, Hilary was saved any further comment by the sound of the front doorbell. Politely excusing herself, she opened the front door to a startled looking Peter, who was busily fixing his tie and buffing up last week's shoe shine on the back of his trousers.

"You're late," she accused as soon as she saw him.

"No, I'm not," he answered defensively. Looking at his watch, he said, "I'm right on time."

Once inside and after Hilary had taken his coat, he asked, "Is this your way of telling me you're glad to see me?"

"Yes," she answered tersely, "but not for the reasons you think." She crooked her finger. "Follow me."

With a look of puzzlement, Peter followed Hilary back to the library where Susan and Jake were waiting in silence, their hands, to Hilary's dismay, unabashedly intertwined. "I guess I don't need to explain," Hilary muttered.

Before Peter could say a word, Stein took the lead. "Listen here, Lieutenant, you need to understand that Susan's an innocent in all this." Putting his arm protectively around her, he said, "Her only fault in this sad little tale was loving me while still married to John, who I might add, was insane, and made Susan's life miserable because of it. He didn't deserve to even be in her same world."

"And you think you do?"

Hilary watched as Peter reached into his front pants pocket, and pulled out a laminated card, well worn, in spite of the protective layering. Still standing, he recited, "It's my responsibility to advise each of you of your Constitutional rights per *Miranda*. In conformance with those protections, you have the right to remain silent. If you choose not to, anything you say or do here today, can and will be used against both of you in a court of law. Each of you has the right to talk with a lawyer of your choice prior to any questioning or the making of any statements, and to have that lawyer present with you while being questioned." Looking up from the card, Peter asked, "Do each of you understand your rights so far?"

Hilary looked at Susan who sat glaring at Peter, and Jake Stein who looked strangely bored. Neither made a sound.

"I take it from your silence that you understand." Peter then continued reading the litany of rights without interruption. When finished, he looked at Susan and Jake. "Do you understand these rights that I have just read to you?" This time, each nodded their head in unison.

Turning to Hilary, Peter asked, "Counselor, would you prefer to have your client questioned first or last?"

Hearing this, Jake blinked his eyes hard and asked in a voice tinged with apprehension, "Can't you represent both Susan *and* me, Hilary?"

Shocked by the question, Hilary momentarily hesitated. It wasn't what she had expected.

"Before you answer that, let me make something clear," interjected Jake. "I would never divide your loyalties. If I need to hire my own talking suit, just tell me and I'll do it. But everyone knows you're the best, so if I can have you represent me too, how 'bout it?"

Trying to handle what had now become a very delicate situation, with a firm but fair response, Hilary unhurriedly walked across the room, sat down in the wing chair next to Susan, and folding her hands in her lap, turned her full attention on Jake. "As Susan well knows, the rules do permit me to represent each of you simultaneously. But there is however, an admonition in there—I may represent you both, but only after each of you has been fully apprised, that in so doing, each client runs an incalculable risk."

Still concentrating on Jake, Hilary explained, "One client may never be sacrificed for the sake of the other. Additionally, each of you must sign a waiver demonstrating that you accept any and all risks that may be part of dual representation." Turning to Susan, Hilary said, "Since I now only represent you, only you can make that decision as to whether such an arrangement would be acceptable."

Three pairs of eyes focused on Susan. Without hesitating, even for a moment, Susan replied in a quiet but assertive voice, "I understand all the negative ramifications of having dual representation. Regardless, I feel no reticence in agreeing to one counsel for both of us." Gazing into Jake's eyes, she added smiling, "Neither separately nor together have we committed a crime."

Hearing this, Hilary opened her briefcase which she had earlier leaned up against the leg of her chair, pulled out a yellow legal pad, and began drafting a waiver that would satisfy the requirements for dual representation. She was grateful to have something physical to do. Emotionally, she felt shaky to say the least, in representing not only Susan who was proving to be a handful, but at the prospect of representing Jake Stein as well.

After several minutes of frantic writing, Hilary finally put down her pen and presented the document to Susan and Jake for their signatures. "Before each of you signs this document, I want to make something else very clear. There may come a time when I feel that dual representation is no longer feasible in protecting your individual interests.

"With that in mind, I accept responsibility in acting as your Counsel, but only on one condition—that in the event I believe that this agreement has become unworkable, for any reason, I may withdraw my representation of both of you. The call will be mine."

Looking now to Peter who had remained appropriately removed from the conversation, Hilary informed him that she would prefer that he begin his questioning with Susan. "Jake, could you remain in the kitchen while Susan is being questioned?"

Jake quickly bent down and embraced Susan, then retired to the kitchen as directed.

Peter turned on the tape recorder.

CHAPTER FORTY-SIX

"My name I s Susan Emmett-Bradley, Circuit Court Judge, Thirtieth Judicial District of Kentucky."

Methodically, Peter asked, "Judge, again for purposes of the record, will you acknowledge the fact that this statement is being recorded, and that you have been fully apprised of your Constitutional rights in conformance with the requirements of *Miranda*?"

"Yes, Lieutenant," Susan answered clearly. "And to further clarify my response, I acknowledge that the statement that I am about to give is being tape-recorded with my permission."

Unused to such precise and articulate responses from a suspect in a criminal investigation, Peter found himself off balance. And that wasn't good when interrogating the likes of Judge Susan Emmett-Bradley. *Concentrate,* he warned himself.

After going through some additional preliminary questioning, customarily included in an individuals's statement against self-interest, Peter asked Susan to begin, by telling in her own words, what had happened on the night her husband was murdered. After she made her general statement, he would ask for more specifics.

Abruptly standing, Susan said, "I hope you don't mind if I walk around the room while I give this statement. And don't worry about losing my answers on tape; I promise to keep well within range of your recorder."

"Okay by me if I'm satisfied that the recorder is picking you up, and also, if you feel physically well enough to do that."

Susan gave him a small smile, then absently rubbed the back of her neck. "Don't worry about my health. I'm just fine." Walking just a few steps away from the sofa, Susan leaned hard against the wooden mantel. Peter could see how tense she was. Her shoulders were stiff, her arms held closely to her sides.

"What I told you before, is essentially true, so there won't be any recantation, just an addendum." For a split second, Susan looked furtively at Hilary, but then continued in what could only be described as a monotone, her sentence structure rambling, disjointed, and out of sequence. The effect was unsettling, disturbing. But Peter was bound and determined to hear her out without interruption.

"On the night John was murdered, I stayed at the office until some time after midnight, then took the back elevator directly to the judges' underground parking garage. Thinking back, I don't recall seeing anyone on my way out who could verify that, but I'm sure you could confirm it somehow, if necessary. There are always guards on duty, regardless of the time.

"As you've already gathered, I didn't go directly home. I made a detour—a stop at Jake Stein's condominium. I told Jake earlier that I expected to be there around eleven and we'd talk then about his meeting with John. When I arrived instead, at about twelve-thirty or so, he was no longer there. I couldn't understand it, especially since I was over an hour late."

"So what did you do?" Peter asked.

"Because of the hour, I let myself into his condo, stayed for awhile, then left a note letting him know that I'd been there, what time I'd left, and that as soon as I got home, I'd try and call him. I was really beginning to worry, so I—"

Interrupting, Peter asked, "Were you worried about his safety, your safety, or worried for another reason?"

"Will you please let me finish a sentence before you try and put words in my mouth?" She gave him a fierce look which unfortunately for her, had no effect on Peter. Angrily, she admitted, "All right, I was worried about what might have gone on between Jake and John earlier that night."

"What do you mean by, 'what might have gone on between Jake and John earlier that night?' Did you know they had planned to meet?"

"As I told you when we talked earlier, I had just gotten back from a judicial conference the day before John's murder. I went quite frankly, because I needed the time away from everyone and everything. Three days later, when I got back to Louisville, Jake and I met at the airport. That's when I told him of my decision to keep his baby in spite of the political, professional, and personal hardships that decision would of course, bring. Since I'm beginning my third month of pregnancy, Jake and I knew our secret would become very public, very soon anyway, especially since John would have known the baby was not his. And even for the sake of the campaign, he wouldn't have pretended it was.

"From the beginning, Jake was adamant that he alone would tell John. That way, I'd be shielded from any more of John's emotional abuse, which, by that time, had become a constant. We were, quite understandably, afraid of what John would say when told. Whatever happened, Jake wanted me out of earshot when the discussion took place."

Susan stopped her narrative, stooped down and poured herself a glass of water from a carafe set out on the coffee table. She took a long slow drink. "We also agreed that the best time and place for Jake to talk with John was at the house where they could be assured of absolute privacy. So Jake scheduled a meeting. Unfortunately, it was scheduled for the night John was murdered."

"Judge, let's backtrack a bit. For the record, tell me what you did before you went back downtown that evening."

"I came home from the office that day, for the first time, in the late afternoon, had a bite to eat, then left the house right afterwards for the courthouse. John wasn't home yet but had left a message on the answering machine reminding me he had an appointment at the house early that evening, and that he would appreciate it if I weren't there. Since I already knew what that meeting was all about, I never asked any questions."

Looking tired as if standing one more minute would be physically impossible, Susan returned to her seat on the sofa, and hunched forward with her elbows touching her knees, her chin resting in her hands. "I know it must seem as though I'm all over the board with this statement, but talking about events as they pop into my mind, even if they're not in chronological order, makes it easier for me to more accurately remember what happened."

Condescendingly she added, "If you have difficulty in following along, just stop me, Lieutenant, and I'll try to put everything in a more orderly fashion."

Peter smiled. She wasn't going to get to him. He knew he had to stay in control. "Don't worry. If I need clarification about something, or help in understanding it, believe me, I'll be sure to ask. Please, go on."

"After I left Jake's, I went directly home. I was worried about the meeting that John and Jake were scheduled to have had that evening."

"Why so worried?" Peter asked.

Twisting her wedding band around and around her finger, she answered sharply, "It's perfectly obvious, isn't it? Because of the nature of the discussion, I logically expected it to get a little testy. I also felt guilty. Jake shouldn't have had to do that alone; he needed my help."

"Your help in doing what?"

"I told you. John could be quite abusive. Jake may talk a good game, but that's not the real Jake. I guess I believed that being there, I might be able to calm the situation."

"So what happened when you finally got back home?"

"I walked in. The house was quiet. Nothing seemed out of the ordinary. Not seeing Jake's car, I immediately made my way back to the library for the purpose of calling him. I figured John had already gone to bed. When I walked in, I didn't notice John's body until I almost tripped over it. When I did, I panicked."

Burying her face in her hands, Susan began crying and slurring her words. "I hope Jake can forgive me for saying this, but I thought at first that he and John had somehow struggled and, in self-defense, Jake had—"

Ever mindful of her condition, even though it was a pivotal point in the interrogation, Peter turned off the recorder. "I think you need to take a break."

"No. No." Susan stammered. "I don't want to prolong this any more than necessary. Please, let's go on with this."

"Okay, it's your call." Looking over at Hilary, Peter felt compelled to ask, "Ms. Adams, do you want your client to take a break?"

Hilary looked at Susan. But again, before Hilary could ask, Susan shook her head, refusing to stop. "Thanks for being considerate of my client's health, but after consultation with her, she indicates she does not want to delay this."

Peter snapped the tape recorder back on, and stated for the record, that they were now continuing the statement. Without any urging, Susan began where she had left off—with the discovery of the body.

"All around him were business papers. Scattered everywhere, some even clutched in his hand. I remember grabbing for his wrist and while doing that, one piece of paper caught my eye. I suppose because it was a different color from the others."

As if guessing what Peter's next question would be, Susan explained, "I know it's odd how your mind works and what it globs onto in times of crisis. For some reason, which I can't explain, I reached down and saw that it was a letter written from a Dr. Parker. Drawn to it, I literally pried it from John's fingers. I don't want to digress, but I think it's important to say, that probably explains why navy blue fibers from my suit were found imbedded under John's fingernails."

Impatiently pushing back rebel strands of hair which had fallen across her face, Susan continued. "Getting back to what was in John's hands—there were two pages to the letter, and on each, heavy streaks of blood. For some reason, I had to know what that letter said. So I took it, holding it with two fingers barely pinching the top right-hand corner, and walked to the other side of the room where I could read it in a better light. The lamp near John had been knocked over and I didn't want to right it. I knew the crime scene needed to be preserved. Silly isn't it? There I was, a lawyer and a judge, and I had already contaminated the area where the body was. So, why was I worried about moving a lamp?" She sighed and shook her head.

Trying to get her back on track, Peter asked, "For the record, what did the letter say?"

"Nothing that made sense. It simply said that John had been tested and re-tested, and neither the doctor nor the lab could find anything physically wrong with him. In the last paragraph, it was recommended that John see one of the persons on the list previously provided, and pick up a copy of his medicals before he kept the appointment. Apparently, the tests which had already been conducted would be important for the referred specialist to review."

"Had your husband been ill?"

"No, so I didn't know what the letter meant. But while I was still reading it, I heard a noise in the hallway. Remembering that I had not locked the door behind me because I thought there was a chance I'd be leaving again to meet Jake, I was terrified. Foolishly stuffing the letter in my pocket, I walked as quietly as I could towards the front door. To my relief, it was Jake. He was worried when I hadn't arrived at the condo by eleven, and had waited around until midnight. Then, when he called the office and I didn't pick up, he drove to the courthouse. We must have just missed each other. When he returned to his condo and found the note, he then drove directly to the house.

"I—I don't remember what I said when I first saw him. By then, as you can imagine, I was in total shock. He asked me why I had been so late and if John was still at home. I don't think I said anything. I just took his hand, led him into the library and pointed. John was still lying in that same contorted position. Blood and papers were everywhere." Closing her eyes, Susan said, "I'll never get that picture out of my mind. There was so much blood, you couldn't even tell how John had died. At first, I thought he had been shot. Later, when I learned he'd been stabbed, I couldn't believe it."

"What did Mr. Stein do when he saw your husband?"

"Jake's reaction was the same as mine. He felt for a pulse, then confirmed what I already knew. John was dead. Jake asked if I was all right and what had happened." Looking down again and tugging at her wedding ring as if trying desperately to remove it, Susan explained, "I'm sure the question wasn't meant to be accusatory, but nonetheless, the inference was clear. Jake truly believed that I had killed John. I was mortified until I realized the first thing I had thought of, was that Jake must have killed John in self-defense.

"After I explained that I had found him like this, I asked Jake what had gone on in their meeting. Jake said that when he got there earlier that evening, he told John the whole story and left within fifteen minutes.

"I knew we needed to call the police, but first, I had to know how John had reacted to the news. Jake told me that after the whole story was out, John laughed so hard, he had to sit down. There was no anger, no recriminations. In fact, according to Jake, John said practically nothing, other than some unintelligible gibberish that when repeated to me didn't make any sense.

Stopping abruptly, Susan said, "That's all I have to say. That's my statement."

Pulling his chair closer to the couch, so that the recorder could pick up his voice, Peter suggested, "That's a start, but let's do what we did before and back up a little bit. As you would expect, I've got some questions."

Settling back in his chair, Peter asked, "First off, what did you do after you and Stein had this conversation in the library? Did Stein just leave after that?"

"He calmed me down, then told me to call 911. I did. Then he left."

"Again, for the record, what happened to Dr. Parker's letter which had been in your husband's hand?"

Looking trapped, Susan whispered, "I put it in my pocket, later transferred it to my briefcase, then gave it to my lawyer. She has since given it to the police." Struggling to talk, Susan sobbed, "When is this going to end? You asked for a statement. I gave it. How much more?"

"I realize that you're not feeling well, but I still have some questions; then we'll end this statement for today.

"Why didn't you disclose your relationship with Jake Stein earlier?"

Sitting up straight, rigid, she answered icily, "I'm running for re-election. Jake Stein was my husband's partner. My husband turns up dead—murdered, and while Jake and I didn't commit the crime, it's awfully tempting for the police to solve the case using only circumstantial evidence. That way, you get the kudos, Jake and I get wrongfully convicted, and the real killer gets away with it. So, I ask you, why would Jake and I make public our relationship? Now, of course, we're left with no choice but to disclose everything. And in disclosing everything, as innocent as everything is, we'll still be crucified."

"Why did you tamper with evidence left at the scene? If what you said in your statement was true, it may have helped you, not hurt you."

Impatiently Susan answered, "Why can't you understand? After I had a chance to read the content of Dr. Parker's letter, I instinctively knew that John's medical problems, whatever they were, should not be made public. What would people think? Public servants are judged by their demeanor, their family, their friends. We're all supposed to be neat little packages. Perfect little cookie cutter shaped politicians, expertly handled by campaign managers, capable at a moment's notice, of spouting philosophies molded by the latest popularity polls."

Rubbing her forehead, Susan said, "Sorry, got a little carried away in telling a long story to make a very short point—that I was trying to protect myself as well as my reputation at all costs. You have to understand. I had to remain judicial and electable. And I knew from past experience that not only would John be the one scrutinized, I would be as well."

Flabbergasted by her inability to understand the significance of what she was saying, Peter just sat back and listened. How could she not see, that it was not her husband's problems that would prove her undoing with the public. It would be her own.

Unaware of the effect her disclosures may have, Susan wearily added, "And that is again all I can tell you. I simply can't take anymore. I'm very tired, and if you're not going to arrest me, I need to go upstairs to bed. If necessary, I promise to make myself available again tomorrow. Believe me, I'm not going anywhere."

"That's fine. We'll end this for today. But you're right, I don't want you going anywhere. That means you stay here where I know I can find you."

Susan got up and walked toward the doorway. "One more thing–" Nervously fingering the door knob, she said, "Jake didn't kill John. I know he didn't. Please believe that, if you believe nothing else I've said here today."

Peter didn't bother to look up as he released the tape from the recorder and placed it in an evidence bag. "I recall you saying that before, Judge." Standing up also, Peter told Hilary that he wished to talk to her second client.

When Jake strode into the library, Peter had just finished putting on his overcoat. He took his time buttoning it and turning up the collar. "Mr. Stein, sorry to tell you this, but you and I are going to take a little trip downtown. You're not under arrest at this time, so I'm asking you to accompany me voluntarily, along with your attorney."

"Why would I want to do that?"

"Because if you give me any grief, I will arrest you and ask the district court judge on call tonight to set one helluva bond on you. You won't see the light of day for at least forty-eight hours. So, what will it be?"

"Well then, since you put it that nicely, what choice do I have?"

CHAPTER FORTY-SEVEN

When they arrived at the station, it was all but deserted except for one night shift secretary, her eyes glued to a computer screen. Peter however, wasn't surprised by the lack of activity. On their way downtown, an update had come in over the radio, reporting a shooting at O'Hara's, a saloon in the very worst part of the worst end of town. So detectives on the four to midnight shift had been immediately dispatched to process and gather information, and to help transport the victim to the hospital or morgue, depending upon what the situation required.

Since radio transmissions continued to be sketchy, even after they got to the station, Peter still had no way of determining whether his detectives were dealing with a serious assault or an actual murder. Therefore, he couldn't judge when the regular shift would be back and able to assist him. All he knew for certain was, he couldn't postpone questioning Jake Stein.

Trying hard to dismiss everything else and concentrate only on the case at hand, Peter directed Hilary and Jake to each take one of the wooden, straight-backed chairs huddled around the scratched and splintered circular conference table.

Closing the door, Peter announced, "For the record, Mr. Stein, I'm going to again advise you of your Constitutional rights."

Jake, with uncharacteristic compliance, acknowledged that he fully understood what he was about to do. Peter noted that the know-it-all attitude, so obvious just a week ago, had all but vanished. But regardless of Stein's new-found cooperative spirit, Peter couldn't help but think it was only temporary—a ruse to impress his newly hired attorney.

"I know I've asked you this several times before, but it's become apparent from the demeanor you demonstrated previously, that it may bear repeating. Do you understand our respective roles here today, and the purpose for which this statement is being given?"

Hilary shot a "if looks could kill" glance at Jake before she answered for him. "Lieutenant, there's no need to browbeat my client. He's here, as you know, voluntarily. So let's get on with it or we'll leave. Since this little meeting has never been characterized as a true custodial interrogation, I assume we're free to go when the spirit moves us."

"That status could change momentarily, Ms. Adams, so don't be too hasty in drawing conclusions like that."

"Give it your best shot then," retorted Hilary.

Turning his full attention to Jake, Peter conceded. "As your counsel has so artfully suggested, let's get down to the issues at hand—now that we understand each other."

Knowing Stein's propensity to deviate from the truth, by expertly side-stepping it when it suited him, Peter knew that an open-ended discussion, similar to the one he and the Judge had earlier that day, was not the best technique to use. Asking tight, simple questions was the way to go with Stein. That format guaranteed the control he needed, at least at first.

"State your full name for the record."

"Jake, no middle initial, Stein."

"Have you ever changed your name, or in the alternative, have you ever gone by a different name?"

"No."

"What is your current residential address?"

"1400 Willow."

"And how long have you resided at that address?"

"Long enough to have the inside painted twice," Stein answered sullenly.

Peter's jaw clenched. "I thought we had this straight. I want facts only. How many years have you resided there?"

"Okay, okay. Four."

"What is your current occupation?"

"I own a small real estate management company, and am the surviving partner in the firm of Bradley & Stein, distributors of prosthetic devises, hospital equipment, and supplies."

"At Bradley & Stein, with whom are you, or were you, in partnership?"

"John Michael Bradley."

"Tell us your whereabouts between the hours of eight o'clock p.m. and two o'clock a.m. on February18th and 19th of this year."

Stein sat back in his chair trying, it appeared, to get comfortable, stretching his long legs out in front of him, and resting his arms in crossed fashion against his chest. "Mind if I smoke?"

"Yes," answered Peter. "So don't." Stein's attitude of entitlement was already getting to him.

"My whereabouts. Well, let's see . . . I had arranged to meet John at his house around eight o'clock. I arrived a little late—about eight-ten. John must have been waiting for me at the front door, because when I knocked, he opened it immediately. Like any good host, he asked if I wanted a drink or just coffee. I remember him saying, 'Name your poison.' I declined both, explaining I didn't intend to stay that long."

Jake stopped and looked expectantly at the Lieutenant. From his expression, it was obvious he wasn't about to volunteer any further information without some kind of prodding. Peter again cautioned himself to remain patient. Right now, he had nothing more on Stein than mere suspicion. But if the interrogation proceeded as Peter anticipated, that could certainly change. The questioning would have to be undertaken very slowly, methodically drawing the suspect into the conversation, in the hopes of eliciting information that fleshed out what Peter had uncovered independently.

After three weeks of intensive investigation, Peter had to admit, John Michael Bradley remained an enigma. Trying to get a good handle on him was like trying to flesh out a shadow. With Stein's help, he hoped to add lines of definition and shades of contour to what were now, just empty spaces of time, opportunity, and motive. All he had to do was wait and listen. Peter went on with the questioning.

"What was Bradley's mood that evening?"

Stein looked thoughtful. "I dunno. I guess, if pushed, I'd say upbeat. At least more positive than it had been." Slowly crossing one long leg over the other, Stein added, "Frankly, looking back, John had an attitude that evening, that for John, could only be described as giddy."

"Anything happen at the office that day which may have accounted for the change in personality?"

"I've told you before, John and I had long ago built an impenetrable Chinese Wall between us. Because of that, if he had a bad day or good day, I wouldn't know the difference." Stein shrugged his shoulders. "Like I said, he had his deals to take care of; I had mine."

"Were you experiencing some problems with Mr. Bradley?"

"You could put it that way, yeah," Stein answered slowly. "John had become combative about bills, and hostile toward customers. I don't know how, or when, it all started. I just know that his less than perfect behavior had begun to effect our bottom line."

"Have you ever had occasion to meet a business client by the name of Richard Waylander?"

"Yes. I met with him after he called, advising that he was going to discontinue doing business with us because of John. That's what I meant when I said that John's behavior was beginning to affect our bottom line. In this case, Waylander was so fired up because of what John had done, that he threatened to take out a warrant if John dared trespass on hospital property again."

"How did you handle this complaint?"

"First, like any good business man, I salvaged the account by personally meeting with Waylander and assuring him that John would no longer have anything to do with the servicing end of it. After I calmed Waylander down, I then went back to the office to hear John's side of it. As usual though, John was somewhere out in left field, going on and on about how people just didn't understand him—that everyone was 'out to get him.'"

"How did you react?"

"I let him rant, rave, and again tell me that he was tired of the partnership and wanted to do only design work on prosthetic devices. And after a day like I'd had, covering up his messes, I wasn't too adverse to dissolving the partnership either. So, we began talking seriously about closing down B & S and each going off on our own."

Jake pressed forward in his chair. "Let's get something straight though. These discussions were very preliminary. We didn't even consult an attorney or accountant. It was just us."

"And what did those initial discussions entail?"

"Oh, we had a vague, sort of general idea how we wanted to handle everything. A simple fifty-fifty split, right down the middle. No buy-out, just a simple get-out for each of us."

"What about a buy-sell clause?"

"I told you before, Lieutenant, I didn't know there wasn't one until after John's death when I phoned that good for nothing lawyer we'd hired when John and I first set up the partnership."

"And who was that?"

"Nick Drummond. We hired him because John and I were pretty fresh out of money at the time we started the partnership. Drummond was all we could afford."

"So, in layman's terms, how does the absence of a buy-sell clause in your partnership agreement effect you now?"

"It means I can't purchase Bradley's share of the business at a fixed price from his heir, Susan, because by law, the business will automatically dissolve." Tilting his head, Stein said, "Trust me, without a buy-sell agreement, I needed Bradley alive. To put it mildly, for business reasons, it wouldn't have been in my best interests to kill him. Do you understand what I'm saying?"

Peter smiled. "Since you asked and we're on the record, killing him could have been in your best interests, based upon any one of several reasons—business and otherwise."

"I don't follow."

"Well then, let me connect the dots. One—you were having an affair with his wife and she inconveniently turns up pregnant. Or, how about motive number two—you killed

Bradley because he was becoming so unglued that he was an albatross around your professional neck? And we all know how important money is to you. Or, maybe motive number three—you killed Bradley because you didn't know about the glitch regarding the absence of a buy-sell clause until after the murder, which, by then, was too late." Glaring at him, Peter asked, "Do any of those reasons work for you?"

With his face red and the vein at his left temple pounding, Stein shouted, "How dare—"

Interrupting, Peter explained, "You killed him because you mistakenly thought that you'd automatically inherit the farm free and clear of any inconvenient encumbrances, didn't you? . . . Excepting of course, Bradley's wife."

"Peter," Hilary interjected. "are you asking questions, or supplying answers? If this continues, I'm going to instruct my client to remain silent. We both know, that right now, you don't have enough to arrest him, so please keep in mind, he's here voluntarily. Do we understand each other?"

She was right, but Peter had to push the envelope every chance he got. He had to keep Stein off balance. That was the only way to get the corroboration he needed.

Nodding Peter allowed, "Maybe we are getting a little off track here. Let's talk about something else. Who else knew about you and the Judge?"

"My secretary, Vivian. If nothing else, she can keep a secret, especially if you pay her well. And I do pay her well."

"Now, Mr. Stein, I'm going to ask you an acutely obvious question. In the last several months, when things started to get out of control with Bradley, why didn't you just extricate yourself from the partnership? It seems to me, the longer you stayed, the more trouble you invited."

"All that's true, but I had another person to consider in this mess—Susan. She was right in the middle of a campaign, and being a judge means everything to her. Understandably, she wanted to keep a lid on everything until after the election. And we would have too, except for her getting pregnant. That changed the timetable for everyone."

"Go on," Peter encouraged.

"Susan decided to keep the baby—a decision which she knew would impact negatively on the election. But she came back from the judicial conference determined to deal with it. That decision was made the day she returned. That's why I had the meeting with John the next night—the night he was murdered."

"So how did you break the news to him?"

"Like I always do—direct and to the point."

Irritated, Peter demanded, "Give me specifics."

"All you had to do was ask," Stein shot back.

"First off, I told him his behavior had become intolerable, and that I wanted an immediate dissolution of the partnership. He was a loose canon; I had to limit my exposure to any further liability. I also told him he needed to get some professional help—fast." Jake smiled, took out a handkerchief from his trouser pocket and absently wiped the face of his watch. "John thought that comment, coming from me, rather uncalled for. Can't imagine why."

Sniggering until he caught Peter glaring at him, Stein obediently continued. "Then John got back on his soap box, repeating that same tired old story—that he was bored, everything and everyone was against him, and he wanted to start all over." Stein stifled a yawn. "We continued talking a little more about what each of us wanted to do with the rest of our lives in the professional sense, then I dropped the big one on him."

"You mean you told him that Susan was pregnant and that you were the father?"

"Well, I was a little more diplomatic than that, but obviously, I was leading up to that, yes." Stein sighed. "I really did try to prepare him for what I thought would be bad news, by telling him I didn't want to be unkind. But hell, let's face it, circumstances had forced my back up against the wall. I had no choice; I had to be blunt. So I told him the whole story—that Susan and I were lovers, and because of our intimate relationship, she wanted a divorce."

As if reliving the memory of that night pleased him no end, Jake stretched his arms forward, and with both hands together and fingers intertwined, cracked his knuckles. Peter looked over and saw Hilary wince. Jake Stein however, oblivious to the social gaffe, continued without batting an eye.

"Looking back on it, the whole conversation was just plain bizarre. After I finished, John just sat there and laughed until tears rolled down his cheeks, literally. When I told him about the baby, he laughed even harder. Then he started mumbling, saying things that made no sense whatsoever—talking about people I didn't know, dropping names I'd never heard before.

"By then, the conversation had ceased being two-sided. It was pretty obvious that John had curled up in a world of his own. He was acting crazy; making no sense."

Suddenly Peter sat up straight in his chair and leaned forward. "Let's back up a bit—can you remember any of those names that he mentioned that night?"

Jake looked startled. Shrugging his shoulders, he said, "I don't know. Why would that matter? It's—"

"Because it may be important," Peter interrupted.

"Then how 'bout giving me a chance to think, okay?"

Stein again leaned back in the chair, this time interlocking his fingers behind his head. He thought for several seconds. "John kept saying over and over again that it had never mattered anyway. And that someone, I can't be sure, but I think his name was Rick, had paid through the nose for absolutely nothing."

Jake fell silent for a moment, then added, "I might remember more if I had the time, but . . . wait, he did mention another name—one that you don't hear very often. Foreign or something." Shaking his head he said, "Oh hell, I can't remember what it was. None of it meant anything to me. Frankly, my mind was on other things that night, so I wasn't exactly making a concentrated effort to make sense out of what he was saying. Sorry."

Scratching his head, Stein added, "But wait a minute. I don't know why this sticks in my brain—probably because we're talking about names, but I remember John kept calling me Mugsy that night. It was strange because it was a name I hadn't heard him use for years."

"Why would he call you Mugsy?"

Peter watched as Jake broke into a grin.

"Ever since I've known him, John loved to play games with people's names. He'd switch letters around, do a play on words, rhyme words with names, anything to rearrange a person's identity. He used this word association routine in med school too, because he had difficulty remembering medical terms. That's how he memorized everything."

"I still don't understand," said Peter.

"The nickname was the result of a combination of words—my name, Stein, which he associated with beer stein or mug, hence Mug, and the name, Bugsy."

Peter shrugged. "I give up. So, where did he come up with the name Bugsy?"

"I was originally from Chicago, and had told him, when half-assed drunk, that I had been arrested once. John associated that with Bugsy Malone and the Chicago mob era, so he put Mug and Bugsy together, and came up with Mugsy.

"Stupid. I agree, but that's just the way his mind worked. It was a compliment if he thought enough of a person to give them a pet name. John explained that it meant he cared enough about someone to remember their existence."

"Did he have a name for Hilary?"

"Yes." Looking in her direction, Jake explained, "He used to call her Dolly, which again, was just a simple reorganization of the name, Lloyd. Before Hilary married Jack Adams, she was known as Hilary Lloyd. That's where John came up with the anagram Dolly."

"I can understand the word associations in order to memorize terms in med school, but why use word associations when remembering people he was close to?"

"I told you—for John, it was a way of playing with people without them knowing it. He loved creating riddles. But his riddles were fascinating only to John; pretty damn stupid to everyone else. When I once asked him how he ever got started doing it, he said that he began jumbling letters around as a child, so that he could have some control over things." Rolling his eyes, Jake added, "He never elaborated, and believe me, I never asked."

For a few minutes, Peter just sat. He didn't ask any questions. Without explanation, he picked up the microphone and haltingly stated he was going off the record for the purpose of conferring with counsel, Hilary Adams.

CHAPTER FORTY-EIGHT

Peter couldn't put his finger on it. He just instinctively knew. This information, provided almost as an afterthought, was important. He put the pen, which he had been doodling with throughout the statement, down on his desk. Looking directly at Hilary, he asked, "Were you aware that Bradley did this kind of thing?"

"Yes. Jake's right.' She shrugged her shoulders. "It was no big deal. Everyone knew John played games by re-arranging letters in names." Laughingly she added, "I'd forgotten all about it until now. The only person John said he could never re-name was Susan because she was perfect just the way she was. But that was years ago. I couldn't tell you whether he continued to use word associations, but I guess it's possible he may still have used them in business. But if he did, I never knew about it. And there would have been no reason for Susan to talk about it." Looking worried, she asked, "Why? Do you think it's important?"

"Maybe," mused Peter. He wasn't about to discuss his suspicions with Hilary, especially in front of her client who still remained the primary suspect. Covering, he said, "Why don't we just continue with the statement." He flipped the switch on the recorder. "We're back on tape.

"Mr. Stein, what happened after this—after you told Bradley all about the Judge, the baby and your desire to immediately dissolve the partnership?"

"Haven't you heard a thing I said? Do I have to re-plow it again?"

Peter nodded. "Humor me."

"As I said before, nothing happened. John just laughed, then told me it didn't matter anyway—that everything and everyone was lost now; nothing was left. Then he said, 'This means I'm free, Mugsy.' To which I said, 'And Susan wants to be free too. This should make it simple for everyone.'

"Then he turned to me, looked right past me, as if I wasn't even there and said, 'You don't understand, Mugsy. I'm not talking about Susan.'

"I asked him if he wasn't talking about Susan, then who was he talking about? Instead of a straight answer though, I got more gibberish."

Shifting in his chair Peter said, "Let's change the focus a little."

"I'm all for that."

"Would you say that your partner was well-off financially?"

"Let's put it this way. He had a lot more money than I ever had. I knew from talking to him and of course, from Susan, that Susan had a pretty hefty trust which was administered by John. Naturally I attributed a lot of his disposable income as originating from her account."

"How about you—what's your financial condition?"

With irritation, Stein shot back. "What's that got to do with anything?"

"Plenty. Perhaps you killed Bradley because you thought it was financially more advantageous to have him out of the picture. After all, you've admitted that you impregnated his wife who was holding the financial purse strings. And you've already admitted you were under the mistaken impression that you could buy the business for a bargain price from his wife, your lover, if your partner turned up conveniently dead. Sounds like a perfect plan to me."

Angrily, Jake rose from his chair. "Listen, I don't need this." Slamming his fist down hard on the table he shouted, "I grew to loathe the son of a bitch, but not enough to kill him." Leaning down, his face just inches from Peter's he said, "You see, besides my interest in Bradley & Stein, I've done very well in real estate investments. In fact, I've done so well, that Bradley & Stein wasn't my main source of income last year. That's why I would have preferred to end the partnership, and be on my own. I wanted to divide my time the way I wanted. I was tired of baby-sitting my business partner."

Slumping back down in his chair, Stein said, "The hassles with John didn't make the effort worth it any longer. But I sure wouldn't have jeopardized everything I had worked so hard for by murdering the bastard. Why in the world would I run the risk of being punished the rest of my life for murder, when divorce and dissolution of the partnership would have done the trick?"

"So who do you think killed Bradley?"

"How the hell should I know who it was who did us all a favor? Aren't you the expert on that?" Jake snorted. "Whoever it was though, I say, 'thank you.'" Bending over, his mouth directly over the microphone, Stein said, "Just remember this—I didn't do it, and Susan didn't do it either. She doesn't have the temperament, and I don't have the stomach, especially if the killing was accomplished by getting close enough to stab him."

"Getting back to that night, what happened after you had your little talk?"

"He told me to get out, which I did, quickly. His jolly good humor was fading fast. Frankly, I didn't want to be around when it all hit the fan."

"Did you leave by the front or back door?"

"The back door. And no, I wasn't trying to hide. I had pulled my car back behind the house when I arrived sometime after eight. I parked it under that big magnolia tree, in a spot next to the patio, just outside the french doors leading to the library. Susan doesn't have any type of drapery there, so when I left, I just opened the french doors and walked out. When I got to my car, for some reason, I looked back. I could see John through the windows."

"What was he doing?"

"Talking to someone on the telephone. That was the last time I saw Bradley alive."

"And what time was this?"

"I guess between eight-thirty, eight-forty-five, or so."

"Where did you go after you left the Bradley residence?"

"Home. I went directly home because I expected Susan to meet me there. It took about ten minutes to get back to my condo."

"Did you see or talk with anyone?"

"At that time of night, what do you think?"

"When did Susan arrive?"

"That's just it. She never did." Quickly correcting himself, he added, "When I was there, that is." Jake loosened his tie and unbuttoned the top button of his shirt. "When we talked earlier, she thought she'd be no later than eleven o'clock, but apparently she was a lot later."

"Why 'apparently?'" asked Peter.

"Because I fell asleep on the couch watching some insipidly stupid video. I didn't wake up until sometime after midnight. I called Susan's office right away, but there was no answer."

"What did you do then?"

"What do you think? I got in my car and drove to the courthouse, but there was no light on in her office window. As usual, her cell phone was turned off. She has a bad habit of doing that. I tried to calm down, convincing myself, that she was fine and probably back at the condo. So I drove back home, but she wasn't there waiting as I had hoped. There was a note though, saying that she had been there, waited awhile, then decided to go home. She'd call when she got there."

"So why didn't you wait until she called?"

"Because I was worried about John's frame of mind and what he might be capable of doing. I thought she might be in trouble. I retraced my steps and drove over to their house. When I got there I didn't bother pulling my car around the back. I knocked on the front door, but there was no answer. Since I heard nothing like arguing going on, I knocked again. Still, there was no answer. I turned the knob. It was unlocked, so I stepped inside. Susan must have heard me by then and came toward the door. She looked awful."

"Can you describe her appearance?"

"She had just found her husband murdered. What do you think she looked like? She looked like hell!"

"What did she say?"

"Absolutely nothing. She just grabbed my hand and dragged me into the library and pointed to where John was lying on the floor. I guess I had just enough med school in me, that the first reaction I had was to go over to where he was and feel for a pulse. There was none. He was dead, and from what I could tell, had been for some time."

"What was running through your head at that time?"

"A lot of things. That Susan needed to call the police, and frankly, if the truth be known, I was thinking I needed to get out of there."

"Did you think Susan had killed him?"

Jake said nothing. He stared at Peter, his jaw clenching. "And why would you ask that?"

"Did you?"

"I didn't know what had happened. All sorts of things go through your mind. I knew that John had been emotionally abusive toward Susan in the past. And after what I had told him earlier that night, I honestly couldn't tell you what I thought Bradley was capable of doing to her. Why do you think I raced like the devil to get back there that night? I thought Susan may be in danger."

"I'm going to ask the same question again. At that moment, did you think that the Judge had killed her husband?"

"No, I did not. And if you want hard evidence to confirm that, let me remind you that you retrieved the suit she was wearing that night. I saw no blood on that suit when I arrived. If there was blood there, it was microscopic. John, on the other hand, was covered in blood. So the person who killed him would have been covered in blood too. That leaves Susan out."

"Maybe," Peter conceded. "But does it leave you out?" Peter opened up a file folder in front of him on the table. He quickly scanned the page for the information he was looking for. "Not to change the subject, but what size shoe do you wear?"

"10 C. Why?"

"Because at the scene we found a partial footprint in the deceased's blood which the crime lab indicates was, guess what? A size 10 C."

Looking stricken, Jake gripped the table. "What do you want me to say? I guess it's possible I stepped in blood at some point that night. I told you I felt for a pulse, and I remember getting blood on my hands when I did that. God knows, it was everywhere."

Peter said nothing. He wanted to see how Stein handled this unexpected news.

"That's the best explanation I can give you. Frankly, it's the only one I've got."

"Do you still have the shoes you had on that night?"

"They cost three hundred and fifty bucks. Of course I still have them."

"Will you voluntarily produce them, or do I need a search warrant?"

"You may have them. Be my guest. I have nothing to hide."

"Before we end this taped statement, let me ask you a little bit more about your background. How long ago were you arrested, and for what?"

"You'll find it out anyway. That's why I volunteered it. At nineteen, I was arrested for trafficking in marijuana. It was later knocked down to possession as part of a plea agreement."

"Is there more?" Peter asked.

"At the risk of sounding like poor me, I grew up on the south side of Chicago. My parents had no money, no education, no skills. Half the time, I never knew from one day to the next, where we'd be living. My old man was a no good drunk. I was just a kid, and if you haven't gotten the picture yet, life sucked, so I got into trouble because there was nothing else to do. But I was good in school—it was all I had to hang onto.

"When I got arrested, I was pre-med, hoping to go to med school. They thought I had a good chance of having a successful career, in spite of my background. So, not only did I get the original charge amended, I got the classification amended too. That way, it didn't affect my status later when I was accepted into med school. All this took place a long, long time ago, almost too long ago to remember. But unfortunately, because of that one small infraction, my prints are still on file. I know I have an FBI rap sheet, because I was stopped for speeding last year and they ran the registration. My rap sheet popped up also."

Peter closed the file folder in front of him. "I appreciate you being honest about it. That goes a long way with me. Truth is, we already ran your prints through our computers. We did that yesterday.

"We lifted a partial at the scene that was initially unidentifiable. It didn't match the occupants, or people whom we knew to be there with any degree of regularity. There were only five prints lifted in all, along with lots and lots of smudges. Fortunately for us, the housekeeper had cleaned the library that afternoon, so those five prints were the only prints found. Two belonged to the deceased; one to Susan; the other to the housekeeper. Until yesterday, that partial print couldn't be identified. Today, it can be. It belongs to you, my friend. Have an explanation?"

"Well, it sure doesn't take a genius to figure out why it was there. I've already admitted to being at the house that night. So what?"

"So why didn't we find another set of prints—those belonging to the killer?"

"Maybe the killer wiped the place clean, or wore gloves. Those explanations work for me." With his eyes turning ice blue Jake asked, "Why are you trying to railroad me? I didn't do it. It's obvious, you just want to make a collar. It doesn't particularly matter who, just so you tag somebody."

"Sorry you feel that way, because it just makes this more difficult." He didn't want to look in Hilary's direction. But he had to do this. It was the only way.

"It's my duty to inform you that you are under arrest for the murder of John Michael Bradley."

"What the fuck are you talking about?"

"Mr. Stein, you admit you were the last person to see John Bradley alive on February 18th. You admit that you were, and are, having a sexual relationship with his wife, Judge Susan Emmett-Bradley. You admit you are the father of the baby she is carrying. You admit you wanted out of the partnership with the deceased. You admit your partner's aberrant behavior exposed you to some liability. You admit that your shoe size is the same size as the bloody shoe print found at the scene. Your fingerprint was lifted from the library in the Bradley residence where the deceased's body was found. And lastly, you have a criminal record which indicates that you're quite capable of breaking the law."

Peter pulled a pair of handcuffs from his back pocket, placed them on Stein's wrists and adjusted them until they snapped shut, digging into his skin. "For all those reasons, you are now under arrest. Larry Benovitz is the Assistant Commonwealth's Attorney assigned to your case. I'll put a call into him advising of your arrest. Your arraignment will be set for tomorrow morning at nine o'clock. At that time, as your lawyer will tell you, bail will be fixed in an amount the court and prosecutor think is appropriate and commensurate with the gravity of the offense.

"Your lawyer may now accompany you through the booking process. This ends the interview."

CHAPTER FORTY-NINE

As usual, Hilary decided, Peter had again arrested the wrong person. "Why do I have to do my job and his too?" she grumbled to herself.

Balancing her brief case in one hand, and a cup of hot coffee in the other, she opened, then kicked her office door closed, behind her. Immediately dumping the bulging brief case on her credenza and the steaming coffee on her desk, she turned and dejectedly plopped down in her chair. She knew Jake was innocent of John's murder. But how could she prove it? He was such a made to order suspect.

No, she thought, *Jake may be guilty of bad taste, bad manners, bad judgement, and most of all, bad timing, but he sure wasn't guilty of murder.*

Frowning, Hilary reached over to a wooden letter tray on her desk and grabbed Susan's file which contained the legal pad she had used several days before when trying to figure out who else, besides Susan, could be considered a viable suspect. Slowly opening the file, she pulled out the writing pad and looked down at the unanswered questions written several days before, that now seemed to be staring right back at her, begging, as was she, for an answer.

Absently she spun herself around and around in her goose-necked swivel chair trying to think. Making herself nothing but dizzy however, Hilary stopped on the forth go-round and pulled her chair flush against her desk. Reflecting back on everything learned in the last forty-eight hours, she tentatively picked up a pen, and tapping it lightly against her cheek, decided her best bet in breaking the mental log jam was to add more questions to her "who, what, and why" list. Maybe writing them out would, this second time, prompt much needed answers.

Leaning hard on her elbow, she flipped to the next page of the legal pad and wrote, (1) Who is Rick O'Neill? (2) Is he the same person whom John referenced when attempting to explain to Susan why he had sexually explicit photos in his coat pocket? (3) What's the significance of John's word associations? (4) If the killer was someone whom John knew, then it follows that that someone was a person whom John either trusted, or for some reason, didn't fear—does that leave out Jake and Susan? (5) Was John murdered by one of the women he paid for sexual performances? (6) Was he killed over a bad business deal? (7) Was the money he took from Susan's trust being used to pay someone off? In parentheses, she added, But then why kill the goose that laid the proverbial golden egg?

For several minutes, Hilary read and re-read what she had just written. But writing questions down today didn't help any more than it had before. Again, no answers came to mind. Discouraged, and more than a little angry with herself as well as with the system, she slammed the file shut and stood up.

"None of this makes sense. Peter must know something I don't. He must."

With a look of determination, she bent down and picked up the phone. Still thinking about what she was going to say, she slowly dialed Peter's private line.

On the second ring he picked up. "Lieutenant. Elliott. May I help you?"

Without words of greeting, she replied, "You know Jake didn't do this, don't you?"

"Nice to hear from you too, Hil, but I know nothing of the sort. All the evidence points to him as the killer and you know it. Accept it. He murdered John Bradley."

"Trust me, he didn't."

"It's not a matter of trust. It's a matter of evidence. Do you have any idea how many defense attorneys call to try and sell me this same line of baloney? Hunches from an accused's lawyer just don't cut it. I'm sorry."

"Listen to me. Obviously, I'm not privy to all your investigative letters, but please, do me a favor and take one more look at those file folders we retrieved from John's desk at home. There's something about those files, that bothers me. I know we've overlooked something, and it's your job to find it."

"Hil, thanks for the heads up, but what you're suggesting is nothing more than an exercise in futility. Quit the amateur sleuthing and keep your day job. We've got our man."

"Stop being so smug and listen to what I'm trying to tell you. It's not as if you've never made a mistake and as a result of that mistake, arrested the wrong person. As I said, please, take one more look at those files. . . . I know I'm right."

"Okay. But only because it's you. No promises though, okay?"

Hilary replaced the receiver and smiled. *Everything's going to turn out just fine. I just know it.*

CHAPTER FIFTY

Just before quitting time, Peter put in an emergency request to the phone company. ASAP, he wanted all records pulled which pertained to any outgoing calls made from the Bradley residence on February 18th and 19th. The records' custodian promised the information by eight-thirty the following morning, explaining that anything faster than next day service was impossible. The computers were up and running only between the hours of eight o'clock a.m. and four o'clock p.m., no exceptions, even for the police. Peter had no choice; he had to wait.

But even knowing he could do nothing until the following morning, Peter couldn't make himself go home. He opted instead to stay late at headquarters, taking all emergency calls personally. Since everyone else was still busy putting prelims together on the O'Hara incident, Peter was still flying solo.

Burjinsky had called in saying he expected to be on his way back to the station within the hour, advising Peter not to worry—the case, which had been officially upgraded from Assault to Murder, was a wrap. They had the suspect, murder weapon, motive, and nine witnesses, each in various stages of drunkenness. "So what do you expect when the murder scene's a bar?" asked Burjinski.

Sitting back in his leather chair which had seen better days, his stocking feet resting comfortably on his desk, Peter took a moment to relax and think about the day. *Here I am busting my ass on this Bradley case, and after two weeks of around-the-clock investigation, we finally make an arrest. But instead of feeling good about it, as usual, I feel something's not right. God, I'm so tired of these second and third guesses. And Hilary's call sure didn't help matters.*

To try and feel better, he reminded himself that Stein had motive, opportunity, and no verifiable alibi to account for his whereabouts at the time of the murder. But somehow, those reasons, which sounded good at the time of Stein's arrest, now weren't very reassuring.

Part of what bothered him was the feeling that, in spite of the evidence, Stein just might have been telling the truth. Peter twisted uncomfortably in his chair Although trying to resist, he couldn't help but relive his recent conversation with Hilary. She had hit a nerve—a year before, in the interests of expediency, Peter had made a wrong decision, resulting in a precipitous arrest. Guiltily, he remembered how cock sure he had been about the case. The arrest had been an error in judgment, made worse because all the signs had been there. Unfortunately, he chose to ignore them. If he had just listened . . .

Peter had vowed never to make that same mistake twice. But in this case, as Hilary warned, could he be sure he wasn't making another one of those errors in judgment?

"Damn!" Restless, he walked the length of his office, stopped in front of the five foot tall file cabinet, nestled in the far corner, labeled, "Current Cases Pending," and pulled out the bottom drawer. Inside were all the investigative letters Peter received and reviewed daily on the Bradley murder. All neatly bound in chronological order, there were five volumes in all, including crime lab reports which measured an intimidating four inches in thickness.

Eerily, Hilary's words kept resonating in his brain—"I know we've overlooked something and it's your job to find it."

Sighing, Peter bent over, reached in and removed the first three black pasteboard files, then returned to his desk and flipped on the green shaded desk lamp. If anyone had stopped in and asked him at that particular moment just what it was he was looking for, Peter would have been hard-pressed to give a cogent reply. But what else did he have to do? Besides, he had promised Hilary.

Opening each file, he looked at the neatly typed table of contents page. Without concern for time, he let his index finger roam aimlessly downward toward the bottom of the page, then slowly move upward in search of something Peter, like Hilary, instinctively knew, had been missed. It was there, a clue as obvious as a name tucked in one of John Bradley's hidden word games, but where exactly was it?

To himself, Peter thought, *to be absolutely sure, I need to check out one more thing—that new piece of evidence, the name, Rick—the same name used by the john tracked down by Rigger—Rick has to be Bradley. And Rick has to be Rick O'Neill—the name Bradley scribbled down when registering at those sleazy flea-bag hotels. By the same token, it couldn't have been just a coincidence that Bradley mentioned the name, Rick, when hit with the news that his wife was 'about to divorce his ass,' as Jake so charitably put it. And, the Rick whom Stein mentioned, has to be the same Rick Hilary heard about from her client's girlfriend, and the same Rick who frequented prostitutes. It all fits.*

Hell, maybe I've been going about this all wrong. Instead of Rick O'Neill being a real person, Rick O'Neill could be one of Bradley's anagrams.

Unfortunately for Peter, however, word games had never been his long suit. Even as a child he hated them. And now, as an adult, he still steered clear of playing the newspaper's daily crossword puzzle, even if desperate for entertainment.

After thirty minutes of tearing his hair out in frustration, trying every which way to transpose letters, Peter was still no further along than when he started. He looked down at the nonsensical scribbles he had written across the note pad in front of him, all originating from the root name, Rick O'Neill. Begrudgingly, he accepted the possibility that Rick O'Neill may not be an anagram.

On a hunch though, he pulled out the center drawer of his desk, grabbed the Greater Louisville phone book and looked up the name O'Neill. He counted two Richard O'Neills and one R. O'Neill. *Great, maybe Rick O'Neill is a real person. So much for anagrams.* To make matters worse, Peter discovered the directory listed three additional ways to spell the name, O'Neill.

"God damn it," he muttered. "This is stupid and probably the biggest waste of time, but I'll give it one last shot and spell it a different way." Choosing the spelling, O'-N-e-a-l, he irritably flipped over the sheet of paper, and on the reverse side, wrote the alternate spelling in oversized letters. Within seconds, he was rewarded when, by rearranging them, he had succeeded in actually forming another word—the word, "alone."

Peter was ecstatic. But his excitement was short-lived when he quickly realized that he still hadn't figured out the *full* anagram, if in fact, the name was an anagram to begin with. He had an anagram for O'Neal, but where was the anagram in the name, Rick?

Again, Peter tried to rearrange letters, swearing all the while, that he should have known nothing could be as easy the second time around. After spending another five minutes staring at the results, he had to admit, that in rearranging them, he only kept repeating the same configuration time and again with no success. Finally giving up, he threw down the pen. Grabbing his jacket, he muttered, "It's time to go home."

But halfway out the door, as he hit the lights, Peter had a brainstorm. "Wait a minute, if Bradley didn't spell O'Neill in the customary way, he could have changed the customary spelling of the name, Rick, too." Throwing his coat down once more across the desk, Peter grabbed the pen and paper he had been using just seconds before. Still standing, he wrote down every possible spelling he could think of for the name, Rick. He came up with two choices—Ric or Rik. But in rearranging those two spellings, he found nothing worked except grouping the letters to read, Cri or Kri. The words sounded phonetically like the real word, "cry," but obviously, neither was spelled correctly. Peter then decided to try reversing the letters of the word, "cry," as he had done previously with the name, O'Neal. This time he came up with, "Ryc," but, shaking his head, immediately scratched it out. That was too easy.

Then thinking better of it after looking at it for the second time, he mumbled, "Who said that the name had to be spelled a certain way? That's it!" he shouted excitedly. "It really doesn't matter how it's spelled, because when Bradley mentioned it out loud to Stein on the night he was murdered, it sounded like, Rick." He looked at the paper in front of him. A genuine double anagram—Cry alone or Ryc alone.

Peter sat back down in his chair. "Does any of this really matter?" he asked himself.

CHAPTER FIFTY-ONE

Peter spent a restless night dreaming about a collage of nightmarish scenarios—Ryc O'Neal, who looked a lot like John Bradley, crying alone in a pool of blood; Jake Stein, who looked a lot scared as he was led to the electric chair screaming he'd been framed by a man with a prosthetic leg; and Hilary, who looked a lot angry as she slammed a door shut screaming, "I told you—you have the wrong guy." Finally, at five o'clock, Peter gave up on the idea of sleep. And even though he wasn't due back at headquarters until eleven, he got up, took a leisurely shower, dressed, ate breakfast, and was out of the house by six-thirty.

Though exhausted, the added jump on his morning's schedule would provide plenty of time for Peter to take care of all routine matters before the Bradley phone logs were ready. If possible, he wanted to see them before Stein's arraignment. And he knew, once the media learned of Stein's arrest, the case would turn into a three-ring circus. He'd never again have any peace and quiet.

Fortunately, the phone company was as good as its word. The records were ready for pickup at eight-fifteen, fifteen minutes ahead of schedule. Not surprisingly, Peter decided to retrieve them personally, and within minutes, the eagerly awaited print-outs were in his hands. In its entirety, the computer generated record measured just three lines across one page, but after reading those three lines, Peter let out a low, slow whistle. Flipping through his spiral note pad, he stopped abruptly. *I thought I recognized that number, and by God, I was right.*

Turning to the phone company's receptionist, he asked, "I feel kind of stupid asking the phone company this question, but I left my cell in the squad car. Do you have a phone I might use?"

Without raising her head from the newspaper propped open in front of her, the receptionist pointed. "There."

Looking in the direction indicated, Peter walked over to a bank of telephones artfully hidden behind the receptionist's cubicle, and dialed the number reflected on the print-out. He allowed the phone to ring four times, then heard the unmistakable click of an answering machine being activated. "No one is available at this time. Please leave your name and a message. Thank you for calling."

The last thing Peter wanted to do was leave his name and accompanying message. And since he knew where he could reach the party, he decided to communicate in person. And if he hurried, he knew he could catch her before she left for court.

CHAPTER FIFTY-TWO

"Good morning. May I help you?" asked the receptionist as she slowly, but pointedly, looked Peter up and down.

"Yes, you can. I guess you don't remember me. Peter Elliott, City Homicide. I'd like to see your boss, please."

Smiling an icy, condescending smile, the receptionist pulled out her message pad. "Sorry, Lieutenant, but she's in conference right now, preparing for a deposition." Between pursed lips, chapped by the cold, she added, "It would be quite impossible for her to meet with you now. Perhaps if you would leave a number where you could be reached sometime later today, I could set up a proper appointment time for you? She's just so—"

Not wanting to listen to her prattle on, Peter interrupted. "Let me make something perfectly clear, Ms.—?"

"Ms. Trevor," she answered while wrinkling her nose and patting her bouffant beehive hairdo.

Peter bent his head and lowered his voice. "This isn't a request. I don't wait on phone calls. That's the beauty of this business I'm in. People talk with me when I want them to talk with me. So, tell your boss I'm here, and that I want to talk with her. Now."

Giving Peter a withering look, Ms. Trevor asked him to take a seat.

Three minutes later, she returned. Holding her head up high she peevishly advised, "Since you won't take 'No' for an answer, she'll see you now, but only for fifteen minutes. She's due in court for a hearing, and will have to leave soon, unless of course, you want to talk with Judge Hamblin. Maybe, in your powerful position, you could explain to him how being a police officer entitles you to certain luxuries that the rest of us don't have."

"I'll keep your time constraints in mind, Ms. Trevor," Peter said, trying hard to be civil. Soundlessly, he followed Ms. Trevor into a small conference room at the end of a long carpeted hallway. She said nothing as she closed the door, more loudly than necessary. Peter got the point.

He took off his coat and waited. Then waited some more. Looking at his watch, he figured he had lost at least ten of the fifteen minutes allotted him, just waiting for her royal highness to make an appearance.

When the door to the conference room finally opened and Caroline Witten appeared, no pleasantries were exchanged. Peter got straight to the point. "Why did John Bradley call you on the night he was murdered?"

Until that moment, Caroline Witten had stood, poised and relaxed, still holding onto the door she had just passed though. Suddenly, she made a jerking movement towards the table, gripped the back of her chair for support, and sat down.

"How did you know?"

"Two words. Phone records."

Chagrined, she answered softly, "Of course. I should have known." She looked down at her hands clasped together in her lap. "I just felt so guilty because I didn't somehow save him that night."

Unwilling to be sidetracked, Peter demanded, "Please answer my question. Why did he call you?"

"I guess to tell me he was divorcing Susan. He said something like, not only would he be free of her, more importantly, he would also be free of the monkey he'd been carrying around on his back. I asked him what he meant, but he didn't explain. He said he just wanted me to know." She shrugged her shoulders. "As I said, we didn't talk long." Softly, she added, "I couldn't. I wasn't alone."

Peter looked at her curiously. "I hate to be so blunt, but why would he call you, of all people? Hadn't you been involved in a nasty breakup with him not too long ago?"

"Yes. But in spite of that, John and I remained in touch, although each for different reasons." Blinking her eyes, trying to hold back tears, she admitted, "I still loved him; he needed a shoulder to cry on. Sick, I admit, but at least it allowed me to stay connected. I needed him, and he knew he could always count on me, no matter what." She grimaced. "A match made in heaven, wouldn't you agree?"

Feeling uncomfortable with her display of self-deprecation, Peter decided to change the focus. "This may seem like a strange question, but did he have a pet name for you?"

Seemingly taken off-guard, Caroline Witten laughed. "What an odd thing to ask. But yes, he did. He used to call me Citten, spelled with a 'C' rather than a 'K'. It was a combination of the letter 'C' in Caroline and my last name, Witten."

She studied him closely as if trying to determine if Peter was mocking her. "It was just a game, Lieutenant. There was no harm done. John loved to rearrange letters in people's names. So what? It didn't matter if the spelling wasn't right, just so it sounded right." Suddenly looking scared she asked, "How is that relevant to the investigation? Are you telling me that the murderer had a pet name too?"

Peter looked at her curiously. "You know, I hadn't thought of that." He wrote a quick notation to himself and stuffed it into his breast pocket. "Here's another off-the-wall question for you, but bear with me. Did you ever know anyone by the name, Rick O'Neill? I'm not sure of the spelling—it could be, O-'-N-e-a-l, but as you said, Bradley didn't care about spelling—just how it sounded. And more importantly, did you ever hear John use that name in any context, or at any time?"

"No, he never mentioned that name to me, and of course, we didn't go out in public together, so I wouldn't have had much of an opportunity to meet any of John's acquaintances or friends."

Persistent, Peter asked, "Does just the name, Rick, mean anything to you with regard to Bradley?"

Visibly shaken by another question she clearly hadn't expected, Caroline Witten answered, "Yes. But its connection may be a little too tenuous even for your purposes."

"Well, why don't you let me determine that."

"Okay. You're the boss, or so you've told my receptionist," she answered sarcastically.

"John told me once that when he was a little boy, whenever he could, he used the name, Rick, instead of his own."

"Did he tell you why?"

"No. I just gathered that the name represented a personality whom John created and turned to as a kind of safety net when necessary. He never came out and said it, but I don't think he had a very loving childhood."

"If John Bradley had been in trouble, would he have turned to you for help?"

Caroline Witten thought for a moment before answering. "If John was going to turn to anyone, I believe it would have been me. Let's put it this way, he wouldn't have turned to the

'Ice Queen,' Judge Susan. But why all the questions—was John in some kind of trouble?"

"He may have thought he was." Peter put his hands in his pockets. "Not to change the subject again, but since you don't have much time, I'll get to the point. When you were seeing Bradley, you mentioned that he spent a lot of money on you."

"Yeah. So?"

"Knowing him as well as you apparently did, do you think it possible for him to have gone through half a million in a little over six months without blinking an eye?"

"No. John was extravagant, but not to that extreme. I assumed, like the rest of us, he had limits too."

Peter stood. "I won't take up any more of your time." He pushed his chair back under the table. "Oh, by the way, you're going to hear about this sooner or later anyway, so I may as well tell you myself. Jake Stein, Bradley's former partner, was arrested last night for Bradley's murder."

Caroline Witten looked at Peter and frowned. "I knew that he and John had their differences as to how the business should be run, but from what John said about Jake personally, I find it difficult to believe that Jake murdered him. Who's representing him?"

"Sorry, job's been taken. Hilary Adams."

Caroline Witten laughed. "Oh, I wouldn't want his business. I prefer nice messy divorces where the parties have assets of at least half a million. Otherwise, it's not worth my time. Besides, everyone knows, Hilary Adams is the best money can buy. He's lucky to have gotten her. But she doesn't come cheap either."

Caroline Witten paused as she walked though the doorway. "Anything else?"

"Do me a favor, Ms. Witten, if you think of anything else that might prove useful, let me know, would you?"

"Are you saying you haven't completed your investigation?" She looked at him suspiciously. "Then why would you make an arrest?"

Irritated, Peter shot back, "Because the evidence supported it. Thanks for your time."

CHAPTER FIFTY-THREE

Again feeling restless, but not for any reason he could put his finger on, Peter returned to the office, pulled two, three-ring binders containing his detectives' investigative letters from the Bradley case, and stacked them, one on top of the other, on his desk. Still standing, he bent down and thumbed listlessly through the voluminous reports, but suddenly stopped short when he came to the name, Liam Leprakalb. According to the reports he now held in his hand, no one had been able to trace the name, either in the phone book, or through the deceased's acquaintances. For all intents and purposes, Liam Leprakalb simply didn't exist. So who was he? And, more importantly, did he have anything at all to do with Bradley's murder? And if Leprakalb didn't, then why was his name so prominently displayed on one of only five file folders left in the deceased's desk? Chuckling, he again remembered Hilary's haunting words—"I know we've overlooked something. And it's your job to find it."

Having nothing else pressing, Peter sat down at his desk, pushed all the reports to one side and again brought out the legal sized note pad he had used the night before when rearranging letters in the name, Rick O'Neill or Rick O'Neal, however one wanted to spell it.

Maybe Liam Leprakalb was an anagram and not the name of a real person. Slowly, he wrote Liam Leprakalb, in one inch letters, tore all the letters from the page in long narrow strips, reduced each to as perfect a square as he could manage, then let them fall from his hands in a lopsided jagged pile. Gingerly picking them up, and righting them, he placed each side by side in a nonsensical line containing a total of thirteen letters. "Thirteen. That's unlucky to begin with," he muttered. Frustrated by what appeared at first, to be a round of *Scrabble* with all consonants and no vowels, Peter removed his glasses and began furiously rubbing his eyes. Weary and discouraged, he looked down to retrieve his glasses and noticed that somehow, four letters had separated from the rest.

Suddenly, Peter slammed his fist on the desk, shouting, "Oh shit," in a voice loud enough for everyone to hear. Immediately picking up the phone, once he found it, hidden under the pile of investigative reports, Peter placed a call to Caroline Witten's office.

This time, Ms. Trevor put him through right away, but not before lecturing him on how fortunate he was to have found Ms. Witten in and available. Politely listening, Peter thought it safer to make no comment. He was put on hold, but not for long.

"Hello again. What may I do for you now?" asked Caroline Witten.

Peter didn't waste any time in conveying how deadly serious his request was. "Answer a couple more questions," he demanded in a sharp, clipped tone. "You mentioned that when John Bradley called you on the night of his murder, you didn't talk long because you weren't alone. Did I understand you correctly?"

"Yes, but why—" she asked, unease in her voice.

Taking a long deep breath before he next spoke, Peter assured her his request was a simple one. He wanted a yes or no answer to a name he would provide. He then posed the question.

Caroline Witten answered simply. "Yes."

Slowly, Peter put down the phone. He sat still for several seconds, trying to put all the pieces together. *Hilary, as usual, was right on the money.*

Suddenly, without saying anything to anyone, he grabbed his coat, headed out the door, and drove the two blocks in between the station and his intended destination. When he arrived, he merely presented his badge to the receptionist and told her whom he was there to see. He didn't bother to take a seat in the plush, perfectly appointed waiting area. He figured right that he wouldn't be waiting long.

When the door to the spacious partner's office closed quietly behind him, Peter strode confidently to the center of the room. "Good morning, Sir. I've come to talk to you about John Bradley."

"Please, have a seat," replied the ever affable Edward Arpel. He turned sharply on his heel, giving Peter his full attention. "Perhaps you don't know this, but I've already answered questions that were asked of me by one of your detectives." He put his hand to his forehead as if physically trying to pull the name from his mind. "I believe his card read, DeAngelo."

"I know all about your previous discussion with Detective DeAngelo. I'm here with some follow-up."

With a wave of his hand, which Peter noticed was trembling, albeit slightly, Arpel announced, "I don't know what else I can do." He raised his eyebrows, as if asking a question. What came out of his mouth however, was an announcement, that judging from Arpel's tone, was news that pleased him. "Besides, I just came from the courthouse where I heard the news about his partner's arrest." Laughing politely he added, "It appears the mystery has been solved. So what more can I do?"

Peter sat down, uninvited. "Let's just say I could use your help in tying up some loose ends."

Arpel removed his reading glasses, blinked several times, then warily slumped down in the chair opposite the Lieutenant. "The whole situation is horrible. Anything to help."

Peter tried a smile. It was difficult.

"For starters, why don't you help by telling me why you killed John Bradley?"

Arpel's eyes narrowed, then locked onto Peter's. "Whatever are you talking about? If this is this some kind of sick joke, I don't see the humor."

"I can assure you, it's no joke," Peter answered evenly. "So, I'm going to ask you one more time. Why did you kill John Bradley?"

"And for the second time, and hopefully for the last, what in God's name are you talking about?"

"I'll have to hand it to you. You were very clever. But unfortunately for you, Bradley's been able to do something I wouldn't have thought possible. He actually succeeded in communicating, so to speak, from his grave."

Arpel's smile vanished, replaced with a look of defiance. "Perhaps I was too hasty. Maybe I want to listen to this ludicrous tale after all. Please, do go on," he encouraged.

"You were blackmailing him, weren't you?"

"Don't be ridiculous!" thundered Arpel.

"Tell me, what exactly did you have on him that was worth all the money he paid you?"

Clutching the arms of his chair with such force that his knuckles looked as though they were about to break through the skin, Arpel argued, "I have no idea what you're talking about. You need to get what my children refer to as a 'grip on things.'"

Peter got up from his chair and moved closer to Arpel whose face had violently contorted into a near apoplectic rage. "Cut the crap, Counselor. I know all about your little dalliance with Caroline Witten. I also know you were with her at her home the night Bradley was murdered." Leaning down, his eyes level with Arpel's, Peter said, "Now why don't you 'get a grip' on the truth and stop wasting my time?"

Arpel pushed his body to the back of his chair in a feeble attempt to put distance between himself and Peter. He tittered nervously. Beads of sweat, forming on his upper lip and forehead betrayed him; the shaking had become more pronounced. Peter could smell the fear.

Brushing back a shock of hair which had fallen across his forehead, Arpel hissed, "So what if I was at Ms. Witten's home on the night Bradley was killed? What the hell does that prove, other than two attorneys got together on a case. And what does that have to do with Bradley? From what I heard he wasn't murdered at Caroline Witten's home, was he?"

Distractedly picking a piece of lint from his dark navy suit, he asked sarcastically, "And if I'm at Caroline Witten's home on the night Bradley was murdered, as you told me I was, don't I have what you professionals in criminal behavior call an alibi?"

Peter ignored his question and asked one of his own. "Let's try another tack. How have you been financing your campaign?"

Arpel snorted in disdain. "How do you think I've been financing my campaign? I'm managing partner of the biggest law firm in the state. Last year, I made in excess of six-hundred thousand. That kind of money goes a long way in financing a judicial race, believe you me!"

Peter continued to stare, not wanting to interrupt what he knew was sure to come. He wanted Arpel to talk; Arpel stupidly obliged.

"Besides what I earn personally, I have a great many supporters who volunteer their time and efforts to what they believe is a worthy cause—my candidacy. I admit the media campaign has cost more than I originally anticipated, but the end result is worth it." Leaning forward in earnest, his jowls shaking in denial, he added, "I'm not saying my opponent isn't worthy, I'm just saying, with as much modesty as possible, I'm the better choice."

There he goes with that asinine Buddha smile again, Peter thought. "Save it Arpel. It's wasted on me."

Arpel stood and walked behind his desk and sat down. "I fail to see the connection between my friendship with Ms. Witten and the murder of my opponent's husband. Therefore, I don't think we have anything more to discuss." With his hand on the intercom, he said, "I'll have my secretary show you out. Good day, Lieutenant."

But Peter didn't move, and Arpel didn't bother to hide his disappointment. He tapped his pen impatiently but soundlessly on the black leather desk pad. He tried again. "As I said, I think this discussion is over."

"Oh, let's not be too hasty. I think we have a lot more to talk about." Peter again took his seat and comfortably crossed his legs. Arpel glared but said nothing.

"Why don't we begin with the rather well-known fact that your financial picture isn't as rosy as you would like everyone to believe. After all, in the last nine months, your firm has been embroiled in a great big, messy investigation involving one of your more junior associates, accused of shaking down a couple of witnesses and losing crucial evidence in a pending criminal matter. All done under the knowing, watchful eyes of some of your fellow partners who saw the scam as a chance to make some fast money." Peter flashed a smile of understanding. "It's no wonder at all, that you want to get out of this snake pit and onto the Bench—if successful, you could effectively distance yourself from inevitable financial disaster."

Peter heard the unmistakable intake of air as Arpel gulped hard and literally squirmed in his seat as if his pants, so precisely creased, were suddenly on fire. Peter continued, enjoying every second of Arpel's visible discomfort.

"I also understand that profit for this current year wasn't as hefty as it had been in the past, due to the firm having to hire its own outside counsel in the hopes of stopping a full blown federal grand jury investigation. In other words, your partnership draw wasn't as obscenely generous as in the past."

Arpel's mouth sagged in disbelief.

"I may work at the local level, but law enforcement agencies cooperate with each other. Up to now, you may have been able to keep it from the public in your campaign, but I know all about your law firm."

Peter knew he had hit a nerve when he noted the color fading from Arpel's face at a rate faster than that of a six week old henna rinse. "Your firm's in big trouble and everyone knows it, especially those of us who have anything to do with the criminal justice system. So, why don't we start where we left off?"

With a look of undisguised disdain, Peter asked for the third time, "Why did you kill John Bradley?"

CHAPTER FIFTY-FOUR

In an instant, Edward Arpel's demeanor changed. The handsome, always in control, public face was gone. In its place, a reflection of terror. Peter watched in fascination as Arpel's hands began shaking uncontrollably, and his eyes darted furtively about the four corners of his office, as if in a desperate search to find a means to escape. Met with the obvious, that there was no place to run or hide, Arpel slumped dejectedly in his chair. Surprisingly however, in spite of his own body language betraying him, Arpel's articulated response to Peter's question did not immediately resonate defeat.

"You think you've got this all figured out, don't you, Lieutenant?" He laughed defiantly. "Let me tell you—you haven't a clue."

"I *do* have it all figured out, so for you to continue denying guilt is not only useless, it's stupid. And since you're far from stupid, why don't you help yourself and give it up."

Seemingly oblivious to what was being said, Arpel didn't bat an eye. Stubbornly, Peter decided to give it one more try.

"I don't think I need to tell you, how ugly a trial will be, or how demeaning it will be awaiting trial for at least a year in the county jail. A jail crammed with inmates accused of everything from murder to sexual assault to the use of illicit drugs. And with the way you look, you'll be easy prey for any young wannabe hustler." Peter let this sink in as he studied him closely. Arpel's jaw clenched. Had Peter finally made some progress in breaking down the seemingly impenetrable Edward Arpel?

Taking the unbroken silence as an opportunity to continue pecking away at Arpel's pride, which Peter believed was perfectly counterbalanced by Arpel's innate cowardice, he asked, "Just how long do you think you'd last? And if you foolishly think you'll receive a 'get out of jail free card' while awaiting trial, think again. With this being a capital offense, bail won't even be an option. No, I'm afraid you'll be in for the long haul."

Met with Arpel's continued lack of contrition, Peter decided to try a different approach. Arpel had to be vulnerable somewhere—perhaps his family was the key. "I understand your wife is very ill. Knowing that, you need to ask yourself, do I really want to put her through all that?"

It didn't take but a second. Peter could see that with his last comment, if nothing else, he finally had Arpel's attention.

Sitting up, Arpel smugly explained, "Even if what you are alleging is true—that I killed Bradley, you can't begin to prove it." Throwing his head back, he smiled dismissively as if scoring a point.

"Just watch me. As I said, you could be facing the death penalty. In taking files and other material from Bradley, you committed not only murder, but robbery too. Not to preach, Counselor, but that's called felony murder, which if convicted, and after all appeals are exhausted, entitles you to a lethal injection, compliments of the great Commonwealth of Kentucky. But if you help yourself by admitting it and telling us why, who knows, the prosecutor may take pity on you and charge you with the lesser offense of Manslaughter. So, what will it be?"

Arpel looked at Peter with a steady gaze. "I could make you work for my confession, you know."

"Again, what'll it be, Mr. Arpel? Are you going to make it easy on yourself and your family, or not?"

For several seconds, Arpel remained expressionless, staring into space as if weighing his options. Suddenly he grunted, then resignedly dropped his head into his hands. "What's the use? It's over." Slowly, he lifted his head, focused expressionless eyes on Peter, and in a voice barely above a whisper demanded, "Read me my rights."

"Do you want to make a statement?"

Arpel again looked hard at Peter before responding.

Impatiently, Peter said, "One more time—are you willing to give me a statement, or not?"

Arpel grimaced, then swallowed hard. "Here's the deal. I'll give you a statement, but only on one condition—I want to do it here, in my office, and in my own way. Let me just talk, get it off my chest, everything out in the open. Then, if you have questions, you can ask me afterwards. Agreed?"

"I'd like to oblige, but I need a recorder,"Peter replied, "so it looks as though no deal."

Saying nothing, Peter watched as Arpel slid open the center drawer of his desk and from inside, pulled out a micro-cassette recorder. Inserting a cassette from an inlaid wooden box found on his desk, he handed the recorder to Peter. "I think this will do nicely."

Peter pushed his thumb down on the slide switch and tested it. The sound and recording level were excellent. *Probably better than the one we have at the station*, he thought. Anxious to get started, Peter placed the recorder in the middle of Arpel's desk and moved his own chair within range of the microphone.

Although figuring out some of the pieces to the puzzle, there remained a lot that Peter still didn't understand, and that bothered him. He needed to hear it all, before Arpel, like other suspects in similar circumstances, changed his mind once he had time to think about the consequences and lawyered up.

Peter clicked on the recorder, identified the parties, the date, time, and location where the statement was being taken. The cassette tape, in the now upright recorder, began spinning soundlessly.

Hunched forward on his elbows, Arpel at first sat motionless, then clearing his throat, began speaking, slowly, almost conversationally. "You're right, you know. I did kill John Bradley. When you first asked me why I killed him, your question shocked me. I don't know whether it was just a lucky guess on your part, or whether you had some hard evidence to back it up, but whatever it was, I knew you had me. . . . Because of my family situation, I don't want to prolong the inevitable." His voice tense, Arpel acknowledged, "Strange, but I'm almost glad this charade's over."

"Just tell me what happened," Peter ordered.

Arpel aimlessly traced the navy blue monogram on his shirt cuff with his right index finger, taking his time before answering. "Please just let me get this out at my own pace. Please." Suddenly bowing his head, he explained, "I know it's no excuse, but it all started and ended with Caroline."

He looked up, expectantly, but Peter wasn't going to make it easy for him. He wasn't surprised that Arpel started his statement by blaming someone else. For all their cloying introspection and disingenuous regret, criminals always seem to find someone else to pin the blame on, or at least someone to share it with. The fault is never theirs alone. For the record though, they always think it sounds good.

"As you seem to have discovered, my wife is terminally ill. Her deteriorating condition, coupled with those problems you talked about at the office, were more than I could handle. If I were younger, perhaps I could have taken it in stride, but all of a sudden, due to old age, or just a latent deficiency in character, I found I could no longer deal with things on my own.

"Out of loneliness, I thoughtlessly turned to someone else for support, and at first, just simple, uncomplicated companionship. As I'm sure you guessed, that person was Caroline Witten."

"When did you initiate this relationship with Ms. Witten?" Peter asked. He should have saved his breath though. It was obvious, Arpel wasn't listening to anything but the sound of his own voice.

"As professionals, she and I had known each other for years but hadn't socialized outside the courtroom until each became counsel for the Hendersons. Since that divorce was a complicated one, and hammering out a satisfactory settlement necessitated a lot of back and forth communications between lawyers and accountants representing each party, it doesn't take much imagination to understand what happened—friendly working lunches soon became intimate dinners, and then, well . . . much more."

Arpel covered his eyes as if embarrassed by revealing something so personal. "I wish I could say I was madly in love with her, but I'm not. Somehow, I guess that would make it less sordid. The sad truth is, I still love my wife, but her illness had long ago eclipsed any intimacy we shared in the past. And, though I'm ashamed to admit it, Caroline, sweet Caroline, answered that need.

"For what it's worth though, I didn't take advantage of her. It was the same type of convenient arrangement for Caroline. We convinced ourselves that since no one knew, no one would get hurt. Looking back, I wonder how foolish two people, who are supposed to be smart, could be?"

Peter decided not to respond.

"When we first started seeing each other, Caroline was trying to get over her rather nasty affair with John Bradley. Devastated to say the least, she was almost to the point of being unable to function. So I helped her; she helped me. Long story short, as part of her self-prescribed healing process, Caroline felt compelled to share every intimate detail she knew about Bradley. Being the woman scorned, at first, she tried to pay him back by exposing his rather unholy, or let's say, less than virtuous social proclivities."

"What do you mean?" asked Peter.

Smirking, Arpel explained, "Especially tantalizing, were her detailed recitals about Bradley's forays into the world of sex, pornography and manic spending. After suffering through unending discourse about these activities for several months, I decided to use the information to my advantage, and pulled a few strings at the bank were Bradley had his accounts. Through discreet inquiries, I found out Bradley had total administrative control over his wife's rather sizeable trust account. Again, it was just too easy to take advantage of another opportunity which Caroline had so innocently presented me."

Arpel let out a chuckle, though politely tried to muffle the sound when Peter didn't join in. "The upshot was, I had a little chat with John about helping me finance my campaign, or I'd make public everything I knew about him, thereby embarrassing his wife into resigning. Strangely, he never asked me how, or from whom, I had gained such information. Like an automaton, he just handed over the money as if grateful to be punished for his sexual sins. I must say, it was a rather bizarre state of affairs—excuse the all too obvious pun. Here was Bradley helping his wife's opponent win the election by pledging his wife's money to her opponent under the table, thereby compromising his wife's chances of winning over an opponent whom he was bankrolling with her money." Throwing his head back and laughing, he asked, "Could anything have been more delicious?"

Peter winced, but said nothing.

"For John, and by extension, Susan, it was nothing but a lose-lose proposition. I never worried about the illegalities of the arrangement. For me, John was a wish come true—a secret cash cow being milked dry—providing all the money I needed, neatly delivered every two weeks in an innocuous looking attache case. No more groveling for campaign money in return for future favors. Most important, I could say to hell with the law firm and its unending problems. I knew I had to get out, and winning the election was my ticket."

"So what happened the night Bradley was murdered?"

"Believe me, there was no intent to kill Bradley that night, or any night for that matter. But something happened that changed all that." Arpel licked dry lips, then reached over and helped himself to a glass of water. Self absorbed, he never bothered to offer any to Peter. Taking a long slow sip, he put the glass down, wiped his mouth with a crisp white linen handkerchief retrieved from his coat pocket, then continued. "I was just about to leave Caroline's that evening when around eight-thirty, the phone rang. Caroline of course picked up immediately, stupidly thinking it was one of her ridiculously rich clients. It became quickly apparent, by the tone of her voice though, that the caller was Bradley. His call was no surprise. Time had healed the bitterness between the two, so I knew they often spoke.

"Since she and I were in the same room, I couldn't help but overhear her side of the conversation. She kept repeating the same question over and over. What did he mean—'the monkey would soon be off his back, and he would be a free man?'" Arpel smiled wistfully. "Poor, stupid Caroline—she must have thought Bradley was going to come crawling back to her." Uncharitably, he added, "She couldn't have been more wrong.

"Of course *I* knew exactly what he meant. I just didn't know *why* he had said it. So during their conversation, I paced back and forth, trying to think. When Caroline hung up, I pretended to be jealous. Trying to humor me, she gleefully explained that Bradley's wife, my esteemed opponent, had asked John for a divorce, and that John's reaction was, 'nothing mattered anymore, and he had nothing and no one to protect.'

"Needless to say, my mind was in chaos. After making my excuses, I left Caroline's and drove over to Bradley's home, hoping against hope, he'd be alone. Since he had called Caroline only minutes before, I figured there was a good chance he was. Due to the campaign, I counted on Susan being out late trying to drum up more money. Still though, I couldn't take any chances, so I parked the car on the next street over."

"Clever."

"Yes, wasn't it?" Arpel agreed. "As luck would have it, when I got there, he was alone and surprisingly, almost glad to see me. As he so laughingly explained, my dropping by afforded him the opportunity to tell me face to face, that he was going to the police. My blackmail scheme was over, and nothing I said or did that night would change his mind.

"Desperate, I even offered to pay back everything he had given me. At first he laughed, then thought better of the offer, deciding that paying him back maybe wasn't such a bad idea after all.

"I remember he walked over to the desk in the library and began doing some handwritten calculations. Apparently, all my files indicating just how much he had paid me were locked in the desk drawers. So, while he was busy crunching numbers, he invited me to go to the kitchen and pour myself a cup of coffee. It was already made he said, just waiting to be poured. I was to bring back a cup for him too. He assured me we needn't hurry–Susan was working late at the office.

"You can't imagine how I felt. Like the whole world was caving in. Barely able to breathe, I remember being grateful for the opportunity to re-group. I gladly trotted out to the kitchen. But I didn't return to the library with a cup of coffee." Suddenly rocking back and forth in his seat, Arpel seemed in another world. He closed his eyes and folded his arms across his chest. "I couldn't tell you exactly what happened. Something just snapped. Here I was, hopelessly caught. There was no way out. I just kept thinking, what am I going to do?

"Since I didn't feel like pouring a cup of coffee for the son of a bitch, on impulse, I pulled open several drawers. It was just something to do. I don't even know what I was looking for. Then I saw the knives. I grabbed the biggest, and with blade pointing downward, held tightly against the outside of my overcoat, carried it back to the library. By that time, John had returned to the couch, his back turned toward the entryway. It couldn't have been more perfect!" cried Arpel as he clasped his hands together.

"I can only assume that before I arrived at the house that night, John had been sitting there doing paper work, since some papers were stacked beside him, others, in anal retentive neat piles, on the floor in front of him.

"I recall standing behind the couch for what must have been several minutes, rubbing my gloved thumb back and forth over what felt like a razor sharp blade, while continuing to carry on some inane conversation. I knew at that moment, whatever decision I made, my world would never be the same. But if I let Bradley go the police, the end result would be ruinous. On the other hand, if I killed Bradley, there was a possibility no one would ever know, and my plans for the judgeship would remain right on track. When I thought of it that way, what choice did I have? Incredible as it sounds, John never turned around or appeared concerned that his back was facing me. The bastard was so trusting. He never once looked up, or even asked where the coffee was." Arpel again laughed that tiny, irritating laugh that was getting on Peter's nerves. "Funny, how you remember those stupid inconsequential things," he mused.

Leaning toward Peter, his arms stretched out over the surface of his desk, he said, "You know, it was almost too easy. I remember thinking, it was meant to be, otherwise, it wouldn't be so simple. God wouldn't permit such an act of vengeance if it weren't meant to be."

Peter couldn't believe what he was hearing—the recitation had all the earmarks of a perfect insanity defense. This man, so suave, so intelligent, so well-respected, was truly mad. Most surprising to Peter, he didn't even have to encourage him. Now, it seemed, Arpel wanted to unload the burden so desperately, he couldn't wait to continue.

"Bradley kept whining about how much he had paid me. To confirm it, he spread out all the records pertaining to our little arrangement on his lap, then gleefully told me how he had religiously maintained everything under lock and key, in a file marked, 'Liam Leprakalb.' Not wanting to prolong this because of Susan's imminent return, but still being curious, I asked him why that name had been applied to a file involving me.

"Bradley laughed, saying something to the effect that, 'It's a game with me, Edward. I like to rearrange letters in people's names. It gives me control. But don't worry, no one would ever guess who Liam Leprakalb really is. But I'll let you in on a little secret—if you reverse the letters, it spells Arpel Blackmail.'

"After hearing that, I remember raising the hand which held the knife high above my head. And in one clean sweep of my arm, I pulled it down *hard,* plunging the knife into his shoulder area. Physically, it was remarkably easy. I had expected some resistence, but it was like I had plunged the knife through soft butter. He struggled of course, but I guess he was so stunned, that his reaction time was slowed, almost to a standstill. I then came around the couch to have better advantage. You see, by then, I had no choice. I had to finish him. But in my haste, I remember tipping over a lamp, causing it to fall to the floor. That further stunned John, who, by that time, was bleeding profusely over the papers, the sofa, and the rug.

"When I finally managed to maneuver past the couch and around the fallen lamp, I struck him again several times in the neck and chest area with everything I had. But it was all happening so fast at that point, I really can't really remember much detail. Anyway, he stumbled then and fell forward, almost on top of me.

"Once he hit the floor, no part of his body moved except his hands. In desperation I guess, he began clutching at the papers that laid strewn around him, but he succeeded in doing nothing but getting blood all over them. Finally, even his hand movements ceased, his eyes closed, and he appeared to be dying."

Peter watched in fascination as Arpel described what he had done. The account was chilling.

"I didn't dare take a chance though, so I stabbed him one more time—again in the chest, close to the heart. To do this, I literally had to stoop down and pull him up by the shirt collar. He let out a moan." Shivering, Arpel added, "I knew then he was finally dead.

"I also knew I couldn't afford to waste any more time, so I grabbed the file marked, 'Liam Leprakalb,' and removed all the remaining papers that were inside, as well as the payment calculations which still lay on the couch. In that spilt second, I stupidly decided to leave behind the empty file folder with the label, 'Liam Leprakalb,' on it." Arpel looked up and straight at Peter. "I guess you figured out the anagram. Who would have thought that John, or his little word games, would, as you say, haunt me from the grave?"

"So how did you get the file back into Bradley's desk drawers?" asked Peter.

"That was easy, really. I wanted it to look as though none of the files had been tampered with, so I took the keys John had conveniently left on the corner of his desk, pulled open the bottom desk drawer and re-filed it. But, as I was doing that, I noticed that all the other file folders in the drawer were full, so I randomly pulled out the papers that were still inside a few of them. That way, my file wouldn't look so conspicuously empty. I also rifled through the other drawers to make sure there was nothing else incriminating left behind. I was in a hurry, so I know they were left in a mess. Then, after I locked the drawer, I placed the keys in one of John's trouser pockets. As I said, it was simple.

"By that time, I was beginning to worry about Susan returning home, even though as I said, John had mentioned that she wasn't expected for a while. I also knew, I had to have sufficient time to clean off the knife still in my hand. The only time I removed my gloves that night was when I washed the knife in the kitchen sink. I then replaced the gloves and put the knife back in the drawer with all the others. Foolishly, I figured that it was in such plain view, it would be overlooked. Practicing only corporate and matrimonial law, I guess I didn't realize all the forensic tests that could be run on things like that."

"Lucky for us, huh?"

Arpel shrugged his shoulders. "After that, I took one last look around the library, pulled some books from the book cases, and dropped them on the floor just to make it look good. I then opened the front door, and left. That's all I can tell you, Lieutenant, because that's all there was."

With that said, Arpel sighed and fell silent. Peter turned off the tape-recorder. For now, he had what he wanted. "I guess I don't need to tell you what the next step is going to be, Counselor."

"No, I guess you don't," Arpel answered softly.

Peter walked around the desk and stood directly in front of Arpel. He pulled out a pair of handcuffs from his pocket and stooped down in anticipation of placing them on Arpel's wrists.

Looking up at him, Arpel asked, "Before you do that, which I know is necessary, could I ask one favor?"

"Depends," Peter answered cautiously.

"Could you give me a moment to call my wife and try to explain. I want her to hear it from me. She's so fragile right now. . . ."

"I don't mean to be cruel, but you should have thought of that before you did what you did." Looking around, Peter hesitated. "Oh what the hell. Two minutes, that's it. I'll be right outside the door."

Since Peter had seen the inside of Arpel's desk drawer when Arpel produced the tape recorder, Peter felt sure there was no gun or knife to worry about. Besides, Peter convinced himself, Arpel was too much of coward to take his own life.

"That's all it will take, Lieutenant. A couple of minutes. I promise not to ask for anything else, but I must do this one last thing before leaving."

Peter nodded, and as promised stepped just outside Arpel's office, but not out of earshot. He left the door conspicuously open half a foot. As he stood there, Peter could hear Arpel talking in low, almost soothing tones, and then he heard another sound—something muffled, a sound Peter couldn't immediately identify. Too late, he realized what it was—locks on a brief case snapping open. Bursting through the door, Peter heard the unmistakable sound of a gunshot. Too late, standing with gun raised, Peter saw its aftermath–Edward Arpel slumped over his desk, a gaping bullet hole in his right temple. Peter walked slowly towards him. Blood had spattered everywhere and was already pooling on the desk surface, just underneath the wound in Arpel's head. There was no need to touch the body. He knew. Edward Arpel was dead. Gently, Peter lifted Arpel's right hand which clutched a small plaque entitled, *Judicial Temperament*. It read:

To be the judge of one's fellow man is a challenge few seek to accept. To be the determinant of right from wrong, is a task few aspire to undertake. But if you do, remember this, brilliant intellect and visionary zeal are qualities unimportant, without the rarest quality of all–Judicial Temperament.

Author Unknown

EPILOGUE

They met at Jack Fry's, Hilary's favorite restaurant. When she arrived, by her watch only five minutes late, Peter was already there waiting, seated in her favorite booth—the one on the right, near the piano player.

Hilary looked around, trying to memorize the moment. It was almost sunset. Soft lights flickered under shaded wall sconces. Starched white tablecloths, impeccably cleaned and pressed, hugged every table like a glove, while simple sprays of white freesia added a subtle scent of spring. Everything was so warm, comfortable, cozy. It was perfect.

Hilary slipped easily into the black leather booth and gave Peter a playful smile. It was the first time they had seen each other since the Bradley case officially closed. Trying to deflect attention from her face, which Hilary could feel burning under his gaze, she said, "You remembered how I love this place."

"How could I forget?" Peter asked quietly. "It hasn't been that long ago, you know."

"Trying to say you're sorry, huh?"

"Something like that."

Hilary reached over and lightly placed her hand on his. "There's no need to apologize, even though you wouldn't listen when I told you Jake didn't do it." She could see his shoulders, which had been so rigid, immediately relax. "Look at it this way—everything turned out fine in the end. Susan now has no opponent in the race; her baby is healthy with no apparent complications; and Jake, well, you know Jake. He's fine too. Just don't look for an invitation to their impending wedding," she added, giggling. "Not to change the subject, but how did you zero in on Edward Arpel as the killer?"

Peter smiled. "I had help from two sources."

Hilary raised her eyebrow. "Don't keep me in suspense. Tell me."

"Remember when you told me that I had overlooked something in the files found in Bradley's desk drawer?"

"Yes," she answered slowly, "but—"

"Well, you were absolutely right. I *had* overlooked something—the name, Liam Leprakalb."

"I remember—the name on one of the file folders." Impatiently she asked, "So who is the mysterious Liam Leprakalb?"

"First let me explain something, then you'll understand. Besides you, the other source of help was Bradley himself."

"I don't understand."

"The anagrams. If it hadn't been for those damnable word games, Arpel may have gotten away with it. The name, Liam Leprakalb, is an anagram for Arpel blackmail."

Hilary blinked hard and shook her head in amazement. "Who would have thought? . . . So that's where the money went. To pay off Arpel."

"Not all of it. Bradley spent some of it on various women and other sexual pleasures. But you're right, the bulk of it had been lining Arpel's pockets for some time, the ante always escalating. From what I can gather, it became a vicious circle—Bradley, though ashamed of what he was doing, couldn't stop; which in turn made Arpel's job easier because the more aberrant Bradley's behavior became, the more he had to hide and the more he had to pay Arpel. Part of Bradley's illness was his need to be redeemed. For him, redemption came in the form of confessing his sins to Caroline Witten, and handing over the cash to Arpel. And as hard as this is to believe, Bradley never even asked Arpel how he had found out about his indiscretions."

Lowering his voice, Peter added, "The real heartbreak is, I think John Bradley truly loved his wife. He just couldn't show her. With her temperament, she couldn't or wouldn't work through it, and he knew it. Sad. And from what I could tell, he tried to replenish the money taken from the Judge's trust account by gouging people like Waylander for money that Bradley & Stein wasn't entitled to receive. I guess though, she has now found true happiness with the likes of Jake Stein."

Shaking her head at the irony of it all, Hilary said, "I guess. It's just so hard to accept though. John gone; Arpel committing suicide instead of facing murder charges; and the company which Jake didn't think he could live without, Bradley & Stein, also gone. In its place, I hear Jake has decided to concentrate his efforts on a new land development/construction business to be known as, Stein and Son, since according to Susan's doctor, Susan is expected to have a boy."

With her most engaging smile, Hilary pronounced, "Another case solved." She touched his arm, coaxing him to face her. "I have to ask. What would you do without me, Lieutenant?"

Peter reached over and took her hand in his. "That, my dearest Hilary, would be a crime I would never want to investigate."